A
Voice in
the Wilderness

GRACE LIVINGSTON HILL

A Voice in the Wilderness

Fleming H. Revell Company
Old Tappan, New Jersey

Library of Congress Cataloging in Publication Data

Hill, Grace Livingston, 1865–1947.
    A voice in the wilderness.

    I. Title.
PS3515.I486V6   1984   813′.52   84-2019
ISBN 0-8007-1209-9

Introduction

As I recall the looks and ways of some of the people our family knew when I was young, I have to smile when I find those ways appearing in my mother's books. Not that any one character is a replica of any person we knew. But certain little humorous—or revolting!—personality traits in the book characters remind me vividly of incidents we used to laugh over, or treasure.

The boy Bud in this book is very like some of the gruff, fun-loving, loyal fellows who were in my mother's Sunday school class. And the pasty-faced preacher who never realized how the girl he aspired to date despised him reminds me of a certain man who held the pastorate in our village church—for a *short* time. Actually, it was I, a teenager then, who was so incensed when he tried to get fresh with me; I called him "that squash!" Even his theology had the consistency of overcooked lukewarm squash.

It is always good to realize, however, as I read over her books, that my mother never lost her love of beauty or romance, or her faith in the faithfulness of God.

RUTH LIVINGSTON HILL

A Voice in the Wilderness

Chapter 1

With a lurch the train came to a dead stop and Margaret Earle, hastily gathering up her belongings, hurried down the aisle and got out into the night.

It occurred to her, as she swung her heavy suitcase down the rather long step to the ground, and then carefully swung herself after it, that it was strange that neither conductor, brakeman, nor porter had come to help her off the train, when all three had taken the trouble to tell her that hers was the next station, but she could hear voices up ahead. Perhaps something was the matter with the engine that detained them and they had forgotten her for the moment.

The ground was rough where she stood, and there seemed no sign of a platform. Did they not have platforms in this wild western land, or was the train so long that her car had stopped before reaching it?

She strained her eyes into the darkness, and tried to make out things from the two or three specks of light that danced about like fireflies in the distance. She could dimly see moving figures away up near the engine, and each one evidently carried a lantern. The train was tremendously long. A sudden feeling of isolation took possession of her. Perhaps she ought not to have gotten out until someone came to help her. Perhaps the train had not pulled into the station yet, and she ought to get back on it and wait. Yet if the train started before she found the conductor she might be carried on somewhere and he justly blame her for a fool.

There did not seem to be any building on that side of the track. It was probably on the other, but she was standing too near the cars to see over. She tried to move back to look, but the ground sloped and she slipped and fell in the cinders, bruising her knee and cutting her wrist.

In sudden panic she arose. She would get back into the train, no matter what the consequences. They had no right to put her out here,

9

away off from the station, at night, in a strange country. If the train started before she could find the conductor she would tell him that he must back it up again and let her off. He certainly could not expect her to get out like this.

She lifted the heavy suitcase up the high step that was even farther from the ground than it had been when she came down, because her fall had loosened some of the earth and caused it to slide away from the track. Then, reaching to the rail of the step, she tried to pull herself up, but as she did so the engine gave a long snort and the whole train, as if it were in league against her, lurched forward crazily, shaking off her hold. She slipped to her knees again, the suitcase toppled from the lower step, descending upon her, and together they slid and rolled down the short bank, while the train, like an irresponsible nurse who had slapped her charge and left it to its fate, ran giddily off into the night.

The horror of being deserted helped the girl to rise in spite of bruises and shock. She lifted imploring hands to the unresponsive cars as they hurried by her—one, two, three, with bright windows, each showing a passenger, comfortable and safe inside, unconscious of her need.

A moment of useless screaming, running, trying to attract someone's attention, a sickening sense of terror and failure, and the last car slatted itself past with a mocking clatter, as if it enjoyed her discomfort.

Margaret stood dazed, reaching out helpless hands, then dropped them at her sides and gazed after the fast retreating train, the light on its last car swinging tauntingly, blinking now and then with a leer in its eye, rapidly vanishing from her sight into the depth of the night.

She gasped and looked about her for the station that but a short moment before had been so real to her mind; and, lo! on this side and on that there was none!

The night was wide like a great floor shut in by a low, vast dome of curving blue set with the largest, most wonderful stars she had ever seen. Heavy shadows of purple-green, smokelike, hovered over earth darker and more intense than the unfathomable blue of the night sky. It seemed like the secret nesting place of mysteries wherein no human foot might dare intrude. It was incredible that such could be but common sagebrush, sand, and greasewood wrapped about with the beauty of the lonely night.

No building broke the inky outlines of the plain, nor friendly light streamed out to cheer her heart. Not even a tree was in sight, except on the far horizon, where a heavy line of deeper darkness might mean a forest. Nothing, absolutely nothing, in the blue, deep, starry dome above and the bluer darkness of the earth below save one sharp shaft ahead like a black mast throwing out a dark arm across the track.

As soon as she sighted it she picked up her baggage and made her painful way toward it, for her knees and wrist were bruised and her baggage was heavy.

A soft drip, drip greeted her as she drew nearer; something splashing down among the cinders by the track. Then she saw the tall column with its arm outstretched, and looming darker among the sagebrush the outlines of a watertank. It was so she recognized the engine's drinking tank, and knew that she had mistaken a pause to water the engine for a regular stop at a station.

Her soul sank within her as she came up to the dripping water and laid her hand upon the dark upright, as if in some way it could help her. She dropped her baggage and stood, trembling, gazing around upon the beautiful, lonely scene in horror; and then, like a mirage against the distance, there melted on her frightened eyes a vision of her father and mother sitting around the library lamp at home, as they sat every evening. They were probably reading and talking at this very minute, and trying not to miss her on this her first venture away from home into the great world to teach. What would they say if they could see their beloved daughter, whom they had sheltered all these years and let go forth so reluctantly now, in all her confidence of youth, bound by almost absurd promises to be careful and not run any risks.

Yet here she was, standing alone beside a water tank in the midst of an Arizona plain, not knowing how many miles from anywhere, at somewhere between nine and ten o'clock at night! It seemed incredible that it had really happened! Perhaps she was dreaming! A few moments before in the bright car, surrounded by drowsy fellow travelers, almost at her journey's end, as she supposed; and now, having merely done as she thought right, she was stranded here!

She rubbed her eyes and looked again up the track, half expecting to see the train come back for her. Surely, surely the conductor, or the porter who had been so kind, would discover that she was gone, and do something about it. They couldn't leave her here alone on the prairie! It would be too dreadful!

That vision of her father and mother off against the purple-green distance, how it shook her! The lamp looked bright and cheerful, and she could see her father's head with its heavy white hair. He turned to look at her mother to tell her of something he read in the paper. They were sitting there, feeling contented and almost happy about her, and she, their little girl—all her dignity as schoolteacher dropped from her like a garment now—she was standing in this empty space alone, with only an engine's water tank to keep her from dying, and only the barren, desolate track to connect her with the world of men and women. She dropped her head upon her breast and the tears came, sobbing, choking, raining down. Then off in the distance she heard a low, rising howl of some snarling, angry beast, and she lifted her head and stood in trembling terror, clinging to the tank.

That sound was coyotes or wolves howling. She had read about them, but had not expected to experience them in such a situation. How confidently had she accepted the position which offered her the opening she had sought for the splendid career that she hoped was to follow! How fearless had she been! Coyotes, nor Indians, nor wild cowboy students—nothing had daunted her courage. Besides, she told her mother it was very different going to a town from what it would be if she were a missionary going to the wilds. It was an important school where she was to teach, where her Latin and German and mathematical achievements had won her the place above several other applicants, and where her well-known tact was expected to work wonders. But what were Latin and German and mathematics now? Could they show her how to climb a water tank? Would tact avail with a hungry wolf?

The howl in the distance seemed to come nearer. She cast frightened eyes to the unresponsive water tank looming high and dark above her. She must get up there somehow. It was not safe to stand here a minute. Besides, from that height she might be able to see farther, and perhaps there would be a light somewhere and she might cry for help.

Investigation showed a set of rude spikes by which the trainmen were wont to climb up, and Margaret prepared to ascend them. She set her suitcase dubiously down at the foot. Would it be safe to leave it there? She had read how coyotes carried off a hatchet from a camping party, just to get the leather thong which was bound about the handle. She could not afford to lose her things. Yet how could she climb and carry that heavy burden with her? A sudden thought came.

Her simple traveling gown was finished with a silken girdle, soft and long, wound twice about her waist and falling in tasseled ends. Swiftly she untied it and knotted one end firmly to the handle of her suitcase, tying the other end securely to her wrist. Then slowly, cautiously, with many a look upward, she began to climb.

It seemed miles, though in reality it was but a short distance. The howling beasts in the distance sounded nearer now and continually, making her heart beat wildly. She was stiff and bruised from her falls, and weak with fright. The spikes were far apart, and each step of progress was painful and difficult. It was good at last to rise high enough to see over the water tank and feel a certain confidence in her defense.

But she had risen already beyond the short length of her silken tether, and the suitcase was dragging painfully on her arm. She was obliged to steady herself where she stood and pull it up before she could go on. Then she managed to get it swung up to the top of the tank in a comparatively safe place. One more long spike step and she was beside it.

The tank was partly roofed over, so that she had room enough to sit on the edge without danger of falling in and drowning. For a few minutes she could only sit still and be thankful and try to get her breath back again after the climb, but presently the beauty of the night began to cast its spell over her. That wonderful blue of the sky! It hadn't ever before impressed her that skies were blue at night. She would have said they were black or gray. As a matter of fact, she didn't remember to have ever seen so much sky at once before, nor to have noticed skies in general until now.

This sky was so deeply, wonderfully blue, the stars so real, alive and sparkling, that all other stars she had ever seen paled before them into mere imitations. The spot looked like one of Taylor's pictures of the Holy Land. She half expected to see a shepherd with his crook and sheep approaching her out of the dim shadows, or a turbaned, white-robed David with his lifted hands of prayer standing off among the depths of purple darkness. It would not have been out of keeping if a walled city with housetops should be hidden behind the clumps of sagebrush farther on. 'Twas such a night and such a scene as this, perhaps, when the wise men started to follow the star!

But one cannot sit on the edge of a water tank in the desert night alone and muse long on art and history. It was cold up here, and the howling seemed nearer than before. There was no sign of a light or a house anywhere, and not even a freight train sent its welcome clatter down the track. All was still and wide and lonely, save that terrifying sound of the beasts; such stillness as she had not ever thought could be—a fearful silence as a setting for the awful voices of the wilds.

The bruises and scratches she had acquired set up a fine stinging, and the cold seemed to sweep down and take possession of her on her high, narrow seat. She was growing stiff and cramped, yet dared not move much. Would there be no train, nor any help? Would she have to sit there all night? It looked so very near to the ground now. Could wild beasts climb, she wondered?

Then in the interval of silence that came between the calling of those wild creatures there stole a sound. She could not tell at first what it was. A slow, regular, plodding sound, and quite far away. She looked to find it, and thought she saw a shape move out of the sagebrush on the other side of the track, but she could not be sure. It might be but a figment of her brain, a foolish fancy from looking so long at the huddled bushes on the dark plain. Yet something prompted her to cry out, and when she heard her own voice she cried again and louder, wondering why she had not cried before.

"Help! Help!" she called, and again: "Help! Help!"

The dark shape paused and turned toward her. She was sure now. What if it were a beast instead of a human! Terrible fear took possession of her; then, to her infinite relief, a nasal voice sounded out:

"Who's thar?"

But when she opened her lips to answer, nothing but a sob would come to them for a minute, and then she could only cry, pitifully:

"Help! Help!"

"Whar be you?" twanged the voice, and now she could see a horse and rider like a shadow moving toward her down the track.

Chapter 2

The horse came to a standstill a little way from the track, and his rider let forth a stream of strange profanity. The girl shuddered and began to think a wild beast might be preferable to some men. However, these remarks seemed to be a mere formality. He paused and addressed her:

"Heow'd yeh git up thar? D'j'yeh drap er climb?"

He was a little, wiry man with a bristly, protruding chin. She could see that, even in the starlight. There was something about the point of that stubby chin that she shrank from inexpressibly. He was not a pleasant man to look upon, and even his voice was unprepossessing. She began to think that even the night with its loneliness and unknown perils was preferable to this man's company.

"I got off the train by mistake, thinking it was my station, and before I discovered it the train had gone and left me," Margaret explained, with dignity.

"Yeh didn't 'xpect it t' sit reound on th' plain while you was gallivantin' up water tanks, did yeh?"

Cold horror froze Margaret's veins. She was dumb for a second. "I am on my way to Ashland station. Can you tell me how far it is from here and how I can get there?" Her tone was like icicles.

"It's a little matter o' twenty miles, more 'r less," said the man protruding his offensive chin. "The walkin's good. I don't know no other way from this p'int at this time o' night. Yeh might set still till th' mornin' freight goes by an' drap atop o' one of the kyars."

"Sir!" said Margaret, remembering her dignity as a teacher.

The man wheeled his horse clear around and looked up at her impudently. She could smell bad whisky on his breath.

"Say, you must be some young highbrow, ain't yeh? Is thet all yeh want o' me? 'Cause ef 'tis I got t' git on t' camp. It's a good five mile yet, an' I 'ain't hed no grub sence noon."

The tears suddenly rushed to the girl's eyes as the horror of being

16

alone in the night again took possession of her. This dreadful man frightened her, but the thought of the loneliness filled her with dismay.

"Oh!" she cried, forgetting her insulted dignity, "you're not going to leave me here alone, are you? Isn't there some place near here where I could stay overnight?"

"Thur ain't no palace hotel round these diggin's, ef that's what you mean," the man leered at her. "You c'n come along t' camp 'ith me ef you ain't too stuck up."

"To camp!" faltered Margaret in dismay, wondering what her mother would say. "Are there any ladies there?"

A loud guffaw greeted her question. "Wal, my woman's thar, sech es she is, but she ain't no highflier like you. We mostly don't hev ladies to camp. But I got t' git on. Ef you want to go too, you better light down pretty speedy, fer I can't wait."

In fear and trembling Margaret descended her rude ladder step by step, primitive man seated calmly on his horse, making no attempt whatever to assist her.

"This ain't no baggage car," he grumbled, as he saw the suitcase in her hand. "Well, h'ist yerself up thar; I reckon we c'n pull through somehow. Gimme the luggage."

Margaret stood appalled beside the bony horse and his uncouth rider. Did he actually expect her to ride with him? "Couldn't I walk?" she faltered, hoping he would offer to do so.

" 'T's up t' you," the man replied, indifferently. "Try 't an' see!"

He spoke to the horse, and it started forward eagerly, while the girl in horror struggled on behind. Over rough, uneven ground, between greasewood, sagebrush, and cactus, back into the trail. The man, oblivious of her presence, rode contentedly on, a silent shadow on a dark horse wending a silent way between the purple-green clumps of other shadows, until, bewildered, the girl almost lost sight of them. Her breath came short, her ankle turned, and she fell with both hands in a stinging bed of cactus. She cried out then and begged him to stop.

"L'arned yer lesson, hev yeh, sweety?" he jeered at her, foolishly. "Well, get in yer box, then."

He let her struggle up to a seat behind himself with very little assistance, but when she was seated and started on her way she began to wish she had stayed behind and taken any perils of the way rather than trust herself in proximity to this creature.

From time to time he took a bottle from his pocket and swallowed a portion of its contents, becoming fluent in his language as they proceeded on their way. Margaret remained silent, growing more and more frightened every time the bottle came out. At last he offered it to her. She declined it with cold politeness, which seemed to irritate the little man, for he turned suddenly fierce.

"Oh, yer too fine to take a drap fer good comp'ny, are yeh? Wal, I'll show yeh a thing er two, my pretty lady. You'll give me a kiss with yer two cherry lips before we go another step. D'yeh hear, my sweetie?" And he turned with a silly leer to enforce his command, but with a cry of horror Margaret slid to the ground and ran back down the trail as hard as she could go, till she stumbled and fell in the shelter of a great sage bush, and lay sobbing on the sand.

The man turned bleared eyes toward her and watched until she disappeared. Then sticking his chin out wickedly, he slung her suitcase after her and called:

"All right, my pretty lady, go yer own gait an' l'arn yer own lesson." He started on again, singing a drunken song.

Under the blue, starry dome alone sat Margaret again, this time with no friendly water tank for her defense, and took counsel with herself. The howling coyotes seemed to be silenced for the time; at least they had become a minor quantity in her equation of troubles. She felt now that man was her greatest menace, and to get away safely from him back to that friendly water tank and the dear old railroad track she would have pledged her next year's salary. She stole softly to the place where she had heard the suitcase fall, and picking it up, started on the weary road back to the tank. Could she ever find the way? The trail seemed so intangible a thing, her sense of direction so confused. Yet there was nothing else to do. She shuddered whenever she thought of the man who had been her companion on horseback.

When the man reached camp he set his horse loose and stumbled into the door of the log bunkhouse, calling loudly for something to eat.

The men were sitting around the room on the rough benches and bunks, smoking their pipes or stolidly staring into the dying fire. Two smoky kerosene lanterns that hung from spikes driven high in the logs cast a weird light over the company, eight men in all, rough and hardened with exposure to stormy life and weather. They were men with unkempt beards and uncombed hair, their coarse cotton shirts open at the neck, their brawny arms bare above the elbow, with crimes and sorrows and hard living written large across their faces.

There was one, a boy in looks, with smooth face and white skin healthily flushed in places like a baby's. His face, too, was hard and set in sternness like a mask, as if life had used him badly, but behind it was a fineness of feature and spirit that could not be utterly hidden. They called him the kid, and thought it was his youth that made him different from them all, for he was only twenty-four, and not one of the rest was under forty. They were doing their best to help him get over that innate fineness that was his natural inheritance, but although he stopped at nothing, and played his part always with the ease of one old in the ways of the world, yet he kept a quiet reserve about him, a kind of charm beyond which they had not been able to go.

He was playing cards with three others at the table when the man came in, and did not look up at the entrance.

The woman, white and hopeless, appeared at the door of the shed room when the man came, and obediently set about getting his supper, but her lifeless face never changed expression.

"Brung a gal 'long of me part way," boasted the man, as he flung himself into a seat by the table. "Thought you fellers might like t' see 'er, but she got too high an' mighty fer me, wouldn't take a pull at th' bottle 'ith me, 'n shrieked like a catamount when I kissed 'er. Found 'er hangin' on th' water tank. Got off 't th' wrong place. One o' yer highbrows out o' th' parlor car! Good lesson fer 'er!"

The boy looked up from his cards sternly, his keen eyes boring through the man. "Where is she now?" he asked, quietly, and all the men in the room looked up uneasily. There was that tone and accent again that made the boy alien from them. What was it?

The man felt it and snarled his answer angrily. "Dropped 'er on th' trail, an' threw her fine lady b'longin's after 'er. 'Ain't got no use fer thet kind. Wonder what they was created fer? Ain't no good to nobody, not even 'emselves." And he laughed a harsh cackle that was not pleasant to hear.

The boy threw down his cards and went out, shutting the door. In a few minutes the men heard two horses pass the end of the bunkhouse toward the trail, but no one looked up nor spoke. You could not have told by the flicker of an eyelash that they knew where the boy had gone.

She was sitting in the deep shadow of a sage bush that lay on the edge of the trail like a great blot, her suitcase beside her, her breath coming short with exertion and excitement, when she heard a cheery whistle in the distance. Just an old love song dating back some years and discarded now as hackneyed even by the street pianos at home; but oh, how good it sounded!

From the desert I come to thee!

The ground was cold, and struck a chill through her garments as she sat there alone in the night. On came the clear, musical whistle, and she peered out of the shadow with eager eyes and frightened heart. Dared she risk it again? Should she call, or should she hold her breath and keep still, hoping he would pass her by unnoticed? Before she could decide two horses stopped almost in front of her and a rider swung himself down. He stood before her as if it were day and he could see her quite plainly.

"You needn't be afraid," he explained, calmly. "I thought I had better look you up after the old man got home and gave his report. He was pretty well tanked up and not exactly a fit escort for ladies. What's the trouble?"

Like an angel of deliverance he looked to her as he stood in the starlight, outlined in silhouette against the wide, wonderful sky: broad shoulders, well-set head, close-cropped curls, handsome contour even in the darkness. There was about him an air of quiet strength which gave her confidence.

"Oh, thank you!" she gasped, with a quick little relieved sob in her voice. "I am so glad you have come. I was—just a little—frightened, I think." She attempted to rise, but her foot caught in her skirt and she sank wearily back to the sand again.

The boy stooped over and lifted her to her feet. "You certainly are some plucky girl!" he commented, looking down at her slender height as she stood beside him. "A little frightened, were you? Well, I should say you had a right to be."

"Well, not exactly frightened, you know," said Margaret, taking a deep breath and trying to steady her voice. "I think perhaps I was more mortified than frightened, to think I made such a blunder as to get off the train before I reached my station. You see I'd made up my mind not to be frightened, but when I heard that awful howl of some beast— And then that terrible man!" She shuddered and put her hands suddenly over her eyes as if to shut out all memory of it.

"More than one kind of beast!" commented the boy, briefly. "Well, you needn't worry about him, he's having his supper and he'll be sound asleep by the time we get back."

"Oh, have we got to go where he is?" gasped Margaret. "Isn't there some other place? Is Ashland very far away? That is where I am going."

"No other place where you could go tonight. Ashland's a good twenty-five miles from here. But you'll be all right. Mom Wallis 'll look out for you. She isn't much of a looker, but she has a kind heart. She pulled me through once when I was just about flickering out. Come on. You'll be pretty tired. We better be getting back. Mom Wallis 'll make you comfortable, and then you can get off good and early in the morning."

Without an apology, and as if it were the common courtesy of the desert, he stooped and lifted her easily to the saddle of the second horse, placed the bridle in her hands, then swung the suitcase up on his own horse and sprang into the saddle.

Chapter 3

He turned the horses about and took charge of her just as if he were accustomed to managing stray ladies in the wilderness every day of his life and understood the situation perfectly, and Margaret settled wearily into her saddle and looked about her with content.

Suddenly, again, the wide wonder of the night possessed her. Involuntarily she breathed a soft little exclamation of awe and delight. Her companion turned to her questioningly:

"Does it always seem so big here—so—limitless?" she asked in explanation. "It is so far to everywhere it takes one's breath away, and yet the stars hang close, like a protection. It gives one the feeling of being alone in the great universe with God. Does it always seem so out here?"

He looked at her curiously, her pure profile turned up to the wide dome of luminous blue above. His voice was strangely low and wondering as he answered, after a moment's silence:

"No, it is not always so," he said. "I have seen it when it was more like being alone in the great universe with the devil."

There was a tremendous earnestness in his tone that the girl felt meant more than was on the surface. She turned to look at the fine young face beside her. In the starlight she could not make out the bitter hardness of lines that were beginning to be carved about his sensitive mouth. But there was so much sadness in his voice that her heart went out to him in pity.

"Oh," she said, gently, "it would be awful that way. Yes, I can understand. I felt so, a little, while that terrible man was with me." And she shuddered again at the remembrance.

Again he gave her that curious look. "There are worse things than Pop Wallis out here," he said, gravely. "But I'll grant you there's some class to the skies. It's a case of 'Where every prospect pleases and only man is vile.'" And with the words his tone grew almost flippant. It hurt her sensitive nature, and without knowing it she half drew away a little farther from him and murmured, sadly:

"Oh!" as if he had classed himself with the man he had been describing. Instantly he felt her withdrawal and grew grave again, as if he would atone.

"Wait till you see this sky at the dawn," he said. "It will burn red fire off there in the east like a hearth in a palace, and all this dome will glow like a great pink jewel set in gold. If you want a classy sky, there you have it! Nothing like it in the East!"

There was a strange mingling of culture and roughness in his speech. The girl could not make him out; yet there had been a palpitating earnestness in his description that showed he had felt the dawn in his very soul.

"You are—a—poet, perhaps?" she asked, half shyly. "Or an artist?" she hazarded.

He laughed roughly and seemed embarrassed. "No, I'm just a— bum! A sort of roughneck out of a job."

She was silent, watching him against the starlight, a kind of embarrassment upon her after his last remark. "You—have been here long?" she asked, at last.

"Three years." He said it almost curtly and turned his head away, as if there were something in his face he would hide.

She knew there was something unhappy in his life. Unconsciously her tone took on a sympathetic sound. "And do you get homesick and want to go back, ever?" she asked.

His tone was fairly savage now. "No!"

The silence which followed became almost oppressive before the boy finally turned and in his kindly tone began to question her about the happenings which had stranded her in the desert alone at night.

So she came to tell him briefly and frankly about herself, as he questioned—how she came to be in Arizona all alone.

"My father is a minister in a small town in New York State. When I finished college I had to do something, and I had an offer of this Ashland school through a friend of ours who had a brother out here. Father and Mother would rather have kept me nearer home, of course, but everybody says the best opportunities are in the West, and this was a good opening, so they finally consented. They would send posthaste for me to come back if they knew what a mess I have made of things right at the start—getting out of the train in the desert."

"But you're not discouraged?" said her companion, half wonderingly. "Some nerve you have with you. I guess you'll manage to hit it off in Ashland. It's the limit as far as discipline is concerned, I understand, but I guess you'll put one over on them. I'll bank on you after tonight, sure thing!"

She turned a laughing face toward him. "Thank you!" she said. "But I don't see how you know all that. I'm sure I didn't do anything particularly nervy. There wasn't anything else to do but what I did, if I'd tried."

"Most girls would have fainted and screamed, and fainted again when they were rescued," stated the boy, out of a vast experience.

"I never fainted in my life," said Margaret Earle, with disdain. "I don't think I should care to faint out in the vast universe like this. It would be rather inopportune, I should think."

Then, because she suddenly realized that she was growing very chummy with this stranger in the dark, she asked the first question that came into her head.

"What was your college?"

That he had not been to college never entered her head. There was something in his speech and manner that made it a foregone conclusion.

It was as if she had struck him forcibly in his face, so sudden and sharp a silence ensued for a second. Then he answered gruffly, "Yale," and plunged into an elaborate account of Arizona in its early ages, including a detailed description of the cliff dwellers and their homes, which were still to be seen high in the rocks of the canyons not many miles to the west of where they were riding.

Margaret was keen to hear it all, and asked many questions, declaring her intention of visiting those cliff caves at her earliest opportunity. It was so wonderful to her to be actually out here where there were all sorts of strange and fascinating things about which she had read and wondered. It did not occur to her, until the next day, to realize that her companion had of intention led her off the topic of himself and kept her from asking any more personal questions.

He told her of the petrified forest just over some low hills off to the left; acres and acres of agatized chips and trunks of great trees all turned to eternal stone, called by the Indians "Yeitso's bones," after the great giant of that name whom an ancient Indian hero killed. He described the coloring of the brilliant days in Arizona, where you stand on the edge of some flat-topped mesa and look off through the clear air to mountains that seem quite near by, but are in reality more than two hundred miles away. He pictured the strange colors and lights of the place; ledges of rock, yellow, white and green, drab and maroon, and tumbled piles of red boulders, shadowy buttes in the distance, serrated cliffs against the horizon, not blue, but rosy pink in the heated haze of the air, and perhaps a great, lonely eagle poised above the silent, brilliant waste.

He told it not in book language, with turn of phrase and smoothly flowing sentences, but in simple, frank words, as a boy might describe a picture to one he knew would appreciate it—for her sake, and not because he loved to put it into words; but in a new, stumbling way letting out the beauty that had somehow crept into his heart in spite of all the rough attempts to keep all gentle things out of his nature.

The girl, as she listened, marveled more and more what manner of youth this might be who had come to her out of the desert night.

She forgot her weariness as she listened, in the thrill of wonder over the new mysterious country to which she had come. She forgot that she was riding through the great darkness with an utter stranger, to a place she knew not, and to experiences most dubious. Her fears had fled and she was actually enjoying herself, and responding to the wonderful story of the place with soft murmured exclamations of delight and wonder.

From time to time in the distance there sounded forth those awful bloodcurdling howls of wild beasts that she had heard when she sat alone by the water tank, and each time she heard a shudder passed through her and instinctively she swerved a trifle toward her companion, then straightened up again and tried to seem not to notice.

The boy saw and watched her brave attempts at self-control with deep appreciation. But suddenly, as they rode and talked, a dark form appeared across their way a little ahead, lithe and stealthy and furry, and two awful eyes like green lamps glared for an instant, then disappeared silently among the mesquite bushes.

She did not cry out nor start. Her very veins seemed frozen with horror, and she could not have spoken if she tried. It was all over in a second and the creature gone, so that she almost doubted her senses and wondered if she had seen right. Then one hand went swiftly to her throat and she shrank toward her companion.

"There is nothing to fear," he said, reassuringly, and laid a strong hand comfortingly across the neck of her horse. "The pussycat was as unwilling for our company as we for hers. Besides, look here!"— and he raised his hand and shot into the air. "She'll not come near us now."

"I am not afraid!" said the girl, bravely. "At least, I don't think I am—very! But it's all so new and unexpected, you know. Do people around here always shoot in that—well—unpremeditated fashion?"

They laughed together.

"Excuse me," he said. "I didn't realize the shot might startle you even more than the wildcat. It seems I'm not fit to have charge of a lady. I told you I was a roughneck."

"You're taking care of me beautifully," said Margaret Earle, loyally, "and I'm glad to get used to shots if that's the thing to be expected often."

Just then they came to the top of the low, rolling hill, and ahead in the darkness there gleamed a tiny, wizened light set in a blotch of blackness. Under the great white stars it burned a sickly red and seemed out of harmony with the night.

"There we are!" said the boy, pointing toward it. "That's the bunkhouse. You needn't be afraid. Pop Wallis 'll be snoring by this time, and we'll come away before he's about in the morning. He always sleeps late after he's been off on a bout. He's been gone three days, selling some cattle, and he'll have a pretty good top on."

The girl caught her breath, gave one wistful look up at the wide, starry sky, a furtive glance at the strong face of her protector, and submitted to being lifted down to the ground.

Before her loomed the bunkhouse, small and mean, built of logs, with only one window in which the flicker of the lanterns menaced, with unknown trials and possible perils for her to meet.

Chapter 4

When Margaret Earle dawned upon that bunk room the men sat up with one accord, ran their rough, red hands through their rough, tousled hair, smoothed their beards, took down their feet from the benches where they were resting. That was as far as their etiquette led them. Most of them continued to smoke their pipes, and all of them stared at her unreservedly. Such a sight of exquisite feminine beauty had not come to their eyes in many a long day. Even in the dim light of the smoky lanterns, and with the dust and weariness of travel upon her, Margaret Earle was a beautiful girl.

"That's what's the matter, Father," said her mother, when the subject of Margaret's going west to teach had first been mentioned. "She's too beautiful to go among savages! If she were homely and old, now, she might be safe. That would be a different matter."

Yet Margaret had prevailed, and was here in the wild country. Now, standing on the threshold of the log cabin, she read, in the unveiled admiration that startled from the eyes of the men, the meaning of her mother's fears.

Yet withal it was a kindly admiration not unmixed with awe. For there was about her beauty a touch of the spiritual which set her above the common run of women, making men feel her purity and sweetness, and inclining their hearts to worship rather than be bold.

The boy had been right. Pop Wallis was asleep and out of the way. From a little shed room at one end his snoring marked time in the silence that the advent of the girl made in the place.

In the doorway of the kitchen offset Mom Wallis stood with her passionless face—a face from which all emotions had long ago been burned by cruel fires—and looked at the girl, whose expression was vivid with her opening life all haloed in a rosy glow.

A kind of wistful contortion passed over Mom Wallis's hopeless countenance, as if she saw before her in all its possibility of perfec-

28

tion the life that she herself had lost. Perhaps it was no longer possible for her features to show tenderness, but a glow of something like it burned in her eyes, though she only turned away with the same old apathetic air, and without a word went about preparing a meal for the stranger.

Margaret looked wildly, fearfully, around the rough assemblage when she first entered the long, low room, but instantly the boy introduced her as "the new teacher for the Ridge School beyond the Junction," and these were Long Bill, Big Jim, the Fiddling Boss, Jasper Kemp, Fadeaway Forbes, Stocky, Croaker, and Fudge. An inspiration fell upon the frightened girl, and she acknowledged the introduction by a radiant smile, followed by the offering of her small gloved hand. Each man in dumb bewilderment instantly became her slave, and accepted the offered hand with more or less pleasure and embarrassment. The girl proved her right to be called tactful, and, seeing her advantage, followed it up quickly by a few bright words. These men were of an utterly different type from any she had ever met before, but they had in their eyes a kind of homage which Pop Wallis had not shown and they were not repulsive to her. Besides, the boy was in the background, and her nerve had returned. The boy knew how a lady should be treated. She was quite ready to "play up" to his lead.

It was the boy who brought the only chair the bunkhouse afforded, a rude, homemade affair, and helped her off with her coat and hat in his easy, friendly way, as if he had known her all his life; while the men, to whom such gallant ways were foreign, sat awkwardly by and watched in wonder and amazement.

Most of all they were astonished at the kid, that he could fall so naturally into intimate talk with this delicate, beautiful woman. She was another of his kind, a creature not made in the same mold as theirs. They saw it now, and watched the fairy play with almost childish interest. Just to hear her call him "Mr. Gardley"—Lance Gardley, that was what he had told them was his name the day he came among them. They had not heard it since. The kid! Mr. Gardley!

There it was, the difference between them! They looked at the girl half jealously, yet proudly at the boy. He was theirs—yes, in a way he was theirs—had they not found him in the wilderness, sick and nigh to death, and nursed him back to life again? He was theirs; but he knew how to drop into her world, too, and not be ashamed. They were glad that he could, even while it struck them with a pang that some day he would go back to the world to which he belonged—and where they could never be at home.

It was a marvel to watch her eat the coarse corn bread and pork that Mom Wallis brought her. It might have been a banquet, the pleasant way she seemed to look at it. Just like a bird she tasted it daintily, and smiled, showing her white teeth. There was nothing of the idea of greediness that each man knew he himself felt after a fast. It was all beautiful, the way she handled the two-tined fork and the old steel knife. They watched and dropped their eyes abashed as at a lovely sacrament. They had not felt before that eating could be an art. They did not know what art meant.

Such strange talk, too! But the kid seemed to understand. About the sky—their old, common sky, with stars that they saw every night—making such a fuss about that, with words like "wide," "infinite," "azure," and "gems." Each man went furtively out that night before he slept and took a new look at the sky to see if he could understand.

The boy was planning so the night would be but brief. He knew the girl was afraid. He kept the talk going enthusiastically, drawing in one or two of the men now and again. Long Bill forgot himself and laughed out a hoarse guffaw, then stopped as if he had been choked. Stocky, red in the face, told a funny story when commanded by the boy, and then dissolved in mortification over his blunders. The Fiddling Boss obediently got down his fiddle from the smoky corner beside the fireplace and played a weird old tune or two, and then they sang. First the men, with hoarse, quavering approach and final roar of wild sweetness; then Margaret and the boy in duet, and finally Margaret alone, with a few bashful chords on the fiddle, feeling their way as accompaniment.

Mom Wallis had long ago stopped her work and was sitting huddled in the doorway on a nail keg with weary, folded hands and a strange wistfulness on her apathetic face. A fine silence had settled over the group as the girl, recognizing her power, and the pleasure she was giving, sang on. Now and then the boy, when he knew the song, would join in with his rich tenor.

It was a strange night, and when she finally lay down to rest on a hard cot with a questionable looking blanket for covering and Mom Wallis as her roommate, Margaret Earle could not help wondering what her mother and father would think now if they could see her. Would they not, perhaps, almost prefer the water tank and the lonely desert for her to her present surroundings?

Nevertheless, she slept soundly after her terrible excitement, and woke with a start of wonder in the early morning, to hear the men outside splashing water and humming or whistling bits of the tunes she had sung to them the night before.

Mom Wallis was standing over her, looking down with a hunger in her eyes at the bright waves of Margaret's hair and the soft, sleep-flushed cheeks.

"You got dretful purty hair," said Mom Wallis, wistfully.

Margaret looked up and smiled in acknowledgment of the compliment.

"You wouldn't b'lieve it, but I was young an' purty oncet. Beats all how much it counts to be young—an' purty! But land! It don't last long. Make the most of it while you got it."

Browning's immortal words came to Margaret's lips—

> Grow old along with me,
> The best is yet to be,
> The last of life for which the first was made—

but she checked them just in time and could only smile mutely. How could she speak such thoughts amid these intolerable surroundings? Then with sudden impulse she reached up to the astonished woman and, drawing her down, kissed her sallow cheek.

"Oh!" said Mom Wallis, starting back and laying her bony hands upon the place where she had been kissed, as if it hurt her, while a dull red stole up from her neck over her cheeks and high forehead to the roots of her hay-colored hair. All at once she turned her back upon her visitor and the tears of the years streamed down her impassive face.

"Don't mind me," she choked, after a minute. "I liked it real good, only it kind of give me a turn." Then, after a second: "It's time t' eat. You c'n wash outside after the men is done."

That, thought Margaret, had been the scheme of this woman's whole life—"After the men is done!"

So, after all, the night was passed in safety, and a wonderful dawning had come. The blue of the morning, so different from the blue of the night sky, was, nevertheless, just as unfathomable; the air seemed filled with straying star beams, so sparkling was the clearness of the light.

But now a mountain rose in the distance with heliotrope and purple bounds to stand across the vision and dispel the illusion of the night that the sky came down to the earth all around like a close-fitting dome. There were mountains on all sides, and a slender, dark line of mesquite set off the more delicate colorings of the plain.

Into the morning they rode, Margaret and the boy, before Pop Wallis was yet awake, while all the other men stood round and watched, eager, jealous for the handshake and the parting smile. They told her they hoped she would come again and sing for them, and each one had an awkward word of parting. Whatever Margaret Earle might do with her school, she had won seven loyal friends in the camp, and she rode away amid their admiring glances, which lingered, too, on the broad shoulders and wide sombrero of her escort riding by her side.

"Wal, that's the end o' him, I 'spose," drawled Long Bill, with a deep sigh, as the riders passed into the valley out of their sight.

"H'm!" said Jasper Kemp, hungrily. "I reck'n *he* thinks it's jes' th' beginnin'!"

"Maybe so! Maybe so!" said Big Jim, dreamily.

The morning was full of wonder for the girl who had come straight from an eastern city. The view from the top of the mesa, or the cool, dim entrance of a canyon where great ferns fringed and feathered its walls, and strange caves hollowed out in the rocks far above, made real the stories she had read of the cavedwellers. It was a new world.

The boy was charming. She could not have picked out among her city acquaintances a man who would have done the honors of the desert more delightfully than he. She had thought him handsome in the starlight and in the lantern light the night before, but now that the morning shown upon him she could not keep from looking at him. His fresh color, which no wind and weather could quite subdue, his gray-blue eyes with that mixture of thoughtfulness and reverence and daring, his crisp, brown curls glinting with gold in the sunlight—all made him good to look upon. There was something about the firm set of his lips and chin that made her feel a hidden strength about him.

When they camped a little while for lunch he showed the thoughtfulness and care for her comfort that many an older man might not have had. Even his talk was a mixture of boyishness and experience and he seemed to know her thoughts before she had them fully spoken.

"I do not understand it," she said, looking him frankly in the eyes at last. "How ever in the world did one like *you* get landed among all those dreadful men! Of course, in their way, some of them are not so bad, but they are not like you, not in the least, and never could be."

They were riding out upon the plain now in the full afternoon light, and a short time would bring them to her destination.

A sad, set look came quickly into the boy's eyes and his face grew almost hard.

"It's an old story. I suppose you've heard it before," he said, and his voice tried to take on a careless note, but failed. "I didn't make good back there"—he waved his hand sharply toward the east—"so I came out here to begin again. But I guess I haven't made good here, either—not in the way I meant when I came."

"You can't, you know," said Margaret. "Not here."

"Why?" He looked at her earnestly, as if he felt the answer might help him.

"Because you have to go back where you didn't make good and pick up the lost opportunities. You can't really make good till you do that *right where you left off.*"

"But suppose it's too late?"

"It's never too late if we're in earnest and not too proud."

There was a long silence then, while the boy looked thoughtfully off at the mountains, and when he spoke again it was to call attention to the beauty of a silver cloud that floated lazily on the horizon. But Margaret Earle had seen the look in his gray eyes and was not deceived.

A few minutes later they crossed another mesa and descended to the enterprising little town where the girl was to begin her winter's work. The very houses and streets seemed to rise briskly and hasten to meet them those last few minutes of their ride.

Now that the experience was almost over, the girl realized that she had enjoyed it intensely, and that she dreaded inexpressibly that she must bid good-bye to this friend of a few hours and face an unknown world. It had been a wonderful day, and now it was almost done. The two looked at each other and realized that their meeting had been an epoch in their lives that neither would soon forget—that neither wanted to forget.

Chapter 5

Slower the horses walked, and slower. The voices of the boy and girl were low when they spoke about the common things by the wayside. Once their eyes met, and they smiled with something both sad and glad in them.

Margaret was watching the young man by her side and wondering at herself. He was different from any man whose life had come near to hers before. He was wild and worldly, she could see that, and unrestrained by many of the things that were vital principles with her, and yet she felt strangely drawn to him and wonderfully at home in his company. She could not understand herself nor him. It was as if his real soul had looked out of his eyes and spoken, untrammeled by the circumstances of birth or breeding or habit, and she knew him for a kindred spirit. And yet he was far from being one in whom she would have expected even to find a friend. Where was her confidence of yesterday? Why was it that she dreaded to have this strong young protector leave her to meet alone a world of strangers, whom yesterday at this time she would have gladly welcomed?

Now, when his face grew thoughtful and sad, she saw the hard, bitter lines that were beginning to be graven about his lips, and her heart ached over what he had said about not making good. She wondered if there was anything else she could say to help him, but no words came to her, and the sad, set look about his lips warned her that perhaps she had said enough. He was not one who needed a long dissertation to bring a thought home to his consciousness.

Gravely they rode to the station to see about Margaret's trunks and make inquiries for the school and the house where she had arranged to board. Then Margaret sent a telegram to her mother to say that she had arrived safely, and so, when all was done and there was no longer an excuse for lingering, the boy realized that he must leave her.

They stood alone for just a moment while the voluble landlady went to attend to something that was boiling over on the stove. It was an ugly little parlor that was to be her reception room for the next year at least, with red and green ingrain carpet of ancient pattern, hideous chromos on the walls, and frantically common furniture setting up in its shining varnish to be pretentious; but the girl had not seen it yet. She was filled with a great homesickness that had not possessed her even when she said good-bye to her dear ones at home. She suddenly realized that the people with whom she was to be thrown were of another world from hers, and this one friend whom she had found in the desert was leaving her.

She tried to shake hands formally and tell him how grateful she was to him for rescuing her from the perils of the night, but somehow words seemed so inadequate, and tears kept crowding their way into her throat and eyes. Absurd it was, and he a stranger twenty hours before, and a man of other ways than hers, besides. Yet he was her friend and rescuer.

She spoke her thanks as well as she could, and then looked up, a swift, timid glance, and found his eyes upon her earnestly and troubled.

"Don't thank me," he said, huskily. "I guess it was the best thing I ever did, finding you. I shan't forget, even if you never let me see you again—and—I hope you will." His eyes searched hers wistfully.

"Of course," she said. "Why not?"

"I thank you," he said in quaint, courtly fashion, bending low over her head. "I shall try to be worthy of the honor."

And so saying, he left her and, mounting his horse, rode away into the lengthening shadows of the afternoon.

She stood in the forlorn little room staring out of the window after her late companion, a sense of utter desolation upon her. For the moment all her brave hopes of the future had fled, and if she could have slipped unobserved out of the front door, down to the station, and boarded some waiting express to her home, she would gladly have done it then and there.

Try as she would to summon her former reasons for coming to this wild, she could not think of one of them, and her eyes were very near to tears.

But Margaret Earle was not given to tears, and as she felt them smart beneath her lids she turned in a panic to prevent them. She could not afford to cry now. Mrs. Tanner would be returning, and she must not find the new schoolteacher weeping.

With a glance she swept the meager, pretentious room, and then, suddenly, became aware of other presences. In the doorway stood a man and a dog, both regarding her intently with open surprise, not unmixed with open appraisement and a marked degree of admiration.

The man was of medium height, slight, with a putty complexion, cold, pale blue eyes, pale, straw-colored hair, and a look of self-indulgence around his rather weak mouth. He was dressed in a city business suit of the latest cut, however, and looked as much out of place in that crude little house as did Margaret Earle herself in her simple gown of dark blue crepe and her undeniable air of style and good taste.

His eyes, as they regarded her, had in them a smile that the girl instinctively resented. Was it a shade too possessive and complacently sure for a stranger?

The dog, a large collie, had great, liquid, brown eyes, menacing or loyal, as circumstances dictated, and regarded her with an air of brief indecision. She felt she was being weighed in the balance by both pairs of eyes. Of the two the girl preferred the dog.

Perhaps the dog understood, for he came a pace nearer and waved his plumy tail tentatively. For the dog she felt a glow of friendliness at once, but for the man she suddenly, and most unreasonably, of course, conceived one of her violent and unexpected dislikes.

Into this tableau bustled Mrs. Tanner. "Well, now, I didn't go to leave you by your lonesome all this time," she apologized, wiping her hands on her apron, "but them beans boiled clean over, and I hed to put 'em in a bigger kettle. You see, I put in more beans 'count o' you bein' here, an' I ain't uset to calca'latin' on two extry." She looked happily from the man to the girl and back again.

"Mr. West, I 'spose, o' course, you interjuced yerself? Bein' a preacher, you don't hev to stan' on ceremony like the rest of mankind. You 'ain't? Well, let me hev the pleasure of interjucin' our new schoolteacher, Miss Margaret Earle. I 'spect you two 'll be awful chummy right at the start, both bein' from the East that way, an' both hevin' ben to college."

Margaret Earle acknowledged the bow with a cool little inclination of her head. She wondered why she didn't hate the garrulous woman who rattled on in this happy, take-it-for-granted way, but there was something so innocently pleased in her manner that she couldn't help putting all her wrath on the smiling man who came forward instantly with a low bow and a voice of fulsome flattery.

"Indeed, Miss Earle, I assure you I am happily surprised. I am sure Mrs. Tanner's prophecy will come true and we shall be the best of friends. When they told me the new teacher was to board here I really hesitated. I have seen something of these western teachers in my time, and scarcely thought I should find you congenial, but I can see at a glance that you are the exception to the rule."

He presented a soft, unmanly white hand, and there was nothing to do but take it or seem rude to her hostess, but her manner was like icicles, and she was thankful she had not yet removed her gloves.

If the reverend gentleman thought he was to enjoy a lingering handclasp he was mistaken, for the gloved fingertips merely touched his hand and were withdrawn, and the girl turned to her hostess with a smile of finality as if he were dismissed. He did not seem disposed to take the hint and withdraw, however, until on a sudden the great dog came and stood between them with open mouthed welcome and joyous greeting in the plumy, wagging tail. He pushed close to her and looked up into her face insistently, his hanging pink tongue and wide, smiling countenance proclaiming that he was satisfied with his investigation.

Margaret looked down at him, and then stooped and put her arms about his neck. Something in his kindly dog expression made her feel suddenly as if she had a real friend.

It seemed the man, however, did not like the situation. He kicked gingerly at the dog's hind legs, and said in a harsh voice:

"Get out of the way, sir. You're annoying the lady. Get out, I say!"

The dog, however, uttered a low growl and merely showed the whites of his menacing eyes at the man, turning his body slightly so that he stood across the lady's way protectingly, as if to keep the man from her.

Margaret smiled at the dog and laid her hand on his head, as if to signify her acceptance of the friendship he had offered her, and he waved his plume once more and attended her from the room, neither of them giving further attention to the man.

"Confound that dog!" said Reverend Frederick West, in almost unpreacherlike tone, as he walked to the window and looked out. Then to himself he mused: "A pretty girl. A *very pretty* girl. I really think it'll be worth my while to stay a month at least."

Up in her room the "very pretty girl" was unpacking her suitcase and struggling with the tears. Not since she was a wee little girl and went to school all alone for the first time had she felt so very forlorn, and it was the little bare bedroom that had done it. At least that had been the final straw that had made too great the burden of keeping down those threatening tears.

It was only a bare, plain room with unfinished walls, rough wood-work, a cheap wooden bed, a bureau with a warped looking glass, and on the floor was a braided rug of rags. A little wooden rocker, another small, straight wooden chair, a hanging wall pocket decorated with purple roses, a hanging bookshelf composed of three thin boards strung together with maroon picture cord, a violently colored picture card of "Moses in the Bulrushes" framed in straws and red worsted, and bright blue paper shades at the windows. That was the room!

How different from her room at home, simply and sweetly finished anew for her homecoming from college! It rose before her homesick vision now. Soft gray walls, rose-colored ceiling, blended by a wreath of exquisite wild roses, whose pattern was repeated in the border of the simple curtains and chair cushions, white enamel furniture, pretty brass bed soft as down in its luxurious mattress, spotless and inviting always. She glanced at the humpy bed with its fringed gray spread and lumpy-looking pillows in dismay. She had not thought of little discomforts like that, yet how they loomed upon her weary vision now!

The tiny wooden stand with its thick, white crockery seemed ill substitute for the dainty white bathroom at home. She had known she would not have her home luxuries, of course, but she had not realized until set down amid these barren surroundings what a difference they would make.

Going to the window and looking out, she saw for the first time the one luxury the little room possessed—a view! And such a view! Wide and wonderful and far it stretched, in colors unmatched by painter's brush, a purple mountain topped by rosy clouds in the distance. For the second time in Arizona her soul was lifted suddenly out of itself and its dismay by a vision of the things that God has made and the largeness of it all.

Chapter 6

For some time she stood and gazed, marveling at the beauty and recalling some of the things her companion of the afternoon had said about his impressions of the place; then suddenly there loomed a dark speck in the near foreground of her meditation, and, looking down annoyed, she discovered the minister like a gnat between the eye and a grand spectacle, his face turned admiringly up to her window, his hand lifted in familiar greeting.

Vexed at his familiarity, she turned quickly and jerked down the shade; then throwing herself on the bed, she had a good cry. Her nerves were terribly wrought up. Things seemed twisted in her mind, and she felt that she had reached the limit of her endurance. Here was she, Margaret Earle, newly elected teacher to the Ashland Ridge School, lying on her bed in tears, when she ought to be getting settled and planning her new life; when the situation demanded her best attention she was wrought up over a foolish little personal dislike. Why did she have to dislike a minister, anyway, and then take to a wild young fellow whose life thus far had been anything but satisfactory even to himself? Was it her perverse nature that caused her to remember the look in the eyes of the boy who had rescued her from a night in the wilderness, and to feel there was far more manliness in his face than in the face of the man whose profession surely would lead one to suppose he was more worthy of her respect and interest? Well, she was tired. Perhaps things would assume their normal relation to one another in the morning. And so, after a few minutes, she bathed her face in the little, heavy, ironstone washbowl, combed her hair, and freshened the collar and ruffles in her sleeves preparatory to going down for the evening meal. Then, with a swift thought, she searched through her suitcase for every available article wherewith to brighten that forlorn room.

The dainty dressing case of Dresden silk with rosy ribbons that her girl friends at home had given as a parting gift covered a generous portion of the pine bureau, and when she had spread it out and bestowed its silver-mounted brushes, combs, hand glass, and pretty sachet, things seemed to brighten up a bit. She hung up a cobweb of a lace boudoir cap with its rose-colored ribbons over the bleary mirror, threw her kimono of flowered challis over the back of the rocker, arranged her soap and toothbrush, her own washrag and a towel brought from home on the washstand, and somehow felt better and more as if she belonged. Last she arranged her precious photographs of father and mother and the dear vine-covered church and manse across in front of the mirror. When her trunks came there would be other things, and she could bear it, perhaps, when she had this room buried deep in the home belongings. But this would have to do for tonight, for the trunk might not come till morning, and, anyhow, she was too weary to unpack.

She ventured one more look out of her window, peering carefully at first to make sure her fellow boarder was not still standing down below on the grass. A pang of compunction shot through her conscience. What would her dear father think of her feeling this way toward a minister, and before she knew the first thing about him, too? It was dreadful! She must shake it off. Of course he was a good man or he wouldn't be in the ministry, and she had doubtless mistaken mere friendliness for forwardness. She would forget it and try to go down and behave to him the way her father would want her to behave toward a fellow minister.

Cautiously she raised the shade again and looked out. The mountain was bathed in a wonderful ruby light fading into amethyst, and all the path between was many-colored like a pavement of jewels set in filigree. While she looked the picture changed, glowed, softened, and changed again, making her think of the chapter about the holy city in Revelation.

She started at last when someone knocked hesitatingly on the door, for the wonderful sunset light had made her forget for the moment where she was, and it seemed a desecration to have mere mortals step in and announce supper, although the odor of pork and cabbage had been proclaiming it dumbly for some time.

She went to the door, and, opening it, found a dark figure standing in the hall. For a minute she half feared it was the minister, until a shy, reluctant backwardness in the whole stocky figure and the stirring of a large furry creature just behind him made her sure it was not.

"Ma says you're to come to supper," said a gruff, untamed voice, and Margaret perceived that the person in the gathering gloom of the hall was a boy.

"Oh!" said Margaret, with relief in her voice. "Thank you for coming to tell me. I meant to come down and not give that trouble, but I got to looking at the wonderful sunset. Have you been watching it?" She pointed across the room to the window. "Look! Isn't that a great color there on the tip of the mountain? I never saw anything like that at home. I suppose you're used to it, though."

The boy came a step nearer the door and looked blankly, half wondering, across at the window, as if he expected to see some phenomenon. "Oh! *That!*" he exclaimed, carelessly. "Sure! We have them all the time."

"But that wonderful silver light pouring down just in that one tiny spot!" exclaimed Margaret. "It makes the mountain seem alive and smiling!"

The boy turned and looked at her curiously. "Gee!" said he, "I c'n show you plenty like that!" But he turned and looked at it a long, lingering minute again.

"But we mustn't keep your mother waiting," said Margaret, remembering and turning reluctantly toward the door. "Is this your dog? Isn't he a beauty! He made me feel really as if he were glad to see me." She stooped and laid her hand on the dog's head and smiled brightly up at his master.

The boy's face lit with a smile, and he turned a keen, appreciative look at the new teacher, for the first time genuinely interested in her. "Cap's a good old scout," he admitted.

"So his name is Cap. Is that short for anything?"

"Cap'n."

"Captain. What a good name for him. He looks as if he were a captain, and he waves that tail grandly, almost as if it might be a badge of office. But who are you? You haven't told me your name yet? Are you Mrs. Tanner's son?"

The boy nodded. "I'm just Bud Tanner."

"Then you are one of my pupils, aren't you? We must shake hands on that." She put out her hand, but she was forced to go out after Bud's reluctant red fist, take it by force in a strange grasp, and do all the shaking; for Bud had never had that experience before in his life, and he emerged from it with a very red face and a feeling as if his right arm had been somehow lifted out of the same class with the rest of his body. It was rather awful, too, that it happened just in the open dining room door, and that preacher-boarder watched the whole performance. Bud put on an extra deep frown and shuffled away from the teacher, making a great show of putting Cap out of the dining room, though he always sat behind his master's chair at meals, much to the discomfiture of the male boarder, who was slightly in awe of his dogship, not having been admitted into friendship as the lady had been.

Mr. West stood back of his chair, awaiting the arrival of the new boarder, an expectant smile on his face, and rubbing his hands together with much the same effect as a wolf licking his lips in anticipation of a victim. In spite of her resolves to like the man, Margaret was again struck with aversion as she saw him standing there, and was intensely relieved when she found that the seat assigned to her was on the opposite side of the table from him, and beside Bud. West, however, did not seem to be pleased with the arrangement, and, stepping around the table, said to his landlady:

"Did you mean me to sit over here?" and he placed a possessive hand on the back of the chair that was meant for Bud.

"No, Mister West, you jest set where you ben settin'," responded Mrs. Tanner. She had thought the matter all out and decided that the minister could converse with the teacher to the better advantage of the whole table if he sat across from her. Mrs. Tanner was a born matchmaker. This she felt was an opportunity not to be despised, even if it sometime robbed the Ridge school of a desirable teacher.

But West did not immediately return to his place at the other side of the table. To Margaret's extreme annoyance he drew her chair and waited for her to sit down. The situation, however, was somewhat relieved of its intimacy by a sudden interference from Cap, who darted away from his frowning master and stepped up authoritatively to the minister's side with a low growl, as if to say:

"Hands off that chair! That doesn't belong to you!"

West suddenly released his hold on the chair without waiting to shove it up to the table, and precipitately retired to his own place. "That dog's a nuisance!" he said, testily, and was answered with a glare from Bud's dark eyes.

Bud came to his seat with his eyes still set savagely on the minister, and Cap settled down protectingly behind Margaret's chair.

Mrs. Tanner bustled in with the coffeepot, and Mr. Tanner came last, having just finished his rather elaborate hair comb at the kitchen glass with the kitchen comb, in full view of the assembled multitude. He was a little, thin, wiry, weather-beaten man, with skin like leather and sparse hair. Some of his teeth were missing, leaving deep hollows in his cheeks, and his kindly protruding chin was covered with scraggy gray whiskers, which stuck out ahead of him like a cow-catcher. He was in his shirtsleeves and collarless, but looked neat and clean, and he greeted the new guest heartily before he sat down, and nodded to the minister:

"Naow, Brother West, I reckon we're ready fer your part o' the performance. You'll please to say grace."

Mr. West bowed his sleek, yellow head and muttered a formal blessing with an offhand manner, as if it were a mere ceremony. Bud stared contemptuously at him the while, and Cap uttered a low rumble as of a distant growl. Margaret felt a sudden desire to laugh, and tried to control herself, wondering what her father would feel about it all.

The genial clatter of knives and forks broke the stiffness after the blessing. Mrs. Tanner bustled back and forth from the stove to the table, talking incessantly. Mr. Tanner joined in with his flat, nasal twang, responding, and the minister, with an air of utter contempt for them both, endeavored to set up a separate and altogether private conversation with Margaret across the narrow table; but Margaret innocently had begun a conversation with Bud about the school, and had to be addressed by name each time before Mr. West could get her attention. Bud, with a boy's keenness, noticed her aversion, and put aside his own backwardness, entering into the contest with remarkably voluble replies. The minister, if he would be in the talk at all, was forced to join in with theirs, and found himself worsted and contradicted by the boy at every turn.

Strange to say, however, this state of things only served to make the man more eager to talk with the lady. She was not anxious for his attention. Ah! She was coy, and the acquaintance was to have the zest of being no lightly won friendship. All the better. He watched her as she talked, noted every charm of lash and lid and curving lip; staring so continually that she finally gave up looking his way at all, even when she was obliged to answer his questions.

Thus, at last, the first meal in the new home was concluded, and Margaret, pleading excessive weariness, went to her room. She felt as if she could not endure another half hour of contact with her present world until she had had some rest. If the world had been just Bud and the dog she could have stayed belowstairs and found out a little more about the new life, but with that oily mouthed minister continually butting in her soul was in a tumult.

When she had prepared for rest she put out her light and drew up the shade. There before her spread the wide wonder of the heavens again, with the soft purple of the mountain under stars, and she was carried back to the experience of the night before with a vivid memory of her companion. Why, just *why* couldn't she be as interested in the minister down there as in the wild young man? Well, she was too tired tonight to analyze it all, and she knelt beside her window in the starlight to pray. As she prayed her thoughts were on Lance Gardley once more, and she felt her heart go out in longing for him, that he might find a way to make good, whatever his trouble had been.

As she rose to retire she heard a step below, and, looking down, saw the minister stalking back and forth in the yard, his hands clasped behind, his head thrown back raptly. He could not see her in her dark room, but she pulled the shade down softly and fled to her hard little bed. Was that man going to obsess her vision everywhere, and must she try to like him just because he was a minister?

So at last she fell asleep.

Chapter 7

The next day was filled with unpacking and with writing letters home. By dint of being very busy Margaret managed to forget the minister, who seemed to obtrude himself at every possible turn of the day, and would have monopolized her if she had given him half a chance.

The trunks, two delightful steamer ones, and a big packing box with her books, arrived the next morning and caused great excitement in the household. Not since they moved into the new house had they seen so many things arrive. Bud helped carry them upstairs, while Cap ran wildly back and forth, giving sharp barks, and the minister stood by the front door and gave ineffectual and unpractical advice to the man who had brought them. Margaret heard the man and Bud exchanging their opinion of West in low growls in the hall as they entered her door, and she couldn't help feeling that she agreed with them, though she might not have expressed her opinion in the same terms.

The minister tapped at her door a little later and offered his services in opening her box and unstrapping her trunks, but she told him Bud had already performed that service for her, and thanked him with a finality that forbade him to linger. She half hoped he heard the vicious little click with which she locked the door after him, and then wondered if she were wicked to feel that way. But all such compunctions were presently forgotten in the work of making over her room.

The trunks, after they were unpacked and repacked with the things she would not need at once, were disposed in front of the two windows with which the ugly little room was blessed. She covered them with two Oriental rugs, relics of her college days, and piled several college pillows from the packing box on each, which made the room instantly assume a homelike air. Then out of the box came other things. Framed pictures of home scenes, college friends and places, pennants, and flags from football, baseball, and basketball games she had attended, photographs, a few prints of rare paintings simply framed, a roll of rose-bordered white scrim like her curtains at home, wherewith she transformed the blue-shadowed windows and the stiff little wooden rocker, and even made a valance and bed-cover over pink cambric for her bed. The bureau and washstand were given pink and white covers, and the ugly walls literally disappeared beneath pictures, pennants, banners, and symbols.

When Bud came up to call her to dinner she flung the door open, and he paused in wide-eyed amazement over the transformation. His eyes kindled at a pair of golf sticks, a hockey stick, a tennis racket, and a big basketball in the corner; and his whole look of surprise was so ridiculous that she had to laugh. He looked as if a miracle had been performed on the room, and actually stepped back into the hall to get his breath and be sure he was still in his father's house.

"I want you to come in and see all my pictures and get acquainted with my friends when you have time," she said. "I wonder if you could make some more shelves for my books and help me unpack and set them up?"

"Sure!" gasped Bud, heartily, albeit with awe. She hadn't asked the minister; she had asked *him—Bud!* Just a boy! He looked around the room with anticipation. What wonder and delight he would have looking at all those things!

Then Cap stepped into the middle of the room as if he belonged, mouth open, tongue lolling, smiling and panting a hearty approval, as he looked about at the strangeness for all the world as a human being might have done. It was plain he was pleased with the change.

There was a proprietary air about Bud during dinner that was pleasant to Margaret and most annoying to West. It was plain that West looked on the boy as an upstart whom Miss Earle was using for the present to block his approach, and he was growing most impatient over the delay. He suggested that perhaps she would like his escort to see something of her surroundings that afternoon; but she smilingly told him that she would be very busy all the afternoon getting settled, and when he offered again to help her, she cast a dazzling smile on Bud and said she didn't think she would need any more help, that Bud was going to do a few things for her, and that was all that was necessary.

Bud straightened up and became two inches taller. He passed the bread, suggested two pieces of pie, and filled her glass of water as if she were his partner. Mr. Tanner beamed to see his son in high favor, but Mrs. Tanner looked a little troubled for the minister. She thought things weren't just progressing as fast as they ought to between him and the teacher.

Bud, with Margaret's instructions, managed to make a very creditable bookcase out of the packing box sawed in half, the pieces set side by side. She covered them deftly with green burlap left over from college days, like her other supplies, and then the two arranged the books. Bud was delighted over the prospect of reading some of the books, for they were not all schoolbooks, by any means, and she had brought plenty of them to keep her from being lonesome on days when she longed to fly back to her home.

At last the work was done, and they stood back to survey it. The books filled up every speck of space and overflowed to the three little hanging shelves over them; but they were all squeezed in at last except a pile of schoolbooks that were saved out to take to the schoolhouse. Margaret set a tiny vase on the top of one part of the packing case and a small brass bowl on the top of the other, and Bud, after a knowing glance, scurried away for a few minutes and brought back a handful of gorgeous cactus blossoms to give the final touch.

"Gee!" he said, admiringly, looking around the room. "Gee! You wouldn't know it fer the same place!"

That evening after supper Margaret sat down to write a long letter home. She had written a brief letter, of course, the night before, but had been too weary to go into detail. The letter read:

DEAR MOTHER AND FATHER—I'm unpacked and settled at last in my room, and now I can't stand it another minute till I talk to you.

Last night, of course, I was pretty homesick, things all looked so strange and new and different. I had known they would, but then I didn't realize at all how different they would be. But I'm not getting homesick already; don't think it. I'm not a bit sorry I came, or at least I shan't be when I get started in school. One of the scholars is Mrs. Tanner's son, and I like him. He's crude, of course, but he has a brain, and he's been helping me this afternoon. We made a bookcase for my books, and it looks fine. I wish you could see it. I covered it with the green burlap, and the books look real happy in smiling rows over on the other side of the room. Bud Tanner got me some wonderful cactus blossoms for my brass bowl. I wish I could send you some. They are gorgeous!

But you will want me to tell about my arrival. Well, to begin with, I was late getting here (Margaret had decided to leave out the incident of the desert altogether, for she knew by experience that her mother would suffer terrors all during her absence if she once heard of that wild adventure) which accounts for the lateness of the telegram I sent you. I hope its delay didn't make you worry any.

A very nice young man named Mr. Gardley piloted me to Mrs. Tanner's house and looked after my trunks for me. He is from the East. It was fortunate for me that he happened along, for he was most kind and gentlemanly and helpful. Tell Jane not to worry lest I'll fall in love with him; he doesn't live here. He belongs to a ranch or camp or something twenty-five miles away. She was so afraid I'd fall in love with an Arizona man and not come back home.

Mrs. Tanner is very kind and motherly according to her lights. She has given me the best room in the house, and she talks a blue streak. She has thin, brown hair turning gray, and she wears it in a funny little knob on the tip-top of her round head to correspond with the funny little tuft of hair on her husband's protruding chin. Her head is set on her neck like a clothespin, only she is squattier than a clothespin. She always wears her sleeves rolled up (at least so far she has) and she always bustles around noisily and apologizes for everything in the jolliest sort of way. I would like her, I guess, if it wasn't for the other boarder, but she has quite made up her mind that I shall like him, and I don't, of course, so she is a bit disappointed in me so far.

Mr. Tanner is very kind and funny, and looks something like a jackknife with the blades half open. He never disagrees with Mrs. Tanner, and I really believe he's in love with her yet, though they must have been married a good while. He calls her "Ma," and seems restless unless she's in the room. When she goes out to the kitchen to get some more soup or hash or bring in the pie, he shouts remarks at her all the time she's gone, and she answers, utterly regardless of the conversation the rest of the family are carrying on. It's like a phonograph wound up for the day.

Bud Tanner is about fourteen, and I like him. He's well developed, strong, and almost handsome, at least he would be if he were fixed up a little. He has fine, dark eyes and a great shock of dark hair. He and I are friends already. And so is the dog. The dog is a peach! Excuse me, Mother, but I just must use a little of the dear old college slang somewhere, and your letters are the only safety valve, for I'm a schoolmarm now and must talk "good and proper" all the time, you know.

The dog's name is Captain, and he looks the part. He has constituted himself my bodyguard, and it's going to be very nice having him. He's perfectly devoted already. He's a great, big, fluffy fellow with keen, intelligent eyes, sensitive ears, and a tail like a spreading plume. You'd love him, I know. He has a smile like the morning sunshine.

And now I come to the only other member of the family, the boarder, and I hesitate to approach the topic, because I have taken one of my violent and naughty dislikes to him, and—awful thought—Mother! Father! *he's a minister!* Yes, he's a *Presbyterian minister!* I know it will make you feel dreadfully, and I thought some of not telling you, but my conscience hurt me so I had to. I just can't *bear* him, so there! Of course, I may get over it, but I don't see how ever, for I can't think of anything that's more like him than *soft soap!* Oh yes, there is one other word. Grandmother used to use it about men she hadn't any use for, and that was "squash." Mother, I can't help it, but he does seem something like a squash. One of that crook-necked, yellow kind with warts all over it, and a great, big, splurgy vine behind it to account for its being there at all. Insipid and thready when it's cooked, you know, and has to have a lot of salt and pepper and butter to make it go down at all. Now I've told you the worst, and I'll try to describe him and see what you think I'd better do about it. Oh, he isn't the regular minister here, or missionary—I guess they call *him.* *He's* located quite a distance off, and only comes once a month to preach here, and, anyhow, *he's* gone East now to take his wife to a hospital for an operation, and won't be back for a couple of months, perhaps, and this man isn't even taking his place. He's just here for his health or for fun or something, I guess. He says he had a large suburban church near New York, and had a nervous breakdown; but I've been wondering if he didn't make a mistake, and it wasn't the church had the nervous breakdown instead. He isn't very big nor very little; he's just insignificant. His hair is like wet straw, and his eyes like a fish's. His hand feels like a dead toad when you have to shake hands, which I'm thankful doesn't have to be done but once. He looks at you with a flat, sickening grin. He has an acquired double chin, acquired to make him look pompous, and he dresses stylishly and speaks of the inhabitants of this country with contempt. He wants to be very affable, and offers to take me to all sorts of places, but so far I've avoided him. I can't think how they ever came to let him be a minister—I really can't. And yet, I suppose it's all my horrid old prejudice, and Father will be grieved and you will think I am perverse. But, really, I'm sure he's not one bit like Father was when he was young. I never saw a minister like him. Perhaps I'll get over it. I do sometimes, you know, so don't begin to worry yet. I'll try real hard. I suppose he'll preach Sunday, and then, perhaps, his sermon will be grand and I'll forget how soft-soapy he looks and think only of his great thoughts.

But I know it will be a sort of comfort to you to know that there is a Presbyterian minister in the house with me, and I'll really try to like him if I can.

There's nothing to complain of in the board. It isn't luxurious, of course, but I didn't expect that. Everything is very plain, but Mrs. Tanner manages to make it taste good. She makes fine corn bread, almost as good as yours—not quite.

My room is all lovely, now that I have covered its bareness with my own things, but it has one great thing that can't compare with anything at home, and that is its view. It is wonderful! I wish I could make you see it. There is a mountain at the end of it that has as many different garments as a queen. Tonight, when sunset came, it grew filmy as if a gauze of many colors had dropped upon it and melted into it, and glowed and melted until it turned to slate blue under the wide, starred blue of the wonderful night sky, and all the dark about was velvet. Last night my mountain was all pink and silver, and I have seen it purple and rose. But you can't think the wideness of the sky, and I couldn't paint it for you with words. You must see it to understand. A great, wide, dark sapphire floor just simply ravished with stars like big jewels!

But I must stop and go to bed, for I find the air of this country makes me very sleepy, and my wicked little kerosene lamp is smoking. I guess you would better send me my student lamp, after all, for I'm surely going to need it.

Now I must turn out the light and say good-night to my mountain, and then I will go to sleep thinking of you. Don't worry about the minister. I'm very polite to him, but I shall never—*no, never*—fall in love with *him*—tell Jane.

Your loving little girl,

MARGARET

Chapter 8

Margaret had arranged with Bud to take her to the schoolhouse the next morning, and he had promised to have a horse hitched up and ready at ten o'clock, as it seemed the school was a magnificent distance from her boarding place. In fact, everything seemed to be located with a view to being as far from everywhere else as possible. Even the town was scattering and widespread and sparse.

When she came down to breakfast she was disappointed to find that Bud was not there, and she was obliged to suffer a breakfast tête-à-tête with West. By dint, however, of asking him questions instead of allowing him to take the initiative, she hurried through her breakfast quite successfully, acquiring a superficial knowledge of her fellow boarder quite distant and satisfactory. She knew where he spent his college days and at what theological seminary he had prepared for the ministry. He had served three years in a prosperous church of a fat little suburb of New York, and was taking a winter off from his severe, strenuous pastoral labors to recuperate his strength, get a new stock of sermons ready, and possibly to write a book of some of his experiences. He flattened his weak, pink chin learnedly as he said this, and tried to look at her impressively. He said that he should probably take a large city church as his next pastorate when his health was fully recuperated. He had come out to study the West and enjoy its freedom, as he understood it was a good place to rest and do as you please unhampered by what people thought. He wanted to get as far away from churches and things clerical as possible. He felt it was due himself and his work that he should. He spoke of the people he had met in Arizona as a kind of tamed savages, and Mrs. Tanner, sitting behind her coffeepot for a moment between bustles, heard his comments meekly and looked at him with awe. What a great man he must be, and how fortunate for the new teacher that he should be there when she came!

54

Margaret drew a breath of relief as she hurried away from the breakfast table to her room. She was really anticipating the ride to the school with Bud. She liked boys, and Bud had taken her fancy. But when she came downstairs with her hat and sweater on she found West standing out in front, holding the horse.

"Bud had to go in another direction, Miss Earle," he said, touching his hat gracefully, "and he has delegated to me the pleasant task of driving you to the school."

Dismay filled Margaret's soul, and rage with young Bud. He had deserted her and left her in the hands of the enemy! And she had thought he understood! Well, there was nothing for it but to go with this man, much as she disliked it. Her father's daughter could not be rude to a minister.

She climbed into the buckboard quickly to get the ceremony over, for her escort was inclined to be too officious about helping her in, and somehow she couldn't bear to have him touch her. Why was it that she felt so about him? Of course he must be a good man.

West made a serious mistake at the very outset of that ride. He took it for granted that all girls like flattery, and he proceeded to try it on Margaret. But Margaret did not enjoy being told how delighted he was to find that instead of the loud, bold old maid he had expected, she had turned out to be so beautiful and young and altogether congenial; and, coolly ignoring his compliments, she began a fire of questions again.

She asked about the country, because that was the most obvious topic of conversation. What plants were those that grew by the wayside? She found he knew greasewood from sagebrush, and that was about all. To some of her questions he hazarded answers that were absurd in the light of the explanations given her by Gardley two days before. However, she reflected that he had been in the country but a short time, and that he was by nature a man not interested in such topics. She tried religious matters, thinking that here at least they must have common interests. She asked him what he thought of Christianity in the West as compared with the East. Did he find these western people more alive and awake to the things of the Kingdom?

West gave a startled look at the clear profile of the young woman beside him, thought he perceived that she was testing him on his clerical side, flattened his chin in his most learned, self-conscious manner, cleared his throat, and put on wisdom.

"Well, now, Miss Earle," he began, condescendingly, "I really don't know that I have thought much about the matter. Ah—you know I have been resting absolutely, and I really haven't had opportunity to study the situation out here in detail, but, on the whole, I should say that everything was decidedly primitive, yes—ah—I might say—ah—well, crude. Yes, *crude* in the extreme! Why, take it in this mission district. The missionary who is in charge seems to be teaching the most absurd of the old dogmas such as our forefathers used to teach. I haven't met him, of course. He is in the East with his wife for a time. I am told she had to undergo some kind of an operation. I have never met him, and really don't care to do so, but to judge from all I hear, he is a most unfit man for a position of the kind. For example, he is teaching such exploded doctrines as the old view of the atonement, the infallibility of the Scriptures, the deity of Christ, belief in miracles, and the like. Of course, in one sense it really matters very little what the poor Indians believe, or what such people as the Tanners are taught. They have but little mind, and would scarcely know the difference, but you can readily see that with such a primitive, unenlightened man at the head of religious affairs, there could scarcely be much broadening and real religious growth. Ignorance, of course, holds sway out here. I fancy you will find that to be the case soon enough. What in the world ever led you to come to a field like this to labor? Surely there must have been many more congenial places open to such as you." He leaned forward and cast a sentimental glance at her, his eyes looking more fishy than ever.

"I came out here because I wanted to get acquainted with this great country, and because I thought there was an opportunity to do good," said Margaret, coldly. She did not care to discuss her own affairs with this man. "But, Mr. West, I don't know that I altogether understand you. Didn't you tell me that you were a Presbyterian minister?"

"I certainly did," he answered, complacently, as though he were honoring the whole great body of Presbyterians by making the statement.

"Well, then, what in the world did you mean? All Presbyterians, of course, believe in the infallibility of the Scriptures and the deity of Jesus—and the atonement!"

"Not necessarily," answered the young man, loftily. "You will find, my dear young lady, that there is a wide, growing feeling in our church in favor of a broader view. The younger men and the great student body of our church have thrown to the winds all their former beliefs and are ready to accept new light with open minds. The findings of science have opened up a vast store of knowledge, and all thinking men must acknowledge that the old dogmas are rapidly vanishing away. Your father doubtless still holds to the old faith, perhaps, and we must be lenient with the older men who have done the best they could with the light they had, but all younger, broadminded men are coming to the new way of looking at things. We have had enough of the days of preaching hellfire and damnation. We need a religion of love to man, and good works. You should read some of the books that have been written on this subject, if you care to understand. I really think it would be worth your while. You look to me like a young woman with a mind. I have a few of the latest with me. I shall be glad to read and discuss them with you if you are interested."

"Thank you, Mr. West," said Margaret, coolly, though her eyes burned with battle. "I think I have probably read most of those books and discussed them with my father. He may be old, but he is not without light, as you call it, and he always believed in knowing all that the other side was saying. He brought me up to look into these things for myself. And, anyhow, I should not care to read and discuss any of these subjects with a man who denies the deity of my Saviour and does not believe in the infallibility of the Bible. It seems to me you have nothing left—"

"Ah! Well—now—my dear young lady—you mustn't misjudge me! I should be sorry indeed to shake your faith, for an innocent faith is, of course, a most beautiful thing, even though it may be unfounded."

"Indeed, Mr. West, that would not be possible. You could not shake my faith in my Christ, because *I know Him.* If I had not ever felt His presence, nor been guided by His leading, such words might

possibly trouble me, but having seen 'Him that is invisible,' *I know.*"
Margaret's voice was steady and gentle. It was impossible for even
that man not to be impressed by her words.

"Well, let us not quarrel about it," he said, indulgently, as to a
little child. "I'm sure you have a very charming way of stating it,
and I'm not sure that it is not a relief to find a woman of the old-
fashioned type now and then. It really is man's place to look into
these deeper questions, anyway. It is woman's sphere to live and love
and make a happy home—"

His voice took on a sentimental purr, and Margaret was fairly
boiling with rage at him, but she would not let her temper give way,
especially when she was talking on the sacred theme of the Christ.
She felt as if she must scream or jump out over the wheel and run
away from this obnoxious man, but she knew she would do neither.
She knew she would sit calmly through the expedition and somehow
control that conversation. There was one relief, anyway. Her father
would no longer expect respect and honor and liking toward a minister who denied the very life and foundation of his faith.

"It can't be possible that the schoolhouse is so far from the town,"
she said, suddenly looking around at the widening desert in front of
them. "Haven't you made some mistake?"

"Why, I thought we should have the pleasure of a little drive first,"
said West, with a cunning smile. "I was sure you would enjoy seeing
the country before you get down to work, and I was not averse myself to a drive in such delightful company."

"I would like to go back to the schoolhouse at once, please," said
Margaret, decidedly, and there was that in her voice that caused the
man to turn the horse around and head it toward the village.

"Why, yes, of course, if you prefer to see the schoolhouse first, we
can go back and look it over, and then, perhaps, you will like to ride
a little farther," he said. "We have plenty of time. In fact, Mrs. Tanner told me she would not expect us home to dinner, and she put a
very promising looking basket of lunch under the seat for us in case
we got hungry before we came back."

"Thank you," said Margaret, quite freezingly now. "I really do not
care to drive this morning. I would like to see the schoolhouse, and

then I must return to the house at once. I have a great many things to do this morning."

Her manner at last penetrated even the thick skin of the self-centered man, and he realized that he had gone a step too far in his attentions. He set himself to undo the mischief, hoping perhaps to melt her yet to take the all-day drive with him. But she sat silent during the return to the village, answering his volubility only by yes or no when absolutely necessary. She let him babble away about college life and tell incidents of his late pastorate, at some of which he laughed immoderately, but he could not even bring a smile to her dignified lips.

He hoped she would change her mind when they got to the school building, and he even stooped to praise it in a kind of contemptuous way as they drew up in front of the large adobe building.

"I suppose you will want to go through the building," he said, affably, producing the key from his pocket and putting on a pleasant anticipatory smile, but Margaret shook her head. She simply would not go into the building with that man.

"It is not necessary," she said again, coldly. "I think I will go home now, please." And he was forced to turn the horse toward the Tanner house, crestfallen, and wonder why this beautiful girl was so extremely hard to win. He flattered himself that he had always been able to interest any girl he chose. She was really quite a bewildering type. But he would win her yet.

He set her down silently at the Tanner door and drove off, lunch basket and all, into the wilderness, vexed that she was so stubbornly unfriendly, and pondering how he might break down the dignity wherewith she had surrounded herself. There would be a way and he would find it. There was a stubbornness about that weak chin of his, when one observed it, and an ugliness in his pale blue eyes, or perhaps you would call it a hardness.

Chapter 9

She watched him furtively from her bedroom window, whither she had fled from Mrs. Tanner's exclamations. He wore his stylish derby tilted down over his left eye and slightly to one side in a most un-ministerial manner, showing too much of his straw-colored back hair, which rose in a cowlick at the point of contact with the hat, and he looked a small, mean creature as he drove off into the vast beauty of the plain. Margaret, in her indignation, could not help comparing him with the young man who had ridden away from the house two days before.

And he to set up to be a minister of Christ's gospel and talk like that about the Bible and Christ! Oh, what was the church of Christ coming to, to have ministers like that? How ever did he get into the ministry, anyway? Of course, she knew there were young men with honest doubts who sometimes slid through nowadays, but a mean little silly man like that? How ever did he get in? What a lot of ridiculous things he had said! He was one of those described in the Bible who "darken counsel with words." He was not worth noticing. And yet, what a lot of harm he could do in an unlearned community. Just see how Mrs. Tanner hung upon his words, as though they were law and gospel! How *could* she?

Margaret found herself trembling yet over the words he had spoken about Christ, the atonement, and the faith. They meant so much to her and to her mother and father. They were not mere empty words of tradition that she believed because she had been taught. She had lived her faith and proved it, and she could not help feeling it like a personal insult to have him speak so of her Saviour. She turned away and took her Bible to try and get a bit of calmness.

She fluttered the leaves for something—she could not just tell what—and her eye caught some of the verses that her father had marked for her before she left home for college, in the days when he was troubled for her going forth into the world of unbelief.

As ye have therefore received Christ Jesus the Lord, so walk ye in him: Rooted and built up in him, and stablished in the faith, as ye have been taught, abounding therein with thanksgiving. Beware lest any man spoil you through philosophy and vain deceit, after the tradition of men, after the rudiments of the world, and not after Christ. For in him dwelleth all the fulness of the Godhead bodily.

How the verses crowded upon one another, standing out clearly from the pages as she turned them, marked with her father's own hand in clear ink underlinings. It almost seemed as if God had looked ahead to these times and set these words down just for the encouragement of his troubled servants who couldn't understand why faith was growing dim. God knew about it, had known it would be, all this doubt, and had put words here just for troubled hearts to be comforted thereby.

For I know whom I have believed [How her heart echoed to that statement!] and am persuaded that he is able to keep that which I have committed unto him against that day.

And on a little further:

Nevertheless the foundation of God standeth sure, having this seal, The Lord knoweth them that are his.

There was a triumphant look to the words as she read them. Then over in Ephesians her eye caught a verse that just seemed to fit that poor blind minister:

Having the understanding darkened, being alienated from the life of God through the ignorance that is in them, because of the blindness of their heart.

And yet he was set to guide the feet of the blind into the way of life! And he had looked on her as one of the ignorant. Poor fellow! He couldn't know the Christ who was her Saviour or he never would have spoken in that way about Him. What could such a man preach? What was there left to preach, but empty words, when one rejected all these doctrines? Would she have to listen to a man like that Sunday after Sunday? Did the scholars in her school, and their parents, and the young man out at the camp, and his rough, simple-hearted companions have to listen to preaching from that man, when they listened to any? Her heart grew sick within her, and she knelt beside her bed for a strengthening word with the Christ who since her little childhood had been a very real presence in her life.

When she arose from her knees she heard the kitchen door slam downstairs and the voice of Bud calling his mother. She went to her door and opened it, listening a moment, and then called the boy.

There was a dead silence for an instant after her voice was heard, and then Bud appeared at the foot of the stairs, with a frown on his face and a surliness in his voice:

"What d'ye want?"

It was plain that Bud was sore.

"Bud"—Margaret's voice was sweet and a bit cool as she leaned over the railing and surveyed the boy; she hadn't yet got over her compulsory ride with that minister—"I wanted to ask you, please, next time you can't keep an appointment with me don't ask anybody else to take your place. I prefer to pick out my own companions. It was all right, of course, if you had to go somewhere else, but I could easily have gone alone or waited until another time. I'd rather not have you ask Mr. West to go anywhere with me again."

Bud's face was a study. It cleared suddenly and his jaw dropped in surprise; his eyes fairly danced with dawning comprehension and pleasure, and then his brow drew down ominously.

"I never ast him," he declared, vehemently. "He told me you wanted him to go, and fer me to get out of the way cause you didn't want to hurt my feelings. Didn't you say nothing to him about it at all this morning?"

"No, indeed!" said Margaret, with flashing eyes.

"Well, I just thought he was that kind of a guy. I told ma he was lying, but she said I didn't understand young ladies, and, of course, you didn't want me when there was a man, and especially a preacher, round. Some preacher he is! This is the second time I've caught him lying. I think he's the limit. I just wish you'd see our missionary. If he was here he'd beat the dust out o' that poor stew. *He's* some man, he is. He's a regular man, *our missionary!* Just you wait till *he* gets back."

Margaret drew a breath of relief. Then the missionary was a real man, after all. Oh, for his return!

"Well, I'm certainly very glad it wasn't your fault, Bud. I didn't feel very happy to be turned off that way," said the teacher, smiling down upon the rough head of the boy.

"You bet it wasn't my fault!" said the boy, vigorously. "I was sore's a pup at you, after you'd made a date and all, to do like that, but I thought if you wanted to go with that guy it was up to you."

"Well, I didn't and I don't. You'll please understand hereafter that I'd always rather have your company than his. How about going down to the schoolhouse some time today? Have you time?"

"Didn't you go yet?" The boy's face looked as if he had received a kingdom, and his voice had a ring of triumph.

"We drove down there, but I didn't care to go in without you, so we came back."

"Wanta go now?" The boy's face fairly shone.

"I'd love to. I'll be ready in three minutes. Could we carry some books down?"

"Sure! Oh—gee! That guy's got the buckboard. We'll have to walk. Doggone him!"

"I shall enjoy a walk. I want to find out just how far it is, for I shall have to walk every day, you know."

"No, you won't, neither, 'nless you wanta. I c'n always hitch up."

"That'll be very nice sometimes, but I'm afraid I'd get spoiled if you babied me all the time that way. I'll be right down."

They went out together into the sunshine and wideness of the morning, and it seemed a new day had been created since she got back from her ride with the minister. She looked at the sturdy, honest-eyed boy beside her, and was glad to have him for a companion.

Just in front of the schoolhouse Margaret paused. "Oh, I forgot! The key! Mr. West has the key in his pocket! We can't get in, can we?"

"Aw, we don't need a key," said her escort. "Just you wait!" And he whisked around to the back of the building, and in about three minutes his shock head appeared at the window. He threw the sash open and dropped out a wooden box. "There!" he said, triumphantly, "you c'n climb up on that, cantcha? Here, I'll holdya steady. Take holta my hand."

And so it was through the front window that the new teacher of the Ridge School first appeared on her future scene of action and surveyed her little kingdom.

Bud threw open the shutters, letting the view of the plains and the sunshine into the big, dusty room, and showed her the new blackboard with great pride.

"There's a whole box o' chalk up on the desk, too; ain't never been opened yet. Dad said that was your property. Want I should open it?"

"Why, yes, you might, and then we'll try the blackboard, won't we?"

Bud went to work gravely opening the chalk box as if it were a small treasure chest, and finally produced a long, smooth stick of chalk and handed it to her with shining eyes.

"You try it first, Bud," said the teacher, seeing his eagerness and the boy went forward awesomely, as if it were a sacred precinct and he unworthy to intrude.

Shyly, awkwardly, with infinite painstaking, he wrote in a cramped hand, "William Budlong Tanner," and then, growing bolder, "Ashland, Arizona," with a big flourish underneath.

"Some class!" he said, standing back and regarding his handiwork with pride. "Say, I like the sound the chalk makes on it, don't you?"

"Yes, I do," said Margaret, heartily, "so smooth and businesslike, isn't it? You'll enjoy doing examples in algebra on it, won't you?"

"Good night! Algebra! Me? No chance. I can't never get through the arithmetic. The last teacher said if he'd come back twenty years from now he'd still find me working compound interest."

"Well, we'll prove to that man that he wasn't much of a judge of boys," said Margaret, with a tilt of her chin and a glint of her teacher mettle showing in her eyes. "If you're not in algebra before two months are over I'll miss my guess. We'll get at it right away and show him."

Bud watched her, charmed. He was beginning to believe that almost anything she tried would come true.

"Now, Bud, suppose we get to work. I'd like to get acquainted with my class a little before Monday. Isn't it Monday school opens? I thought so. Well, suppose you give me the names of the scholars and I'll write them down, and that will help me to remember them. Where will you begin? Here, suppose you sit down in the front seat and tell me who sits there and a little bit about him, and I'll write the name down, and then you move to the next seat and tell me about the next one, and so on. Will you?"

"Sure!" said Bud, entering into the new game. "But it ain't a 'he' sits there. It's Susie Johnson. She's Bill Johnson's smallest girl. She has to sit front 'cause she giggles so much. She has yellow curls and she ducks her head down and snickers right out this way when anything funny happens in school." And Bud proceeded to duck and wriggle in perfect imitation of the small Susie.

Margaret saw the boy's power of imitation was remarkable, and laughed heartily at his burlesque. Then she turned and wrote "Susie Johnson" on the board in beautiful script.

Bud watched with admiration, saying softly under his breath; "Gee! That's great, that blackboard, ain't it?"

Amelia Schwartz came next. She was long and lank, with the buttons off the back of her dress, and hands and feet too large for her garments. Margaret could not help but see her in the clever pantomime the boy carried on. Next was Rosa Rogers, daughter of a wealthy cattleman, the pink-cheeked, blue-eyed beauty of the school, with all the boys at her feet and a perfect knowledge of her power over them. Bud didn't, of course, state it that way, but Margaret gathered as much from his simpering smile and the coy way he looked out of the corner of his eyes as he described her.

Down the long list of scholars he went, row after row, and when he came to the seats where the boys sat his tone changed. She could tell by the shading of his voice which boys were the ones to look out for.

Jed Brower, it appeared, was a name to conjure with. He could ride any horse that ever stood on four legs, he could outshoot most of the boys in the neighborhood, and he never allowed any teacher to tell him what to do. He was Texas Brower's only boy, and always had his own way. His father was on the school board. Jed Brower was held in awe, even while his methods were despised, by some of the younger boys. He was big and powerful, and nobody dared fool with him. Bud did not exactly warn Margaret that she must keep on the right side of Jed Brower, but he conveyed that impression without words. Margaret understood. She knew also that Tad Brooks, Larry Parker, Jim Long, and Dake Foster were merely henchmen of the worthy Jed, and of no particular concern when taken by themselves. But over the name of Timothy Forbes—"Delicate Forbes," Bud explained was his nickname—the boy lingered with that loving inflection of admiration that a younger boy will sometimes have for a husky, courageous older lad. The second time Bud spoke of him he called him "Forbeszy," and Margaret perceived that here was Bud's model of manhood. Delicate Forbes could outshoot and outride even Jed Brower when he chose, and his courage with cattle was that of a man. Moreover, he was good to the younger boys and wasn't above pitching baseball with them when he had nothing better afoot. It became evident from the general description that Delicate Forbes was not called so from any lack of inches to his stature. He had a record of having licked every man teacher in the school, and beaten by guile every woman teacher they had had in six years. Bud was loyal to his admiration, yet it could be plainly seen that he felt Margaret's greatest hindrance in the school would be Delicate Forbes.

Margaret mentally underlined the names in her memory that belonged to the back seats in the first and second rows of desks, and went home praying that she might have wisdom and patience to deal with Jed Brower and Timothy Forbes, and through them to manage the rest of her school.

She surprised Bud at the dinner table by handing him a neat diagram of the schoolroom desks with the correct names of all but three or four of the scholars written on them. Such a feat of memory raised her several notches in his estimation.

"Say, that's going some! Guess you won't forget nothing, no matter how much they try to make you."

Chapter 10

The minister did not appear until late in the evening, after Margaret had gone to her room, for which she was sincerely thankful. She could hear his voice, fretful and complaining, as he called loudly for Bud to take the horse. It appeared he had lost his way and wandered many miles out of the trail. He blamed the country for having no better trails, and the horse for not being able to find his way better. Mr. Tanner had gone to bed, but Mrs. Tanner bustled about and tried to comfort him.

"Now that's too bad! Dearie me! Bud oughta hev gone with you, so he ought. Bud! *Oh,* Bud, you ain't gonta sleep yet, hev you? Wake up and come down and take this horse to the barn."

But Bud declined to descend. He shouted some sleepy directions from his loft where he slept, and said the minister could look after his own horse, he "wasn'ta gonta!" There was "plentya corn in the bin."

The minister grumbled his way to the barn, highly incensed at Bud, and disturbed the calm of the evening view of Margaret's mountain by his complaints when he returned. He wasn't accustomed to handling horses, and he thought Bud might have stayed up and attended to it himself. Bud chuckled in his loft and stole down the back kitchen roof while the minister ate his late supper. Bud would never leave the old horse to that amateur's tender mercies, but he didn't intend to make it easy for the amateur. Margaret, from her window seat watching the night in the darkness, saw Bud slip off the kitchen roof and run to the barn, and she smiled to herself. She liked that boy. He was going to be a good comrade.

The Sabbath morning dawned brilliantly, and to the homesick girl there suddenly came a sense of desolation on waking. A strange land was this, without church bells or sense of Sabbath fitness. The mountain, it is true, greeted her with a holy light of gladness, but mountains are not dependent upon humankind for being in the spirit on the Lord's day. They are "continually praising Him." Margaret wondered how she was to get through this day, this dreary first Sabbath away from her home and her Sabbath school class, and her dear old church with Father preaching. She had been away, of course, a great many times before, but never to a churchless community. It was beginning to dawn upon her that that was what Ashland was—a churchless community. As she recalled the walk to the school and the ride through the village she had seen nothing that looked like a church, and all the talk had been of the missionary. They must have services of some sort, of course, and probably that flabby, fish-eyed man, her fellow boarder, was to preach, but her heart turned sick at thought of listening to a man who had confessed to the unbeliefs that he had. Of course, he would likely know enough to keep such doubts to himself, but he had told her, and nothing he could say now would help or uplift her in the least.

She drew a deep sigh and looked at her watch. It was late. At home the early Sabbath school bells would be ringing, and little girls in white, with bunches of late fall flowers for their teachers, and holding hands with their little brothers, would be hurrying down the street. Father was in his study, going over his morning sermon, and Mother putting her little pearl pin in her collar, getting ready to go to her Bible class. Margaret decided it was time to get up and stop thinking of it all.

She put on a little white dress that she wore to church at home and hurried down to discover what the family plans were for the day, but found, to her dismay, that the atmosphere belowstairs was just like that of other days. Mr. Tanner sat tilted back in a dining room chair, reading the weekly paper, Mrs. Tanner was bustling in with hot corn bread, Bud was on the front door steps teasing the dog, and the minister came in with an air of weariness upon him, as if he quite intended taking it out on his companions that he had experienced a trying time on Saturday. He did not look in the least like a man who expected to preach in a few minutes. He declined to eat his egg because it was cooked too hard, and poor Mrs. Tanner had to try it twice before she succeeded in producing a soft-boiled egg to suit him. Only the radiant outline of the great mountain, which Margaret could see over the minister's head, looked peaceful and Sabbathlike.

"What time do you have service?" Margaret asked, as she rose from the table.

"Service?" It was Mr. Tanner who echoed her question as if he did not quite know what she meant.

Mrs. Tanner raised her eyes from her belated breakfast with a worried look, like a hen stretching her neck about to see what she ought to do next for the comfort of the chickens under her care. It was apparent that she had no comprehension of what the question meant. It was the minister who answered, condescendingly:

"Um! Ah! There is no church edifice here, you know, Miss Earle. The mission station is located some miles distant."

"I know," said Margaret, "but they surely have some religious service?"

"I really don't know," said the minister, loftily, as if it were something wholly beneath his notice.

"Then you are not going to preach this morning?" In spite of herself there was relief in her tone.

"Most certainly not," he replied, stiffly. "I came out here to rest, and I selected this place largely because it was so far from a church. I wanted to be where I should not be annoyed by requests to preach. Of course, ministers from the East would be a curiosity in these western towns, and I should really get no rest at all if I had gone where my services would have been in constant demand. When I came out here I was in much the condition of our friend the minister of whom you have doubtless heard. He was starting on his vacation, and he said to a brother minister, with a smile of joy and relief, 'No preaching, no praying, no reading of the Bible for six whole weeks!'"

"Indeed!" said Margaret, freezingly. "No, I am not familiar with ministers of that sort." She turned with dismissal in her manner and appealed to Mrs. Tanner. "Then you really have no Sabbath service of any sort whatever in town?" There was something almost tragic in her face. She stood aghast at the prospect before her.

Mrs. Tanner's neck stretched up a little longer, and her lips dropped apart in her attempt to understand the situation. One would scarcely have been surprised to hear her say, "Cut-cut-cut-ca-daw-cut?" so fluttered did she seem.

Then up spoke Bud. "We gotta Sunday school, Ma!" There was

pride of possession in Bud's tone, and a kind of triumph over the minister, albeit Bud had abjured Sunday school since his early infancy. He was ready now, however, to be offered on the altar of Sunday school, even, if that would please the new teacher—and spite the minister. "I'll take you ef you wanta go." He looked defiantly at the minister as he said it.

But at last Mrs. Tanner seemed to grasp what was the matter. "Why!—why!—why! You mean preaching service!" she clucked out. "Why, yes, Mr. West, wouldn't that be fine? You could preach for us. We could have it posted up at the saloon, and the crossings, and out a ways on both trails, and you'd have quite a crowd. They'd come from over to the camp, and up the canyon way, and roundabouts. They'd do you credit, they surely would, Mr. West. And you could have the schoolhouse for a meeting house. Pa, there, is one of the school board. There wouldn't be a bit of trouble—"

"Um! Ah! Mrs. Tanner, I assure you it's quite out of the question. I told you I was here for absolute rest. I couldn't think of preaching. Besides, it's against my principles to preach without remuneration. It's a wrong idea. The workman is worthy of his hire, you know, Mrs. Tanner, the Good Book says." Mr. West's tone took on a self-righteous inflection.

"Oh! Ef that's all, that 'u'd be all right!" she said, with relief. "You could take up a collection. The boys would be real generous. They always are when any show comes along. They'd appreciate it, you know, and I'd like fer Miss Earle here to hear you preach. It 'u'd be a real treat to her, her being a preacher's daughter and all." She turned to Margaret for support, but that young woman was talking to Bud. She had promptly closed with his offer to take her to Sunday school, and now she hurried away to get ready, leaving Mrs. Tanner to make her clerical arrangements without aid.

The minister, meantime, looked after her doubtfully. Perhaps, after all, it would have been a good move to have preached. He might have impressed that difficult young woman better that way than any other, seeing she posed as being so interested in religious matters. He turned to Mrs. Tanner and began to ask questions about the feasibility of a church service. The word "collection" sounded good to him. He was not averse to replenishing his somewhat depleted treasury if it could be done so easily as that.

Meantime Margaret, up in her room, was wondering again how such a man as Mr. West ever got into the Christian ministry.

West was still endeavoring to impress the Tanners with the importance of his late charge in the East as Margaret came downstairs. His pompous tones, raised to favor the deafness that he took for granted in Mr. Tanner, easily reached her ears.

"I couldn't, of course, think of doing it every Sunday, you understand. It wouldn't be fair to myself nor my work which I have just left, but, of course, if there were sufficient inducement I might consent to preach some Sunday before I leave."

Mrs. Tanner's little satisfied cluck was quite audible as the girl closed the front door and went out to the waiting Bud.

The Sunday school was a desolate affair, presided over by an elderly and very illiterate man, who nursed his elbows and rubbed his chin meditatively between the slow questions which he read out of the lesson leaf. The woman who usually taught the children was called away to nurse a sick neighbor, and the children were huddled together in a restless group. The singing was poor, and the whole of the exercises dreary, including the prayer. The few women present sat and stared in a kind of awe at the visitor, half belligerently, as if she were an intruder. Bud lingered outside the door and finally disappeared altogether, reappearing when the last hymn was sung. Altogether the new teacher felt exceedingly homesick as she wended her way back to the Tanners' beside Bud.

"What do you do with yourself on Sunday afternoons, Bud?" she asked, as soon as they were out of hearing of the rest of the group.

The boy turned wondering eyes toward her. "Do?" he repeated, puzzled. "Why, we pass the time away, like most any day. There ain't much difference."

A great desolation possessed her. No church! Worse than no minister! No Sabbath! What kind of a land was this to which she had come?

The boy beside her smelled of tobacco smoke. He had been off somewhere smoking while she was in the dreary little Sunday school.

She looked at his careless boy-face furtively as they walked along. He smoked, of course, like most boys of his age, probably, and he did a lot of other things he ought not to do. He had no interest in God or righteousness, and he did not take it for granted that the Sabbath was different from any other day. A sudden heart sinking came upon her. What was the use of trying to do anything for such as he? Why not give it up now and go back where there was more promising material to work upon and where she would be welcome indeed? Of course, she had known things would be discouraging, but somehow it had seemed different from a distance. It all looked utterly hopeless now, and herself crazy to have thought she could do any good in a place like this.

And yet the place needed somebody! That pitiful little Sunday school! How forlorn it all was! She was almost sorry she had gone. It gave her an unhappy feeling for the morrow, which was to be her first day of school.

Then, all suddenly, just as they were nearing the Tanner house, there came one riding down the street with all the glory of the radiant morning in his face, and a light in his eyes at seeing her that lifted away her desolation, for here at last was a friend!

She wondered at herself. An unknown stranger, and a self-confessed failure so far in his young life, and yet he seemed so good a sight to her amid these uncongenial surroundings!

Chapter 11

This stranger of royal bearing, riding a rough western pony as if it were decked with golden trappings, with his bright hair gleaming like Roman gold in the sun, and his blue-gray eyes looking into hers with the gladness of his youth; this one who had come to her out of the shadows of the wilderness and led her into safety! Yes, she was glad to see him.

He dismounted and greeted her, his wide hat in his hand, his eyes upon her face, and Bud stepped back, watching them in pleased surprise. This was the man who had shot all the lights out the night of the big riot in the saloon. He had also risked his life in a number of foolish ways at recent festal carouses. Bud would not have been a boy had he not admired the young man beyond measure; and his boy worship of the teacher yielded her to a fitting rival. He stepped behind and walked beside the pony, who was following his master meekly, as though he, too, were under the young man's charm.

"Oh, and this is my friend, William Tanner," spoke Margaret, turning toward the boy loyally. (Whatever good angel made her call him William? Bud's soul swelled with new dignity as he blushed and acknowledged the introduction by a grin.)

"Glad to know you, Will," said the newcomer, extending his hand in a hearty shake that warmed the boy's heart in a trice. "I'm glad Miss Earle has so good a protector. You'll have to look out for her. She's pretty plucky and is apt to stray around the wilderness by herself. It isn't safe, you know, boy, for such as her. Look after her, will you?"

"Right I will," said Bud, accepting the commission as if it were heaven-sent, and thereafter walked behind the two with his head in the clouds. He felt that he understood this great hero of the plains and was one with him at heart. There could be no higher honor than to be the servitor of this man's lady. Bud did not stop to question how the new teacher became acquainted with the young rider of the plains. It was enough that both were young and handsome and seemed to belong together. He felt they were fitting friends.

The little procession walked down the road slowly, glad to prolong the way. The young man had brought her handkerchief, a filmy trifle of an excuse that she had dropped behind her chair at the bunkhouse, where it had lain unnoticed till she was gone. He produced it from his inner pocket, as though it had been too precious to carry anywhere but over his heart, yet there was in his manner nothing presuming, not a hint of any intimacy other than their chance acquaintance of the wilderness would warrant. He did not look at her with any such look as West had given every time he spoke to her. She felt no desire to resent his glance when it rested upon her almost worshipfully, for there was respect and utmost humility in his look.

The men had sent gifts: some arrowheads and a curiously fashioned vessel from the canyon of the cave dwellers, some chips from the petrified forest, a fern with wonderful fronds, root and all, and a sheaf of strange, beautiful blossoms carefully wrapped in wet paper, and all fastened to the saddle.

Margaret's face kindled with interest as he showed them to her one by one, and told her the history of each and a little message from the man who had sent it. Mom Wallis, too, had baked a queer little cake and sent it. The young man's face was tender as he spoke of it. The girl saw that he knew what her coming had meant to Mom Wallis. Her memory went quickly back to those few words the morning she had wakened in the bunkhouse and found the withered old woman watching her with tears in her eyes. Poor Mom Wallis, with her pretty girlhood all behind her and such a blank, dull future ahead! Poor, tired, ill-used, worn-out Mom Wallis! Margaret's heart went out to her.

"They want to know," said the young man, half hesitatingly, "if some time, when you get settled and have time, you would come to them again and sing? I tried to make them understand, of course, that you would be busy, your time taken with other friends and your work, and you would not want to come, but they wanted me to tell you they never enjoyed anything so much in years as your singing.

Why, I heard Long Jim singing 'Old Folks at Home' this morning when he was saddling his horse. And it's made a difference. The men sort of want to straighten up the bunkroom. Jasper made a new chair yesterday. He said it would do when you came again." Gardley laughed diffidently, as if he knew their hopes were all in vain.

But Margaret looked up with sympathy in her face. "I'll come! Of course I'll come sometime," she said, eagerly. "I'll come as soon as I can arrange it. You tell them we'll have more than one concert yet."

The young man's face lit up with a quick appreciation, and the flash of his eyes as he looked at her would have told any onlooker that he felt here was a girl in a thousand, a girl with an angel spirit, if ever such a one walked the earth.

Now it happened that Reverend Frederick West was walking impatiently up and down in front of the Tanner residence, looking down the road about that time. He had spent the morning in looking over the small bundle of "show sermons" he had brought with him in case of emergency, and had about decided to accede to Mrs. Tanner's request and preach in Ashland before he left. This decision had put him in so self-satisfied a mood that he was eager to announce it before his fellow boarder. Moreover, he was hungry, and he could not understand why that impudent boy and that coquettish young woman should remain away at Sunday school such an interminable time.

Mrs. Tanner was frying chicken. He could smell it every time he took a turn toward the house. It really was ridiculous that they should keep dinner waiting this way. He took one more turn and began to think over the sermon he had decided to preach. He was just recalling a particularly eloquent passage when he happened to look down the road once more, and there they were, almost upon him! But Bud was no longer walking with the maiden. She had acquired a new escort, a man of broad shoulders and fine height. Where had he seen that fellow before? He watched them as they came up, his small, pale eyes narrowing under their yellow lashes with a glint of slyness, like some mean little animal that meant to take advantage of its prey. It was wonderful how many different things that man could look like for a person as insignificant as he really was!

Well, he saw the look between the man and maiden; the look of sympathy and admiration and a fine kind of trust that is not founded on mere outward show, but has found some hidden fineness of the soul. Not that the reverend gentleman understood that, however. He had no fineness of soul himself. His mind had been too thoroughly taken up with himself all his life for him to have cultivated any.

Simultaneous with the look came his recognition of the man or, at least, of where he had last seen him, and his little soul rejoiced at the advantage he instantly recognized.

He drew himself up importantly, flattened his chin upward until his lower lip protruded in a pink roll across his mouth, drew down his yellow brows in a frown of displeasure, and came forward mentorlike to meet the little party as it neared the house. He had the air of coming to investigate and possibly oust the stranger, and he looked at him keenly, critically, offensively, as if he had the right to protect the lady. They might have been a pair of naughty children come back from a forbidden frolic, from the way he surveyed them. But the beauty of it was that neither of them saw him, being occupied with each other, until they were fairly upon him. Then, there he stood offensively, as if he were a great power to be reckoned with.

"Well, well, well, Miss Margaret, you have got home at last!" he said, pompously and condescendingly, and then he looked into the eyes of her companion as if demanding an explanation of *his* presence there.

Margaret drew herself up haughtily. His use of her Christian name in that familiar tone annoyed her exceedingly. Her eyes flashed indignantly, but the whole of it was lost unless Bud saw it, for Gardley had faced his would-be adversary with a keen, surprised scrutiny, and was looking him over coolly. There was that in the young man's eye that made the eye of Frederick West quail before him. It was only an instant the two stood challenging each other, but in that short time each knew and marked the other for an enemy. Only a brief instant and then Gardley turned to Margaret, and before she had time to think what to say, he asked:

"Is this man a friend of yours, Miss *Earle?*" with marked emphasis on the last word.

"No," said Margaret, coolly, "not a friend—a boarder in the house." Then most formally, "Mr. West, my *friend* Mr. Gardley."

If the minister had not been possessed of the skin of a rhinoceros he would have understood himself to be dismissed at that; but he was not a man accustomed to accepting dismissal, as his recent church in New York State might have testified. He stood his ground, his chin flatter than ever, his little eyes mere slits of condemnation. He did not acknowledge the introduction by so much as the inclination of his head. His hands were clasped behind his back, and his whole attitude was one of righteous belligerence.

Gardley gazed steadily at him for a moment, a look of mingled contempt and amusement gradually growing upon his face. Then he turned away as if the man were too small to notice.

"You will come in and take dinner with me?" asked Margaret, eagerly. "I want to send a small package to Mrs. Wallis if you will be so good as to take it with you."

"I'm sorry I can't stay to dinner, but I have an errand in another direction and at some distance. I am returning this way, however, and, if I may, will call and get the package toward evening."

Margaret's eyes spoke her welcome, and with a few formal words the young man sprang on his horse, said, "So long, Will!" to Bud, and, ignoring the minister, rode away.

They watched him for an instant, for, indeed, he was a goodly sight upon a horse, riding as if he and the horse were utterly one in spirit; then Margaret turned quickly to go into the house.

"Um! Ah! Miss Margaret!" began the minister, with a commandatory gesture for her to stop.

Margaret was the picture of haughtiness as she turned and said, "Miss *Earle,* if you please!"

"Um! Ah! Why, certainly, Miss-ah-*Earle,* if you wish it. Will you kindly remain here for a moment? I wish to speak with you. Bud, you may go on."

"I'll go when I like, and it's none of your business!" muttered Bud, ominously, under his breath. He looked at Margaret to see if she wished him to go. He had an idea that this might be one of the times when he was to look after her.

She smiled at him understandingly. "William may remain, Mr. West," she said, sweetly. "Anything you have to say to me can surely be said in his presence," and she laid her hand lightly on Bud's sleeve.

Bud looked down at the hand proudly and grew inches taller enjoying the minister's frown.

"Um! Ah!" said West, unabashed. "Well, I merely wished to warn you concerning the character of that person who has just left us. He is really not a proper companion for you. Indeed, I may say he is quite the contrary, and that to my personal knowledge—"

"He's as good as you are and better!" growled Bud, ominously.

"Be quiet, boy! I wasn't speaking to you!" said West, as if he were addressing a slave. "If I hear another word from your lips I shall report it to your father!"

"Go 's far 's you like and see how much I care!" taunted Bud, but was stopped by Margaret's gentle pressure on his arm.

"Mr. West, I thought I made you understand that Mr. Gardley is my friend."

"Um! Ah! Miss Earle, then all I have to say is that you have formed a most unwise friendship, and should let it proceed no further. Why, my dear young lady, if you knew all there is to know about him you would not think of speaking to that young man."

"Indeed! Mr. West, I suppose that might be true of a good many people, might it not, *if we knew all there is to know about them?* Nobody but God could very well get along with some of us."

"But, my dear young lady, you don't understand. This young person is nothing but a common ruffian, a gambler, in fact, and an habitué at the saloons. I have seen him myself sitting in a saloon at a very late hour playing with a vile, dirty pack of cards and in the company of a lot of low-down creatures—"

"May I ask how you came to be in a saloon at that hour, Mr. West?" There was a gleam of mischief in the girl's eyes, and her mouth looked as if she were going to laugh, but she controlled it.

The minister turned very red indeed. "Well, I—ah—I had been

called from my bed by shouts and the report of a pistol. There was a fight going on in the room adjoining the bar, and I didn't know but my assistance might be needed!" (At this juncture Bud uttered a sort of snort and, placing his hands over his heart, ducked down as if a sudden pain had seized him.) "But imagine my pain and astonishment when I was informed that the drunken brawl I was witnessing was but a nightly and common occurrence. I may say I remained for a few minutes, partly out of curiosity, as I wished to see all kinds of life in this new world for the sake of a book I am thinking of writing. I therefore took careful note of the persons present, and was thus able to identify the person who has just ridden away as one of the chief factors in the evening's entertainment. He was, in fact, the man who, when he had pocketed all the money on the gaming table, arose and, taking out his pistol, shot out the lights in the room, a most dangerous and irregular proceeding—"

"Yes, and you came within an ace of being shot, Pa says. The kid's a dead shot, he is, and you were right in the way. Served you right for going where you had no business!"

"I did not remain longer in that place, as you may imagine," went on West, ignoring Bud, "for I found it was no place for a—for—a—ah—minister of the gospel; but I remained long enough to hear from the lips of this person with whom you have just been walking some of the most terrible language my ears have ever been permitted to—ah—witness!"

But Margaret had heard all that she intended to listen to on that subject. With decided tone she interrupted the voluble speaker, who was evidently enjoying his own eloquence.

"Mr. West, I think you have said all that it is necessary to say. There are still some things about Mr. Gardley that you evidently do not know, but I think you are in a fair way to learn them if you stay in this part of the country long. William, isn't that your mother calling us to dinner? Let us go in; I'm hungry."

Bud followed her up the walk with a triumphant wink at the discomfited minister, and they disappeared into the house; but when Margaret went up to her room and took off her hat in front of the little warped looking glass there were angry tears in her eyes. She never felt more like crying in her life. Chagrin and anger and disappointment were all struggling in her soul, yet she must not cry, for dinner would be ready and she must go down. Never should that mean little meddling man see that his words had pierced her soul.

For, angry as she was at the minister, much as she loathed his petty, jealous nature and saw through his tale-bearing, something yet told her that his picture of young Gardley's wildness was probably true, and her soul sank within her at the thought. It was just what had come in shadowy, instinctive fear to her heart when he had hinted at his being a roughneck, yet to have it put baldly into words by an enemy hurt her deeply, and she looked at herself in the glass half frightened. *Margaret Earle, have you come out to the wilderness to lose your heart to the first handsome sower of wild oats that you meet?* her true eyes asked her face in the glass, and Margaret Earle's heart turned sad at the question and shrank back. Then she dropped upon her knees beside her gay little rocking chair and buried her face in its flowered cushions and cried to her Father in heaven:

"Oh, my Father, let me not be weak, but with all my heart I cry to Thee to save this young, strong, courageous life and not let it be a failure. Help him to find Thee and serve Thee, and if his life has been all wrong—and I suppose it has—oh, make it right for Jesus' sake! If there is anything that I can do to help, show me how, and don't let me make mistakes. Oh, Jesus, Thy power is great. Let this young man feel it and yield himself to it."

She remained silently praying for a moment more, putting her whole soul into the prayer and knowing that she had been called thus to pray for him until her prayer was answered.

She came down to dinner a few minutes later with a calm, serene face, on which was no hint of her recent emotion, and she managed to keep the table conversation wholly in her own hands, telling Mr. Tanner about her home town and her father and mother. When the meal was finished the minister had no excuse to think that the new teacher was careless about her friends and associates, and he was well informed about the high principles of her family.

But West had retired into a sulky mood and uttered not a word except to ask for more chicken and coffee and a second helping of pie. It was, perhaps, during that dinner that he decided it would be best for him to preach in Ashland on the following Sunday. The young lady could be properly impressed with his dignity in no other way.

Chapter 12

W hen Lance Gardley came back to the Tanners' the sun was preparing the glory of its evening setting, and the mountain was robed in all its rosiest veils.

Margaret was waiting for him, with the dog Captain beside her, wandering back and forth in the unfenced dooryard and watching her mountain. It was a relief to her to find that the minister occupied a room on the first floor in a kind of ell on the opposite side of the house from her own room and her mountain. He had not been visible that afternoon, and with Captain by her side and Bud on the front doorstep reading *The Sky Pilot* she felt comparatively safe. She had read to Bud for an hour and a half, and he was thoroughly interested in the story, but she was sure he would keep the minister away at all costs. As for Captain, he and the minister were sworn enemies by this time. He growled every time West came near or spoke to her.

She made a picture standing with her hand on Captain's shaggy, noble head, the lace of her sleeve falling back from the white arm, her other hand raised to shade her face as she looked away to the glorified mountain, a slim, white figure looking wistfully off at the sunset. The young man took off his hat and rode his horse more softly, as if in the presence of the holy.

The dog lifted one ear, and a tremor passed through his frame as the rider drew near; otherwise he did not stir from his position, but it was enough. The girl turned, on the alert at once, and met him with a smile, and the young man looked at her as if an angel had deigned to smile upon him. There was a humility in his fine face that sat well with the courage written there, and smoothed away all hardness for the time, so that the girl, looking at him in the light of the revelations of the morning, could hardly believe it had been true, yet an inner fineness of perception taught her that it was.

The young man dismounted and left his horse standing quietly by the roadside. He would not stay, he said, yet lingered by her side, talking for a few minutes, watching the sunset and pointing out its changes.

She gave him the little package for Mom Wallis. There was a simple lace collar in a little white box, and a tiny leather-bound book done in russet suede with gold lettering.

"Tell her to wear the collar and think of me whenever she dresses up."

"I'm afraid that'll never be, then," said the young man, with a pitying smile. "Mom Wallis never dresses up."

"Tell her I said she must dress up evenings for supper, and I'll make her another one to change with that and bring it when I come."

He smiled upon her again, that wondering, almost worshipful smile, as if he wondered if she were real, after all, so different did she seem from his idea of girls.

"And the little book," she went on, apologetically, "I suppose it was foolish to send it, but something she said made me think of some of the lines in the poem. I've marked them for her. She reads, doesn't she?"

"A little, I think. I see her now and then read the papers that Pop brings home with him. I don't fancy her literary range is very wide, however."

"Of course, I suppose it is ridiculous! And maybe she'll not understand any of it, but tell her I sent her a message. She must see if she can find it in the poem. Perhaps you can explain it to her. It's Browning's *Rabbi Ben Ezra*. You know it, don't you?"

"I'm afraid not. I was intent on other things about the time when I was supposed to be giving my attention to Browning, or I wouldn't be what I am today, I suppose. But I'll do my best with what wits I have. What's it about? Couldn't you give me a pointer or two?"

"It's the one beginning:

"Grow old along with me!
   The best is yet to be,
   The last of life, for which the first was made:

Our times are in His hand
Who saith, 'A whole I planned,
Youth shows but half; trust God: see all, nor be afraid!' "

He looked down at her still with that wondering smile. "Grow old along with you!" he said, gravely, and then sighed. "You don't look as if you ever would grow old."

"That's it," she said, eagerly. "That's the whole idea. We don't ever grow old, and get done with it all, we just go on to bigger things, wiser and better and more beautiful, till we come to understand and be a part of the whole great plan of God!"

He did not attempt an answer, nor did he smile now, but just looked at her with that deeply quizzical, grave look as if his soul were turning over the matter seriously. She held her peace and waited, unable to find the right word to speak. Then he turned and looked off, an infinite regret growing in his face.

"That makes living a different thing from the way most people take it," he said, at last, and his tone showed that he was considering it deeply.

"Does it?" she said, softly, and looked with him toward the sunset, still half seeing his quiet profile against the light. At last it came to her that she must speak. Half fearfully she began: "I've been thinking about what you said on the ride. You said you didn't make good. I—wish you would. I—I'm sure you could—"

She looked up wistfully and saw the gentleness come into his face as if the fountain of his soul, long sealed, had broken up, and as if he saw a possibility before him for the first time through the words she had spoken.

At last he turned to her with that wondering smile again. "Why should you care?" he asked. The words would have sounded harsh if his tone had not been so gentle.

Margaret hesitated for an answer. "I don't know how to tell it," she said slowly. "There's another verse, a few lines more in that poem, perhaps you know them?—

'All I could never be, All, men ignored in me,
This, I was worth to God, whose wheel the pitcher shaped.'

I want it because—well, perhaps because I feel you are worth all that to God. I would like to see you be that."

He looked down at her again, and was still so long that she felt she had failed miserably.

"I hope you will excuse my speaking," she added. "I— It seems there are so many grand possibilities in life, and for you—I couldn't bear to have you say you hadn't made good, as if it were all over."

"I'm glad you spoke," he said quickly. "I guess perhaps I have been all kinds of a fool. You have made me feel how many kinds I have been."

"Oh no!" she protested.

"You don't know what I have been," he said, sadly, and then with sudden conviction, as if he read her thoughts: "You *do* know! That prig of a parson has told you! Well, it's just as well you should know. It's right!"

A wave of misery passed over his face and erased all its brightness and hope. Even the gentleness was gone. He looked haggard and drawn with hopelessness all in a moment.

"Do you think it would matter to me—*anything* that man would say?" she protested, all her woman's heart going out in pity.

"But it was true, all he said, probably, and more—"

"It doesn't matter," she said, eagerly. "The other is true, too. Just as the poem says, 'All that man ignores in you, just that you are worth to God!" And you *can* be what He meant you to be. I have been praying all the afternoon that He would help you to be."

"Have you?" he said, and his eyes lit up again as if the altar fires of hope were burning once more. "Have you? I thank you."

"You came to me when I was lost in the wilderness," she said, shyly. "I wanted to help *you* back—if—I might."

"You will help—you have!" he said, earnestly. "And I was far enough off the trail, too, but if there's any way to get back I'll get there." He grasped her hand and held it for a second. "Keep up that praying," he said. "I'll see what can be done."

Margaret looked up. "Oh, I'm so glad, so glad!"

He looked reverently into her eyes, all the manhood in him stirred to higher, better things. Then, suddenly, as they stood together, a sound smote their ears as from another world.

"Um! Ah!—"

The minister stood within the doorway, barred by Bud in scowling defiance, and guarded by Cap, who gave an answering growl.

Gardley and Margaret looked at each other and smiled, then turned and walked slowly down to where the pony stood. They did not wish to talk here in that alien presence. Indeed, it seemed that more words were not needed—they would be a desecration.

So he rode away into the sunset once more with just another look and a handclasp, and she turned, strangely happy at heart, to go back to her dull surroundings and her uncongenial company.

"Come, William, let's have a praise service," she said, brightly, pausing at the doorway, but ignoring the scowling minister.

"A praise service! What's a praise service?" asked the wondering Bud, shoving over to let her sit down beside him.

She sat with her back to West, and Cap came and lay at her feet with the white of one eye on the minister and a growl ready to gleam between his teeth any minute. There was just no way for the minister to get out unless he jumped over them or went out the back door, but the people in the doorway had the advantage of not having to look at him, and he couldn't very well dominate the conversation standing so behind them.

"Why, a praise service is a service of song and gladness, of course. You sing, don't you? Of course. Well, what shall we sing? Do you know this?" And she broke softly into song:

> "When peace like a river attendeth my way;
>   When sorrows like sea-billows roll;
>   Whatever my lot Thou hast taught me to say,
>   It is well, it is well with my soul."

Bud did not know the song, but he did not intend to be balked with the minister standing right behind him, ready, no doubt, to jump in and take the precedence; so he growled away at a note in the bass, turning it over and over and trying to make it fit, like a dog gnawing at a bare bone, but he managed to keep time and make it sound a little like singing.

The dusk was falling fast as they finished the last verse, Margaret singing the words clear and distinct, Bud growling unintelligibly and snatching at words he had never heard before. Once more Margaret sang:

> "Abide with me; fast falls the eventide;
> The darkness deepens; Lord, with me abide!
> When other refuge fails and comforts flee,
> Help of the helpless, oh, abide with me!"

Out on the lonely trail wending his way toward the purple mountain—the silent way to the bunkhouse at the camp—in that clear air where sound travels a long distance the traveler heard the song, and something thrilled his soul. A chord that never had been touched in him before was vibrating, and its echoes would be heard through all his life.

On and on sang Margaret, just because she could not bear to stop and hear the commonplace talk which would be about her. Song after song thrilled through the night's wideness. The stars came out in thick clusters. Father Tanner had long ago dropped his weekly paper and tilted his chair back against the wall, with his eyes half closed to listen, and his wife had settled down comfortably on the carpet sofa, with her hands nicely folded in her lap, as if she were at church. The minister, after silently surveying the situation for a song or two, attempted to join his voice to the chorus. He had a voice like a cross-cut saw, but he didn't do much harm in the background that way, though Cap did growl now and then, as if it put his nerves on edge. And by and by Mr. Tanner quavered in with a note or two.

Finally Margaret sang:

> "Sun of my soul, Thou Saviour dear,
> It is not night if Thou art near,
> Oh, may no earth-born cloud arise
> To hide Thee from Thy servant's eyes."

During this hymn the minister had slipped out the back door and gone around to the front of the house. He could not stand being in the background any longer, but as the last note died away Margaret arose and, bidding Bud good night, slipped up to her room.

There, presently, beside her darkened window, with her face toward the mountain, she knelt to pray for the wanderer who was trying to find his way out of the wilderness.

Chapter 13

Monday morning found Margaret at the schoolhouse nerved for her new task.

One by one the scholars trooped in, shyly or half defiantly, hung their hats on the hooks, put their dinner pails on the shelf, looked furtively at her, and sank into their accustomed seats; that is, the seats they had occupied during the last term of school. The big boys remained outside until Bud, acting under instructions from Margaret—after she had been carefully taught the ways of the school by Bud himself—rang the big bell. Even then they entered reluctantly and as if it were a great condescension that they came at all, Jed and "Delicate" coming in last, with scarcely a casual glance toward the teacher's desk, as if she were a mere fraction in the scheme of the school. She did not need to be told which was Timothy and which was Jed. Bud's description had been perfect. Her heart, by the way, instantly went out to Timothy. Jed was another proposition. He had thick, overhanging eyebrows, and a mouth that loved to make trouble and laugh over it. He was going to be hard to conquer. She wasn't sure the conquering would be interesting, either.

Margaret stood by the desk, watching them all with a pleasant smile. She did not frown at the unnecessary shuffling of feet nor the loud remarks of the boys as they settled into their seats. She just stood and watched them interestedly, as though her time had not yet come.

Jed and Timothy were carrying on a rumbling conversation. Even after they took their seats they kept it up. It was no part of their plan to let the teacher suppose they saw her or minded her in the least. They were the dominating influences in that school, and they wanted her to know it, right at the start; then a lot of trouble would be saved. If they didn't like her and couldn't manage her they didn't intend she should stay, and she might as well understand that at once.

Margaret understood it fully. Yet she stood quietly and watched them with a look of deep interest on her face and a light almost of mischief in her eyes, while Bud grew redder and redder over the way his two idols were treating the new teacher. One by one the school became aware of the twinkle in the teacher's eyes, and grew silent to watch, and one by one they began to smile over the coming scene when Jed and Timothy should discover it, and, worst of all, find out that it was actually directed against them. They would expect severity, or fear, or a desire to placate, but a twinkle—it was more than the school could decide what would happen under such circumstances. No one in that room would ever dare to laugh at either of those two boys. But the teacher was almost laughing now, and the twinkle had taken the rest of the room into the secret, while she waited amusedly until the two should finish the conversation.

The room grew suddenly deathly still, except for the whispered growls of Jed and Timothy, and still the silence deepened, until the two young giants themselves perceived that it was time to look up and take account of stock.

The perspiration by this time was rolling down the back of Bud's neck. He was about the only one in the room who was not on a broad grin, and he was wretched. What a fearful mistake the new teacher was making right at the start! She was antagonizing the two boys who held the whole school in their hands. There was no telling what they wouldn't do to her now. And he would have to stand up for her. Yes, no matter what they did, he would stand up for her! Even though he lost his best friends, he must be loyal to her; but the strain was terrible! He did not dare to look at them, but fastened his eyes upon Margaret, as if keeping them glued there was his only hope. Then suddenly he saw her face break into one of the sweetest, merriest smiles he ever witnessed, with not one single hint of reproach or offended dignity in it, just a smile of comradeship, understanding, and pleasure in the meeting, and it was directed to the two seats where Jed and Timothy sat.

With wonder he turned toward the two big boys, and saw, to his amazement, an answering smile upon their faces; reluctant, tis true, half sheepish at first, but a smile with lifted eyebrows of astonishment and real enjoyment of the joke.

A little ripple of approval went round in half-breathed syllables, but Margaret gave no time for any restlessness to start. She spoke at once, in her pleasantest partnership tone, such as she had used to Bud when she asked him to help her build her bookcase. So she spoke now to that school, and each one felt she was speaking just to him especially, and felt a leaping response in his soul. Here, at least, was something new and interesting, a new kind of teacher. They kept silence to listen.

"Oh, I'm not going to make a speech now," she said, and her voice sounded glad to them all. "I'll wait till we know one another before I do that. I just want to say how do you do to you, and tell you how glad I am to be here. I hope we shall like one another immensely and have a great many good times together. But we've got to get acquainted first, of course, and perhaps we'd better give most of the time to that today. First, suppose we sing something. What shall it be? What do you sing?"

Little Susan Johnson, by virtue of having seen the teacher at Sunday school, made bold to raise her hand and suggest, "Thar-thpangle Banner, pleath!" And so they tried it, but when Margaret found that only a few seemed to know the words, she said, "Wait!" Lifting her arm with a pretty, imperative gesture, and taking a piece of chalk from the box on her desk, she went to the new blackboard that stretched its shining black length around the room.

The school was breathlessly watching the graceful movement of the beautiful hand and arm over the smooth surface, leaving behind it the clear, perfect script. Such wonderful writing they had never seen; such perfect, easy curves and twirls. Every eye in the room was fastened on her, every breath was held as they watched and spelled out the words one by one.

"Gee!" said Bud, softly, under his breath, nor knew that he had spoken, but no one else moved.

"Now," she said, "let us sing," and when they started off again Margaret's strong, clear soprano leading, every voice in the room growled out the words and tried to get in step with the tune.

They had gone thus through two verses when Jed seemed to think it was about time to start something. Things were going altogether too smoothly for an untried teacher, if she *was* handsome and un-abashed. If they went on like this the scholars would lose all respect for him. So, being quite able to sing a clear tenor, he nevertheless puckered his lips impertinently, drew his brows in an ominous frown, and began to whistle a somewhat erratic accompaniment to the song. He watched the teacher closely, expecting to see the color flame in her cheeks, the anger flash in her eyes; he had tried this trick on other teachers and it always worked. He gave the wink to Timo-thy, and he too left off his glorious bass and began to whistle.

But instead of the anger and annoyance they expected, Margaret turned appreciative eyes toward the two back seats, nodding her head a trifle and smiling with her eyes as she sang, and when the verse was done she held up her hand for silence and said:

"Why, boys, that's beautiful! Let's try that verse once more, and you two whistle the accompaniment a little stronger in the chorus, or how would it do if you just came in on the chorus? I believe that would be more effective. Let's try the first verse that way; you boys sing during the verse and then whistle the chorus just as you did now. We really need your voices in the verse part, they are so strong and splendid. Let's try it now." And she started off again, the two big as-tonished fellows meekly doing as they were told, and really the effect was beautiful. What was their surprise when the whole song was fin-ished to have her say, "Now everybody whistle the chorus softly," and then pucker up her own soft lips to join in. That completely fin-ished the whistling stunt. Jed realized that it would never work again, not while she was here, for she had turned the joke into beauty and made them all enjoy it. It hadn't annoyed her in the least.

Somehow by that time they were all ready for anything she had to suggest, and they watched again breathlessly as she wrote another song on the blackboard, taking the other side of the room for it, and this time a hymn—"I Need Thee Every Hour."

When they began to sing it, however, Margaret found the tune went slowly, uncertainly.

"Oh, how we need a piano!" she exclaimed. "I wonder if we can't get up an entertainment and raise money to buy one. How many will help?"

Every hand in the place went up, Jed's and Timothy's last and only a little way, but she noted with triumph that they went up.

"All right; we'll do it! Now let's sing that verse correctly." And she began to sing again, while they all joined anxiously in, really trying to do their best.

The instant the last verse died away, Margaret's voice took their attention.

"Two years ago in Boston two young men, who belonged to a little group of Christian workers who were going from place to place holding meetings, sat talking together in their room in the hotel one evening."

There was instant quiet, a kind of a breathless quiet. This was not like the beginning of any lesson any other teacher had ever given them. Every eye was fixed on her.

"They had been talking over the work of the day, and finally one of them suggested that they choose a Bible verse for the whole year—"

There was a movement of impatience from one backseat, as if Jed had scented an incipient sermon, but the teacher's voice went steadily on:

"They talked it over, and at last they settled on 2 Timothy 2:15. They made up their minds to use it on every possible occasion. It was time to go to bed, so the man whose room adjoined got up and instead of saying good-night, he said, 'Well, 2 Timothy 2:15,' and went to his room. Pretty soon, when he put out his light, he knocked on the wall and shouted '2 Timothy 2:15,' and the other man responded, heartily, 'All right, 2 Timothy 2:15.' The next morning when they wrote their letters each of them wrote '2 Timothy 2:15' on the lower left-hand corner of the envelope, and sent out a great handful of letters to all parts of the world. Those letters passed through the Boston post office, and some of the clerks who sorted them saw that queer legend written down in the lower left-hand corner of the envelope, and they wondered at it, and one or two wrote it down, to look it up afterward. The letters reached other cities and were put into the hands of mail carriers to distribute, and they saw the queer little sentence, '2 Timothy 2:15,' and they wondered, and some of them looked it up."

By this time the entire attention of the school was upon the story, for they perceived that it was a story.

"The men left Boston and went across the ocean to hold meetings in other cities, and one day at a little railway station in Europe a group of people were gathered, waiting for a train, and those two men were among them. Pretty soon the train came, and one of the men got on the back end of the last car, while the other stayed on the platform, and as the train moved off the man on the last car took off his hat and said, in a good, loud, clear tone, 'Well, take care of yourself, 2 Timothy 2:15,' and the other one smiled and waved his hat and answered, 'Yes, 2 Timothy 2:15.' The man on the train, which was moving fast now, shouted back, '2 Timothy 2:15,' and the man on the platform responded still louder, waving his hat, '2 Timothy 2:15,' and back and forth the queer sentence was flung until the train was too far away for them to hear each other's voices. In the meantime all the people on the platform had been standing there listening and wondering what in the world such a strange salutation could mean. Some of them recognized what it was, but many did not know, and yet the sentence was said over so many times that they could not help remembering it, and some went away to recall it and ask their friends what it meant. A young man from America was on that platform and heard it, and he knew it stood for a passage in the Bible, and his curiosity was so great that he went back to his boardinghouse and hunted up the Bible his mother had packed in his trunk when he came away from home, and he hunted through the Bible until he found the place, 2 Timothy 2:15, and read it, and it made him think about his life and decide that he wasn't doing as he ought to do. I can't tell you all the story about that queer Bible verse, how it went here and there and what a great work it did in people's hearts; but one day those Christian workers went to Australia to hold some meetings, and one night, when the great auditorium was crowded, a man who was leading the meeting got up and told the story of this verse, how it had been chosen, and how it had gone over the world in strange ways, even told about the morning at the little railway station when the two men said good-bye. Just as he got to that place in his story a man in the audience stood up and said: 'Brother, just let me say a word, please. I never knew anything about all this before, but I was at that railway station, and I heard those two men shout that strange good-bye, and I went home and read that verse, and it's made a great difference in my life.'

"There was a great deal more to the story, how some Chicago policemen got to be good men through reading that verse, and how the story of the Australia meetings was printed in an Australian paper and sent to a lady in America who sent it to a friend in England to read about the meetings. And this friend in England had a son in the army in India, to whom she was sending a package, and she wrapped it around something in that package, and the young man read all about it, and it helped to change his life. Well, I thought of that story this morning when I was trying to decide what to read for our opening chapter, and it occurred to me that perhaps you would be interested to take that verse for our school verse this term, and so if you would like it I will put it on the blackboard. Would you like it, I wonder?"

She paused wistfully, as if she expected an answer, and there was a low, almost inaudible growl of assent; a keen listener might almost have said it had an impatient quality in it, as if they were in a hurry to find out what the verse was that had made such a stir in the world.

"Very well," said Margaret, turning to the board, "then I'll put it where we all can see it, and while I write it will you please say over where it is, so that you will remember it and hunt it up for yourselves in your Bibles at home?"

There was a sort of snicker at that, for there were probably not half a dozen Bibles, if there were so many, represented in that school, but they took her hint as she wrote, and chanted, "Two Timothy 2:15, 2 Timothy 2:15," and then spelled out after her rapid crayon, "Study to show thyself approved unto God, a workman that needeth not to be ashamed."

They read it together at her bidding, with a wondering, half-serious look in their faces, and then she said, "Now, shall we pray?"

The former teacher had not opened her school with prayer. It had never been even suggested in that school. It might have been a dangerous experiment if Margaret had attempted it sooner in her program. As it was, there was a shuffling of feet in the back seats at her first word, but the room grew quiet again, perhaps out of curiosity to hear a woman's voice in prayer:

"Our heavenly Father, we want to ask Thee to bless us in our work together, and to help us to be such workmen that we shall not need to be ashamed to show our work to Thee at the close of the day. For Christ's sake we ask it. Amen."

They did not have time to resent that prayer before she had them interested in something else. In fact, she had planned her whole first day out so that there should not be a minute for misbehavior. She had argued that if she could just get time to become acquainted with them she might prevent a lot of trouble before it ever started. Her first business was to win her scholars. After that she could teach them easily if they were once willing to learn.

She had a set of mental arithmetic problems ready which she propounded to them next, some of them difficult and some easy enough for the youngest child who could think, and she timed their answers and wrote on the board the names of those who raised their hands first and had the correct answers. The questions were put in a fascinating way, many of them having curious little catches in them for the scholars who were not on the alert, and Timothy presently discovered this and set himself to get every one, coming off victorious at the end. Even Jed roused himself and was interested, and some of the girls quite distinguished themselves.

When a half hour of this was over she put the word "TRANSFIGURATION" on the blackboard, and set them to playing a regular game out of it. If some of the schoolboard had come in just then they might have lifted up hands of horror at the idea of the new teacher setting the whole school to playing a game. But they certainly would have been delightfully surprised to see a quiet and orderly room with bent heads and knit brows, all intent upon papers and pencils. Never before in the annals of that school had the first day held a full period of quiet or orderliness. It was expected to be a day of battle, a day of trying out the soul of the teacher and proving whether he or she were worthy to cope with the active minds and bodies of the young bullies of Ashland. But the expected battle had been forgotten. Every mind was busy with the matter in hand.

Margaret had given them three minutes to write as many words as they could think of, of three letters or more, beginning with T, and using only the letters in the word she had put on the board. When time was called there was a breathless rush to write a last word, and then each scholar had to tell how many words he had, and each was called upon to read his list. Some had only two or three, some had ten or eleven. They were allowed to mark their words, counting one for each person present who did not have that word and doubling if it were two syllables, and so on. Excitement ran high when it was discovered that some had actually made a count of thirty or forty, and when they started writing words beginning with R every head was bent intently from the minute time was started.

Never had three minutes seemed so short to those unused brains, and Jed yelled out: "Aw, gee! I only got three!" when time was called next.

It was recess time when they finally finished every letter in that word, and, adding all up, found that Timothy had won the game. Was that school? Why, a barbecue couldn't be named beside it for fun! They rushed out to the school yard with a shout, and the boys played leapfrog loudly for the first few minutes. Margaret, leaning her tired head in her hands, elbows on the window seat, closing her eyes and gathering strength for the after-recess session, heard one boy say: "Wal, how d'ye like 'er?" And the answer came: "Gee! I didn't think she'd be that kind of a guy! I thought she'd be some mean old maid! Ain't she a peach, though?" She lifted up her head and laughed triumphantly to herself, her eyes alight, herself now strengthened for the fray. She wasn't wholly failing then?

After recess there was a spelling match, choosing sides, of course, "Because this is only the first day, and we must get acquainted before we can do real work, you know," she explained.

The spelling match proved an exciting affair also, with new features that Ashland had never seen before. Here the girls began to shine into prominence, but there were very few good spellers, and they were presently reduced to two girls—Rosa Rogers, the beauty of the school, and Amanda Bounds, a stolid, homely girl with deep eyes and a broad brow.

"I'm going to give this as a prize to the one who stands up the longest," said Margaret, with sudden inspiration as she saw the boys in their seats getting restless, and she unpinned a tiny blue silk bow that fastened her white collar.

The girls all said "Oh-h-h!" and immediately everyone in the room straightened up. The next few minutes those two girls spelled for dear life, each with her eye fixed upon the tiny blue bow in the teacher's white hands. To own that bow, that wonderful, strange bow of the heavenly blue, with the graceful twist to the tie! What delight! The girl who won that would be the admired of all the school. Even the boys sat up and took notice, each secretly thinking that Rosa, the beauty, would get it, of course.

But she didn't; she slipped up on the word "receive," after all, putting the i before the e; and her stolid companion, catching her breath awesomely, slowly spelled it right and received the blue prize, pinned gracefully at the throat of her old brown gingham by the teacher's own soft, white fingers, while the school looked on admiringly and the blood rolled hotly up the back of her neck and spread over her face and forehead. Rosa, the beauty, went crestfallen to her seat.

It was at noon, while they ate their lunch, that Margaret tried to get acquainted with the girls, calling most of them by name, to their great surprise, and hinting of delightful possibilities in the winter's work. Then she slipped out among the boys and watched their sports, laughing and applauding when someone made a particularly fine play, as if she thoroughly understood and appreciated.

She managed to stand near Jed and Timothy just before Bud rang the bell. "I've heard you are great sportsmen," she said to them, confidingly. "And I've been wondering if you'll teach me some things I want to learn? I want to know how to ride and shoot. Do you suppose I could learn?"

"Sure!" they chorused, eagerly, their embarrassment forgotten. "Sure, you could learn fine! Sure, *we'll learn* you!"

And then the bell rang and they all went in.

The afternoon was a rather informal arrangement of classes and schedule for the next day, Margaret giving out slips of paper with questions for each to answer, that she might find out just where to place them; and while they wrote she went from one to another, getting acquainted, advising, and suggesting about what they wanted to study. It was all so new and wonderful to them! They had not been used to caring what they were to study. Now it almost seemed interesting.

But when the day was done, the schoolhouse locked, and Bud and Margaret started for home, she realized that she was weary. Yet it was a weariness of success and not of failure, and she felt happy in looking forward to the morrow.

Chapter 14

The minister had decided to preach in Ashland, and on the following Sabbath. It became apparent that if he wished to have any notice at all from the haughty new teacher he must do something at once to establish his superiority in her eyes. He had carefully gone over his store of sermons that he always carried with him, and decided to preach on "The Dynamics of Altruism."

Notices had been posted up in saloons and stores and post office. He had made them himself after completely tabooing Mr. Tanner's kindly and blundering attempt, and they gave full information concerning the Reverend Frederick West, Ph.D., of the vicinity of New York City, who had kindly consented to preach in the schoolhouse on "The Dynamics of Altruism."

Several of these elaborately printed announcements had been posted up on big trees along the trails, and in other conspicuous places, and there was no doubt but that the coming Sabbath services were more talked of than anything else in that neighborhood for miles around, except the new teacher and her extraordinary way of making all the scholars fall in love with her. It is quite possible that the Reverend Frederick might not have been so flattered at the size of his audience when the day came if he could have known how many of them came principally because they thought it would be a good opportunity to see the new teacher.

However, the announcements were read, and the preacher became an object of deep interest to the community when he went abroad. Under this attention he swelled, grew pleased, bland, and condescending, wearing an oily smile and bowing most conceitedly whenever anybody noticed him. He even began to drop his severity and silence at the table, toward the end of the week, and expanded into dignified conversation, mainly addressed to Mr. Tanner about the political situation in the state of Arizona. He was trying to impress the teacher with the fact that he looked upon her as a most insignificant mortal who had forfeited her right to his smiles by her headstrong and unseemly conduct when he had warned her about "that young ruffian."

Out on the trail Long Bill and Jasper Kemp paused before a tree that bore the Reverend Frederick's church notice, and read in silence while the wide wonder of the desert spread about them.

"What d'ye make out o' them cuss words, Jap?" asked Long Bill, at length. "D'ye figger the parson's goin' to preach oon swearin' ur gunpowder?"

"Blowed ef I know," answered Jasper, eyeing the sign ungraciously, "but by the looks of him he can't say much to suit me on neither one. He resembles a yaller cactus bloom out in a rainstorm as to head, an' his smile is like some of them prickles on the plant. He can't be no 'sky-pilot' to me, not just yet."

"You don't allow he b'longs in any way to *her?*" asked Long Bill, anxiously, after they had been on their way for a half hour.

"B'long to *her?* Meanin' the schoolmarm?"

"Yes; he ain't sweet on her nor nothin'?"

"Wal, I guess not," said Jasper, contentedly. "She's got eyes sharp's a needle. You don't size her up so small she's goin' to take to a sickly parson with yaller hair an' sleek ways when she's seen the kid, do you?"

"Wal, no, it don't seem noways reasonable, but you never can tell. Women gets notions."

"She ain't that kind! You mark my words, *she ain't that kind.* I'd lay she'd punch the breeze like a coyote ef he'd make up to her. Just you wait till you see him. He's the most no-'count, mealeyest little thing that ever called himself a man. My word! I'd like to see him try to ride that colt o' mine. I really would. It would be some sight for sore eyes, it sure would."

"Mebbe he's got a intellec'," suggested Long Bill, after another mile. "That goes a long ways with womenfolks with a education."

"No chance!" said Jasper, confidently. "Ain't got room fer one under his yaller thatch. You wait till you set your lamps on him once before you go to gettin' excited. Why, he ain't one-two-three with our missionary! Gosh! I wish *he'd* come back an' see to such goin's-on—I certainly do."

"Was you figgerin' to go to that gatherin' Sunday?"

"I sure was," said Jasper. "I want to see the show, an', besides, we might be needed ef things got too high-soundin'. It ain't good to have a creature at large that thinks he knows all there is to know. I heard him talk down to the post office the day after that little party we had when the kid shot out the lights to save Bunchy from killin' Crapster, an' it's my opinion he needs a good spankin, but I'm agoin' to give him a fair show. I ain't much on religion myself, but I do like to see a square deal, especially in a parson. I've sized it up he needs a lesson."

"I'm with ye, Jap," said Long Bill, and the two rode on their way in silence.

Margaret was so busy and so happy with her school all the week that she quite forgot her annoyance at the minister. She really saw very little of him, for he was always late to breakfast, and she took hers early. She went to her room immediately after supper, and he had little opportunity for pursuing her acquaintance. Perhaps he judged that it would be wise to let her alone until after he had made his grand impression on Sunday, and let her "make up" to him.

It was not until Sunday morning that she suddenly recalled that he was to preach that day. She had indeed seen the notices, for a very large and elaborate one was posted in front of the schoolhouse, and some anonymous artist had produced a fine caricature of the preacher in red clay underneath his name. Margaret had been obliged to remain after school Friday and remove as much of this portrait as she was able, not having been willing to make it a matter of discipline to discover the artist. In fact, it was so true to the model that the young teacher felt a growing sympathy for the one who had perpetrated it.

Margaret started to the schoolhouse early Sunday morning, attended by the faithful Bud. Not that he had any more intention of going to Sunday school than he had the week before, but it was pleasant to be the chosen escort of so popular a teacher. Even Jed and Timothy had walked home with her twice during the week. He did not intend to lose his place as nearest to her. There was only one to whom he would surrender that, and he was too far away to claim it often.

Margaret had promised to help in the Sunday school that morning, for the woman who taught the little ones was still away with her sick neighbor, and on the way she persuaded Bud to help her.

"You'll be secretary for me, won't you, William?" she asked, brightly. "I'm going to take the left-front corner of the room for the children, and seat them on the recitation benches, and that will leave all the back part of the room for the older people. Then I can use the blackboard and not disturb the rest."

"Secretary?" asked the astonished Bud. He was, so to speak, growing accustomed to surprises. Secretary did not sound like being a nice little Sunday school boy.

"Why, yes! Take up the collection, and see who is absent, and so on. I don't know all the names, perhaps, and, anyhow, I don't like to do that when I have to teach!"

Artful Margaret! She had no mind to leave Bud floating around outside the schoolhouse, and though she had ostensibly prepared her lesson and her blackboard illustration for the little children, she had hidden in it a truth for Bud—poor, neglected, devoted Bud!

The inefficient old man who taught the older people that day gathered his forces together and, seated with his back to the platform, his spectacles extended upon his long nose, he proceeded with the questions in the textbook, as usual, being more than ordinarily unfamiliar with them, but before he was half through he perceived by the long pauses between the questions and answers that he did not have the attention of his class. He turned slowly around to see what they were all looking at, and became so engaged in listening to the lesson the new teacher was drawing on the blackboard that he completely forgot to go on, until Bud, very important in his new position, rang the tiny desk bell for the close of school, and Margaret, looking up, saw in dismay that she had been teaching the whole school.

While they were singing a closing hymn the room began to fill up, and presently came the minister, walking importantly beside Mr. Tanner, his chin flattened upward as usual, but bent in till it made a double roll over his collar, his eyes rolling importantly, showing much of their whites, his sermon, in an elaborate leather cover, carried conspicuously under his arm, and the severest of clerical coats and collars setting out his insignificant face.

Walking behind him in single file, measured step, just so far apart, came the eight men from the bunkhouse—Long Bill, Big Jim, Fiddling Boss, Jasper Kemp, Fadeaway Forbes, Stocky, Croaker, and Fudge; and behind them, looking like a scared rabbit, Mom Wallis scuttled into the back seat and sank out of sight. The eight men, however, ranged themselves across in front of the room on the recitation bench, directly in front of the platform, removing a few small children for that purpose.

They had been lined up in a scowling row along the path as the minister entered, looking at them askance under his aristocratic yellow eyebrows, and as he neared the door the last man followed in his wake, then the next, and so on.

Margaret, in her seat halfway back at the side of the schoolhouse near a window, saw through the trees a wide sombrero over a pair of broad shoulders; but, though she kept close watch, she did not see her friend of the wilderness enter the schoolhouse. If he had really come to meeting, he was staying outside.

The minister was rather nonplussed at first that there were no hymnbooks. It almost seemed that he did not know how to go on with divine service without hymnbooks, but at last he compromised on the long-meter doxology, pronounced with deliberate unction. Then, looking about for a possible pipe organ and choir, he finally started it himself; but it is doubtful whether anyone would have recognized the tune enough to help it on if Margaret had not for very shame's sake taken it up and carried it along, and so they came to the prayer and Bible reading.

These were performed with a formal, perfunctory style calculated to impress the audience with the importance of the preacher rather than the words he was speaking. The audience was very quiet, having the air of reserving judgment for the sermon.

Margaret could not just remember afterward how it was she missed the text. She had turned her eyes away from the minister, because it somehow made her feel homesick to compare him with her dear, dignified father. Her mind had wandered, perhaps, to the sombrero she had glimpsed outside, and she was wondering how its owner was coming on with his resolves, and just what change they would mean in his life, anyway. Then suddenly she awoke to the fact that the sermon had begun.

Chapter 15

"Considered in the world of physics," began the lordly tones of the Reverend Frederick, "dynamics is that branch of mechanics that treats of the effects of forces in producing motion, and of the laws of motion thus produced—sometimes called kinetics, opposed to statics. It is the science that treats of the laws of force, whether producing equilibrium or motion; in this sense including both statics and kinetics. It is also applied to the forces producing or governing activity or movement of any kind, also the methods of such activity."

The big words rolled out magnificently over the awed gathering, and the minister flattened his chin and rolled his eyes up at the people in his most impressive way.

Margaret's gaze hastily sought the row of rough men on the front seat, sitting with folded arms in an attitude of attention, each man with a pair of intelligent eyes under his shaggy brows regarding the preacher as they might have regarded an animal in a zoo. Did they understand what had been said? It was impossible to tell from their serious faces.

"Philanthropy has been called the dynamics of Christianity; that is to say, it is Christianity in action," went on the preacher. "It is my purpose this morning to speak upon the dynamics of altruism. Now altruism is the theory that inculcates benevolence to others in subordination to self-interest; interested benevolence as opposed to disinterested; also, the practice of this theory."

He lifted his eyes to the audience once more and nodded his head slightly, as if to emphasize the deep truth he had just given them, and the battery of keen eyes before him never flinched from his face. They were searching him through and through. Margaret wondered if he had no sense of the ridiculous, that he could, to such an audience, pour forth such a string of technical definitions. They sounded strangely like dictionary language. She wondered if anybody present besides herself knew what the man meant or got any inkling of what his subject was. Surely he would drop to simpler language, now that he had laid out his plan.

It never occurred to her that the man was trying to impress *her* with his wonderful fluency of language and his marvelous store of wisdom. On and on he went in much the same trend he had begun, with now and then a flowery sentence or whole paragraph of meaningless eloquence about the "brotherhood of man"—with a roll to the r's in brotherhood.

Fifteen minutes of this profitless oratory those men of the wilderness endured, stolidly and with fixed attention; then, suddenly, a sentence of unusual simplicity struck them and an almost visible thrill went down the front seat.

"For years the church has preached a dead faith, without works, my friends, and the time has come to stop preaching faith! I repeat it—fellowmen. I repeat it. The time has come *to stop preaching faith* and begin to do good works!" He thumped the desk vehemently. "Men don't need a superstitious belief in a Saviour to save them from their sins. They need to go to work and save themselves! As if a man dying two thousand years ago on a cross could do any good to you and me today!"

It was then that the thrill passed down that front line, and Long Bill, sitting at their head, leaned slightly forward and looked full and frowning into the face of Jasper Kemp, and the latter, frowning back, solemnly winked one eye. Margaret sat where she could see the whole thing.

Immediately, still with studied gravity, Long Bill cleared his throat impressively, arose, and, giving the minister a full look in the eye, of the nature almost of a challenge, he turned and walked slowly, noisily down the aisle and out the front door.

The minister was visibly annoyed, and for the moment a trifle flustered, but, concluding his remarks had been too deep for the rough creature, he gathered up the thread of his argument and proceeded:

"We need to get to work at our duty toward our fellowmen. We need to down trusts and give the laboring man a chance. We need to stop insisting that men shall believe in the inspiration of the entire Bible and get to work at something practical!"

The impressive pause after this sentence was interrupted by a sharp, rasping sound of Big Jim clearing his throat and shuffling to his feet. He, too, looked the minister full in the face with a searching gaze, shook his head sadly, and walked leisurely down the aisle and out of the door. The minister paused again and frowned. This was becoming annoying.

Margaret sat in startled wonder. Could it be possible that these rough men were objecting to the sermon from a theological point of view, or was it just a happening that they had gone out at such pointed moments. She sat back after a minute, telling herself that of course the men must just have been weary of the long sentences, which no doubt they could not understand. She began to hope that Gardley was not within hearing. It was not probable that many others understood enough to get harm from the sermon, but her soul boiled with indignation that a man could go forth and call himself a minister of an evangelical church and yet talk such terrible heresy.

Big Jim's steps died slowly away on the clay path outside, and the preacher resumed his discourse.

"We have preached long enough of hell and torment. It is time for a gospel of love to our brothers. Hell is a superstition of the Dark Ages. *There is no hell!*"

Fiddling Boss turned sharply toward Jasper Kemp, as if waiting for a signal, and Jasper gave a slight, almost imperceptible nod. Whereupon Fiddling Boss cleared his throat loudly and arose, faced the minister, and marched down the aisle, while Jasper Kemp remained quietly seated as if nothing had happened, a vacancy each side of him.

By this time the color began to rise in the minister's cheeks. He looked at the retreating back of Fiddling Boss, and then suspiciously down at the row of men, but every one of them sat with folded arms and eyes intent upon the sermon, as if their comrades had not left them. The minister thought he must have been mistaken and took up the broken thread once more, or tried to, but he had hopelessly lost the place in his manuscript, and the only clue that offered was a quotation of a poem about the devil; to be sure, the connection was somewhat abrupt, but he clutched it with his eye gratefully and began reading it dramatically:

"Men don't believe in the devil now
    As their fathers used to do—"

But he got no further when a whole clearinghouse of throats
sounded, and Fadeaway Forbes stumbled to his feet frantically,
bolting down the aisle as if he had been sent for. He had not quite
reached the door when Stocky clumped after him, followed at inter-
vals by Croaker and Fudge, and each just as the minister had begun:
    "Um! Ah! To resume—"
And now only Jasper Kemp remained of the front-seaters, his fine
gray eyes boring through and through the minister as he floundered
through the remaining portion of his manuscript up to the point
where it began, "And finally—" which opened with another poem:

        "I need no Christ to die for me."

The sturdy, gray-haired Scotchman suddenly lowered his folded
arms, slapping a hand resoundingly on each knee, bent his shoulders
the better to pull himself to his feet, pressing his weight on his hands
till his elbows were akimbo, uttered a deep sigh and a, "Yes—well—
ah!"
    With that he got to his feet and dragged them slowly out of the
schoolhouse.
    By this time the minister was ready to burst with indignation.
Never before in all the bombastic days of his egotism had he been so
grossly insulted, and by such rude creatures! And yet there was really
nothing that could be said or done. These men appeared to be simple
creatures who had wandered in idly, perhaps for a few moments'
amusement, and, finding the discourse above their caliber, had innocently wandered out again. That was the way it had been made to
appear. But his plans had been cruelly upset by such actions, and he
was mortified in the extreme. His face was purple with his emotions,
and he struggled and spluttered for a way out of his trying dilemma.
At last he spoke, and his voice was absurdly dignified:
    "Is there—ah—any other—ah—auditor—ah—who is desirous of
withdrawing before the close of service? If so he may do so now,
or—ah—" He paused for a suitable ending, and familiar words

rushed to his lips without consciousness for the moment of their meaning—"or forever after hold their peace—ah!"

There was a deathly silence in the schoolhouse. No one offered to go out, and Margaret suddenly turned her head and looked out of the window. Her emotions were almost beyond her control.

Thus the closing eloquence proceeded to its finish, and at last the service was over. Margaret looked about for Mom Wallis, but she had disappeared. She signed to Bud, and together they hastened out, but a quiet Sabbath peace reigned about the door of the schoolhouse, and not a man from the camp was in sight; no, or even the horses upon which they had come.

And yet, when the minister had finished shaking hands with the worshipful women and a few men and children, and came with Mr. Tanner to the door of the schoolhouse, those eight men stood in a solemn row, four on each side of the walk, each holding his chin in his right hand, his right elbow in his left hand, and all eyes on Jasper Kemp, who kept his eyes thoughtfully up in the sky.

"H'w aire yeh, Tanner? Pleasant 'casion. Mind steppin' on a bit? We men wanta have a word with the parson."

Mr. Tanner stepped on hurriedly, and the minister was left standing nonplussed and alone in the doorway of the schoolhouse.

Chapter 16

"Um! Ah!" began the minister, trying to summon his best clerical manner to meet—what? He did not know. It was best to assume they were a penitent band of inquirers for the truth. But the memory of their recent exodus from the service was rather too clearly in his mind for his pleasantest expression to be uppermost toward these rough creatures. Insolent fellows! He ought to give them a good lesson in behavior!

"Um! Ah!" he began again, but found to his surprise that his remarks thus far had had no effect whatever on the eight stolid countenances before him. In fact, they seemed to have grown grim and menacing even in their quiet attitude, and their eyes were fulfilling the promise of the look they had given him when they left the service.

"What does all this mean, anyway?" he burst forth, suddenly.

"Calm yourself, elder! Calm yourself," spoke up Long Bill. "There ain't any occasion to get excited."

"I'm not an elder; I'm a minister of the gospel," exploded West, in his most pompous tones. "I should like to know who you are and what all this means?"

"Yes, parson, we understand who you are. We understand quite well, an' we're agoin' to tell you who we are. We're a band of altruists! That's what we are. We're *altruists!*" It was Jasper Kemp of the keen eyes and sturdy countenance who spoke. "And we've come here in brotherly love to exercise a little of that dynamic force of altruism you was talkin' about. We just thought we'd begin on you so's you could see that we got some works to go 'long with our faith."

"What do you mean, sir?" said West, looking from one grim countenance to another. "I—I don't quite understand." The minister was beginning to be frightened, he couldn't exactly tell why. He wished he had kept Brother Tanner with him. It was the first time he had ever thought of Mr. Tanner as "brother."

"We mean just this, parson; you been talkin' a lot of lies in there about there bein' no Saviour an' no hell, ner no devil, an' while we ain't much credit to God ourselves, bein' just common men, we know all that stuff you said ain't true about the Bible an' the devil bein' superstitions, an' we thought we better exercise a little of that there altruism you was talkin' about an' teach you better. You see, it's real brotherly kindness, parson. An' now we're goin' to give you a sample of that dynamics you spoke about. Are you ready, boys?"

"All ready," they cried as one man.

There seemed to be no concerted motion, nor was there warning. Swifter than the weaver's shuttle, sudden as the lightning's flash, the minister was caught from where he stood pompously in that doorway, hat in hand, all grandly as he was attired, and hurled from man to man. Across the walk and back, across and back, across and back, until it seemed to him it was a thousand miles all in a minute of time. He had no opportunity to prepare for the onslaught. He jammed his high silk hat, wherewith he had thought to overawe the community, upon his sleek head, and grasped his precious sermon case to his breast; the sermon, as it well deserved, was flung to the four winds of heaven and fortunately was no more—that is, existing as a whole. The time came when each of those eight men recovered and retained a portion of that learned oration, and Mom Wallis, not quite understanding, pinned up and used as a sort of shrine the portion about doubting the devil; but as a sermon the parts were never assembled on this earth, nor could be, for some of it was ground to powder under eight pairs of ponderous heels. But the minister at that trying moment was too much otherwise engaged to notice that the child of his brain lay scattered on the ground.

Seven times he made the round up and down, up and down that merciless group, tossed like a thistledown from man to man. And at last, when his breath was gone, when the world had grown black before him, and he felt smaller and more inadequate than he had ever felt in his whole conceited life before, he found himself bound, helplessly bound, and cast ignominiously into a wagon. And it was a strange thing that, though seemingly but five short minutes before the place had been swarming with worshipful admirers thanking him for his sermon, now there did not seem to be a creature within hearing, for he called and cried aloud and roared with his raucous voice until it would seem that all the surrounding states might have heard that cry from Arizona, yet none came to his relief.

They carried him away somewhere, he did not know where; it was a lonely spot and near a waterhole. When he protested and loudly blamed them, threatening all the law in the land upon them, they regarded him as one might a naughty child who needed chastisement, leniently and with sorrow, but also with determination.

They took him down by the water's side and stood him up among them. He began to tremble with fear as he looked from one to another, for he was not a man of courage, and he had heard strange tales of this wild, free land, where every man was a law unto himself. Were they going to drown him then and there? Then up spoke Jasper Kemp:

"Mr. Parson," he said, and his voice was kind but firm. One might almost say there was a hint of humor in it, and there surely was a twinkle in his eye; but the sternness of his lips belied it, and the minister was in no state to appreciate humor—"Mr. Parson, we've brought you here to do you good, an' you oughtn't to complain. This is altruism, an' we're but actin' out what you been preachin'. You're our brother an' we're tryin' to do you good, an' now we're about to show you what a dynamic force we are. You see, Mr. Parson, I was brought up by a good Scotch grandmother, an' I know a lie when I hear it, an' when I hear a man preach error I know it's time to set him straight, so now we're agoin' to set you straight. I don't know where you come from, nor who brang you up, nor what church set you afloat, but I know enough by all my grandmother taught me—even if I hadn't been a-listenin' off and on for two years back to Mr. Brownleigh, our missionary—to know you're a dangerous man to have at large. I'd as soon have a mad dog let loose. Why, what you preach ain't the gospel, an' it ain't the truth, and the time has come for you to know it, an' own it and recant. Recant! That's what they call it. That's what we're here to see 't you do, or we'll know the reason why. That's the *dynamics* of it. See?"

The minister saw. He saw the deep, muddy water hole. He saw nothing more.

"Folks are all too ready to believe them there things you was gettin' off without havin' 'em *preached* to justify 'em in their evil ways. We gotta think of those poor ignorant brothers of ours that might listen to you. See? That's the *altruism* of it!"

"What do you want me to do?" The wretched man's tone was not merely humble—it was abject. His grand Prince Albert coat was torn in three places; one tail hung down dejectedly over his hip; one sleeve was ripped halfway out. His collar was unbuttoned and the ends rode up hilariously over his cheeks. His necktie was gone. His sleek hair stuck out in damp wisps about his frightened eyes, and his hat had been "stove in" and jammed down as far as it would go until his ample ears stuck out like sails at half-mast. His feet were embedded in the heavy mud on the margin of the waterhole, and his fine silk socks, which had showed at one time above the erstwhile neat tyings, were torn and covered with mud.

"Well, in the first place," said Jasper Kemp, with a slow wink around at the company, "that little matter about hell needs adjustin'. Hell ain't no superstition. I ain't dictatin' what kind of a hell there is. You can make it fire or water or anything else you like, but *there is a hell,* an' *you believe in it.* D'ye understand? We's just like to have you make that statement publicly right here an' now."

"But how can I say what I don't believe?" whined West, almost ready to cry. He had come proudly through a trial by presbytery on these very same points, and had posed as being a man who had the courage of his convictions. He could not thus easily surrender his pride of original thought and broad-mindedness. He had received congratulations from a number of noble martyrs who had left their chosen church for just such reasons, congratulating him on his brave stand. It had been the first notice from big men he had ever been able to attract to himself, and it had gone to his head like wine. Give that up for a few miserable cowboys! It might get into the papers and go back East. He must think of his reputation.

"That's just where the dynamics of the thing comes in, brother," said Jasper Kemp, patronizingly. "We're here to *make* you believe in a hell. We're the force that will bring you back into the right way of thinkin' again. Are you ready, boys?"

The quiet utterance brought gooseflesh up to West's very ears, and his eyes bulged with horror.

"Oh, that isn't necessary! I believe—yes, I believe in hell!" he shouted, as they seized him.

But it was too late. The Reverend Frederick West was plunged into the waterhole, from whose sheep-muddied waters he came up spluttering, "Yes, I believe in *hell!*" and for the first time in his life, perhaps, he really did believe in it, and thought that he was in it.

The men were standing knee-deep in the water and holding their captive lightly by his arms and legs, their eyes upon their leader, waiting now.

Jasper Kemp stood in the water, also, looking down benevolently upon his victim, his chin in his hand, his elbow in his other hand, an attitude which carried a feeling of hopelessness to the frightened minister.

"An' now there's that little matter of the devil," said Jasper Kemp, reflectively. "We'll just fix that up next while we're near his place of residence. You believe in the devil, Mr. Parson, from now on? If you'd ever tried resistin' him I figger you'd have b'lieved in him long ago. But *you believe in him* from *now on,* an' you *don't preach against him any more!* We're not goin' to have our Arizona men gettin' off their guard an' thinkin' their enemy is dead. There *is* a devil, parson, and you believe in him! Duck him, boys!"

Down went the minister into the water again, and came up spluttering. "Yes, I—I—I—believe—in—the—devil." Even in this strait he was loath to surrender his pet theme—no devil.

"Very well so far as it goes," said Jasper Kemp, thoughtfully. "But now, boys, we're comin' to the most important of all, and you better put him under about three times, for there mustn't be no mistake about this matter. You believe in the Bible, parson—*the whole Bible?*"

"Yes!" gasped West, as he went down the first time and got a mouthful of the bitter water, "I believe—" The voice was fairly anguished. Down he went again. Another mouthful of water. *"I believe in the whole Bible!"* he screamed, and went down the third time. His voice was growing weaker, but he came up and reiterated it without request, and was lifted out upon the mud for a brief respite. The men of the bunkhouse were succeeding better than the presbytery back in the East had been able to do. The conceit was no longer visible in the face of the Reverend Frederick. His teeth were chattering, and he was beginning to see one really needed to believe in something when one came as near to his end as this.

"There's just one more thing to reckon with," said Jasper Kemp, thoughtfully. "That line of talk you was handin' out about a man dyin' on a cross two thousand years ago bein' nothin' to you. You said you *an' me,* but you can speak for *yourself.* We may not be much to look at, but we ain't goin' to stand for no such slander as that. Our missionary preaches all about that Man on the Cross, an' if you don't need Him before you get through this little campaign of life I'll miss my guess. Mebbe we haven't been all we might have been, but we ain't agoin' to let you ner no one else go back on that there Cross!"

Jasper Kemp's tone was tender and solemn. As the minister lay panting upon his back in the mud he was forced to acknowledge that at only two other times in his life had a tone of voice so arrested his attention and filled him with awe; once when as a boy he had been caught copying off another's paper at examination time, and he had been sent to the principal's office; and again on the occasion of his mother's funeral, as he sat in the dim church a few years ago and listened to the old minister. For a moment now he was impressed with the wonder of the Cross, and it suddenly seemed as if he were being arraigned before the eyes of Him with whom we all have to do. A kind of shame stole into his pale, flabby face, all the smugness and complacence gone, and he a poor wretch in the hands of his accusers. Jasper Kemp, standing over him on the bank, looking down grimly upon him, seemed like the emissary of God sent to condemn him, and his little, self-centered soul quailed within him.

"Along near the end of that *dis*course of yours you mentioned that sin was only misplaced energy. Well, if that's so there's a heap of your energy gone astray this mornin', an' the time has come for you to pay up. Speak up now an' say what you believe or whether you want another duckin'—an' it'll be seven times this time!"

The man on the ground shut his eyes and gasped. The silence was very solemn. There seemed no hint of the ridiculous in the situation. It was serious business now to all those men. Their eyes were on their leader.

"Do you solemnly declare before God—I s'pose you still believe in a God, as you didn't say nothin' to the contrary—that from now on you'll stand for that there Cross and for Him that hung on it?"

The minister opened his eyes and looked up into the wide brightness of the sky, as if he half expected to see horses and chariots of fire standing about to do battle with him then and there, and his voice was awed and frightened as he said:

"I do!"

There was silence, and the men stood with half bowed heads, as if some solemn service were being performed that they did not quite understand, but in which they fully sympathized. Then Jasper Kemp said, softly:

"Amen!" And after a pause: "I ain't any sort of a Christian myself, but I just can't stand it to see a parson floatin' round that don't even know the name of the firm he's workin' for. Now, parson, there's just one more requirement, an' then you can go home."

The minister opened his eyes and looked around with a frightened appeal, but not one moved, and Jasper Kemp went on:

"You say you had a church in New York. What was the name and *ad*dress of your workin' boss up there?"

"What do you mean? I hadn't any boss."

"Why, him that hired you an' paid you. The chief elder or whatever you called him."

"Oh!" The minister's tone expressed lack of interest in the subject, but he answered languidly, "Ezekiel Newbold, Hazelton."

"Very good. Now, parson, you'll just kindly write two copies of a letter to Mr. Ezekiel Newbold statin' what you've just said to us concernin' your change of faith, sign your name, address one to Mr. Newbold, an' give the duplicate to me. We just want this little matter put on record so you can't change your mind any in the future. Do you get my idea?"

"Yes," said the minister, dispiritedly.

"Will you do it?"

"Yes," apathetically.

"Well, now I got a piece of advice for you. It would be just as well for your health for you to leave Arizona about as quick as you can find it convenient to pack, but you won't be allowed to leave this town, day or night, cars or afoot, until them there letters are all O.K. Do you get me?"

"Yes," pathetically.

"I might add, by way of explainin', that if you had come to Arizona an' minded your own business you wouldn't have been interfered with. You mighta preached whatever bosh you darned pleased so far as we was concerned, only you wouldn't have had no sorta audience after the first try of that stuff you give today. But when you come to Arizona an' put your fingers in other folks' pie, when you tried to squeal on the young gentleman who was keen enough to shoot out the lights to save a man's life, why, we 'ain't no further use for you. In the first place, you was all wrong. You thought the kid shot out the lights to steal the gamin' money, but he didn't. He put it all in the hands of the sheriff some hours before your 'private information' reached him through the mail. You thought you were awful sharp, you little sneak! But I wasn't the only man present who saw you put your foot out an' cover a gold piece that rolled on the floor just when the fight began. You thought nobody was a-lookin', but you'll favor us, please, with that identical gold piece along with the letter before you leave. Well, boys, that'll be about all, then. Untie him!"

In silence and with a kind of contemptuous pity in their faces the strong men stooped and unbound him. Then, without another word, they left him, tramping solemnly away single file to their horses, standing at a little distance.

Jasper Kemp lingered for a moment, looking down at the wretched man. "Would you care to have us carry you back to the house?" he asked, reflectively.

"No!" said the minister, bitterly. "No!" And without another word Jasper Kemp left him.

Into the mesquite bushes crept the minister, his glory all departed, and hid his misery from the light, groaning in bitterness of spirit. He who had made the hearts of a score of old ministers to sorrow for Zion, who had split in two a pleasantly united congregation, disrupted a session, and brought about a scandalous trial in presbytery was at last conquered. The Reverend Frederick West had recanted!

Chapter 17

When Margaret left the schoolhouse with Bud she had walked but a few steps when she remembered Mom Wallis and turned back to search for her, but nowhere could she find a trace of her, and the front of the schoolhouse was as empty of any people from the camp as if they had not been there that morning. The curtain had not yet risen for the scene of the undoing of West.

"I suppose she must have gone home with them," said the girl, wistfully. "I'm sorry not to have spoken with her. She was good to me."

"You mean Mom Wallis?" said the boy. "No, she ain't gone home. She's hiking 'long to our house to see you. The kid went along of her. See, there—down by those cottonwood trees? That's them."

Margaret turned with eagerness and hurried along with Bud now. She knew who it was they called the kid in that tone of voice. It was the way the men had spoken of and to him, a mingling of respect and gentling that showed how much beloved he was. Her cheeks wore a heightened color, and her heart gave a pleasant flutter of interest.

They walked rapidly and caught up with their guests before they had reached the Tanner house, and Margaret had the pleasure of seeing Mom Wallis's face flush with shy delight when she caught her softly round the waist, stealing quietly up behind, and greeted her with a kiss. There had not been many kisses for Mom Wallis in the later years, and the two that were to Margaret Earle's account seemed very sweet to her. Mom Wallis's eyes shone as if she had been a young girl as she turned with a smothered "Oh!" She was a woman not given to expressing herself; indeed, it might be said that the last twenty years of her life had been mainly of self-repression. She gave that one little gasp of recognition and pleasure, and then she relapsed into embarrassed silence beside the two young people who found pleasure in their own greetings. Bud, boylike, was a cottontail, along with Cap, who had appeared from no one knew where and was attending the party joyously.

Mom Wallis, in her big, rough shoes, on the heels of which her scant brown calico gown was lifted as she walked, trudged shyly along between the two young people, as carefully watched and helped over the humps and bumps of the way as if she had been a princess. Margaret noticed with a happy approval how Gardley's hand was ready under the old woman's elbow to assist her as politely as he might have done for her own mother had she been walking by his side.

Presently Bud and Cap returned, and Bud, with observant eye, soon timed his step to Margaret's on her other side and touched her elbow lightly to help her over the next rut. This was his second lesson in manners from Gardley. He had his first the Sunday before, watching the two while he and Cap walked behind. Bud was learning. He had keen eyes and an alert brain. Margaret smiled understandingly at him, and his face grew deep red with pleasure.

"He was bringin' me to see where you was livin'," explained Mom Wallis, suddenly, nodding toward Gardley as if he had been a king. "We wasn't hopin' to see you, except mebbe just as you come by goin' in."

"Oh, then I'm so glad I caught up with you in time. I wouldn't have missed you for anything. I went back to look for you. Now you're coming in to dinner with me, both of you," declared Margaret, joyfully. "William, your mother will have enough dinner for us all, won't she?"

"Sure!" said Bud, with that assurance born of his life acquaintance with his mother, who had never failed him in a trying situation so far as things to eat were concerned.

Margaret looked happily from one of her invited guests to the other, and Gardley forgot to answer for himself in watching the brightness of her face, and wondering why it was so different from the faces of all other girls he knew anywhere.

But Mom Wallis was overwhelmed. A wave of red rolled dully up from her withered neck in its gala collar over her leathery face to the roots of her thin, gray hair.

"Me! Stay to dinner! Oh, I couldn't do that nohow! Not in these here clo'es. 'Course I got that pretty collar you give me, but I couldn't never go out to dinner in this old dress an' these shoes. I know what folks ought to look like an' I ain't goin' to shame you."

"Shame me? Nonsense! Your dress is all right, and who is going to see your shoes? Besides, I've just set my heart on it. I want to take you up to my room and show you the pictures of my father and mother and home and the church where I was christened, and everything."

Mom Wallis looked at her with wistful eyes, but still shook her head. "Oh, I'd like to mighty well. It's good of you to ast me. But I couldn't. I just couldn't. 'Sides, I gotta go home an' git the men's grub ready."

"Oh, can't she stay this time, Mr. Gardley?" appealed Margaret. "The men won't mind for once, will they?"

Gardley looked into her true eyes and saw she really meant the invitation. He turned to the withered old woman by his side. "Mom, we're going to stay," he declared joyously. "She wants us, and we have to do whatever she says. The men will run along. They all know how to cook. Mom, *we're going to stay.*"

"That's beautiful!" declared Margaret. "It's so nice to have some company of my own." Then her face suddenly sobered. "Mr. Wallis won't mind, will he?" And she looked with troubled eyes from one of her guests to the other. She did not want to prepare trouble for poor Mom Wallis when she went back.

Mom Wallis turned startled eyes toward her. There was contempt in her face and outraged womanhood. "Pop's gone off," she said, significantly. "He went yist'day. But he 'ain't got no call t' mind. I ben waitin' on Pop nigh on to twenty year, an' I guess I'm goin' to a dinner party, now 't I'm invited. Pop 'd better *not* mind, I guess!"

And Margaret suddenly saw how much, how very much, her invitation had been to the starved old soul. Margaret took her guests into the stiff little parlor and slipped out to interview her landlady. She found Mrs. Tanner, as she had expected, a large-minded woman who was quite pleased to have more guests to sit down to her generous dinner, particularly as her delightful boarder had hinted of ample recompense in the way of board money; and she fluttered about, sending Tanner after another jar of pickles, some more apple-butter, and added another pie to the menu.

Well pleased, Margaret left Mr. Tanner and slipped back to her guests. She found Gardley making arrangements with Bud to run back to the church and tell the men to leave the buckboard for them, as they would not be home for dinner. While this was going on she took Mom Wallis up to her room to remove her bonnet and smooth her hair.

It is doubtful whether Mom Wallis ever did see such a room in her life; for when Margaret swung open the door the poor little woman stopped short on the threshold, abashed, and caught her breath, looking around with wondering eyes and putting out a trembling hand to steady herself against the doorframe. She wasn't quite sure whether things in that room were real, or whether she might not by chance have caught a glimpse into heaven, so beautiful did it seem to her. It was not till her eyes, in the roving, suddenly rested on the great mountain framed in the open window that she felt anchored and sure that this was a tangible place. Then she ventured to step her heavy shoe inside the door. Even then she drew her ugly calico back apologetically, as if it were a desecration to the lovely room.

But Margaret seized her and drew her into the room, placing her gently in the rose-ruffled rocking chair as if it were a throne and she a queen, and the poor little woman sat entranced, with tears springing to her eyes and trickling down her cheeks.

Perhaps it was an impossibility for Margaret to conceive what the vision of that room meant to Mom Wallis. The realization of all the dreams of a starved soul concentrated into a small space; the actual, tangible proof that there might be a heaven some day—who knew?—since beauties and comforts like these could be real in Arizona.

Margaret brought the pictures of her father and mother, of her dear home and the dear old church. She took her about the room and showed her the various pictures and reminders of her college days, and when she saw that the poor creature was overwhelmed and speechless she turned her about and showed her the great mountain again, like an anchorage for her soul.

Mom Wallis looked at everything speechlessly, gasping as her attention was turned from one object to another, as if she were unable to rise beyond her excitement, but when she saw the mountain again her tongue was loosed, and she turned and looked back at the girl wonderingly.

"Now, ain't it strange! Even that old mounting looks diffrunt—it do look diffrunt from a room like this. Why, it looks like it got its hair combed an' its best collar on!" And Mom Wallis looked down with pride and patted the simple net ruffle about her withered throat. "Why, it looks like a picter painted an' hung up on this yere wall, that's what that mounting looks like! Its kinda ain't no mounting anymore; it's jest a picter in your room!"

Margaret smiled. "It is a picture, isn't it? Just look at that silver light over the purple place. Isn't it wonderful? I like to think it's mine—my mountain. And yet the beautiful thing about it is that it's just as much yours, too. It will make a picture of itself framed in your bunkhouse window if you let it. Try it. You just need to let it."

Mom Wallis looked at her wonderingly. "Do you mean," she said, studying the girl's lovely face, "that ef I should wash them there bunkhouse winders, an' string up some posy caliker, an' stuff a chair, an' have a pincushion, I could make that there mounting come in an' set fer me like a picter the way it does here fer you?"

"Yes, that's what I mean," said Margaret, softly, marveling how the uncouth woman had caught the thought. "That's exactly what I mean. God's gifts will be as much to us as we will let them, always. Try it and see."

Mom Wallis stood for some minutes looking out reflectively at the mountain. "Wal, mebbe I'll try it!" she said, and turned back to survey the room again.

And now the mirror caught her eye, and she saw herself, a strange self in a soft white collar, and went up to get a nearer view, laying a toil-worn finger on the lace and looking half embarrassed at sight of her own face.

"It's a real purty collar," she said, softly, with a choke in her voice. "It's too purty fer me. I told him so, but he said as how you wanted I should dress up every night fer supper in it. It's 'most as strange as havin 'a mounting come an' live with you, to wear a collar like that—me!"

Margaret's eyes were suddenly bright with tears. Who would have suspected Mom Wallis of having poetry in her nature? Then, as if her thoughts anticipated the question in Margaret's mind, Mom Wallis went on:

"He brang me your little book," she said. "I ain't goin' to say thank yeh, it ain't a big 'nuf word. An' he read me the poetry words it says. I got it wropped in a hankercher on the top o' the beam over my bed. I'm goin' to have it buried with me when I die. Oh, I *read* it. I couldn't make much out of it, but I read the words *thor*ough. An' then *he* read 'em—the kid did. He reads just beautiful. He's got education, he has. He read it, and he talked a lot about it. Was this what you mean? Was it that we ain't really growin' old at all, we're jest goin' on, *gettin'* there, if we go right? Did you mean you think Him as planned it all wanted some old woman right thar in the bunkhouse, an' it's *me?* Did you mean there was agoin' to be a chanct fer me to be young an' beautiful somewheres in creation yit, 'fore I get through?"

The old woman had turned around from looking into the mirror and was facing her hostess. Her eyes were very bright, her cheeks had taken on an excited flush, and her knotted hands were clutching the bureau. She looked into Margaret's eyes earnestly, as though her very life depended upon the answer, and Margaret, with a great leap of her heart, smiled and answered:

"Yes, Mrs. Wallis, yes, that is just what I meant. Listen, these are God's own words about it: 'For I reckon that the sufferings of this present time are not worthy to be compared with the glory that shall be revealed in us.' "

A kind of glory shone in the withered old face now. "Did you say them was God's words?" she asked in an awed voice.

"Yes," said Margaret, "they are in the Bible."

"But you couldn't be sure it meant *me?*" she asked, eagerly. "They wouldn't go to put *me* in the Bible, o' course."

"Oh, yes, you could be quite sure, Mrs. Wallis," said Margaret, gently. "Because if God was making you and had a plan for you, as the poem says, He would be sure to put down something in His book about it, don't you think? He would want you to know."

"It does sound reasonablelike now, don't it?" said the woman, wistfully. "Say them glory words again, won't you?"

Margaret repeated the text slowly and distinctly.

"Glory!" repeated Mom Wallis, wonderingly. "Glory! Me!" and turned incredulously toward the glass. She looked a long time wistfully at herself, as if she could not believe it, and pulled reproachfully at the tight hair drawn away from her weather-beaten face. "I useta have purty hair onct," she said, sadly.

"Why, you have pretty hair now!" said Margaret, eagerly. "It just wants a chance to show its beauty. Here, let me fix it for dinner, will you?"

She whisked the bewildered old woman into a chair and began unwinding the hard, tight knot of hair at the back of her head and shaking it out. The hair was thin and gray now, but it showed signs of having been fine and thick once.

"It's easy to keep your hair looking pretty," said the girl, as she worked. "I'm going to give you a little box of my nice sweet-smelling soap powder that I use to shampoo my hair. You take it home and wash your hair with it every week and you'll see it will make a difference in a little while. You just haven't taken time to take care of it, that's all. Do you mind if I wave the front here a little? I'd like to fix your hair the way my mother wears hers."

Now nothing could have been further apart than this little weather-beaten old woman and Margaret's gentle, dovelike mother, with her abundant soft gray hair, her cameo features, and her pretty, gray dresses, but Margaret had a vision of what glory might bring to Mom Wallis, and she wanted to help it along. She believed that heavenly glory can be hastened a good deal on earth if one only tries, and so she set to work. Glancing out the window, she saw with relief that Gardley was talking interestedly with Mr. Tanner and seemed entirely content with their absence.

Mom Wallis hadn't any idea what waving her hair meant, but she readily consented to anything this wonderful girl proposed, and she sat entranced, looking at her mountain and thrilling with every touch of Margaret's satin fingers against her leathery old temples. And so, Sunday though it was, Margaret lighted her little alcohol lamp and heated a tiny curling iron which she kept for emergencies. In a few minutes' time Mom Wallis's astonished old gray locks lay soft and fluffy about her face, and pinned in a smooth coil behind, instead of the tight knot, making the most wonderful difference in the world in her old, tired face.

"Now look!" said Margaret, and turned her about to the mirror. "If there's anything at all you don't like about it I can change it, you know. You don't have to wear it so if you don't like it."

The old woman looked, and then looked back at Margaret with frightened eyes, and back to the vision in the mirror again.

"My soul!" she exclaimed in an awed voice. "My soul! It's come a'ready! Glory! I didn't think I could look like that! I wonder what Pop 'd say! My land! Would you mind ef I kep' it on a while an' wore it back to camp this way? Pop might uv come home an' I'd like to see ef he'd take notice to it. I used to be purty onct, but I never expected no sech thing like this again on earth. Glory! Glory! Mebbe I *could* get some glory, *too.*"

" 'The glory that shall be revealed' is a great deal more wonderful than this," said Margaret, gently. "This was here all the time, only you didn't let it come out. Wear it home that way, of course, and wear it so all the time. It's very little trouble, and you'll find your family will like it. Men always like to see a woman looking her best, even when she's working. It helps to make them good. Before you go home I'll show you how to fix it. It's quite simple. Come, now, shall we go downstairs? We don't want to leave Mr. Gardley alone too long, and, besides, I smell the dinner. I think they'll be waiting for us pretty soon. I'm going to take a few of these pictures down to show Mr. Gardley."

She hastily gathered a few photographs together and led the bewildered little woman downstairs again, and out in the yard, where Gardley was walking up and down now, looking off at the mountain. It came to Margaret, suddenly, that the minister would be returning to the house soon, and she wished he wouldn't come. He would be a false note in the pleasant harmony of the little company.

He would be disagreeable to manage, and perhaps hurt poor Mom Wallis's feelings. Perhaps he had already come. She looked furtively around as she came out the door, but no minister was in sight, and then she forgot him utterly in the look of bewildered astonishment with which Gardley was regarding Mom Wallis.

He had stopped short in his walk across the little yard, and was staring at Mom Wallis, recognition gradually growing in his gaze. When he was fully convinced he turned his eyes to Margaret, as if to ask: "How did you do it? Wonderful woman!" and a look of deep reverence for her came over his face.

Then suddenly he noticed the shy embarrassment on the old woman's face and swiftly came toward her, his hands outstretched, and, taking her bony hands in his, bowed low over them as a courtier might do.

"Mom Wallis, you are beautiful. Did you know it?" he said, gently, and led her to a little stumpy rocking chair with a gay red and blue rag cushion that Mrs. Tanner always kept sitting by the front door in pleasant weather. Then he stood off and surveyed her, while the red stole into her cheeks becomingly. "What has Miss Earle been doing to glorify you?" he asked, again looking at her earnestly.

The old woman looked at him in awed silence. There was that word again—glory! He had said the girl had glorified her. There was then some glory in her, and it had been brought out by so simple a thing as the arrangement of her hair. It frightened her, and tears came and stood in her tired old eyes.

It was well for Mom Wallis's equilibrium that Mr. Tanner came out just then with the paper he had gone after, for the stolidity of her lifetime was about breaking up. But, as he turned, Gardley gave her one of the rarest smiles of sympathy and understanding that a young man can give to an old woman, and Margaret, watching, loved him for it. It seemed to her one of the most beautiful things a young man had ever done.

They had discussed the article in the paper thoroughly, and had looked at the photographs that Margaret had brought down, and Mrs. Tanner had come to the door numberless times, looking out in a troubled way down the road, only to trot back again, look in the oven, peep in the kettle, sigh, and trot out to the door again. At last she came and stood, arms akimbo, and looked down the road once more.

"Pa, I don't just see how I can keep the dinner waitin' a minute longer. The potatoes 'll be sp'iled. I don't see what's keepin' that preacher man. He musta been invited out, though I don't see why he didn't send me word."

"That's it, likely, Ma," said Tanner. He was growing hungry. "I saw Mis' Bacon talkin' to him. She's likely invited him there. She's always tryin' to get ahead o' you, Ma, you know, 'cause you got the prize fer your marble cake."

Mrs. Tanner blushed and looked down apologetically at her guests. "Well, then, ef you'll just come in and set down, I'll dish up. My land! Ain't that Bud comin' down the road, Pa? He's likely sent word by Bud. I'll hurry in an' dish up."

Bud slid into his seat hurriedly after a brief ablution in the kitchen, and his mother questioned him sharply.

"Bud, wher you be'n? Did the minister get invited out?"

The boy grinned and slowly winked one eye at Gardley. "Yes, he's invited out, all right," he said, meaningly. "You don't need to wait fer him. He won't be home fer some time, I don't reckon."

Gardley looked keenly, steadily, at the boy's dancing eyes, and re-solved to have a fuller understanding later, and his own eyes met the boy's in a gleam of mischief and sympathy.

It was the first time in twenty years that Mom Wallis had eaten anything which she had not prepared herself, and now, with fried chicken and company preserves before her, she could scarcely swal-low a mouthful. To be seated beside Gardley and waited on like a queen! To be smiled at by the beautiful young girl across the table, and deferred to by Mr. and Mrs. Tanner as "Mrs. Wallis," and asked to have more pickles and another helping of jelly, and did she take cream and sugar in her coffee! It was too much, and Mom Wallis was struggling with the tears. Even Bud's round, blue eyes regarded her with approval and interest. She couldn't help thinking, if her own baby boy had lived, would he ever have been like Bud? And once she smiled at him, and Bud smiled back, a real boylike, frank, hearty grin. It was all like taking dinner in the kingdom of Heaven to Mom Wallis, and getting glory aforetime.

It was a wonderful afternoon, and seemed to go on swift wings. Gardley went back to the schoolhouse, where the horses had been left, and Bud went with him to give further particulars about that wink at the dinnertable. Mom Wallis went up to the rose-garlanded room and learned how to wash her hair, and received a roll of flowered scrim wherewith to make curtains for the bunkhouse. Margaret had originally intended it for the schoolhouse windows in case it proved necessary to make that place habitable, but the schoolroom could wait.

And there in the rose room, with the new curtains in her trembling hands, and the great old mountain in full view, Mom Wallis knelt beside the little gay rocking chair, while Margaret knelt beside her and prayed that the heavenly Father would show Mom Wallis how to let the glory be revealed in her now on the earth.

Then Mom Wallis wiped the furtive tears away with her calico sleeve, tied on her funny old bonnet, and rode away with her handsome young escort into the silence of the desert, with the glory beginning to be revealed already in her countenance.

Quite late that evening the minister returned.

He came in slowly and wearily, as if every step were a pain to him, and he avoided the light. His coat was torn and his garments were mud-covered. He murmured of a "slight accident" to Mrs. Tanner, who met him solicitously in a flowered dressing gown with a candle in her hand. He accepted greedily the half a pie, with cheese and cold chicken and other articles, she proffered on a plate at his door, and in the reply to her query as to where he had been for dinner, and if he had a pleasant time, he said:

"Very pleasant, indeed, thank you! The name? Um—ah—I disremember! I really didn't ask—That is—"

The minister did not get up to breakfast. In fact, he remained in bed for several days, professing to be suffering with an attack of rheumatism. He was solicitously watched over and fed by the anxious Mrs. Tanner, who was much disconcerted at the state of affairs, and couldn't understand why she could not get the schoolteacher more interested in the invalid.

On the fourth day, however, the Reverend Frederick crept forth, white and shaken, with his sleek hair elaborately combed to cover a long scratch on his forehead, and announced his intention of departing from the state of Arizona that evening.

He crept forth cautiously to the station as the shades of evening drew on, but found Long Bill awaiting him, and Jasper Kemp not far away. He had the two letters ready in his pocket, with the gold piece, though he had entertained hopes of escaping without forfeiting them, but he was obliged to wait patiently until Jasper Kemp had read both letters through twice, with the train in momentary danger of departing without him, before he was finally allowed to get on board. Jasper Kemp's parting word to him was:

"Watch your steps spry, parson. I'm going' to see that you're shadowed wherever you go. You needn't think you can get shy on the Bible again. It won't pay."

There was menace in the dry remark, and the Reverend Frederick's professional egotism withered before it. He bowed his head, climbed on board the train, and vanished from the scene of his recent discomfiture. But the bitterest thing about it all was that he had gone without capturing the heart or even the attention of that haughty little schoolteacher. "And she was such a pretty girl," he said, regretfully, to himself. "Such a *very* pretty girl!" He sighed deeply to himself as he watched Arizona speed by the window. "Still," he reflected, comfortably, after a moment, "there are always plenty more! What was that remarkably witty saying I heard just before I left home? 'Never run after a streetcar or a woman. There'll be another one along in a minute.' Um—ah—yes—very true—there'll be another one along in a minute."

Chapter 18

School had settled down to real work by the opening of the new week. Margaret knew her scholars and had gained a personal hold on most of them already. There was enough novelty in her teaching to keep the entire school in a pleasant state of excitement and wonder as to what she would do next, and the word had gone out through all the country round about that the new teacher had taken the school by storm. It was not infrequent for men to turn out of their way on the trail to get a glimpse of the school as they were passing, just to make sure the reports were true. Rumor stated that the teacher was exceedingly pretty, that she would take no nonsense, not even from the big boys, that she never threatened nor punished, but that every one of the boys was her devoted slave. There had been no uprising, and it almost seemed as if that popular excitement was to be omitted this season, and school was to sail along in an orderly and proper manner. In fact, the entire school as well as the surrounding population were eagerly talking about the new piano, which seemed really to be a coming fact. Not that there had been anything done toward it yet, but the teacher had promised that just as soon as everyone was really studying hard and doing his best, she was going to begin to get them ready for an entertainment to raise money for that piano. They couldn't begin until everybody was in good working order, because they didn't want to take the interest away from the real business of school, but it was going to be a Shakespeare play, whatever that was, and therefore of grave import. Some people talked learnedly about Shakespeare and hinted of poetry, but the main part of the community spoke the name joyously and familiarly and without awe, as if it were milk and honey in their mouths. Why should they reverence Shakespeare more than anyone else?

Margaret had grown used to seeing a head appear suddenly at one of the schoolroom windows and look long and frowningly first at her, then at the school, and then back to her again, as if it were a nine days' wonder. Whoever the visitor was, he would stand quietly, watching the process of the hour as if he were at a play, and Margaret would turn and smile pleasantly, then go right on with her work. The visitor would generally take off a wide hat and wave it cordially, smile back a curious, softened smile, and by and by he would mount his horse and pass on reflectively down the trail, wishing he could be a boy and go back again to school—such a school!

Oh, it was not all smooth, the way that Margaret walked. There were hitches, and unpleasant days when nothing went right, and when some of the girls got silly and rebellious, and the boys followed in their lead. She had her trials as any teacher, skillful as she was, and not the least of them became Rosa Rogers, the petted beauty, who presently manifested a childish jealousy of her in her influence over the boys. Noting this, Margaret went out of her way to win Rosa, but found it a difficult matter.

Rosa was proud, selfish, and unprincipled. She never forgave anyone who frustrated her plans. She resented being made to study like the rest. She had always compelled the teacher to let her do as she pleased and still give her a good report. This she found she could not do with Margaret, and for the first time in her career she was compelled to work or fall behind. It presently became not a question of how the new teacher was to manage the big boys and the bad boys of the Ashland Ridge School, but how she was to prevent Rosa Rogers and a few girls who followed her from upsetting all her plans. The trouble was, Rosa was pretty and knew her power over the boys. If she chose she could put them all in a state of insubordination, and this she chose very often during those first few weeks.

But there was one visitor who did not confine himself to looking in at the window.

One morning a fine black horse came galloping up to the schoolhouse at recess time, and a well-set-up young man in wide sombrero and jaunty leather trappings sprang off and came into the building. His shining spurs caught the sunlight and flashed as he moved. He walked with the air of one who regards himself of far more importance than all who may be watching him. The boys in the yard stopped their ball game, and the girls huddled close in whispering groups and drew near to the door. He was a young man from a ranch near the fort some thirty miles away, and he had brought an invitation for the new schoolteacher to come over to dinner on Friday evening and stay until the following Monday morning. The invitation was from his sister, the wife of a wealthy cattleman whose home and hospitality were noted for miles around. She had heard of the coming of the beautiful young teacher, and wanted to attach her to her social circle.

The young man was deference itself to Margaret, openly admiring her as he talked, and said the most gracious things to her; and then, while she was answering the note, he smiled over at Rosa Rogers, who had slipped into her seat and was studiously preparing her algebra with the book upside down.

Margaret, looking up, caught Rosa's smiling glance and the tail end of a look from the young man's eyes, and felt a passing wonder whether he had ever met the girl before. Something in the boldness of his look made her feel that he had not. Yet he was all smiles and deference to herself, and his open admiration and pleasure that she was to come to help brighten this lonely country, and that she was going to accept the invitation, was really pleasant to the girl, for it was desolate being tied down to only the Tanner household and the school, and she welcomed any bit of social life.

The young man had light hair, combed very smooth, and light blue eyes. They were bolder and handsomer than the minister's, but the girl had a feeling that they were the very same cold color. She wondered at her comparison, for she liked the handsome young man, and in spite of herself was a little flattered at the nice things he had said to her. Nevertheless, when she remembered him afterward it was always with that uncomfortable feeling that if he hadn't been so handsome and polished in his appearance he would have seemed just a little bit like the minister, and she couldn't for the life of her tell why.

After he was gone she looked back at Rosa, and there was a narrowing of the girl's eyes and a frown of hate on her brows. Margaret turned with a sigh back to her school problem—what to do with Rosa Rogers?

But Rosa did not stay in the schoolhouse. She slipped out and walked arm in arm with Amanda Bounds down the road.

Margaret went to the door and watched. Presently she saw the rider wheel and come galloping back to the door. He had forgotten to tell her that an escort would be sent to bring her as early on Friday afternoon as she would be ready to leave the school, and he intimated that he hoped he might be detailed for that pleasant duty.

Margaret looked into his face and warmed to his pleasant smile. How could she have thought him like West? He touched his hat and rode away, and a moment later she saw him draw rein beside Rosa and Amanda, and presently dismount.

Bud rang the bell just then, and Margaret went back to her desk with a lingering look at the three figures in the distance. It was full half an hour before Rosa came in, with Amanda looking scared behind her, and troubled Margaret watched the sly look in the girl's eyes and wondered what she ought to do about it. As Rosa was passing out the door after school she called her to the desk.

"You were late in coming in after recess, Rosa," said Margaret, gently. "Have you any excuse?"

"I was talking to a friend," said Rosa, with a toss of her head which said, as plainly as words could have done, "I don't intend to give an excuse."

"Were you talking to the gentleman who was here?"

"Well, if I was, what is that to you, Miss Earle?" said Rosa, haughtily. "Did you think you could have all the men and boys to yourself?"

"Rosa," said Margaret, trying to speak calmly, but her voice trembling with suppressed indignation, "don't talk that way to me. Child, did you ever meet Mr. Forsythe before?"

"I'm not a child, and it's none of your business!" flouted Rosa, angrily, and she twitched away and flung herself out of the schoolhouse.

Margaret, trembling from the disagreeable encounter, stood at the window and watched the girl going down the road, and felt for the moment that she would rather give up her school and go back home than face the situation. She knew in her heart that this girl, once an enemy, would be a bitter one, and this her last move had been a most unfortunate one, coming out, as it did, with Rosa in the lead. She could, of course, complain to Rosa's family, or to the school board, but such was not the policy she had chosen. She wanted to be able to settle her own difficulties. It seemed strange that she could not reach this one girl—who was in a way the key to the situation. Perhaps the play would be able to help her. She spent a long time that evening going over the different plays in her library, and finally, with a look of apology toward a little photographed head of Shakespeare, she decided on "A Midsummer Night's Dream." What if it was away above the heads of them all, wouldn't a few get something from it? And wasn't it better to take a great thing and try to make her scholars and a few of the community understand it, rather than to take a silly little play that would not amount to anything in the end? Of course, they couldn't do it well, that went without saying. Of course it would be away beyond them all, but at least it would be a study of something great for her pupils, and she could meantime teach them a little about Shakespeare and perhaps help some of them to learn to love his plays and study them.

The play she had selected was one in which she herself had acted the part of Puck, and she knew it by heart. She felt reasonably sure that she could help some of the more adaptable scholars to interpret their parts, and, at least, it would be good for them just as a study in literature. As for the audience, they would not be critics. Perhaps they would not even be able to comprehend the meaning of the play, but they would come and they would listen, and the experiment was one worth trying.

Carefully she went over the parts, trying to find the one which she thought would best fit Rosa Rogers, and please her as well, because it gave her opportunity to display her beauty and charm. She really was a pretty girl, and would do well. Margaret wondered whether she were altogether right in attempting to win the girl through her vanity, and yet what other weak place was there in which to storm the silly little citadel of her soul?

And so the work of assigning parts and learning them began that very week, though no one was allowed a part until his work for the day had all been handed in.

At noon Margaret made one more attempt with Rosa Rogers. She drew her to a seat beside her and put aside as much as possible her own remembrance of the girl's disagreeable actions and impudent words.

"Rosa," she said, and her voice was very gentle, "I want to have a little talk with you. You seem to feel that you and I are enemies, and I don't want you to have that attitude. I hoped we'd be the best of friends. You see, there isn't any other way for us to work well together. And I want to explain why I spoke to you as I did yesterday. It was not, as you hinted, that I want to keep all my acquaintances to myself. I have no desire to do that. It was because I feel responsible for the girls and boys in my care, and I was troubled lest perhaps you had been foolish—"

Margaret paused. She could see by the bright hardness of the girl's eyes that she was accomplishing nothing. Rosa evidently did not believe her.

"Well, Rosa," she said, suddenly, putting an impulsive, kindly hand on the girl's arm, "suppose we forget it this time, put it all away, and be friends. Let's learn to understand each other if we can, but in the meantime I want to talk to you about the play."

And then, indeed, Rosa's hard manner broke, and she looked up with interest, albeit there was some suspicion in the glance. She wanted to be in that play with all her heart; she wanted the very showiest part in it, too, and she meant to have it, although she had a strong suspicion that the teacher would want to keep that part for herself, whatever it was.

But Margaret had been wise. She had decided to take time and explain the play to her, and then let her choose her own part. She wisely judged that Rosa would do better in the part in which her interest centered, and perhaps the choice would help her to understand her pupil better.

And so for an hour she patiently stayed after school and went over the play, explaining it carefully, and it seemed at one time as though Rosa was about to choose to be Puck, because with quick perception she caught the importance of that character, but when she learned that the costume must be a quiet hood and skirt of green and brown she scorned it, and chose, at last, to be Titania, queen of the fairies.

So, with a sigh of relief, and a keen insight into the shallow nature, Margaret began to teach the girl some of the fairy steps, and found her quick and eager to learn. In the first lesson Rosa forgot for a little while her animosity and became almost as one of the other pupils. The play was going to prove a great means of bringing them all together.

Before Friday afternoon came the parts had all been assigned and the plans for the entertainment were well under way.

Jed and Timothy had been as good as their word about giving the teacher riding lessons, each vying with the other to bring a horse and make her ride at noon hour, and she had already had several good lessons and a long ride or two in company with both her teachers.

The thirty-mile ride for Friday, then, was not such an undertaking as it might otherwise have been, and Margaret looked forward to it with eagerness.

Chapter 19

The little party of escort arrived before school was closed on Friday afternoon, and came down to the schoolhouse in full force to take her away with them. The young man Forsythe, with his sister, the hostess herself, and a young army officer from the fort, comprised the party. Margaret dismissed school ten minutes early and went back with them to the Tanners' to make a hurried change in her dress and pick up her suitcase, which was already packed. As they rode away from the schoolhouse Margaret looked back and saw Rosa Rogers posing in one of her sprite dances in the schoolyard, saw her kiss her hand laughingly toward their party, and saw the flutter of a handkerchief in young Forsythe's hand. It was all very general and elusive, a passing bit of fun, but it left an uncomfortable impression on the teacher's mind. She looked keenly at the young man as he rode up smiling beside her, and once more experienced that strange, sudden change of feeling about him.

She took opportunity during that long ride to find out if the young man had known Rosa Rogers before, but he frankly told her that he had just come west to visit his sister, was bored to death because he didn't know a soul in the whole state, and until he had seen her had not laid eyes on one whom he cared to know. Yet while she could not help enjoying the gay badinage, she carried a sense of uneasiness whenever she thought of the young girl Rosa in her pretty fairy pose, with her fluttering pink fingers and her saucy, smiling eyes. There was something untrustworthy, too, in the handsome face of the man beside her.

There was just one shadow over this bit of a holiday. Margaret had a little feeling that possibly someone from the camp might come down on Saturday or Sunday, and she would miss him. Yet nothing had been said about it, and she had no way of sending word that she would be away. She had meant to send Mom Wallis a letter by the next messenger that came that way. It was all written and lying on her bureau, but no one had been down all the week. She was, therefore, greatly pleased when an approaching rider in the distance proved to be Gardley, and with a joyful little greeting she drew rein and hailed him, giving him a message for Mom Wallis.

Only Gardley's eyes told what this meeting was to him. His demeanor was grave and dignified. He acknowledged the introductions to the rest of the party gracefully, touched his hat with the ease of one to the manner born, and rode away, flashing her one gleam of a smile that told her he was glad of the meeting, but throughout the brief interview there had been an air of question and hostility between the two men, Forsythe and Gardley. Forsythe surveyed Gardley rudely, almost insolently, as if his position beside the lady gave him rights beyond the other, and he resented the coming of the stranger. Gardley's gaze was cold, too, as he met the look, and his eyes searched Forsythe's face keenly, as though they would find out what manner of man was riding with his friend.

When he was gone Margaret had the feeling that he was somehow disappointed, and once she turned in the saddle and looked wistfully after him, but he was riding furiously into the distance, sitting his horse as straight as an arrow and already far away upon the desert.

"Your friend is a reckless rider," said Forsythe, with a sneer in his voice that Margaret did not like, as they watched the speck in the distance clear a steep descent from the mesa at a bound and disappear from sight in the mesquite beyond.

"Isn't he fine looking? Where did you find him, Miss Earle?" asked Mrs. Temple, eagerly. "I wish I'd asked him to join us. He left so suddenly I didn't realize he was going."

Margaret felt a wondering and pleasant sense of possession and pride in Gardley as she watched, but she quietly explained that the young stranger was from the East, and that he was engaged in some kind of cattle business at a distance from Ashland. Her manner was reserved, and the matter dropped. She naturally felt a reluctance to tell how her acquaintance with Gardley began. It seemed something between themselves. She could fancy the gushing Mrs. Temple saying, "How romantic!" She was that kind of a woman. It was evident that she was romantically inclined herself, for she used her fine eyes with effect on the young officer who rode with her, and Margaret found herself wondering what kind of a husband she had and what her mother would think of a woman like this.

There was no denying that the luxury of the ranch was a happy relief from the simplicity of life at the Tanners'. Iced drinks and cushions and easy chairs, feasting and music and laughter! There were books, too, and magazines, and all the little things that go to make up a cultured life; and yet they were not people of Margaret's world, and when Saturday evening was over she sat alone in the room they had given her and, facing herself in the glass, confessed to herself that she looked back with more pleasure to the Sabbath spent with Mom Wallis than she could look forward to a Sabbath here. The morning proved her forebodings well founded.

Breakfast was a late, informal affair, filled with hilarious gaiety. There was no mention of any church service, and Margaret found it was quite too late to suggest such a thing when breakfast was over, even if she had been sure there was any service.

After breakfast was over there were various forms of amusement proposed for her pleasure, and she really felt very much embarrassed for a few moments to know how to avoid what to her was pure Sabbath-breaking. Yet she did not wish to be rude to these people who were really trying to be kind to her. She managed at last to get them interested in music, and, grouping them around the piano after a few preliminary performances by herself at their earnest solicitation, coaxed them into singing hymns.

After all, they really seemed to enjoy it, though they had to get along with one hymnbook for the whole company, but Margaret knew how to make hymn singing interesting, and her exquisite voice was never more at its best than when she led off with "My Jesus, as Thou Wilt," or "Jesus, Saviour, Pilot Me."

"You would be the delight of Mr. Brownleigh's heart," said the hostess, gushingly, at last, after Margaret had finished singing "Abide With Me" with wonderful feeling.

"And who is Mr. Brownleigh?" asked Margaret. "Why should I delight his heart?"

"Why, he is our missionary—that is, the missionary for this region—and you would delight his heart because you are so religious and sing so well," said the superficial little woman. "Mr. Brownleigh is really a very cultured man. Of course, he's narrow. All clergymen are narrow, don't you think? They have to be to a certain extent. He's really *quite* narrow. Why, he believes in the Bible *literally*, the whale and Jonah, and the Flood, and making bread out of stones, and all that sort of thing, you know. Imagine it! But he does. He's sincere! Perfectly sincere. I suppose he has to be. It's his business. But sometimes one feels it a pity that he can't relax a little, just among us here, you know. We'd never tell. Why, he won't even play a little game of poker! And he doesn't smoke! *Imagine* it—*not even when he's by himself, and no one would know!* Isn't that odd? But he can preach. He's really very interesting, only a little too utopian in his ideas. He thinks everybody ought to be good, you know, and all that sort of thing. He really thinks it's possible, and he lives that way himself. He really does. But he is a wonderful person, only I feel sorry for his wife sometimes. She's quite a cultured person. Has been wealthy, you know. She was a New York society girl. Just imagine it, out in these wilds taking food to the unfortunate Indians! How she ever came to do it! Of course she adores him, but I can't really believe she is happy. No woman could be quite blind enough to give up everything in the world for one man, no matter how good he was. Do you think she could? It wasn't as if she didn't have plenty of other chances. She gave them all up to come out and marry him. She's a pretty good sport, too; she never lets you know she isn't perfectly happy."

"She *is* happy, Mother, she's happier than *anybody* I ever saw," declared the fourteen-year-old daughter of the house, who was home from boarding school for a brief visit during an epidemic of measles in the school.

"Oh yes, she manages to make people think she's happy," said her mother, indulgently, "but you can't make me believe she's satisfied to give up her house on Fifth Avenue and live in a two-roomed log cabin in the desert, with no society."

"Mother, you don't know! Why, *any* woman would be satisfied if her husband adored her the way Mr. Brownleigh does her."

"Well, Ada, you're a romantic girl, and Mr. Brownleigh is a handsome man. You've got a few things to learn yet. Mark my words, I don't believe you'll see Mrs. Brownleigh coming back next month with her husband. This operation was all well enough to talk about, but I'll not be surprised to hear that he has come back alone or else that he has accepted a call to some big city church. And he's equal to the city church, too, that's the wonder of it. He comes of a fine family himself, I've heard. Oh, people can't keep up the pose of saints forever, even though they do adore each other. But Mr. Brownleigh *certainly is* a good man!"

The vapid little woman sat looking reflectively out of the window for a whole minute after this deliverance. Yes, certainly Mr. Brownleigh was a good man. He was the one man of culture, education, refinement, who had come her way in many a year who had patiently and persistently and gloriously refused her advances at a mild flirtation, and refused to understand them, yet remained her friend and reverenced hero. He was a good man, and she knew it, for she was a very pretty woman and understood her art well.

Before the day was over Margaret had reason to feel that a Sabbath in Arizona was a very hard thing to find. The singing could not last all day, and her friends seemed to find more amusements on Sunday that did not come into Margaret's code of Sabbath-keeping than one knew how to say no to. Neither could they understand her feeling, and she found it hard not to be rude in gently declining one plan after another.

She drew the children into a wide, cozy corner after dinner and began a Bible story in the guise of a fairy tale, while the hostess slipped away to take a nap. However, several other guests lingered about, and Mr. Temple strayed in. They sat with newspapers before their faces and got into the story, too, seeming to be deeply interested, so that, after all, Margaret did not have an unprofitable Sabbath.

But altogether, though she had a gay and somewhat frivolous time, a good deal of admiration and many invitations to return as often as possible, Margaret was not sorry when she said good-night to know that she was to return in the early morning to her work.

Mr. Temple himself was going part way with them, accompanied by his niece, Forsythe, and the young officer who came over with them. Margaret rode beside Mr. Temple until his way parted from theirs, and had a delightful talk about Arizona. He was a kindly old fellow who adored his frivolous little wife and let her go her own gait, seeming not to mind how much she flirted.

The morning was pink and silver, gold and azure, a wonderful specimen of an Arizona sunrise for Margaret's benefit, and a glorious beginning for her day's work in spite of the extremely early hour. The company was gay and blithe, and the eastern girl felt as if she were passing through a wonderful experience.

They loitered a little on the way to show Margaret the wonders of a fern-plumed canyon and it was almost school time when they came up the street, so that Margaret rode straight to the schoolhouse instead of stopping at Tanners'. On the way to the school they passed a group of girls, of whom Rosa Rogers was the center. A certain something in Rosa's narrowed eyelids as she said good morning caused Margaret to look back uneasily, and she distinctly saw the girl give a signal to young Forsythe, who, for answer, only tipped his hat and gave her a peculiar smile.

In a moment more they had said good-bye, and Margaret was left at the schoolhouse door with a cluster of eager children about her, and several shy boys in the background, ready to welcome her back as if she had been gone a month.

In the flutter of opening school Margaret failed to notice that Rosa Rogers did not appear. It was not until the roll was called that she noticed her absence, and she looked uneasily toward the door many times during the morning, but Rosa did not come until after recess, when she stole smilingly in, as if it were quite the thing to come to school late. When questioned about her tardiness she said she had torn her dress and had to go home and change it. Margaret knew by the look in her eyes that the girl was not telling the truth, but what was she to do? It troubled her all morning and went with her to a sleepless pillow that night. She was beginning to see that life as a schoolteacher in the far West was not all she had imagined it to be. Her father had been right. There would likely be more thorns than roses on her way.

Chapter 20

The first time Lance Gardley met Rosa Rogers riding with Archie Forsythe he thought little of it. He knew the girl by sight, because he knew her father in a business way. That she was very young and one of Margaret's pupils was all he knew about her. For the young man he had conceived a strong dislike, but as there was no reason whatever for it he put it out of his mind as quickly as possible.

The second time he met them it was toward evening and they were so wholly absorbed in each other's society that they did not see him until he was close upon them. Forsythe looked up with a frown and a quick hand to his hip, where gleamed a weapon.

He scarcely returned the slight salute given by Gardley, and the two young people touched up their horses and were soon out of sight in the mesquite. But something in the frightened look of the girl's eyes caused Gardley to turn and look after the two.

Where could they be going at that hour of the evening? It was not a trail usually chosen for rides. It was lonely and unfrequented, and led out of the way of travelers. Gardley himself had been on a far errand for Jasper Kemp, and had taken this short trail back because it cut off several miles and he was weary. Also, he was anxious to stop in Ashland and leave Mom Wallis's request that Margaret would spend the next Sabbath at the camp and see the new curtains. He was thinking what he should say to her when he saw her in a little while now, and this interruption to his thoughts was unwelcome. Nevertheless, he could not get away from that frightened look in the girl's eyes. Where could they have been going? That fellow was a newcomer in the region; perhaps he had lost his way. Perhaps he did not know that the road he was taking the girl led into a region of outlaws, and that the only habitation along the way was a cabin belonging to an old woman of weird reputation, where wild orgies were sometimes celebrated, and where men went who loved darkness rather than light, because their deeds were evil.

Twice Gardley turned in his saddle and scanned the desert. The sky was darkening, and one or two pale stars were impatiently shadowing forth their presence. And now he could see the two riders again. They had come up out of the mesquite in the top of the mesa, and were outlined against the sky sharply. They were still on the trail to old Ouida's cabin!

With a quick jerk Gardley reined in his horse and wheeled about, watching the riders for a moment, and then, setting spurs to his beast, he was off down the trail after them on one of his wild, reckless rides. Down through the mesquite he plunged, through the darkening grove, out, and up to the top of the mesa. He had lost sight of his quarry for the time, but now he could see them again riding more slowly in the valley below, their horses close together, and even as he watched the sky took on its wide night look and the stars blazed forth.

Suddenly Gardley turned sharply from the trail and made a detour through a grove of trees, riding with reckless speed, his head down to escape low branches, and in a minute or two he came with unerring instinct back to the trail some distance ahead of Forsythe and Rosa. Then he wheeled his horse and stopped stock-still, awaiting their coming.

By this time the great full moon was risen and, strangely enough, was at Gardley's back, making a silhouette of man and horse as the two riders came on toward him.

They rode out from the cover of the grove, and there he was across their path. Rosa gave a scream, drawing nearer her companion, and her horse swerved and reared, but Gardley's horse stood like an image carved in ebony against the silver of the moon, and Gardley's quiet voice was in strong contrast to the quick, unguarded exclamation of Forsythe, as he sharply drew rein and put his hand hastily to his hip for his weapon.

"I beg your pardon, Mr. Forsythe"—Gardley had an excellent memory for names—"but I thought you might not be aware, being a newcomer in these parts, that the trail you are taking leads to a place where ladies do not like to go."

"Really! You don't say so!" answered the young man, insolently. "It is very kind of you, I'm sure, but you might have saved yourself the trouble. I know perfectly where I am going, and so does the lady, and we choose to go this way. Move out of the way, please. You are detaining us."

But Gardley did not move out of the way. "I am sure the lady does not know where she is going," he said, firmly. "I am sure that she does not know that it is a place of bad reputation, even in this un-conventional land. At least, if she knows, I am sure that *her father* does not know, and I am well acquainted with her father."

"Get out of the way, sir," said Forsythe, hotly. "It certainly is none of your business, anyway, whoever knows what. Get out of the way or I shall shoot. This lady and I intend to ride where we please."

"Then I shall have to say you *cannot*," said Gardley, and his voice still had that calm that made his opponent think him easy to con-quer.

"Just how do you propose to stop us?" sneered Forsythe, pulling out his pistol.

"This way," said Gardley, lifting a tiny silver whistle to his lips and sending forth a peculiar, shrilling blast. "And this way," went on Gardley, calmly lifting both hands and showing a weapon in each, wherewith he covered the two.

Rosa screamed and covered her face with her hands, cowering in her saddle.

Forsythe lifted his weapon, but looked around nervously. "Dead men tell no tales," he said, angrily.

"It depends upon the man," said Gardley, meaningly, "especially if he were found on this road. I fancy a few tales could be told if you happened to be the man. Turn your horses around at once and take this lady back to her home. My men are not far off, and if you do not wish the whole story to be known among your friends and hers you would better make haste."

Forsythe dropped his weapon and obeyed. He decidedly did not wish his escapade to be known among his friends. There were finan-cial reasons why he did not care to have it come to the ears of his brother-in-law just now.

Silently in the moonlight the little procession took its way down the trail, the girl and the man side by side, their captor close behind, and when the girl summoned courage to glance fearsomely behind her she saw three more men riding like three grim shadows yet behind. They had fallen into the trail so quietly that she had not heard them when they came. They were Jasper Kemp, Long Bill, and Big Jim. They had been out for other purposes, but without question followed the call of the signal.

It was a long ride back to Rogers's ranch, and Forsythe glanced nervously behind now and then. It seemed to him that the company was growing larger all the time. He half expected to see a regiment each time he turned. He tried hurrying his horse, but when he did so the followers were just as close without any seeming effort. He tried to laugh it all off.

Once he turned and tried to placate Gardley with a few shakily jovial words:

"Look here, old fellow, aren't you the man I met on the trail the day Miss Earle went over to the fort? I guess you've made a mistake in your calculations. I was merely out on a pleasure ride with Miss Rogers. We weren't going anywhere in particular, you know. Miss Rogers chose this way, and I wanted to please her. No man likes to have his pleasure interfered with, you know. I guess you didn't recognize me?"

"I recognized you," said Gardley. "It would be well for you to be careful where you ride with ladies, especially at night. The matter, however, is one that you would better settle with Mr. Rogers. My duty will be done when I have put it into his hands."

"Now, my good fellow," said Forsythe, patronizingly, "you surely don't intend to make a great fuss about this and go telling tales to Mr. Rogers about a trifling matter—"

"I intend to do my duty, Mr. Forsythe," said Gardley, and Forsythe noticed that the young man still held his weapons. "I was set this night to guard Mr. Rogers's property. That I did not expect his daughter would be a part of the evening's guarding has nothing to do with the matter. I shall certainly put the matter into Mr. Rogers's hands."

Rosa began to cry softly.

"Well, if you want to be a fool, of course," laughed Forsythe, disagreeably, "but you will soon see Mr. Rogers will accept my explanation."

"That is for Mr. Rogers to decide," answered Gardley, and said no more.

The reflections of Forsythe during the rest of that silent ride were not pleasant, and Rosa's intermittent crying did not tend to make him more comfortable.

The silent procession at last turned in at the great ranch gate and rode up to the house. Just as they stopped and the door of the house swung open, letting out a flood of light, Rosa leaned toward Gardley and whispered:

"Please, Mr. Gardley, don't tell Papa. I'll do *anything* in the world for you if you won't tell Papa."

He looked at the pretty, pitiful child in the moonlight. "I'm sorry, Miss Rosa," he said, firmly. "But you don't understand. I must do my duty."

"Then I shall hate you!" she hissed. "Do you hear? I shall *hate* you forever, and you don't know what that means. It means I'll take my *revenge* on you and on *everybody you like.*"

He looked at her half pityingly as he swung off his horse and went up the steps to meet Mr. Rogers, who had come out and was standing on the top step of the ranch house in the square of light that flickered from a great fire on the hearth of the wide fireplace. He was looking from one to another of the silent group, and as his eyes rested on his daughter he said, sternly:

"Why, Rosa, what does this mean? You told me you were going to bed with a headache!"

Gardley drew his employer aside and told what had happened in a few low-toned sentences, and then stepped down and back into the shadow, his horse by his side, the three men from the camp grouped behind him. He had the delicacy to withdraw after his duty was done.

Mr. Rogers, his face stern with sudden anger and alarm, stepped down and stood beside his daughter. "Rosa, you may get down and go into the house to your own room. I will talk with you later," he said. And then to the young man, "You, sir, will step into my office. I wish to have a plain talk with you."

A half hour later Forsythe came out of the Rogers house and

mounted his horse, while Mr. Rogers stood silently and watched him.

"I will bid you good evening, sir," he said, formally, as the young man mounted his horse and silently rode away. His back had a defiant look in the moonlight as he passed the group of men in the shadow, but they did not turn to watch him.

"That will be all tonight, Gardley, and I thank you very much," called the clear voice of Mr. Rogers from his front steps.

The four men mounted their horses silently and rode down a little distance behind the young man, who wondered in his heart just how much or how little Gardley had told Rosa's father.

The interview to which young Forsythe had just been subjected had been chastening in character, of a kind to baffle curiosity concerning the father's knowledge of details, and to discourage any further romantic rides with Miss Rosa. It had been left in abeyance whether or not the Temples should be made acquainted with the episode, dependent upon the future conduct of both young people. It had not been satisfactory from Forsythe's point of view. That is, he had not been so easily able to disabuse the father's mind of suspicion, nor to establish his own guileless character as he had hoped, and some of the remarks Rogers made led Forsythe to think that the father understood just how unpleasant it might become for him if his brother-in-law found out about the escapade.

This is why Archie Forsythe feared Lance Gardley, although there was nothing in the least triumphant about the set of that young man's shoulders as he rode away in the moonlight on the trail toward Ashland. And this is how it came about that Rosa Rogers hated Lance Gardley, handsome and daring though he was, and because of him hated her teacher, Margaret Earle.

An hour later Lance Gardley stood in the little dim Tanner parlor, talking to Margaret.

"You look tired," said the girl, compassionately, as she saw the haggard shadows on the young face, showing in spite of the light of pleasure in his eyes. "You look *very* tired. What in the world have you been doing?"

"I went out to catch cattle thieves," he said, with a sigh, "but I found there were other kinds of thieves abroad. It's all in the day's work. I'm not tired now." And he smiled at her with beautiful reverence.

Margaret, as she watched him, could not help thinking that the lines in his face had softened and strengthened since she had first seen him, and her eyes let him know that she was glad he had come.

"And so you will really come to us, and it isn't going to be asking too much?" he said, wistfully. "You can't think what it's going to be to the men—to *us!* And Mom Wallis is so excited she can hardly get her work done. If you had said no I would be almost afraid to go back." He laughed, but she could see there was deep earnestness under his tone.

"Indeed I will come," said Margaret. "I'm just looking foward to it. I'm going to bring Mom Wallis a new bonnet like one I made for Mother, and I'm going to teach her how to make corn gems and steamed apple dumplings. I'm bringing some songs and some music for the violin, and I've got something for you to help me do, too, if you will?"

He smiled tenderly down on her. What a wonderful girl she was, to be willing to come out to the old shack among a lot of rough men and one uncultured old woman and make them happy, when she was fit for the finest in the land!

"You're *wonderful!*" he said, taking her hand with a quick pressure for good-bye. "You make everyone want to do his best."

He hurried out to his horse and rode away in the moonlight. Margaret went up to her "mountain window" and watched him far out on the trail, her heart swelling with an unnamed gladness over his last words.

"Oh, God, keep him, and help him to make good!" she prayed.

Chapter 21

The visit to the camp was a time to be remembered long by all the inhabitants of the bunkhouse, and even by Margaret herself. Margaret wondered Friday evening, as she sat up late, working away braiding a lovely gray bonnet out of folds of malines, and fashioning it into form for Mom Wallis, why she was looking forward to the visit with so much more real pleasure than she had done to the one the week before at the Temples'. And so subtle is the heart of a maid that she never fathomed the real reason.

The Temples', of course, was interesting and delightful as being something utterly new in her experience. It was comparatively luxurious, and there were pleasant, cultured people there, more from her own social class of life. But it was going to be such fun to surprise Mom Wallis with that bonnet and see her old face light up when she saw herself in the little folding three-leaved mirror she was taking along with her and meant to leave for Mom Wallis's log boudoir. She was quite excited over selecting some little thing for each of the men—books, pictures, a piece of music, a bright cushion, and a pile of picture magazines. It made a big bundle when she had them together, and she was dubious if she ought to try to carry them all, but Bud, whom she consulted on the subject, said, loftily, it "wasn't a fleabite for the kid; he could carry *any*thing on a horse."

Bud was just a little jealous to have his beloved teacher away from home so much, and rejoiced greatly when Gardley, Friday afternoon, suggested that he come along, too. He made quick time to his home, and secured a hasty permission and wardrobe, appearing like a footman on his father's old horse when they were half a mile down the trail.

Mom Wallis was out at the door to greet her guest when she arrived, for Margaret had chosen to make her visit last from Friday afternoon after school, until Monday morning. It was the generosity of her nature that she gave to her utmost when she gave.

The one fear she had entertained about coming had been set at rest on the way when Gardley told her that Pop Wallis was off on one of his long trips, selling cattle, and would probably not return for a week. Margaret, much as she trusted Gardley and the men, could not help dreading to meet Pop Wallis again.

There was a new trimness about the old bunkhouse. The clearing had been cleaned up and made neat, the grass cut, some vines set out and trained up limply about the door, and the windows shone with Mom Wallis's washing.

Mom Wallis herself was wearing her best white apron, stiff with starch, her lace collar, and her hair in her best imitation of the way Margaret had fixed it, although it must be confessed she hadn't quite caught the knack of arrangement yet. But the one great difference Margaret noticed in the old woman was the illuminating smile on her face. Mom Wallis had learned how to let the glory gleam through all the hard sordidness of her life, and make earth brighter for those about her.

The curtains certainly made a great difference in the looks of the bunkhouse, together with a few other changes. The men had made some chairs—three of them, one out of a barrel, and together they had upholstered them roughly. The cots around the walls were blazing with their red blankets folded smoothly and neatly over them, and on the floor in front of the hearth, which had been scrubbed, Gardley had spread a Navajo blanket he had bought from an Indian.

The fireplace was piled with logs ready for the lighting at night, and from somewhere a lamp had been rigged up and polished till it shone in the setting sun that slanted long rays in at the shining windows.

The men were washed and combed, and had been huddled at the back of the bunkhouse for an hour, watching the road, and now they came forward awkwardly to greet their guest, their horny hands scrubbed to an unbelievable whiteness. They did not say much, but they looked their pleasure, and Margaret greeted every one as if he were an old friend, the charming part about it all to the men being that she remembered everyone's name and used it.

Bud hovered in the background and watched with starry eyes. Bud was having the time of his life. He preferred the teacher's visiting the camp rather than the fort. The "Howdy, sonny!" which he had received from the men, and the "Make yourself at home, Bill" from Gardley, had given him great joy, and the whole thing seemed somehow to link him to the teacher in a most distinguishing manner.

Supper was ready almost immediately, and Mom Wallis had done her best to make it appetizing. There was a lamb stew with potatoes, and fresh corn bread with coffee. The men ate with relish, and watched their guest of honor as if she had been an angel come down to abide with them for a season. There was a tablecloth on the old table, too—a *white* tablecloth. It looked remarkably like an old sheet, to be sure, with a seam through the middle where it had been worn and turned and sewed together, but it was a tablecloth now, and a marvel to the men. And the wonder about Margaret was that she could eat at such a table and make it seem as though that tablecloth were the finest damask, and the two-tined forks the heaviest of silver.

After the supper was cleared away and the lamp lighted, the gifts were brought out. A book of Scotch poetry for Jasper Kemp, bound in tartan covers of the Campbell clan, a small illustrated pamphlet of Niagara Falls for Big Jim, because he had said he wanted to see the place and never could manage it, a little pictured folder of Washington City for Big Jim, a book of old ballad music for Fiddling Boss, a book of jokes for Fadeaway Forbes, a framed picture of a beautiful shepherd dog for Stocky, a big, red, ruffled denim pillow for Croaker, because when she was there before he was always complaining about the seats being hard, a great blazing crimson pennant bearing the name HARVARD in big letters for Fudge, because she had remembered he was from Boston, and for Mom Wallis a framed text beautifully painted in watercolors, done in rustic letters twined with stray forget-me-nots, the words, "Come unto Me, all ye that labor and are heavy laden, and I will give you rest." Margaret had made that during the week and framed it in a simple raffia braid of brown and green.

It was marvelous how these men liked their presents, and while they were examining them and laughing about them and putting their pictures and Mom Wallis's text on the walls, the pillow on a bunk, and the pennant over the fireplace, Margaret shyly held out a tiny box to Gardley.

"I thought perhaps you would let me give you this," she said. "It isn't much; it isn't even new, and it has some marks in it, but I thought it might help with your new undertaking."

Gardley took it with a lighting of his face and opened the box. In it was a little, soft, leather-bound Testament, showing the marks of usage, yet not worn. It was a tiny thing, very thin, easily fitting in a vest pocket, and not a burden to carry. He took the little book in his hand, removed the silken rubber band that bound it, and turned the leaves reverently in his fingers, noting that there were pencil marks here and there. His face was all emotion as he looked up at the giver.

"I thank you," he said, in a low tone, glancing about to see that no one was noticing them. "I shall prize it greatly. It surely will help. I will read it every day. Was that what you wanted? And I will carry it with me always."

His voice was very earnest, and he looked at her as though she had given him a fortune. With another glance about at the preoccupied room—even Bud was busy studying Jasper Kemp's oldest gun—he snapped the band on the book again and put it carefully in his inner breast pocket. The book would henceforth travel next to his heart and be his guide. She thought he meant her to understand that, as he put out his hand unobtrusively and pressed her fingers gently with a quick, low "Thank you!"

Then Mom Wallis's bonnet was brought out and tied on her, and the poor old woman blushed like a girl when she stood with meek hands folded at her waist and looked primly about on the family for their approval at Margaret's request. But that was nothing to the way she stared when Margaret got out the threefold mirror and showed herself in the new headgear. She trotted away at last, the wonderful bonnet in one hand, the box in the other, a look of awe on her face, and Margaret heard her murmur as she put it away: "Glory! *Me!* Glory!"

Then Margaret had to read one or two of the poems for Jasper Kemp, while they all sat and listened to her Scotch and marveled at her. A woman like that condescending to come to visit them!

She gave a lesson in note-reading to the Fiddling Boss, pointing one by one with her white fingers to the notes until he was able to creep along and pick out "Suwanee River" and "Old Folks at Home" to the intense delight of the audience.

Margaret never knew just how it was that she came to be telling the men a story, one she had read not long before in a magazine, a story with a thrilling national interest and a keen personal touch that searched the hearts of men, but they listened as they had never listened to anything in their lives before.

And then there was singing, more singing, until it bade fair to be morning before they slept, and the little teacher was weary indeed when she lay down on the cot in Mom Wallis's room, after having knelt beside the old woman and prayed.

The next day there was a wonderful ride with Gardley and Bud to the canyon of the cave dwellers, and a coming home to the apple dumplings she had taught Mom Wallis to make before she went away. All day Gardley and she, with Bud for delighted audience, had talked over the play she was getting up at the school, Gardley suggesting about costumes and tree boughs for scenery, and promising to help in any way she wanted. Then after supper there were jokes and songs around the big fire, and some popcorn one of the men had gone a long ride that day to get. They called for another story, too, and it was forthcoming.

It was Sunday morning after breakfast, however, that Margaret suddenly wondered how she was going to make the day helpful and different from the other days.

She stood for a moment looking out of the clear little window thoughtfully, with just the shadow of a sigh on her lips, and as she turned back to the room she met Gardley's questioning glance.

"Are you homesick?" he asked, with a sorry smile. "This must all be very different from what you are accustomed to."

"Oh, no, it isn't that." She smiled, brightly. "I'm not a baby for home, but I do get a bit homesick about church time. Sunday is such a strange day to me without a service."

"Why not have one, then?" he suggested, eagerly. "We can sing and—you could—do the rest!"

Her eyes lighted at the suggestion, and she cast a quick glance at the men. Would they stand for that sort of thing?

Gardley followed her glance and caught her meaning. "Let them answer for themselves," he said quickly in a low tone, and then, raising his voice: "Speak up, men. Do you want to have church? Miss Earle here is homesick for a service, and I suggest that we have one, and she conduct it."

"Sure!" said Jasper Kemp, his face lighting. "I'll miss my guess if she can't do better than the parson we had last Sunday. Get into your seats, boys, we're goin' to church."

Margaret's face was a study of embarrassment and delight as she saw the alacrity with which the men moved to get ready for church. Her quick brain turned over the possibility of what she could read or say to help this strange congregation thus suddenly thrust upon her.

It was a testimony to her upbringing by a father whose great business of life was to preach the gospel that she never thought once of hesitating or declining the opportunity, but welcomed it as an opportunity, and only deprecated her unreadiness for the work.

The men stirred about, donned their coats, furtively brushing their hair, and Long Bill insisted that Mom Wallis put on her new bonnet, which she obligingly did, and sat down carefully in the barrel chair, her hands neatly crossed in her lap, supremely happy. It really was wonderful what a difference that bonnet made in Mom Wallis.

Gardley arranged a comfortable seat for Margaret at the table and put in front of her one of the hymnbooks she had brought. Then, after she was seated, he took the chair beside her and brought out the little Testament from his breast pocket, gravely laying it on the hymnbook.

Margaret met his eyes with a look of quick appreciation. It was wonderful the way these two were growing to understand each other. It gave the girl a thrill of wonder and delight to have him do this simple little thing for her, and the smile that passed between them was beautiful to see. Long Bill turned away his head and looked out of the window with an improvised sneeze to excuse the sudden mist that came into his eyes.

Margaret chose "My Faith Looks up to Thee" for the first hymn, because Fiddling Boss could play it, and while he was tuning up his fiddle she hastily wrote out two more copies of the words. And so the queer service started with a quaver of the old fiddle and the clear, sweet voices of Margaret and Gardley leading off, while the men growled on their way behind, and Mom Wallis, in her new gray bonnet, with her hair all fluffed softly gray under it, sat with eyes shining like a girl's.

So absorbed in the song were they all that they failed to hear the sound of a horse coming into the clearing. But just as the last words of the final verse died away the door of the bunkhouse swung open, and there in the doorway stood Pop Wallis!

The men sprang to their feet with one accord, ominous frowns on their brows, and poor old Mom Wallis sat petrified where she was, the smile of relaxation frozen on her face, a look of fear growing in her tired old eyes.

Now Pop Wallis, through an unusual combination of circumstances, had been for some hours without liquor and was comparatively sober. He stood for a moment staring amazedly at the group around his fireside. Perhaps because he had been so long without his usual stimulant his mind was weakened and things appeared as a strange vision to him. At any rate, he stood and stared, and as he looked from one to another of the men, at the beautiful stranger, and across to the strangely unfamiliar face of his wife in her new bonnet, his eyes took on a frightened look. He slowly took his hand from the doorframe and passed it over his eyes, then looked again, from one to another, and back to his glorified wife.

Margaret had half risen at her end of the table, and Gardley stood beside her as if to reassure her, but Pop Wallis was not looking at any of them any more. His eyes were on his wife. He passed his hand once more over his eyes and took one step gropingly into the room, a hand reached out in front of him, as if he were not sure but he might run into something on the way, the other hand on his forehead, a dazed look in his face.

"Why, Mom—that ain't really—*you,* now, *is* it?" he said, in a gentle, insinuating voice like one long unaccustomed to making a hasty prayer.

The tone made a swift change in the old woman. She gripped her bony hands tight and a look of beatific joy came into her wrinkled face.

"Yes, it's really *me,* Pop!" she said, with a kind of triumphant ring to her voice.

"But—but—you're right *here,* ain't you? You ain't *dead,* an'—an'—gone to—gl-oo-ry, be you? You're right *here?*"

"Yes, I'm right *here,* Pop. I ain't dead! Pop—glory's *come to me!*"

"Glory?" repeated the man, dazedly. "Glory?" And he gazed around the room and took in the new curtains, the pictures on the wall, the cushions and chairs, and the bright, shining windows. "You don't mean it's *heav'n,* do you, Mom? 'Cause I better go back—*I* don't belong in heav'n. Why, Mom, it can't be glory, *'cause* it's the same old bunkhouse outside, anyhow."

"Yes, it's the same old bunkhouse, and it ain't heaven, but it's *goin'* to be. The glory's come all right. You sit down, Pop, we're goin' to have church, and this is my new bonnet. *She* brang it. This is the new schoolteacher, Miss Earle, and she's goin' to have church. She done it *all!* You sit down and listen."

Pop Wallis took a few hesitating steps into the room and dropped into the nearest chair. He looked at Margaret as if she might be an angel holding open the portal to a kingdom in the sky. He looked and wondered and admired, and then he looked back to his glorified old wife again in wonder.

Jasper Kemp shut the door, and the company dropped back into their places. Margaret, because of her deep embarrassment, and a kind of inward trembling that had taken possession of her, announced another hymn.

It was a solemn little service, quite unique, with a brief, simple prayer and an expository reading of the story of the blind man from the ninth chapter of John. The men sat attentively, their eyes upon her face as she read, but Pop Wallis sat staring at his wife, an awed light upon his scared old face, the wickedness and cunning all faded out, and only fear and wonder written there.

In the early dawning of the pink and silver morning Margaret went back to her work, Gardley riding by her side, and Bud riding at a discreet distance behind, now and then going off at a tangent after a stray cottontail. It was wonderful what good sense Bud seemed to have on occasion.

The horse that Margaret rode, a sturdy little western pony, with nerve and grit and a gentle common sense for humans, was to remain with her in Ashland, a gift from the men of the bunkhouse. During the week that followed Archie Forsythe came riding over with a beautiful shining saddle horse for her use during her stay in the West, but when he went riding back to the ranch the shining saddle horse was still in his train, riderless, for Margaret told him that she already had a horse of her own. Neither had Margaret accepted the invitation to the Temples' for the next weekend. She had other plans for the Sabbath, and that week there appeared on all the trees and posts about the town, and on the trails, a little notice of a Bible class and vesper service to be held in the schoolhouse on the following Sabbath afternoon. And so Margaret, true daughter of her minister-father, took up her mission in Ashland for the Sabbaths that were to follow, for the schoolboard had agreed with alacrity to such use of the schoolhouse.

Chapter 22

Now when it became noised abroad that the new teacher wanted above all things to purchase a piano, and that to that end she was staging a wonderful Shakespeare play in which the scholars were to act upon a stage set with tree boughs after the manner of some new kind of players, the whole community round about began to be excited.

Mrs. Tanner talked much about it. Was not Bud to be a prominent character? Mr. Tanner talked about it everywhere he went. The mothers and fathers and sisters talked about it, and the work of preparing the play went on.

Margaret had discovered that one of the men at the bunkhouse played a flute, and she was working hard to teach him and Fiddling Boss and Croaker to play a portion of the elfin dance to accompany the players. The work of making costumes and training the actors became more and more strenuous, and in this Gardley proved a fine assistant. He undertook to train some of the older boys for their parts, and did it so well that he was presently in the forefront of the battle of preparation and working almost as hard as Margaret herself.

The beauty of the whole thing was that every boy in the school adored him, even Jed and Timothy, and life took on a different aspect to them in company with this highborn college-bred, eastern young man who yet could ride and shoot with the daringest among the westerners.

Far and wide went forth the fame of the play that was to be. The news of it reached to the fort and the ranches, and brought offers of assistance and costumes and orders for tickets. Margaret purchased a small duplicator and set her school to printing tickets and selling them, and before the play was half ready to be acted tickets enough were sold for two performances, and people were planning to come from fifty miles around. The young teacher began to quake at the thought of her big audience and her poor little amateur players, and yet for children they were doing wonderfully well, and were growing quite Shakespearean in their manner of conversation.

"What say you, sweet Amanda?" would be a form of frequent address to that stolid maiden Amanda Bounds; and Jed, instead of shouting for "Delicate" at recess, as in former times, would say, "My good Timothy, I swear to thee by Cupid's strongest bow, by his best arrow with the golden head"—until all the schoolyard rang with classic phrases, and the whole country round was being addressed in phrases of another century by the younger members of their households.

Then Rosa Rogers's father one day stopped at the Tanners' and left a contribution with the teacher of fifty dollars toward the new piano, and after that it was rumored that the teacher said the piano could be sent for in time to be used at the play. Then other contributions of smaller amounts came in, and before the date of the play had been set there was money enough to make a first payment on the piano. That day the English exercise for the whole school was to compose the letter to the eastern piano firm where the piano was to be purchased, ordering it to be sent on at once. Weeks before this Margaret had sent for a number of piano catalogues beautifully illustrated, showing by cuts how the whole instruments were made, with full illustrations of the factories where they were manufactured, and she had discussed the selection with the scholars, showing them what points were to be considered in selecting a good piano. At last the order was sent out, the actual selection itself to be made by a musical friend of Margaret's in New York, and the school waited in anxious suspense to hear that it had started on its way.

The piano arrived at last, three weeks before the time set for the play, which was coming on finely now and seemed to the eager scholars quite ready for public performance. Not so to Margaret and Gardley, as daily they pruned, trained, and patiently went over and over again each part, drawing all the while nearer to the ideal they had set. It could not be done perfectly, of course, and when they had done all they could there would yet be many crudities, but Margaret's hope was to bring out the meaning of the play and give both audience and performers the true idea of what Shakespeare meant when he wrote it.

The arrival of the piano was naturally a great event in the school. For three days in succession the entire school marched in procession down to the incoming eastern train to see if their expected treasure had arrived, and when at last it was lifted from the freight car and set upon the station platform the school stood awestruck and silent, with half-bowed heads and bated breath, as though at the arrival of some great and honorable guest.

They attended it on the roadside as it was carted by the biggest wagon in town to the schoolhouse door. They stood in silent rows while the great box was peeled off and the instrument taken out and carried into the schoolroom; then they filed in soulfully and took their accustomed seats without being told, touching shyly the shining case as they passed. By common consent they waited to hear its voice for the first time. Margaret took the little key from the envelope tied to the frame, unlocked the cover, and, sitting down, began to play. The rough men who had brought it stood in awesome adoration around the platform. The silence that spread over that room would have done honor to Paderewski or Josef Hofmann.

Margaret played and played, and they could not hear enough. They would have stayed all night listening, perhaps, so wonderful was it to them. And then the teacher called each one and let him or her touch a few chords, just to say they had played on it. After which she locked the instrument and sent them all home. That was the only afternoon during that term that the play was forgotten for a while.

After the arrival of the piano the play went forward with great strides, for now Margaret accompanied some of the parts with the music, and the flute and violin were also practiced in their elfin dance with much better effect. It was about this time that Archie Forsythe discovered the rehearsals and offered his assistance, and, although it was declined, he frequently managed to ride over about rehearsal time, finding ways to make himself useful in spite of Margaret's polite refusals. Margaret always felt annoyed when he came, because Rosa Rogers instantly became another creature on his arrival, and because Gardley simply froze into a polite statue, never speaking except when spoken to. As for Forsythe, his attitude toward Gardley was that of a contemptuous master toward a slave, and yet he took care to cover it always with a form of courtesy, so that Margaret could say or do nothing to show her displeasure, except to be grave and dignified. At such times Rosa Rogers's eyes would be upon her with a gleam of hatred, and the teacher felt that the scholar was taking advantage of the situation. Altogether it was a trying time for Margaret when Forsythe came to the schoolhouse. Also, he discovered to them that he played the violin, and offered to assist in the orchestral parts. Margaret really could think of no reason to decline this offer, but she was sadly upset by the whole thing. His manner to her was too pronounced, and she felt continually uncomfortable under it, what with Rosa Rogers's jealous eyes upon her and Gardley's eyes turned haughtily away.

She planned a number of special rehearsals in the evenings, when it was difficult for Forsythe to get there, and managed in this way to avoid his presence; but the whole matter became a source of much vexation, and Margaret even shed a few tears wearily into her pillow one night when things had gone particularly hard and Forsythe had hurt the feelings of Fiddling Boss with his insolent directions about playing. She could not say or do anything much in the matter, because the Temples had been very kind in helping to get the piano, and Mr. Temple seemed to think he was doing the greatest possible kindness to her in letting Forsythe off duty so much to help with the play. The matter became more and more of a distress to Margaret, and the Sabbath was the only day of real delight.

The first Sunday after the arrival of the piano was a great day. Everybody in the neighborhood turned out to the Sunday afternoon class and vesper service, which had been growing more and more in popularity, until now the schoolroom was crowded. Every man from the bunkhouse came regularly, often including Pop Wallis, who had not yet recovered fully from the effect of his wife's new bonnet and fluffy arrangement of hair, but treated her like a lady visitor and deferred to her absolutely when he was at home. He wasn't quite sure even yet but he had strayed by mistake into the outermost courts of heaven and ought to get shooed out. He always looked at the rose-wreathed curtains with a mingling of pride and awe.

Margaret had put several hymns on the blackboard in clear, bold printing, and the singing that day was wonderful. Not the least part of the service was her own playing over of the hymns before the singing began, which was listened to with reverence as if it had been the music of an angel playing on a heavenly harp.

Gardley always came to the Sunday services, and helped her with the singing, and often they two sang duets together.

The service was not always of set form. Usually Margaret taught a short Bible lesson, beginning with the general outline of the Bible, its books, their form, substance, authors—all very brief and exceedingly simple, putting a wide space of music between this and the vesper service, into which she wove songs, bits of poems, passages from the Bible, and often a story which she told dramatically, illustrating the scripture read.

But the very Sunday before the play, just the time Margaret had looked forward to as being her rest from all the perplexities of the week, a company from the fort, including the Temples, arrived at the schoolhouse right in the midst of the Bible lesson.

The ladies were daintily dressed, and settled their frills and ribbons amusedly as they watched the embarrassed young teacher trying to forget that there was company present. They were in a distinct sense company, for they had the air, as they entered, of having come to look on and be amused, not to partake in the worship with the rest.

Margaret found herself trembling inwardly as she saw the supercilious smile on the lips of Mrs. Temple and the amused stares of the other ladies of the party. They did not take notice of the other people present anymore than if they had been so many puppets set up to show off the teacher. Their air of superiority was offensive. Not until Rosa Rogers entered with her father, a little later, did they condescend to bow in recognition, and then with that pretty little atmosphere as if they would say, "Oh, you've come, too, to be amused."

Gardley was sitting up in front, listening to her talk, and she thought he had not noticed the strangers. Suddenly it came to her to try to keep her nerve and let him see that they were nothing to her, and with a strong effort and a swift prayer for help she called for a hymn. She sat coolly down at the piano, touching the keys with a tender chord or two and beginning to sing almost at once. She had sent home for some old hymnbooks from the Christian Endeavor Society in her father's church, so the congregation was supplied with the notes and words now, and everybody took part eagerly, even the people from the fort condescendingly joining in.

But Gardley was too much alive to every expression on that vivid face of Margaret's to miss knowing that she was annoyed and upset. He did not need to turn and look back to immediately discover the cause. He was a young person of keen intuition. It suddenly gave him great satisfaction to see that look of consternation on Margaret's face. It settled for him a question he had been in great and anxious doubt about, and his soul was lifted up with peace within him. When, presently, according to arrangement, he rose to sing a duet with Margaret, no one could have possibly told by so much as the lifting of an eyelash that he knew there was an enemy of his in the back of the room. He sang, as did Margaret, to the immediate audience in front of him, those admiring children and adoring men in the forefront who felt the schoolhouse had become for them the gate of heaven for the time being, and he sang with marvelous feeling and sympathy, letting out his voice at its best.

"Really," said Mrs. Temple, in a loud whisper to the wife of one of the officers, "that young man has a fine voice, and he isn't bad-looking, either. I think he'd be worth cultivating. We must have him up and try him out."

But when she repeated this remark in another stage whisper to Forsythe he frowned haughtily.

The one glimpse Margaret caught of Forsythe during that afternoon's service was when he was smiling meaningly at Rosa Rogers, and she had to resolutely put the memory of their look from her mind or the story which she was about to tell would have fled.

It was the hunger in Jasper Kemp's eyes that finally anchored Margaret's thoughts and helped her to forget the company at the back of the room. She told her story, and she told it wonderfully and with power, interpreting it now and then for the row of men who sat in the center of the room drinking in her every word, and when the simple service was concluded with another song, in which Gardley's voice rang forth with peculiar tenderness and strength, the men filed forth silently, solemnly, with bowed heads and thoughtful eyes. But the company from the fort flowed up around Margaret like floodtide let loose and gushed upon her.

"Oh, my dear!" said Mrs. Temple. "How beautifully you do it! And such attention as they give you! No wonder you are willing to forego all other amusements to stay here and preach! But it was perfectly sweet the way you made them listen and the way you told that story. I don't see how you do it. I'd be scared to death!"

They babbled about her awhile, much to her annoyance, for there were several people to whom she had wanted to speak, who drew away and disappeared when the newcomers took possession of her. At last, however, they mounted and rode away, to her great relief. Forsythe, it is true, tried to make her go home with them, tried to escort her to the Tanners', tried to remain in the schoolhouse with her awhile when she told him she had something to do there, but she would not let him, and he rode away half sulky at the last, a look of injured pride upon his face.

Margaret went to the door finally, and looked down the road. He was gone, and she was alone. A shade of sadness came over her face. She was sorry that Gardley had not waited. She had wanted to tell him how much she liked his singing, what a pleasure it was to sing with him, and how glad she was that he came up to her need so well with the strangers there and helped to make it easy. But Gardley had melted away as soon as the service was over, and had probably gone home with the rest of the men. It was disappointing, for she had come to consider their little time together on Sunday as a very pleasant hour, this few minutes after the service when they would talk about real living and the vital things of existence. But he was gone!

She turned, and there he was, quite near the door, coming toward her. Her face lighted up with a joy that was unmistakable, and his own smile in answer was a revelation of his deeper self.

"Oh, I'm so glad you are not gone!" she said, eagerly. "I wanted to tell you—" And then she stopped, and the color flooded her face rosily, for she saw in his eyes how glad he was and forgot to finish her sentence.

He came up gravely, after all, and, standing just a minute so beside the door, took both her hands in both his. It was only for a second that he stood so, looking down into her eyes. I doubt if either of them knew till afterward that they had been holding hands. It seemed the right and natural thing to do, and meant so much to each of them. Both were glad beyond their own understanding over that moment and its tenderness.

It was all very decorous, and over in a second, but it meant much to remember afteward, that look and handclasp.

"I wanted to tell you," he said, tenderly, "how much that story did for me. It was wonderful, and it helped me to decide something I have been perplexed over—"

"Oh, I am glad!" she said, half breathlessly.

So, talking in low, broken sentences, they went back to the piano and tried over several songs for the next Sunday, lingering together, just happy to be there with each other, and not half knowing the significance of it all. As the purple lights on the schoolroom wall grew long and rose-edged, they walked slowly to the Tanner house and said good-night.

There was a beauty about the young man as he stood for a moment looking down upon the girl in parting, the kind of beauty there is in any strong, wild thing made tame and tender for a great love by a great uplift. Gardley had that look of self-surrender, and power made subservient to right, that crowns a man with strength and more than physical beauty. In his fine face there glowed high purpose, and deep devotion to the one who had taught it to him. Margaret, looking up at him, felt her heart go out with that great love, half maiden, half divine, that comes to some favored women even here on earth, and she watched him down the road toward the mountain in the evening light and marveled how her trust had grown since first she met him, marveled and reflected that she had not told her mother and father much about him yet. It was growing time to do so, yes—*it was growing time!* Her cheeks grew pink in the darkness and she turned and fled to her room.

That was the last time she saw him before the play.

Chapter 23

The play was set for Tuesday. Monday afternoon and evening were to be the final rehearsals, but Gardley did not come to them. Fiddling Boss came late and said the men had been off all day and had not yet returned. He himself found it hard to come at all. They had important work on. But there was no word from Gardley.

Margaret was disappointed. She couldn't get away from it. Of course they could go on with the rehearsal without him. He had done his work well, and there was no real reason why he had to be there. He knew every part by heart, and could take any boy's place if anyone failed in any way. There was nothing further really for him to do until the performance, as far as that was concerned, except be there and encourage her. But she missed him, and an uneasiness grew in her mind. She had so looked forward to seeing him, and now to have no word! He might at least have sent her a note when he found he could not come.

Still she knew this was unreasonable. His work, whatever it was— he had never explained it very thoroughly to her, perhaps because she had never asked—must, of course, have kept him. She must excuse him without question and go on with the business of the hour.

Her hands were full enough, for Forsythe came presently and was more trying than usual. She had to be very decided and put her foot down about one or two things, or some of her actors would have gone home in the sulks, and Fiddling Boss, whose part in the program meant much to him, would have given it up entirely.

She hurried everything through as soon as possible, knowing she was weary, and longing to get to her room and rest. Gardley would come and explain tomorrow, likely in the morning on his way somewhere.

But the morning came and no word. Afternoon came and he had not sent a sign yet. Some of the little things that he had promised to do about the setting of the stage would have to remain undone, for it was too late now to do it herself, and there was no one else to call upon.

Into the midst of her perplexity and anxiety came the news that Jed on his way home had been thrown from his horse, which was a young and vicious one, and had broken his leg. Jed was to act the part of Nick Bottom that evening, and he did it well! Now what in the world was she to do? If only Gardley would come!

Just at this moment Forsythe arrived.

"Oh, it is you, Mr. Forsythe!" And her tone showed plainly her disappointment. "Haven't you seen Mr. Gardley today? I don't know what I shall do without him."

"I certainly have seen Gardley," said Forsythe, a spice of vindictiveness and satisfaction in his tone. "I saw him not two hours ago, drunk as a fish, out at a place called Old Ouida's Cabin, as I was passing. He's in for a regular spree. You'll not see him for several days, I fancy. He's utterly helpless for the present, and out of the question. What is there I can do for you? Present your request. It's yours—to the half of my kingdom."

Margaret's heart grew cold as ice and then like fire. Her blood seemed to stop utterly and then to go pounding through her veins in leaps and torrents. Her eyes grew dark, and things swam before her. She reached out to a desk and caught at it for support, and her white face looked at him a moment as if she had not heard. But when in a second she spoke, she said, quite steadily:

"I thank you, Mr. Forsythe, there is nothing just at present—or, yes, there is, if you wouldn't mind helping Timothy put up those curtains. Now, I think I'll go home and rest a few minutes. I am very tired."

It wasn't exactly the job Forsythe coveted, to stay in the schoolhouse and fuss over those curtains, but she made him do it, then disappeared, and he didn't like the memory of her white face. He hadn't thought she would take it that way. He had expected to have her exclaim with horror and disgust. He watched her out of the door, and then turned impatiently to the waiting Timothy.

Margaret went outside the schoolhouse to call Bud, who had been sent to gather sagebrush for filling in the background, but Bud was already out of sight far on the trail toward the camp on Forsythe's horse, riding for dear life. Bud had come near to the schoolhouse door with his armful of sagebrush just in time to hear Forsythe's flippant speech about Gardley and see Margaret's white face. Bud had gone for help!

But Margaret did not go home to rest. She did not even get half-way home. When she had gone a very short distance outside the schoolhouse she saw someone coming toward her, and in her distress of mind she could not tell who it was. Her eyes were blinded with tears, her breath was constricted, and it seemed to her that a demon unseen was gripping her heart. She had not yet taken her bearings to know what she thought. She had only just come dazed from the shock of Forsythe's words, and had not the power to think. Over and over to herself, as she walked along, she kept repeating the words: "I *do not* believe it! It is *not* true!" but her inner consciousness had not had time to analyze her soul and be sure that she believed the words wherewith she was comforting herself.

So now, when she saw someone coming, she felt the necessity of bringing her telltale face to order and getting ready to answer whoever she was to meet. As she drew nearer she became suddenly aware that it was Rosa Rogers coming with her arms full of bundles and more piled up in front of her on her pony. Margaret knew at once that Rosa must have seen Forsythe go by her house, and had returned promptly to the schoolhouse on some pretext or other. It would not do to let her go there alone with the young man; she must go back and stay with them. She could not be sure that if she sent Rosa home with orders to rest she would be obeyed. Doubtless the girl would take another way around and return to the school again. There was nothing for it but to go back and stay as long as Rosa did.

Margaret stooped and, hastily plucking a great armful of sagebrush, turned around and retraced her steps, her heart like lead, her feet suddenly grown heavy. How could she go back and hear them laugh and chatter, answer their many silly, unnecessary questions, and stand it all? How could she, with that great weight at her heart?

She went back with a wonderful self-control. Forsythe's face lighted, and his reluctant hand grew suddenly eager as he worked. Rosa came presently, and others, and the laughing chatter went on quite as Margaret had known it would. And she—so great is the power of human will under pressure—went calmly about and directed here and there, planned and executed, put little, dainty, wholly unnecessary touches to the stage, and never let anyone know that her heart was being crushed with the weight of a great, awful fear, and yet steadily upborne by the rising of a great, deep trust. As she worked and smiled and ordered, she was praying: "Oh, God, don't let it be true! Keep him! Save him! Bring him! Make him true! I *know* he is true! Oh, God, bring him safely *soon!*"

Meantime there was nothing she could do. She could not send Forsythe after him. She could not speak of the matter to one of those present, and Bud—where was Bud? It was the first time since she came to Arizona that Bud had failed her. She might not leave the schoolhouse, with Forsythe and Rosa there, to go and find him, and she might not do anything else. There was nothing to do but work on feverishly and pray as she had never prayed before.

By and by one of the smaller boys came, and she sent him back to the Tanners' to find Bud, but he returned with the message that Bud had not been home since morning, and so the last hours before the evening, that would otherwise have been so brief for all there was to be done, dragged their weary length away and Margaret worked on.

She did not even go back for supper at the last, but sent one of the girls to her room for a few things she needed, and declined even the nice little chicken sandwich that thoughtful Mrs. Tanner sent back along with the things. And then, at last, the audience began to gather.

By this time her anxiety was so great for Gardley that all thought of how she was to supply the place of the absent Jed had gone from her mind, which was in a whirl. Gardley! Gardley! If only Gardley would come! That was her one thought. What should she do if he didn't come at all? How should she explain things to herself afterward? What if it had been true? What if he were the kind of man Forsythe had suggested? How terrible life would look to her! But it was not true. No, it was *not* true! She trusted him! With her soul she trusted him! He would come back sometime and he would explain all. She could not remember his last look at her on Sunday and not trust him. He was true! He would come!

Somehow she managed to get through the terrible interval, to slip into the dressing room and make herself sweet and comely in the little white gown she had sent for, with its delicate blue ribbons and soft lace ruffles. Somehow she managed the expected smiles as one and another of the audience came around to the platform to speak to her. There were dark hollows under her eyes, and her mouth was drawn and weary, but they laid that to the excitement. Two bright red spots glowed on her cheeks, but she smiled and talked with her usual gaiety. People looked at her and said how beautiful she was, and how bright and untiring, and how wonderful it was that Ashland School had drawn such a prize of a teacher. The seats filled, the noise and the clatter went on. Still no sign of Gardley or anyone from the camp, and still Bud had not returned! What could it mean?

But the minutes were rushing rapidly now. It was more than time to begin. The girls were in a flutter in one cloak-room at the right of the stage, asking more questions in a minute than one could answer in an hour; the boys in the other cloakroom wanted all sorts of help, and three or four of the actors were attacked with stage fright as they peered through a hole in the curtain and saw some friend or relative arrive and sit down in the audience. It was all a mad whirl of seemingly useless noise and excitement, and she could not, no, she *could not,* go on and do the necessary things to start that awful play. Why, oh, *why* had she ever been left to think of getting up a play?

Forsythe, up behind the piano, whispered to her that it was time to begin. The house was full. There was not room for another soul. Margaret explained that Fiddling Boss had not yet arrived, and caught a glimpse of the cunning designs of Forsythe in the shifty turning away of his eyes as he answered that they could not wait all night for him, that if he wanted to get into it he ought to have come early. But even as she turned away she saw the little, bobbing, eager faces of Pop and Mom Wallis away back by the door, and the grim, towering figure of the Boss, his fiddle held high, making his way to the front amid the crowd.

She sat down and touched the keys, her eyes watching eagerly for a chance to speak to Boss and see if he knew anything of Gardley, but Forsythe was close beside her all the time, and there was no opportunity. She struck the opening chords of the overture they were to attempt to play, and somehow got through it. Of course, the audience was not a critical one, and there were few real judges of music present, but it may be that the truly wonderful effect she produced upon the listeners was due to the fact that she was playing a prayer with her heart as her fingers touched the keys, and that instead of a preliminary to a fairy revel the music told the story of a great soul struggle, and reached hearts as it tinkled and rolled and swelled on to the end. It may be, too, the Fiddling Boss was more in sympathy that night with his accompanist than was the other violinist, and that was why his old fiddle brought forth such weird and tender tones.

Almost to the end, with her heart sobbing its trouble to the keys, Margaret looked up sadly, and there, straight before her through a hole in the curtain made by some rash youth to glimpse the audience, or perhaps even put there by the owner of the nose itself, she saw the little, freckled, turned-up member belonging to Bud's face. A second more and a big, bright eye appeared and solemnly winked at her twice, as if to say, "Don't you worry, it's all right!"

She almost started from the stool, but kept her head enough to finish the chords, and as they died away she heard a hoarse whisper in Bud's familiar voice:

"Whoop her up, Miss Earle. We're all ready. Raise the curtain there, you guy. Let her rip. Everything's okay."

With a leap of light into her eyes Margaret turned the leaves of the music and went on playing as she should have done if nothing had been the matter. Bud was there, anyway, and that somehow cheered her heart. Perhaps Gardley had come or Bud had heard of him—and yet, Bud didn't know he had been missing, for Bud had been away himself.

Nevertheless, she summoned courage to go on playing. Nick Bottom wasn't in this first scene, anyway, and this would have to be gone through with somehow. By this time she was in a state of daze that only thought from moment to moment. The end of the evening seemed to her as far off as the end of a hale old age seems at the beginning of a lifetime. Somehow she must walk through it, but she could only see a step at a time.

Once she turned half sideways to the audience and gave a hurried glance about, catching sight of Fudge's round, near-sighted face, and that gave her encouragement. Perhaps the others were somewhere present. If only she could get a chance to whisper to someone from the camp and ask when they had seen Gardley last! But there was no chance, of course!

The curtain was rapidly raised and the opening scene of the play began, the actors going through their parts with marvelous ease and dexterity, and the audience silent and charmed, watching those strangers in queer costumes that were their own children, marching around there at their ease and talking weird language that was not used in any class of society they had ever come across on sea or land before.

But Margaret, watching her music as best she could, and playing mechanically rather than with her mind, could not tell if they were doing well or ill, so loudly did her heart pound out her fears—so stoutly did her heart proclaim her trust.

And thus, without a flaw or mistake in the execution of the work she had struggled so hard to teach them, the first scene of the first act drew to its close, and Margaret struck the final chords of the music and felt that in another minute she must reel and fall from that piano stool. And yet she sat and watched the curtain fall with a face as controlled as if nothing at all were the matter.

A second later she suddenly knew that to sit in that place calmly another second was a physical impossibility. She must get somewhere to the air at once or her senses would desert her.

With a movement so quick that no one could have anticipated it, she slipped from her piano stool, under the curtain to the stage, and was gone before the rest of the orchestra had noticed her intention.

Chapter 24

Since the day that he had given Margaret his promise to make good, Gardley had been regularly employed by Mr. Rogers, looking after important matters of his ranch. Before that he had lived a free and easy life, working a little now and then when it seemed desirable to him, having no set interest in life, and only endeavoring from day to day to put as far as possible from his mind the life he had left behind him. Now, however, all things became different. He brought to his service the keen mind and ready ability that had made him easily a winner at any game, a brave rider, and a never-failing shot. Within a few days Rogers saw what material was in him, and as the weeks went by grew to depend more and more upon his advice in matters.

There had been much trouble with cattle thieves, and so far no method of stopping the loss or catching the thieves had been successful. Rogers finally put the matter into Gardley's hands to carry out his own ideas, with the men of the camp at his command to help him, the camp itself being only a part of Rogers's outlying possessions, one of several such centers from which he worked his growing interests.

Gardley had formulated a scheme by which he hoped eventually to get hold of the thieves and put a stop to the trouble, and he was pretty sure he was on the right track, but his plan required slow and cautious work, that the enemy might not suspect and take to cover. He had for several weeks suspected that the thieves made their headquarters in the region of old Ouida's cabin, and made their raids from that direction. It was for this reason that of late the woods and trails in the vicinity of Ouida's had been secretly patrolled day and night, and every passerby taken note of, until Gardley knew just who were the frequenters of that way and mostly what was their business. This work was done alternately by the men of the Wallis camp and two other camps, Gardley being the head of all and carrying all responsibility, and not the least of that young man's offenses in the eyes of Rosa Rogers was that he was so constantly at her father's house and yet never lifted an eye in admiration of her pretty face. She longed to humiliate him, and through him to humiliate Margaret, who presumed to interfere with her flirtations, for it was a bitter thing to Rosa that Forsythe had no eyes for her when Margaret was about.

When the party from the fort rode homeward that Sunday after the service at the schoolhouse, Forsythe lingered behind to talk to Margaret, and then rode around by the Rogers place, where Rosa and he had long ago established a trysting place.

Rosa was watching for his passing, and he stopped a half hour or so to talk to her. During this time she casually disclosed to Forsythe some of the plans she had overhead Gardley laying before her father. Rosa had very little idea of the importance of Gardley's work to her father, or perhaps she would not have so readily prattled of his affairs. Her main idea was to pay back Gardley for his part in her humiliation with Forsythe. She suggested that it would be a great thing if Gardley could be prevented from being at the play Tuesday evening, and told what she had overheard him saying to her father merely to show Forsythe how easy it would be to have Gardley detained on Tuesday. Forsythe questioned Rosa keenly. Did she know whom they suspected? Did she know what they were planning to do to catch them, and when?

Rosa innocently enough disclosed all she knew, little thinking how dishonorable to her father it was, and perhaps caring as little, for Rosa had ever been a spoiled child, accustomed to subordinating everything within reach to her own uses. As for Forsythe, he would just as soon get rid of Gardley, and he saw more possibilities in Rosa's suggestion than she had seen herself. When at last he bade Rosa good night and rode unobtrusively back to the trail he was already formulating a plan.

It was, therefore, quite in keeping with his wishes that he should meet a dark-browed rider a few miles farther up the trail whose identity he had happened to learn a few days before.

Now Forsythe would, perhaps, not have dared to enter into any compact against Gardley with men of such ill repute had it been a matter of money and bribery, but, armed as he was with information valuable to the criminals, he could so word his suggestion about Gardley's detention as to make the hunted men think it to their advantage to catch Gardley sometime the next day when he passed their way and imprison him for a while. This would appear to be but a friendly bit of advice from a disinterested party deserving a good turn sometime in the future and not get Forsythe into any trouble. As such it was received by the wretch, who clutched at the information with ill-concealed delight and rode away into the twilight like a serpent threading his secret, gliding way among the darkest places, scarcely rippling the air, so stealthily did he pass.

As for Forsythe, he rode blithely to the Temple ranch, with no thought of the forces he had set going, his life as yet one round of trying to please himself at others' expense, if need be, but please himself, *anyway,* with whatever amusement the hour afforded.

At home in the East, where his early life had been spent, a splendid girl awaited his dilatory letters and set herself patiently to endure the months of separation until he should have attained a home and a living and be ready for her to come to him.

In the South, where he had idled six months before he went west, another lovely girl cherished mementoes of his tarrying and wrote him loving letters in reply to his occasional erratic epistles.

Out on the Californian shore a girl with whom he had traveled west in her uncle's luxurious private car, with a gay party of friends and relatives, cherished fond hopes of a visit he had promised to make her during the winter.

Innumerable maidens of this world, wise in the wisdom that crushes hearts, remembered him with a sigh now and then, but held no illusions concerning his kind.

Pretty little Rosa Rogers cried her eyes out every time he cast a languishing look at her teacher, and several of the ladies of the fort sighed that the glance of his eye and the gentle pressure of his hand could only be a passing joy. But the gay Lothario passed on his way as yet without a scratch on the hard enamel of his heart, till one wondered if it were a heart, indeed, or perhaps only a metal imitation. But girls like Margaret Earle, though they sometimes were attracted by him, invariably distrusted him. He was like a beautiful spotted snake that was often caught menacing something precious, but you could put him down anywhere after punishment or imprisonment and he would slide on his same slippery way and still be a spotted, deadly snake.

When Gardley left the camp that Monday morning following the walk home with Margaret from the Sabbath service, he fully intended to be back at the schoolhouse Monday by the time the afternoon rehearsal began. His plans were so laid that he thought relays from other camps were to guard the suspected ground for the next three days and he could be free. It had been a part of the information that Forsythe had given the stranger that Gardley would likely pass a certain lonely crossing of the trail at about three o'clock that afternoon, and, had that arrangement been carried out, the men who lay in wait for him would doubtless have been pleased to have their plans mature so easily, but they would not have been pleased long, for Gardley's men were so near at hand at that time, watching that very spot with eyes and ears and long-distance glasses, that their chief would soon have been rescued and the captors be themselves the captured.

But the men from the farther camp, called "Lone Fox" men, did not arrive on time, perhaps through some misunderstanding, and Gardley and Kemp and their men had to do double time. At last, later in the afternoon, Gardley volunteered to go to Lone Fox and bring back the men.

As he rode his thoughts were of Margaret, and he was seeing again the look of gladness in her eyes when she found he had not gone yesterday, feeling again the thrill of her hands in his, the trust of her smile! It was incredible, wonderful, that God had sent a veritable angel into the wilderness to bring him to himself, and now he was wondering, could it be that there was really hope that he could ever make good enough to dare to ask her to marry him. The sky and the air were rare, but his thoughts were rarer still, and his soul was lifted up with joy. He was earning good wages now. In two more weeks he would have enough to pay back the paltry sum for the lack of which he had fled from his old home and come to the wilderness. He would go back, of course, and straighten out the old score. Then what? Should be stay in the East and go back to the old business wherewith he had hoped to make his name honored and gain wealth, or should he return to this wild, free land again and start anew?

His mother was dead. Perhaps if she had lived and cared he would have made good in the first place. His sisters were both married to wealthy men and not deeply interested in him. He had disappointed and mortified them; their lives were filled with social duties; they had never missed him. His father had been dead many years. As for his uncle, his mother's brother, whose heir he was to have been before he got himself into disgrace, he decided not to go near him. He would stay as long as he must to undo the wrong he had done. He would call on his sisters and then come back; come back and let Margaret decide what she wanted him to do—that is, if she would consent to link her life with one who had been once a failure. Margaret! How wonderful she was! If Margaret said he ought to go back and be a lawyer, he would go—yes, even if he had to enter his uncle's office as an underling to do it. His soul loathed the idea, but he would do it for Margaret, if she thought it best. And so he mused as he rode!

When the Lone Fox camp was reached and the men sent out on their belated task, Gardley decided not to go with them back to meet Kemp and the other men, but sent word to Kemp that he had gone the shortcut to Ashland, hoping to get to a part of the evening rehearsal yet.

Now that shortcut led him to the lonely crossing of the trail much sooner than Kemp and the others could reach it from the rendezvous, and there in cramped positions, and with much unnecessary cursing and impatience, four strong masked men had been concealed for four long hours.

Through the stillness of the twilight rode Gardley, thinking of Margaret, and for once utterly off his guard. His long day's work was done, and though he had not been able to get back when he planned, he was free now, free until the day after tomorrow. He would go at once to her and see if there was anything she wanted him to do.

Then, as if to help along his enemies, he began to hum a song, his clear, high voice reaching keenly to the ears of the men in ambush:

> "Oh, the time is long, mavourneen,
> Till I come again, O mavourneen—"

"And the toime 'll be longer thun iver, oim thinkin', ma purty little voorneen!" said an unmistakable voice of Erin through the gathering dusk.

Gardley's horse stopped and Gardley's hand went to his revolver, while his other hand lifted the silver whistle to his lips, but four guns bristled at him in the twilight, the whistle was knocked from his lips before his breath had even reached it, someone caught his arms from behind, and his own weapon was wrenched from his hand as it went off. The cry which he at once sent forth was stifled in its first whisper in a great muffling garment flung over his head and drawn tightly about his neck. He was in a fair way to strangle, and his vigorous efforts at escape were useless in the hands of so many. He might have been plunged at once into a great abyss of limitless, soundless depths, so futile did any resistance seem. And so, as it was useless to struggle, he lay like one dead and put all his powers into listening. But neither could he hear much, muffled as he was, and bound hand and foot now, with a gag in his mouth and little care taken whether he could even breathe.

They were leading him off the trail and up over rough ground, so much he knew, for the horse stumbled and jolted and strained to carry him. To keep his whirling senses alive and alert he tried to think where they might be leading him, but the darkness and the suffocation dulled his powers. He wondered idly if his men would miss him and come back when they got home to search for him, and then remembered with a pang that they would think him safely in Ashland, helping Margaret. They would not be alarmed if he did not return that night, for they would suppose he had stopped at Rogers's on the way and perhaps stayed all night, as he had done once or twice before. *Margaret!* When should he see Margaret now? What would she think?

And then he collapsed.

When he came somewhat to himself he was in a close, stifling room where candlelight from a distance threw weird shadows over the adobe walls. The witchlike voices of a woman and a girl in harsh, cackling laughter, half suppressed, were not far away, and someone, whose face was covered, was holding a glass to his lips. The smell was sickening, and he remembered that he hated the thought of liquor. It did not fit with those who companied with Margaret. He had never cared for it, and had resolved never to taste it again. But whether he chose or not, the liquor was poured down his throat. Huge hands held him and forced it, and he was still bound and too weak to resist, even if he had realized the necessity.

The liquid burned its way down his throat and seethed into his brain, and a great darkness, mingled with men's wrangling voices and much cursing, swirled about him like some furious torrent of angry waters that finally submerged his consciousness. Then came deeper darkness and a blank relief from pain.

Hours passed. He heard sounds sometimes, and dreamed dreams which he could not tell from reality. He saw his friends with terror written on their faces, while he lay apathetically and could not stir. He saw tears on Margaret's face, and once he was sure he heard Forsythe's voice in contempt: "Well, he seems to be well occupied for the present! No danger of his waking up for a while!" and then the voices all grew dim and far away again, and only an old crone and the harsh girl's whisper over him; and then Margaret's tears—tears that fell on his heart from far above, and seemed to melt out all his early sins and flood him with their horror. Tears and the consciousness that he ought to be doing something for Margaret now and could not. Tears—and more darkness!

Chapter 25

When Margaret arrived behind the curtain she was aware of many cries and questions hurled at her like an avalanche, but, ignoring them all, she sprang past the noisy, excited group of young people, darted through the dressing room to the right and out into the night and coolness. Her head was swimming, and things went black before her eyes. She felt that her breath was going, going, and she must get to the air.

But when she passed the hot wave of the schoolroom, and the sharp air of the night struck her face, consciousness seemed to turn and come back into her again, for there over her head was the wideness of the vast, starry Arizona night, and there, before her, in Nick Bottom's somber costume, eating one of the chicken sandwiches that Mrs. Tanner had sent down to her, stood Gardley! He was pale and shaken from his recent experience, but he was undaunted, and when he saw Margaret coming toward him through the doorway with her soul in her eyes and her spirit all aflame with joy and relief, he came to meet her under the stars, and, forgetting everything else, just folded her gently in his arms!

It was a most astonishing thing to do, of course, right there outside the dressing room door, with the curtain just about to rise on the scene and Gardley's wig was not on yet. He had not even asked nor obtained permission. But the soul sometimes grows impatient waiting for the lips to speak, and Margaret felt her trust had been justified and her heart had found its home. Right there behind the schoolhouse, out in the great wide night, while the crowded, clamoring audience waited for them, and the young actors grew frantic, they plighted their troth, his lips upon hers, and with not a word spoken.

Voices from the dressing room roused them. "Come in quick, Mr. Gardley; it's time for the curtain to rise, and everybody is ready.

Where on earth has Miss Earle vanished? Miss Earle! Oh, Miss Earle!"

There was a rush to the dressing room to find the missing ones, but Bud, as ever, present where was the most need, stood with his back to the outside world in the door of the dressing room and called loudly:

"They're comin', all right. Go on! Get to your places. Miss Earle says to get to your places."

The two in the darkness groped for each other's hands as they stood suddenly apart, and with one quick pressure and a glance hurried in. There was not any need for words. They understood, these two, and trusted.

With her cheeks glowing now, and her eyes like two stars, Margaret fled across the stage and took her place at the piano again, just as the curtain began to be drawn, and Forsythe, who had been slightly uneasy at the look on her face as she left them, wondered now and leaned forward to tell her how well she was looking.

He kept his honeyed phrase to himself, however, for she was not heeding him. Her eyes were on the rising curtain, and Forsythe suddenly remembered that this was the scene in which Jed was to have appeared—and Jed had a broken leg! What had Margaret done about it? It was scarcely a part that could be left out. Why hadn't he thought of it sooner and offered to take it? He could have bluffed it out somehow—he had heard it so much—made up words where he couldn't remember them all, and it would have been a splendid opportunity to do some real lovemaking with Rosa. Why hadn't he thought of it? Why hadn't Rosa? Perhaps she hadn't heard about Jed soon enough to suggest it.

The curtain was fully open now, and Bud's voice as Peter Quince, a trifle high and cracked with excitement, broke the stillness, while the awed audience gazed upon this new, strange world presented to them.

"Is all our company here?" lilted out Bud, excitely, and Nick Bottom replied with Gardley's voice:

"You were best to call them generally, man by man, according to the script."

Forsythe turned deadly white. Jasper Kemp, whose keen eye was upon him, saw it through the tan, saw his lips go pale and purple points of fear start in his eyes, as he looked and looked again, and could not believe his senses.

Furtively he darted a glance around, like one about to steal away; then, seeing Jasper Kemp's eyes upon him, settled back with a strained look upon his face. Once he stole a look at Margaret and caught her face all transfigured with great joy, looked again and felt rebuked somehow by the pureness of her maiden joy and trust.

Not once had she turned her eyes to his. He was forgotten, and somehow he knew the look he would get if she should see him. It would be contempt and scorn that would burn his very soul. It is only a maid now and then to whom it is given thus to pierce and bruise the soul of a man who plays with love and trust and womanhood for selfishness. Such a woman never knows her power. She punishes all unconscious to herself. It was so that Margaret Earle, without being herself aware, and by her very indifference and contempt, showed the little soul of this puppet man to himself.

He stole away at last when he thought no one was looking, and reached the back of the schoolhouse at the open door of the girls' dressing room, where he knew Titania would be posing in between the acts. He beckoned her to his side and began to question her in quick, eager, almost angry tones, as if the failure of their plans were her fault. Had her father been at home all day? Had anything happened—anyone been there? Did Gardley come? Had there been any report from the men? Had that short, thickset Scotchman with the ugly grin been there? She must remember that she was the one to suggest the scheme in the first place, and it was her business to keep a watch. There was no telling now what might happen. He turned, and there stood Jasper Kemp close to his elbow, his short stature drawn to its full, his thickset shoulders squaring themselves, his ugly grin standing out in bold relief, menacingly, in the night.

The young man let forth some words not in a gentleman's code, and turned to leave the frightened girl, who by this time was almost crying, but Jasper Kemp kept pace with Forsythe as he walked.

"Was you addressing me?" he asked, politely, "because I could tell you a few things a sight more appropriate for you than what you just handed to me."

Forsythe hurried around to the front of the schoolhouse, making no reply.

"Nice, pleasant evening to be *free,*" went on Jasper Kemp, looking up at the stars. "Rather unpleasant for some folks that have to be shut up in jail."

Forsythe wheeled upon him. "What do you mean?" he demanded, angrily, albeit he was white with fear.

"Oh, nothing much," drawled Jasper, affably. "I was just thinking how much pleasanter it was to be a free man than shut up in prison on a night like this. It's so much healthier, you know."

Forsythe looked at him a moment, a kind of panic of intelligence growing in his face; then he turned and went toward the back of the schoolhouse, where he had left his horse some hours before.

"Where are you going?" demanded Jasper. "It's 'most time you went back to your fiddling, ain't it?"

But Forsythe answered him not a word. He was mounting his horse hurriedly—his horse, which, all unknown to him, had been many miles since he last rode him.

"You think you have to go, then?" said Jasper, deprecatingly. "Well, now, that's a pity, seeing you was fiddling so nice an' all. Shall I tell them you've gone for your health?"

Thus recalled, Forsythe stared at his tormentor wildly for a second. "Tell her—tell her"—he muttered, hoarsely—"tell her I've been taken suddenly ill." And he was off on a wild gallop toward the fort.

"I'll tell her you've gone for your health!" called Jasper Kemp, with his hands to his mouth like a megaphone. "I reckon he won't return again very soon, either," he chuckled. "This country's better off without such pests as him an' that measley parson." Then, turning, he beheld Titania, the queen of the fairies, white and frightened, staring wildly into the starry darkness after the departed rider. "Poor little fool!" he muttered under his breath as he looked at the girl and turned away. "Poor, pretty little fool!" Suddenly he stepped up to her side and touched her white-clad shoulder gently. "Don't you go for to care, lassie," he said in a tender tone. "He ain't worth a tear from your pretty eye. He ain't fit to wipe your feet on—your pretty wee feet!"

But Rosa turned angrily and stamped her foot.

"Go away! You bad old man!" she shrieked. "Go away! I shall tell my father!" And she flouted herself into the schoolhouse.

Jasper stood looking ruefully after her, shaking his head. "The little de'il!" he said aloud, "the poor, pretty little de'il. She'll get her dues aplenty afore she's done." And Jasper went back to the play.

Meantime, inside the schoolhouse, the play went gloriously on to the finish, and Gardley as Nick Bottom took the house by storm. Poor absent Jed's father, sent by the sufferer to report it all, stood at the back of the house while tears of pride and disappointment rolled down his cheeks—pride that Jed had been so well represented, disappointment that it couldn't have been his son up there playacting like that.

The hour was late when the play was over, and Margaret stood at last in front of the stage to receive the congratulations of the entire countryside, while the young actors posed and laughed and chattered excitedly, then went away by twos and threes, their tired, happy voices sounding back along the road. The people from the fort had been the first to surge around Margaret with their eager congratulations and gushing sentiments: "So sweet, my dear! So perfectly wonderful. You really have got some dandy actors!" And, "Why don't you try something lighter—something simpler, don't you know. Something really popular that these poor people could understand and appreciate? A little farce! I could help you pick one out!"

And all the while they gushed Jasper Kemp and his men, grim and forbidding, stood like a cordon drawn about her to protect her, with Gardley in the center, just behind her, as though he had a right there and meant to stay, till at last the fort people hurried away and the schoolhouse grew suddenly empty with just those two and the eight men behind, and by the door Bud, talking to Pop and Mom Wallis in the buckboard outside.

Amid this admiring bodyguard at last Gardley took Margaret home. Perhaps she wondered a little that they all went along, but she laid it to their pride in the play and their desire to talk it over.

They had sent Mom and Pop Wallis home horseback, after all, and put Margaret and Gardley in the buckboard, Margaret never dreaming that it was because Gardley was not fit to walk. Indeed, he did not realize himself why they all stuck so closely to him. He had lived through so much since Jasper and his men had burst into his prison and freed him, bringing him in hot haste to the schoolhouse, with Bud wildly riding ahead. But it was enough for him to sit beside Margaret in the sweet night and remember how she had come out to him under the stars. Her hand lay beside him on the seat, and without intending it his own brushed it. Then he laid his gently, reverently, down upon hers with a quiet pressure, and her smaller fingers thrilled and nestled in his grasp.

In the shadow of a big tree beside the house he bade her good-bye, the men busying themselves with turning about the buckboard noisily, and Bud discreetly taking himself to the back door to get one of the men a drink of water.

"You have been suffering in some way," said Margaret, with sudden intuition, as she looked up into Gardley's face. "You have been in peril, somehow—"

"A little," he answered, lightly. "I'll tell you about it tomorrow. I mustn't keep the men waiting now. I shall have a great deal to tell you tomorrow—if you will let me. Good night, *Margaret!*" Their hands lingered in a clasp, and then he rode away with his bodyguard.

But Margaret did not have to wait until the morrow to hear the story, for Bud was just fairly bursting.

Mrs. Tanner had prepared a nice little supper—more cold chicken, pie, doughnuts, coffee, some of her famous marble cake, and preserves—and she insisted on Margaret's coming into the dining room and eating it, though the girl would much rather have gone with her happy heart up to her own room by herself.

Bud did not wait on ceremony. He began at once when Margaret was seated, even before his mother could get her properly waited on.

"Well, we had *some ride,* we sure did! The kid's a great old scout."

Margaret perceived that this was a leader. "Why, that's so, what became of you, William? I hunted everywhere for you. Things were pretty strenuous there for a while, and I needed you dreadfully."

"Well, I know," Bud apologized. "I'd oughta let you know before I went, but there wasn't time. You see, I had to pinch that guy's horse to go, and I knew it was just a chance if we could get back, anyway,

but I had to take it. You see, if I could 'a gone right to the cabin it
would have been a dead cinch, but I had to ride to camp for the men,
and then, taking the short trail across, it was some ride to Ouida's
cabin!"

Mrs. Tanner stopped aghast as she was cutting a piece of dried-
apple pie for Margaret. "Now, Buddie—Mother's boy—you don't
mean to tell me *you* went to *Ouida's cabin?* Why, sonnie, that's an
awful place! Don't you know your pa told you he'd whip you if you
ever went on that trail?"

"I should worry, Ma! I *had* to go. They had Mr. Gardley tied up
there, and we had to go and get him rescued."

"*You* had to go, Buddie—now what could *you* do in that awful
place?" Mrs. Tanner was almost reduced to tears. She saw her off-
spring at the edge of perdition at once.

But Bud ignored his mother and went on with his tale. "You jest
oughta seen Jap Kemp's face when I told him what that guy said to
you! Some face, b'lieve me! He saw right through the whole thing,
too. I could see that! He ner the men hadn't had a bite o' supper yet;
they'd just got back from somewheres. They thought the kid was
over here all day helping you. He said yesterday when he left 'em
here's where he's a-comin' "—Bud's mouth was so full he could
hardly articulate—"an' when I told 'em, he jest blew his little whistle—like what they all carry—three times, and those men every one
jest stopped right where they was, whatever they was doin'. Long Bill
had the comb in the air gettin' ready to comb his hair, an' he left it
there and come away, and Big Jim never stopped to wipe his face on
the roller towel, he just let the wind dry it, and they all hustled on
their horses fast as ever they could and beat it after Jap Kemp. Jap,
he rode alongside o' me and asked me questions. He made me tell all
what the guy from the fort said over again, three or four times, and
then he ast what time he got to the schoolhouse, and whether the kid
had been there at all yest'iday ur t'day, and a lot of other questions,
and then he rode alongside each man and told him in just a few
words where we was goin' and what the guy from the fort had said.
Gee! but you'd oughta heard what the men said when he told 'em!
Gee! but they was some mad! Bimeby we came to the woods round

the cabin, and Jap Kemp made me stick alongside Long Bill, and he sent the men off in different directions all in a big circle, and waited till each man was in his place, and then we all rode hard as we could and came softly up round that cabin just as the sun was goin' down. Gee! but you'd oughta seen the scairt look on them women's faces; there was two of 'em—an old un an' a skinny-looking long-drink-o'-pump-water. I guess she was a girl. I don't know. Her eyes looked real old. There was only three men in the cabin, the rest was off somewheres. They wasn't looking for anybody to come that time o' day, I guess. One of the men was sick on a bunk in the corner. He had his head tied up, and his arm, like he'd been shot, and the other two men came jumping up to the door with their guns, but when they saw how many men *we* had they looked awful scairt. *We* all had *our* guns out, too!—Jap Kemp gave me one to carry—" Bud tried not to swagger as he told this, but it was almost too much for him. "Two of our men held the horses, and all the rest of us got down and went into the cabin. Jap Kemp sounded his whistle and all our men done the same just as they went in the door—some kind of signals they have for the Lone Fox Camp! The two men in the doorway aimed straight at Jap Kemp and fired, but Jap was onto 'em and jumped one side, and our men fired, too, and we soon had 'em tied up and went in—that is, Jap and me and Long Bill went in, the rest stayed by the door—and it wasn't long 'fore their other men came riding back hot haste; they'd heard the shots, you know—and some more of *our* men—why, most twenty or thirty there was, I guess, altogether; some from Lone Fox Camp that was watching off in the woods came, and when we got outside again there they all were, like a big army. Most of the men belonging to the cabin was tied and harmless by that time, for our men took 'em one at a time as they came riding in. Two of 'em got away, but Jap Kemp said they couldn't go far without being caught, 'cause there was a watch out for 'em—they'd been stealing cattle long back something terrible. Well, so Jap Kemp and Long Bill and I went into the cabin after the two men that shot was tied with ropes we'd brung along, and handcuffs, and we went hunting for the kid. At first we couldn't find him at all. Gee! It was something fierce! And the old woman kep' a-crying and saying we'd kill her sick son, and she didn't know nothing about the man we was hunting for. But pretty soon I spied the kid's foot stickin' out from under the cot where the sick man was, and when I told Jap Kemp that sick man pulled out a gun he had under the blanket and aimed it right at me!'

"Oh, Mother's little Buddie!" whimpered Mrs. Tanner, with her apron to her eyes.

"*Aw, Ma,* cut it out! *He* didn't *hurt* me! The gun just went off crooked, and grazed Jap Kemp's hand a little, not much. Jap knocked it out of the sick man's hand just as he was pullin' the trigger. Say, Ma, ain't you got anymore of those cucumber pickles? It makes a man mighty hungry to do all that riding and shooting. Well, it certainly was something fierce— Say, Miss Earle, you take that last piece o' pie. Oh, g'wan! *Take* it! *You* worked hard. No, I don't want it, really! Well, if you won't take it *anyway,* I might eat it just to save it. Got any more coffee, Ma?"

But Margaret was not eating. Her face was pale and her eyes were starry with unshed tears, and she waited in patient but breathless suspense for the vagaries of the story to work out to the finish.

"Yes, it certainly was something fierce, that cabin," went on the narrator. "Why, Ma, it looked as if it had never been swept under that cot when we hauled the kid out. He was tied all up in knots, and great heavy ropes wound tight from his shoulders down to his ankles. Why, they were wound so tight they made great heavy welts in his wrists and shoulders and round his ankles when we took 'em off, and they had a great big rag stuffed into his mouth so he couldn't yell. Gee! It was something fierce! He was 'most dippy, too, but Jap Kemp brought him round pretty quick and got him outside in the air. That was the worst place I ever was in myself. You couldn't breathe, and the dirt was something fierce. It was like a pigpen. I sure was glad to get outdoors again. And then—well, the kid came around all right and they got him on a horse and gave him something out of a bottle Jap Kemp had, and pretty soon he could ride again. Why, you'd oughta seen his nerve. He just sat up there as straight, his lips all white yet and his eyes looked some queer; but he straightened up and he looked those rascals right in the eye, and told 'em a few things, and he gave orders to the other men from Lone Fox Camp what to do with 'em; and he had the two women disarmed—they had guns, too—and carried away, and the cabin nailed up, and a notice put on the door, and every one of those men were handcuffed—the sick one and all—and he told 'em to bring a wagon and put the sick one's cot in and take 'em over to Ashland to the jail, and he sent word to Mr. Rogers. Then we rode home and got to the schoolhouse just when you was playing the last chords of the ov'rtcher. Gee! It was some fierce ride and some *close shave!* The kid he hadn't had a thing to eat since Monday noon, and he was some hungry! I found a sandwich on the window of the dressing room, and he ate it while he got togged up—'course I told him 'bout Jed soon's we left the cabin, and Jap Kemp said he'd oughta go right home to camp after all he had been through, but he wouldn't, he said he was goin' to *act.* So 'course he had his way! But, gee! You could see it wasn't any cinch game for him! He 'most fell over every time after the curtain fell. You see, they gave him some kind of drugged whisky up there at the cabin that made his head feel queer. Say, he thinks that guy from the fort came in and looked at him once while he was asleep. He says it was only a dream, but I bet he did. Say, Ma, ain't you gonta give me another doughnut?"

In the quiet of her chamber at last, Margaret knelt before her window toward the purple, shadowy mountain under the starry dome, and gave thanks for the deliverance of Gardley, while Bud, in his comfortable loft, lay down to his well-earned rest and dreamed of pirates and angels and a hero who looked like the kid.

Chapter 26

The Sunday before Lance Gardley started east on his journey of reparation two strangers slipped quietly into the back of the school-house during the first hymn and sat down in the shadow by the door.

Margaret was playing the piano when they came in, and did not see them, and when she turned back to her Scripture lesson she had time for but the briefest of glances. She supposed they must be some visitors from the fort, as they were speaking to the captain's wife—who came over occasionally to the Sunday service, perhaps because it afforded an opportunity for a ride with one of the young officers. These occasional visitors who came for amusement and curiosity had ceased to trouble Margaret. Her real work was with the men and women and children who loved the services for their own sake, and she tried as much as possible to forget outsiders. So, that day everything went on just as usual, Margaret, putting her heart into the prayer, the simple, storylike reading of the Scripture, and the other story-sermon which followed it. Gardley sang unusually well at the close, a wonderful bit from an oratorio that he and Margaret had been practicing.

But when toward the close of the little vesper service Margaret gave opportunity, as she often did, for others to take part in sentence prayers, one of the strangers from the back of the room stood up and began to pray. And such a prayer! Heaven seemed to bend low, and earth to kneel and beseech as the stranger-man, with a face like an archangel, and a body of an athlete clothed in a brown flannel shirt and khakis, besought the Lord of heaven for a blessing on this gathering and on the leader of this little company who had so wonderfully led them to see the Christ and their need of salvation through the lesson of the day. And it did not need Bud's low-breathed whisper, "The missionary!" to tell Margaret who he was. His face told her. His prayer thrilled her, and his strong, young, true voice made her sure that here was a man of God in truth.

When the prayer was over and Margaret stood once more shyly facing her audience, she could scarcely keep the tremble out of her voice:

"Oh," said she, casting aside ceremony, "if I had known the missionary was here I should not have dared to try and lead this meeting today. Won't you please come up here and talk to us for a little while now, Mr. Brownleigh?"

At once he came forward eagerly, as if each opportunity were a pleasure. "Why, surely, I want to speak a word to you, just to say how glad I am to see you all, and to experience what a wonderful teacher you have found since I went away, but I wouldn't have missed this meeting today for all the sermons I ever wrote or preached. You don't need any more sermon than the remarkable story you've just been listening to, and I've only one word to add: and that is, that I've found since I went away that Jesus Christ, the only begotten Son of God, is just the same Jesus to me today that He was the last time I spoke to you. He is just as ready to forgive your sin, to comfort you in sorrow, to help you in temptation, to raise your body in the resurrection, and to take you home to a mansion in His Father's house as He was the day He hung upon the cross to save your soul from death. I've found I can rest just as securely upon the Bible as the word of God as when I first tested its promises. Heaven and earth may pass away, but His Word shall *never* pass away."

"Go to it!" said Jasper Kemp under his breath in the tone some men say "Amen!" and his brows were drawn as if he were watching a battle. Margaret couldn't help wondering if he were thinking of the Reverend Frederick West just then.

When the service was over the missionary brought his wife forward to Margaret, and they loved each other at once. Just another sweet girl like Margaret. She was lovely, with a delicacy of feature that betokened the highborn and highbred, but dressed in a dainty khaki riding costume, if that uncompromising fabric could ever be called dainty. Margaret, remembering it afterward, wondered what it had been that gave it that unique individuality, and decided it was perhaps a combination of cut and finish and little dainty accessories. A bit of creamy lace at the throat of the rolling collar, a touch of golden-brown velvet in a golden clasp, the flash of a wonderful jewel on her finger, the modeling of the small, brown cap with its suede band—all set the little woman apart and made her fit to enter any well-dressed company of riders in some great city park or fashionable drive. Yet here in the wilderness she was not overdressed.

The eight men from the camp stood in solemn row, waiting to be recognized, and behind them, abashed and grinning with embarrassment, stood Pop and Mom Wallis, Mom with her new gray bonnet glorifying her old face till the missionary's wife had to look twice to be sure who she was.

"And now, surely, Hazel, we must have these dear people come over and help us with the singing sometimes. Can't we try something right now?" said the missionary, looking first at his wife and then at Margaret and Gardley. "This man is a newcomer since I went away, but I'm mighty sure he is the right kind, and I'm glad to welcome him—or perhaps I would better ask if he will welcome me?" And with his rare smile the missionary put out his hand to Gardley, who took it with an eager grasp. The two men stood looking at each other for a moment, as rare men, rarely met, sometimes do even on a sinful earth, and after that clasp and that look they turned away, brothers for life.

That was a most interesting song rehearsal that followed. It would be rare to find four voices like those even in a cultivated musical center, and they blended as if they had been made for one another. The men from the bunkhouse and a lot of other people silently dropped again into their seats to listen as the four sang on. The missionary took the bass, and his wife the alto, and the four made music worth listening to. The rare and lovely thing about it was that they sang to souls, not alone for ears, and so their music, classical though it was and of the highest order, appealed keenly to the hearts of these rough men, and made them feel that heaven had opened for them, as once before for untaught shepherds, and let down a ladder of angelic voices.

"I shall feel better about leaving you out here while I am gone, since they have come," said Gardley that night when he was bidding Margaret good night. "I couldn't bear to think there were none of your own kind about you. The others are devoted and would do for you with their lives if need be, as far as they know, but I like you to have *real friends*—real *Christian* friends. This man is what I call a Christian. I'm not sure but he is the first minister that I have ever come close to who has impressed me as believing what he preaches, and living it. I suppose there are others. I haven't known many. That man West that was here when you came was a mistake!"

"He didn't even preach much," smiled Margaret, "so how could he live it? This man is real. And there are others. Oh, I have known a lot of them that are living lives of sacrifice and loving service and are yet just as strong and happy and delightful as if they were millionaires. But they are the men who have not thrown away their Bibles and their Christ. They believe every promise in God's Word, and rest on them day by day, testing them and proving them over and over. I wish you knew my father!"

"I am going to," said Gardley, proudly. "I am going to him just as soon as I have finished my business and straightened out my affairs, and I am going to tell him *everything*—with your permission, Margaret!"

"Oh, how beautiful!" cried Margaret, with happy tears in her eyes. "To think you are going to see Father and Mother. I have wanted them to know the real you. I couldn't half *tell* you, the real you, in a letter!"

"Perhaps they won't look on me with your sweet blindness, dear," he said, smiling tenderly down on her. "Perhaps they will see only my dark, past life—for I mean to tell your father everything. I'm not going to have any skeletons in the closet to cause pain hereafter. Perhaps your father and mother will not feel like giving their daughter to me after they know. Remember, I realize just what a rare prize she is."

"No, Father is not like that, Lance," said Margaret, with her rare smile lighting up her happy eyes. "Father and Mother will understand."

"But if they should not?" There was the shadow of sadness in Gardley's eyes as he asked the question.

"I belong to you, dear, anyway," she said, with sweet surrender. "I trust you though the whole world were against you!"

For answer Gardley took her in his arms, a look of awe upon his face, and, stooping, laid his lips upon hers in tender reverence.

"Margaret—you wonderful Margaret!" he said. "God has blessed me more than other men in sending you to me! With His help I will be worthy of you!"

Three days more and Margaret was alone with her school work, her two missionary friends thirty miles away, her eager watching for the mail to come, her faithful attendant, Bud, and for comfort the purple mountain with its changing glory in the distance.

A few days before Gardley left for the East he had been offered a position by Rogers as general manager of his estate at a fine salary, and after consultation with Margaret he decided to accept it, but the question of their marriage they had left by common consent unsettled until Gardley should return and be able to offer his future wife a record made as fair and clean as human effort could make it after human mistakes had unmade it. As Margaret worked and waited, wrote her charming letters to Father and Mother and lover, and thought her happy thoughts with only the mountain for confidant, she did not plan for the future except in a dim and dreamy way. She would make those plans with Gardley when he returned. Probably they must wait some time before they could be married. Gardley would have to earn some money, and she must earn, too. She must keep the Ashland School for another year. It had been rather understood, when she came out, that if at all possible she would remain two years at least. It was hard to think of not going home for the summer vacation, but the trip cost a great deal and was not to be thought of. There was already a plan suggested to have a summer session of the school, and if that went through, of course she must stay right in Ashland. It was hard to think of not seeing her father and mother for another long year, but perhaps Gardley would be returning before the summer was over, and then it would not be so hard. However, she tried to put these thoughts out of her mind and do her work happily. It was incredible that Arizona should have become suddenly so blank and uninteresting since the departure of a man whom she had not known a few short months before.

Margaret had long since written to her father and mother about

Gardley's first finding her in the desert. The thing had become history and was not likely to alarm them. She had been in Arizona long enough to be acquainted with things, and they would not be always thinking of her as sitting on stray water tanks in the desert, so she told them about it, for she wanted them to know Gardley as he had been to her. The letters that had traveled back and forth between New York and Arizona had been full of Gardley, and still Margaret had not told her parents how it was between them. Gardley had asked that he might do that. Yet it had been a blind father and mother who had not long ago read between the lines of those letters and understood. Margaret fancied she detected a certain sense of relief in her mother's letters after she knew that Gardley had gone east. Were they worrying about him, she wondered, or was it just the natural dread of a mother to lose her child?

So Margaret settled down to school routine, and more and more made a confidant of Bud concerning little matters of the school. If it had not been for Bud at that time Margaret would have been lonely indeed.

Two or three times since Gardley left, the Brownleighs had ridden over to Sunday service, and once had stopped for a few minutes during the week on their way to visit some distant need. These occasions were a delight to Margaret, for Hazel Brownleigh was a kindred spirit. She was looking forward with pleasure to the visit she was to make them at the mission station as soon as school closed. She had been there once with Gardley before he left, but the ride was too long to go often, and the only escort available was Bud. Besides, she could not get away from school and the Sunday service at present, but it was pleasant to have something to look forward to.

Meantime the spring commencement was coming on and Margaret had her hands full. She had undertaken to inaugurate a real commencement with class day and as much form and ceremony as she could introduce in order to create a good school spirit, but such things are not done with the turn of a hand, and the young teacher sadly missed Gardley in all these preparations.

At this time Rosa Rogers was Margaret's particular thorn in the flesh.

Since the night that Forsythe had quit the play and ridden forth into the darkness Rosa had regarded her teacher with baleful eyes. Gardley, too, she hated, and was only waiting with smoldering wrath until her wild, ungoverned soul could take its revenge. She felt that but for those two Forsythe would still have been with her.

Margaret, realizing the passionate, untaught nature of the motherless girl and her great need of a friend to guide her, made attempt after attempt to reach and befriend her, but every attempt was met with repulse and the sharp word of scorn. Rosa had been too long the petted darling of a father who was utterly blind to her faults to be other than spoiled. Her own way was the one thing that ruled her. By her will she had ruled every nurse and servant about the place, and wheedled her father into letting her do anything the whim prompted. Twice her father, through the advice of friends, had tried the experiment of sending her away to school, once to an eastern finishing school, and once to a convent on the Pacific Coast, only to have her return shortly by request of the school, more willful than when she had gone away. And now she ruled supreme in her father's home, disliked by most of the servants save those whom she chose to favor because they could be made to serve her purposes. Her father, engrossed in his business and away much of the time, was bound up in her and saw few of her faults. It is true that when a fault of hers did come to his notice, however, he dealt with it most severely, and grieved over it in secret, for the girl was much like the mother whose loss had emptied the world of its joy for him. But Rosa knew well how to manage her father and wheedle him, and also how to hide her own doings from his knowledge.

Rosa's eyes, dimples, pink cheeks, and coquettish little mouth were not idle in those days. She knew how to have every pupil at her feet and ready to obey her slightest wish. She wielded her power to its fullest extent as the summer drew near, and day after day saw a slow torture for Margaret. Some days the menacing air of insurrection fairly bristled in the room, and Margaret could not understand how some of her most devoted followers seemed to be in the forefront of battle, until one day she looked up quickly and caught the lynx-eyed glance of Rosa as she turned from smiling at the boys in the backseat. Then she understood. Rosa had cast her spell upon the boys, and they were acting under it and not of their own clear judgment. It was the world-old battle of sex, of woman against woman for the winning of the man to do her will. Margaret, using all the charm of her lovely personality to uphold standards of right, truth, purity, high living, and earnest thinking; Rosa striving with her impish beauty to lure them into *any* mischief so it foiled the other's purposes. And one day Margaret faced the girl alone, looking steadily into her eyes with sad, searching gaze, and almost a yearning to try to lead the pretty child to finer things.

"Rosa, why do you always act as if I were your enemy?" she said, sadly.

"Because you are!" said Rosa, with a toss of her independent head.

"Indeed I'm not, dear child," she said, putting out her hand to lay it on the girl's shoulder kindly. "I want to be your friend."

"I'm not a child!" snapped Rosa, jerking her shoulder angrily away; "and you can *never* be my friend, because I *hate* you!"

"Rosa, look here!" said Margaret, following the girl toward the door, the color rising in her cheeks and a desire growing in her heart to conquer this poor, passionate creature and win her for better things. "Rosa, I cannot have you say such things. Tell me why you hate me? What have I done that you should feel that way? I'm sure if we should talk it over we might come to some better understanding."

Rosa stood defiant in the doorway. "We could never come to any better understanding, Miss Earle," she declared in a cold, hard tone, "because I understand you now and I hate you. You tried your best to get my friend away from me, but you couldn't do it, and you would like to keep me from having any boyfriends at all, but you can't do that, either. You think you are very popular, but you'll find out I always do what I like, and you needn't try to stop me. I don't have to come to school unless I choose, and as long as I don't break your rules you have no complaint coming, but you needn't think you can pull the wool over my eyes the way you do the others by pretending to be friends. I won't be friends! I hate you!" And Rosa turned grandly and marched out of the schoolhouse.

Margaret stood gazing sadly after her and wondering if her failure here were her fault—if there was anything else she ought to have done—if she had let her personal dislike of the girl influence her conduct. She sat for some time at her desk, her chin in her hands, her eyes fixed on vacancy with a hopeless, discouraged expression in them, before she became aware of another presence in the room. Looking around quickly, she saw that Bud was sitting motionless at his desk, his forehead wrinkled in a fierce frown, his jaw set belligerently, and a look of such unutterable pity and devotion in his eyes that her heart warmed to him at once and a smile of comradeship broke over her face.

"Oh, William! Were you here? Did you hear all that? What do you suppose is the matter? Where have I failed?"

"You 'ain't failed anywhere! You should worry 'bout her! She's a nut! If she was a boy I'd punch her head for her! But seeing she's only a girl, *you should worry!* She always was the limit!"

Bud's tone was forcible. He was the only one of all the boys who never yielded to Rosa's charms, but sat in glowering silence when she exercised her powers on the school and created pandemonium for the teacher. Bud's attitude was comforting. It had a touch of manliness and gentleness about it quite unwonted for him. It suggested beautiful possibilities for the future of his character, and Margaret smiled tenderly.

"Thank you, dear boy!" she said, gently. "You certainly are a comfort. If everyone was as splendid as you are we should have a model school. But I do wish I could help Rosa. I can't see why she should hate me so! I must have made some big mistake with her in the first place to antagonize her."

"Naw!" said Bud, roughly. "No chance! She's just a *nut,* that's all. She's got a case on that Forsythe guy, the worst kind, and she's afraid somebody'll get him away from her, the poor stew, as if anybody would get a case on a tough guy like that! Gee! You should worry! Come on, let's take a ride over t' camp!"

With a sigh and a smile Margaret accepted Bud's consolations and went on her way, trying to find some manner of showing Rosa what a real friend she was willing to be. But Rosa continued obdurate and hateful, regarding her teacher with haughty indifference except when she was called upon to recite, which she did sometimes with scornful condescension, sometimes with pert perfection, and sometimes with saucy humor which convulsed the whole room. Margaret's patience was almost ceasing to be a virtue, and she meditated often whether she ought not to request that the girl be withdrawn from the school. Yet she reflected that it was a very short time now until commencement, and that Rosa had not openly defied any rules. It was merely a personal antagonism. Then, too, if Rosa were taken from the school there was really no other good influence in the girl's life at present. Day by day Margaret prayed about the matter and hoped that something would develop to make plain her way.

After much thought in the matter she decided to go on with her plans, letting Rosa have her place in the commencement program and her part in the class-day doings as if nothing were the matter. Certainly there was nothing laid down in the rules of a public school that proscribed a scholar who did not love her teacher. Why should the fact that one had incurred the hate of a pupil unfit that pupil for her place in her class so long as she did her duties? And Rosa did hers promptly and deftly, with a certain piquant originality that Margaret could not help but admire.

Sometimes, as the teacher cast a furtive look at the pretty girl working away at her desk, she wondered what was going on behind the lovely mask. But the look in Rosa's eyes, when she raised them, was both deep and sly.

Rosa's hatred was indeed deep-rooted. Whatever heart she had not frivoled away in willfulness had been caught and won by Forsythe, the first grown man who had ever dared to make real love to her. Her jealousy of Margaret was the most intense thing that had ever come into her life. To think of him looking at Margaret, talking to Margaret, smiling at Margaret, walking or riding with Margaret, was enough to send her writhing upon her bed in the darkness of a wakeful night. She would clench her pretty hands until the nails dug into the flesh and brought the blood. She would bite the pillow or the blankets with an almost fiendish clenching of her teeth upon them and mutter, as she did so: "I hate her! I *hate her!* I could *kill* her!"

The day her first letter came from Forsythe, Rosa held her head high and went about the school as if she were a princess royal and Margaret were the dust under her feet. Triumph sat upon her like a crown and looked forth regally from her eyes. She laid her hand upon her heart and felt the crackle of his letter inside her blouse. She dreamed with her eyes upon the distant mountain and thought of the tender names he had called her: "Little wild Rose of my heart," "No rose in all the world until you came," and a lot of other meaningful sentences. A real love letter all her own! No sharing him with any hateful teachers! He had implied in her letter that she was the only one of all the people in that region to whom he cared to write. He had said he was coming back someday to get her. Her young, wild heart throbbed exultantly, and her eyes looked forth their triumph malignantly. When he did come she would take care that he stayed close by her. No conceited teacher from the East should lure him from her side. She would prepare her guiles and smile her sweetest. She would wear fine garments from abroad, and show him she could far outshine that quiet, common Miss Earle, with all her airs. Yet to this end she studied hard. It was no part of her plan to be left behind at graduating-time. She would please her father by taking a prominent part in things and outdoing all the others. Then he would give her what she liked—jewels and silk dresses, and all the things a girl should have who had won a lover like hers.

The last busy days before commencement were especially trying for Margaret. It seemed as if the children were possessed with the very spirit of mischief, and she could not help but see that it was Rosa who, sitting demurely in her desk, was the center of it all. Only Bud's steady, frowning countenance of all that rollicking, roistering crowd kept loyalty with the really beloved teacher. For, indeed, they loved her, every one but Rosa, and would have stood by her to a man and girl when it really came to the pinch, but in a matter like a little bit of fun in these last few days of school, and when challenged to it by the school beauty who did not usually condescend to any but a few of the older boys, where was the harm? They were so flattered by Rosa's smiles that they failed to see Margaret's worn, weary wistfulness.

Bud, coming into the schoolhouse late one afternoon in search of her after the other scholars had gone, found Margaret with her head down upon the desk and her shoulders shaken with soundless sobs. He stood for a second silent in the doorway, gazing helplessly at her grief, then with the delicacy of one boy for another he slipped back outside the door and stood in the shadow, grinding his teeth.

"Gee!" he said, under his breath. "Oh, gee! I'd like to punch her fool head. I don't care if she is a girl! She needs it. Gee! if she was a boy wouldn't I settle her, the little darned mean sneak!"

His remarks, it is needless to say, did not have reference to his beloved teacher.

It was in the atmosphere everywhere that something was bound to happen if this strain kept up. Margaret knew it and felt utterly inadequate to meet it. Rosa knew it and was awaiting her opportunity. Bud knew it and could only stand and watch where the blow was to strike first and be ready to ward it off. In these days he wished fervently for Gardley's return. He did not know just what Gardley could do about "that little fool," as he called Rosa, but it would be a relief to be able to tell someone all about it. If he only dared leave he would go over and tell Jasper Kemp about it, just to share his burden with somebody. But as it was he must stick to the job for the present and bear his great responsibility, and so the days hastened by to the last Sunday before commencement, which was to be on Monday.

Chapter 27

Margaret had spent Saturday in rehearsals, so that there had been no rest for her. Sunday morning she slept late, and awoke from a troubled dream, unrested. She almost meditated whether she would not ask someone to read a sermon at the afternoon service and let her go on sleeping. Then a memory of the lonely old woman at the camp, and the men, who came so regularly to the service, roused her to effort once more, and she arose and tried to prepare a little something for them.

She came into the schoolhouse at the hour, looking exhausted, with dark circles under her eyes, and the loving eyes of Mom Wallis already in her front seat watched her keenly.

"It's time for *him* to come back," she said, in her heart. "She's gettin' peaked! I wisht he'd come!"

Margaret had hoped that Rosa would not come. The girl was not always there, but of late she had been quite regular, coming in late with her father just a little after the story had begun, and attracting attention by her smiles and bows and giggling whispers, which sometimes were so audible as to create quite a diversion from the speaker.

But Rosa came in early today and took a seat directly in front of Margaret, in about the middle of the house, fixing her eyes on her teacher with a kind of settled intention that made Margaret shrink as if from a danger she was not able to meet. There was something bright and hard and daring in Rosa's eyes as she stared unwinkingly, as if she had come to search out a weak spot for her evil purposes, and Margaret was so tired she wanted to lay her head down on her desk and cry. She drew some comfort from the reflection that if she should do so childish a thing she would be at once surrounded by a strong battalion of friends from the camp, who would shield her with their lives if necessary.

It was silly, of course, and she must control this choking in her throat, only how was she ever going to talk, with Rosa looking at her that way? It was like a nightmare pursuing her. She turned to the piano and kept them all singing for a while, so that she might pray in her heart and grow calm, and when, after her brief, earnest prayer, she lifted her eyes to the audience, she saw with intense relief that the Brownleighs were in the audience.

She started a hymn that they all knew, and when they were well in the midst of the first verse she slipped from the piano stool and walked swiftly down the aisle to Brownleigh's side.

"Would you please talk to them a little while?" she pleaded, wistfully. "I am so tired I feel as if I just couldn't, today."

Instantly Brownleigh followed her back to the desk and took her place, pulling out his little, worn Bible and opening it with familiar fingers to a beloved passage:

"Come unto me, all ye that labour and are heavy laden, and I will give you rest."

The words fell on Margaret's tired heart like balm, and she rested her head back against the wall and closed her eyes to listen. Sitting so away from Rosa's stare, she could forget for a while the absurd burdens that had got on her nerves, and could rest down hard upon her Saviour. Every word that the man of God spoke seemed meant just for her, and brought strength, courage, and new trust to her heart. She forgot the little crowd of other listeners and took the message to herself, drinking it in eagerly as one who has been a long time giving herself to others. When she moved to the piano again for the closing hymn she felt new strength within her to bear the trials of the week that were before her. She turned, smiling and brave, to speak to those who always crowded around to shake hands and have a word before leaving.

Hazel, putting a loving arm around her as soon as she could get up to the front, began to speak soothingly: "You poor, tired child!" she said; "you are almost worn to a frazzle. You need a big change, and I'm going to plan it for you just as soon as I possibly can. How would you like to go with us on our trip among the Indians? Wouldn't it be great? It'll be several days, depending on how far we go, but John wants to visit the Hopi reservation, if possible, and it'll be so interesting. They are a most fascinating people. We'll have a delightful trip, sleeping out under the stars, you know. Don't you just love it? I do. I wouldn't miss it for the world. I can't be sure, for a few days yet, when we can go, for John has to make a journey in the other direction first, and he isn't sure when he can return, but it might be this week. How soon can you come to us? How I wish we could take you right home with us tonight. You need to get away and rest. But your commencement is tomorrow, isn't it? I'm so sorry we can't be here, but this other matter is important, and John has to go early in the morning. Someone very sick who wants to see him before he dies— an old Indian who didn't know a thing about Jesus till John found him one day. I suppose you haven't anybody who could bring you over to us after your work is done here tomorrow night or Tuesday, have you? Well, we'll see if we can't find someone to send for you soon. There's an old Indian who often comes this way, but he's away buying cattle. Maybe John can think of a way we could send for you early in the week. Then you would be ready to go with us on the trip. You would like to go, wouldn't you?"

"Oh, so much!" said Margaret, with a sigh of wistfulness. "I can't think of anything pleasanter!"

Margaret turned suddenly, and there, just behind her, almost touching her, stood Rosa, that strange, baleful gleam in her eyes like a serpent who was biding her time, drawing nearer and nearer, knowing she had her victim where she could not move before she struck.

It was a strange fancy, of course, and one that was caused by sick nerves, but Margaret drew back and almost cried out, as if for someone to protect her. Then her strong common sense came to the rescue and she rallied and smiled at Rosa a faint little sorry smile. It was hard to smile at the bright, baleful face with the menace in the eyes.

Hazel was watching her. "You poor child! You're quite worn out! I'm afraid you're going to be sick."

"Oh, no," said Margaret, trying to speak cheerfully, "things have just got on my nerves, that's all. It's been a particularly trying time. I shall be all right when tomorrow night is over."

"Well, we're going to send for you very soon, so be ready!" and Hazel followed her husband, waving her hand in gay parting.

Rosa was still standing just behind her when Margaret turned back to her desk, and the younger girl gave her one last dagger look, a glitter in her eyes so sinister and vindictive that Margaret felt a shudder run through her whole body, and was glad that just then Rosa's father called to her that they must be starting home. Only one more day now of Rosa, and she would be done with her, perhaps forever. The girl was through the school course and was graduating. It was not likely she would return another year. Her opportunity was over to help her. She had failed. Why, she couldn't tell, but she had strangely failed, and all she asked now was not to have to endure the hard, cold, young presence any longer.

"Sick nerves, Margaret!" she said to herself. "Go home and go to bed. You'll be all right tomorrow!" And she locked the schoolhouse door and walked quietly home with the faithful Bud.

The past month had been a trying time also for Rosa. Young, wild, and motherless, passionate, willful and impetuous, she was finding life tremendously exciting just now. With no one to restrain her or warn her she was playing with forces that she did not understand.

She had subjugated easily all the boys in school, keeping them exactly where she wanted them for her purpose, and using methods that would have done credit to a woman of the world. But by far the greatest force in her life was her infatuation for Forsythe.

The letters had traveled back and forth many times between them since Forsythe wrote that first love letter. He found a whimsical pleasure in her deep devotion and naive readiness to follow as far as he cared to lead her. He realized that, young as she was, she was no innocent, which made the acquaintance all the more interesting. He, meantime, idled away a few months on the Pacific coast, making mild love to a rich California girl and considering whether or not he was ready yet to settle down.

In the meantime his correspondence with Rosa took on such a nature that his volatile, impulsive nature was stirred with a desire to see her again. It was not often that once out of sight he looked back to a victim, but Rosa had shown a daring and a spirit in her letters that sent a challenge to his sated senses. Moreover, the California heiress was going on a journey; besides, an old enemy of his who knew altogether too much of his past had appeared on the scene, and as Gardley had been removed from the Ashland vicinity for a time, Forsythe felt it might be safe to venture back again. There was always that pretty, spirited little teacher if Rosa failed to charm. But why should Rosa not charm? And why should he not yield? Rosa's father was a good sort and had all kinds of property. Rosa was her father's only heir. On the whole, Forsythe decided that the best move he could make next would be to return to Arizona. If things turned out well he might even think of marrying Rosa.

This was somewhat the train of thought that led Forsythe at last to write to Rosa that he was coming, throwing Rosa into a panic of joy and alarm. For Rosa's father had been most explicit about her ever going out with Forsythe again. It had been the most relentless command he had ever laid upon her, spoken in a tone she hardly ever disobeyed. Moreover, Rosa was fearfully jealous of Margaret. If Forsythe should come and begin to hang around the teacher Rosa felt she would go wild, or do something terrible, perhaps even kill somebody. She shut her sharp little white teeth fiercely down into her red under lip and vowed with flashing eyes that he should never see Margaret again if power of hers could prevent it.

The letter from Forsythe had reached her on Saturday evening, and she had come to the Sunday service with the distinct idea of trying to plan how she might get rid of Margaret. It would be hard enough to evade her father's vigilance if he once found out the young man had returned, but to have him begin to go and see Margaret again was a thing she could not and would not stand.

The idea obsessed her to the exclusion of all others, and made her watch her teacher as if by her very concentration of thought upon her some way out of the difficulty might be evolved, as if Margaret herself might give forth a hint of weakness somewhere that would show her how to plan.

To that intent she had come close in the group with the others around the teacher at the close of meeting, and, so standing, had overheard all that the Brownleighs had said. The lightning flash of triumph that she cast at Margaret as she left the schoolhouse was her own signal that she had found a way at last. Her opportunity had come, and just in time. Forsythe was to arrive in Arizona some time on Tuesday, and wanted Rosa to meet him at one of their old trysting places, out some distance from her father's house. He knew that school would just be over, for she had written him about commencement, and so he understood that she would be free. But he did not know that the place he had selected to meet her was on one of Margaret's favorite trails where she and Bud often rode in the late afternoons, and that above all things Rosa wished to avoid any danger of meeting her teacher, for she not only feared that Forsythe's attention would be drawn away from her, but also that Margaret might feel it her duty to report to her father about her clandestine meeting.

Rosa's heart beat high as she rode demurely home with her father, answering his pleasantries with smiles and dimples and a coaxing word, just as he loved to have her. But she was not thinking of her father, though she kept well her mask of interest in what he had to say. She was trying to plan how she might use what she had heard to get rid of Margaret Earle. If only Mrs. Brownleigh would do as she had hinted and send someone Tuesday morning to escort Miss Earle over to her home, all would be clear sailing for Rosa, but she dared not trust to such a possibility. There were not many escorts coming their way from Ganado, and Rosa happened to know that the old Indian who frequently escorted parties was off in another direction. She could not rest on any such hope. When she reached home she went at once to her room and sat beside her window, gazing off at the purple mountains in deep thought. Then she lighted a candle and went in search of a certain little Testament, long since neglected and covered with dust. She found it at last on the top of a pile of books in a dark closet, and dragged it forth, eagerly turning the pages. Yes, there it was, and in it a small envelope directed to "Miss Rosa Rogers" in a fine angular handwriting. The letter was from the missionary's wife to the little girl who had recited her texts so beautifully as to earn the Testament.

Rosa carried it to her desk, secured a good light, and sat down to read it over carefully.

No thought of her innocent childish exultation over that letter came to her now. She was intent on one thing—the handwriting. Could she seize the secret of it and reproduce it? She had before often done so with great success. She could imitate Miss Earle's writing so perfectly that she often took an impish pleasure in changing words in the questions on the blackboard and making them read absurdly for the benefit of the school. It was such a good sport to see the amazement on Margaret's face when her attention would be called to it by a hilarious class, and to watch her troubled brow when she read what she supposed she had written.

When Rosa was but a little child she used to boast that she could write her father's name in perfect imitation of his signature, and often signed some trifling receipt for him just for amusement. A dangerous gift in the hands of a conscienceless girl! Yet this was the first time that Rosa had really planned to use her art in any serious way. Perhaps it never occurred to her that she was doing wrong. At present her heart was too full of hate and fear and jealous love to care for right or wrong or anything else. It is doubtful if she would have hesitated a second even if the thing she was planning had suddenly appeared to her in the light of a great crime. She seemed sometimes almost like a creature without moral sense, so swayed was she by her own desires and feelings. She was blind now to everything but her great desire to get Margaret out of the way and have Forsythe to herself.

Long after her father and the servants were asleep Rosa's light burned while she bent over her desk, writing. Page after page she covered with careful copies of Mrs. Brownleigh's letter written to herself almost three years before. Finally she wrote out the alphabet, bit by bit as she picked it from the words, learning just how each letter was habitually formed, the small letters and the capitals, with the peculiarities of connection and ending. At last, when she lay down to rest, she felt herself capable of writing a pretty fair letter in Mrs. Brownleigh's handwriting. The next thing was to make her plan and compose her letter. She lay staring into the darkness and trying to think just what she could do.

In the first place, she settled it that Margaret must be gotten to

Walpi at least. It would not do to send her to Ganado, where the mission station was, for that was a comparatively short journey, and she could easily go in a day. When the fraud was discovered, as of course it would be when Mrs. Brownleigh heard of it, Margaret would perhaps return to find out who had done it. No, she must be sent all the way to Walpi if possible. That would take at least two nights and the most of two days to get there. Forsythe had said his stay was to be short. By the time Margaret got back from Walpi Forsythe would be gone.

But how manage to get her to Walpi without her suspicions being aroused? She might word the note so that Margaret would be told to come halfway, expecting to meet the missionaries, say at Keams. There was a trail straight up from Ashland to Keams, cutting off quite a distance and leaving Ganado off at the right. Keams was nearly forty miles west of Ganado. That would do nicely. Then if she could manage to have another note left at Keams, saying they could not wait and had gone on, Margaret would suspect nothing and go all the way to Walpi. That would be fine and would give the school-teacher an interesting experience which wouldn't hurt her in the least. Rosa thought it might be rather interesting than otherwise. She had no compunctions whatever about how Margaret might feel when she arrived in that strange Indian town and found no friends awaiting her. Her only worry was where she was to find a suitable escort, for she felt assured that Margaret would not start out alone with one man servant on an expedition that would keep her out overnight. And where in all that region could she find a woman whom she could trust to send on the errand? It almost looked as though the thing were an impossibility. She lay tossing and puzzling over it till gray dawn stole into the room. She mentally reviewed every servant on the place on whom she could rely to do her bidding and keep her secret, but there was some reason why each one would not do. She scanned the country, even considering old Ouida, who had been living in a shack over beyond the fort ever since her cabin had been raided, but old Ouida was too notorious. Mrs. Tanner would keep Margaret from going with her, even if Margaret herself did not know the old woman's reputation. Rosa considered if there were any way of wheedling Mom Wallis into the affair, and gave that up, remembering the suspicious little twinkling eyes of Jasper Kemp. At last she fell asleep, with her plan still unformed but her determination to carry it through just as strong as ever. If worst came to worst she would send the Indian cook from the ranch kitchen and put something in the note about his expecting to meet his sister an hour's ride out on the trail. The Indian would do anything in the world for money, and Rosa had no trouble in getting all she wanted of that commodity. But the Indian was an evil-looking fellow, and she feared lest Margaret would not like to go with him. However, he should be a last resort. She would not be balked in her purpose.

Chapter 28

Rosa awoke very early, for her sleep had been light and troubled. She dressed hastily and sat down to compose a note which could be altered slightly in case she found someone better than the Indian; but before she was half through the phrasing she heard a slight disturbance below her window and a muttering in guttural tones from a strange voice. Glancing hastily out, she saw some Indians below, talking with one of the men. The Indian motioned to his wife, sitting on a dilapidated little moth-eaten burro with a small papoose in her arms and looking both dirty and miserable. He muttered as though he were pleading for something.

We believe that God's angels follow the feet of little children and needy ones to protect them. Does the devil also send his angels to lead unwary ones astray, and to protect the plans of the erring ones? If so then he must have sent these Indians that morning to further Rosa's plans, and instantly she recognized her opportunity. She leaned out of her window and spoke in a clear, reproving voice:

"James, what does he want? Breakfast? You know Father wouldn't want any hungry person to be turned away. Let them sit down on the bench there and tell Dorset I said to give them a good hot breakfast, and get some milk for the baby. Be quick about it, too!"

James started and frowned at the clear, commanding voice. The wife turned grateful eyes up to the little beauty in the window, muttering some inarticulate thanks, while the stolid Indian's eyes glittered hopefully, though the muscles of his masklike countenance changed not an atom.

Rosa smiled radiantly and ran down to see that her orders were obeyed. She tried to talk a little with the woman, but found she understood very little English. The Indian spoke better and gave her their brief story. They were on their way to the Navajo reservation to

213

the far north. They had been unfortunate enough to lose their last scanty provisions by prowling coyotes during the night, and were in need of food. Rosa gave them a place to sit down and a plentiful breakfast, and ordered that a small store of provisions should be prepared for their journey after they had rested. Then she hurried up to her room to finish her letter. She had her plan well fixed now. These strangers should be her willing messengers. Now and then, as she wrote she lifted her head and gazed out of the window, where she could see the young mother busy with her little one, and her eyes fairly glittered with satisfaction. Nothing could have been better planned than this.

She wrote her note carefully:

DEAR MARGARET [she had heard Hazel call Margaret by her first name, and rightly judged that their new friendship was already strong enough to justify this intimacy],—I have found just the opportunity I wanted for you to come to us. These Indians are thoroughly trustworthy and are coming in just the direction to bring you to a point where we will meet you. We have decided to go on to Walpi at once, and will probably meet you near Keams, or a little farther on. The Indian knows the way, and you need not be afraid. I trust him perfectly. Start at once, please, so that you will meet us in time. John has to go on as fast as possible. I know you will enjoy the trip, and am so glad you are coming.

Lovingly,
HAZEL RADCLIFFE BROWNLEIGH

Rosa read it over, comparing it carefully with the little yellow note from her Testament, and decided that it was a very good imitation. She could almost hear Mrs. Brownleigh saying what she had written. Rosa really was quite clever. She had done it well.

She hastily sealed and addressed her letter, and then hurried down to talk with the Indians again.

The place she had ordered for them to rest was at some distance from the kitchen door, a sort of outshed for the shelter of certain implements used about the ranch. A long bench ran in front of it, and a big tree made a goodly shade. The Indians had found their temporary camp quite inviting.

Rosa made a detour of the shed, satisfied herself that no one was within hearing, and then sat down on the bench, ostensibly playing with the baby, dangling a red ball on a ribbon before his dazzled eyes and bringing forth a gurgle of delight from the dusky little one. While she played she talked idly with the Indians. Had they money enough for their journey? Would they like to earn some? Would they act as guide to a lady who wanted to go to Walpi? At least she wanted to go as far as Keams, where she might meet friends, missionaries, who were going on with her to Walpi to visit the Indians. If they didn't meet her she wanted to be guided all the way to Walpi. Would they undertake it? It would pay them well. They would get money enough for their journey and have some left when they got to the reservation. And Rosa displayed two gold pieces temptingly in her small palms.

The Indian uttered a sort of gasp at sight of so much money, and sat upright. He gasped again, indicating by a solemn nod that he was agreeable to the task before him, and the girl went gaily on with her instructions:

"You will have to take some things along to make the lady comfortable. I will see that those are gotten ready. Then you can have the things for your own when you leave the lady at Walpi. You will have to take a letter to the lady and tell her you are going this afternoon, and she must be ready to start at once or she will not meet the missionary. Tell her you can only wait until three o'clock to start. You will find the lady at the schoolhouse at noon. You must not come till noon—" Rosa pointed to the sun and then straight overhead. The Indian watched her keenly and nodded.

"You must ask for Miss Earle and give her this letter. She is the schoolteacher."

The Indian looked at the white missive in Rosa's hand, noting once more the gleam of the gold pieces.

"You must wait till the teacher goes to her boardinghouse and packs her things and eats her dinner. If anybody asks where you came from you must say the missionary's wife from Ganado sent you. Don't tell anybody anything else. Do you understand? More money if you don't say anything." Rosa clinked the gold pieces softly.

The strange, sphinxlike gaze of the Indian narrowed comprehensively. He understood. His native cunning was being bought for this girl's own purposes. He looked greedily at the money. Rosa had put her hand in her pocket and brought out yet another gold piece.

"See! I give you this one now"—she laid one gold piece in the Indian's hand—"and these two I put in an envelope and pack with some provisions and blankets on another horse. I will leave the horse tied to a tree up where the big trail crosses this big trail out that way. You know?"

Rosa pointed in the direction she meant, and the Indian looked and nodded, his eyes returning to the two gold pieces in her hand. It was a great deal of money for the little lady to give. Was she trying to cheat him? He looked down at the gold he already held. It was good money. He was sure of that. He looked at her keenly.

"I shall be watching and I shall know whether you have the lady or not," went on the girl, sharply. "If you do not bring the lady with you there will be no money and no provisions waiting for you. But if you bring the lady you can untie the horse and take him with you. You will need the horse to carry the things. When you get to Walpi you can set him free. He is branded and he will likely come back. We shall find him. See, I will put the gold pieces in this tin can."

She picked up a sardine tin that lay at her feet, slipped the gold pieces in an envelope from her pocket, stuffed it in the tin, bent down the cover, and held it up.

"This can will be packed on the top of the other provisions, and you can open it and take the money out when you untie the horse. Then hurry on as fast as you can and get as far along the trail as possible tonight before you camp. Do you understand?"

The Indian nodded once more, and Rosa felt that she had a confederate worthy of her need.

She stayed a few minutes more, going carefully over her directions, telling the Indian to be sure his wife was kind to the lady, and that on no account he should let the lady get uneasy or have cause to complain of her treatment, or trouble would surely come to him. At last she felt sure she had made him understand, and she hurried away to slip into her pretty white dress and rose-colored ribbons and ride to school. Before she left her room she glanced out of the window at the Indians, and saw them sitting motionless, like a group of bronze. Once the Indian stirred and, putting his hand in his bosom, drew forth the white letter she had given him, gazed at it a moment, and hid it in his breast again. She nodded her satisfaction as she turned from the window. The next thing was to get to school and play her own part in the commencement exercises.

The morning was bright, and the schoolhouse was already filled to overflowing when Rosa arrived. Her coming, as always, made a little stir among admiring groups, for even those who feared her admired her from afar. She fluttered into the schoolhouse and up the aisle with the air of a princess who knew she had been waited for and was condescending to come at all.

Rosa was in everything—the drills, the march, the choruses, and the crowning oration. She went through it all with the perfection of a bright mind and an adaptable nature. One would never have dreamed, to look at her pretty dimpling face and her sparkling eyes, what diabolical things were moving in her mind, nor how those eyes, lynx-soft with lurking sweetness and treachery, were watching all the time furtively for the appearance of the Indian.

At last she saw him, standing in a group just outside the window near the platform, his tall form and stern countenance marking him among the crowd of familiar faces. She was receiving her diploma from the hand of Margaret when she caught his eye, and her hand trembled just a quiver as she took the dainty roll tied with blue and white ribbons. That he recognized her she was sure; that he knew she did not wish him to make known his connection with her she felt equally convinced he understood. His eye had that comprehending look of withdrawal. She did not look up directly at him again. Her eyes were daintily downward. Nevertheless, she missed not a turn of his head, not a glance from that stern eye, and she knew the moment when he stood at the front door of the schoolhouse with the letter in his hand, stolid and indifferent, yet a great force to be reckoned with.

Someone looked at the letter, pointed to Margaret, called her, and she came. Rosa was not far away all the time, talking with Jed, her eyes downcast, her cheeks dimpling, missing nothing that could be heard or seen.

Margaret read the letter. Rosa watched her, knew every curve of every letter and syllable as she read, held her breath, and watched Margaret's expression. Did she suspect? No. A look of intense relief and pleasure had come into her eyes. She was glad to have found a way to go. She turned to Mrs. Tanner.

"What do you think of this, Mrs. Tanner? I'm to go with Mrs. Brownleigh on a trip to Walpi. Isn't that delicious? I'm to start at once. Do you suppose I could have a bite to eat? I won't need much. I'm too tired to eat and too anxious to be off. If you give me a cup of tea and a sandwich I'll be all right. I've got things about ready to go, for Mrs. Brownleigh told me she would send someone for me."

"H'm!" said Mrs. Tanner, disapprovingly. "Who you goin' with? Just *him?* I don't much like *his* looks!"

She spoke in a low tone so the Indian would not hear, and it was almost in Rosa's very ear, who stood just behind. Rosa's heart stopped a beat and she frowned at the toe of her slipper. Was this common little Tanner woman going to be the one to balk her plans?

Margaret raised her head now for her first good look at the Indian, and it must be admitted a chill came into her heart. Then, as if he comprehended what was at stake, the Indian turned slightly and pointed down the path toward the road. By common consent the few who were standing about the door stepped back and made a vista for Margaret to see the woman sitting statuelike on her scraggy little pony, gazing off at the mountain in the distance, as if she were sitting for her picture, her solemn little baby strapped to her back.

Margaret's troubled eyes cleared. The family aspect made things all right again. "You see, he has his wife and child," she said. "It's all right. Mrs. Brownleigh says she trusts him perfectly, and I'm to meet them on the way. Read the letter."

She thrust the letter into Mrs. Tanner's hand, and Rosa trembled for her scheme once more. Surely, surely Mrs. Tanner would not be able to detect the forgery!

"H'm! Well, I s'pose it's all right if she says so, but I'm sure I don't relish them pesky Injuns, and I don't think that wife of his looks any great shakes, either. They look to me like they needed a good scrub with Bristol brick. But then, if you're set on going, you'll go, 'course.

I jest wish Bud hadn't a gone home with that Jasper Kemp. He might a gone along, an' then you'd a had somebody to speak English to."

"Yes, it would have been nice to have William along," said Margaret, "but I think I'll be all right. Mrs. Brownleigh wouldn't send anybody that wasn't nice."

"H'm! I dun'no'! She's an awful crank. She just loves them Injuns, they say. But I, fer one, draw the line at holdin' 'em in my lap. I don't b'lieve in mixin' folks up that way. Preach to 'em if you like, but let 'em keep their distance, I say."

Margaret laughed and went off to pick up her things. Rosa stood smiling and talking to Jed until she saw Margaret and Mrs. Tanner go off together, the Indians riding slowly along behind.

Rosa waited until the Indians had turned off the road down toward the Tanners', and then she mounted her own pony and rode swiftly home.

She rushed up to her room and took off her fine apparel, arraying herself quickly in a plain little gown, and went down to prepare the provisions. There was none too much time, and she must work rapidly. It was well for her plans that she was all-powerful with the servants and could send them about at will to get them out of her way. She invented a duty for each now that would take them for a few minutes well out of sight and sound; then she hurried together the provisions in a basket, making two trips to get them to the shelter where she had told the Indian he would find the horse tied. She had to make a third trip to bring the blankets and a few other things she knew would be indispensable, but the whole outfit was carelessly gotten together, and it was just by chance that some things got in at all.

It was not difficult to find the old cayuse she intended using for a packhorse. He was browsing around in the corral, and she soon had a halter over his head, for she had been quite used to horses from her babyhood.

She packed the canned things, tinned meats, vegetables, and fruit into a couple of large sacks, adding some fodder for the horses, a box of matches, some corn bread, of which there was always plenty on hand in the house, some salt pork, and a few tin dishes. These she slung pack fashion over the old horse, fastened the sardine tin con-taining the gold pieces where it would be easily found, tied the horse to a tree, and retired behind a shelter of sagebrush to watch.

It was not long before the little caravan came, the Indians riding ahead single file, like two graven images, moving not a muscle of their faces, and Margaret a little way behind on her own pony, her face as happy and relieved as if she were a child let out from a hard task to play.

The Indian stopped beside the horse, a glitter of satisfaction in his eyes as he saw that the little lady had fulfilled her part of the bargain. He indicated to his wife and his charge that they might move on down the trail, and he would catch up with them, and then dis-mounted, pouncing warily upon the sardine tin at once. He looked furtively about, then took out the money and tested it with his teeth to make sure it was genuine.

He grunted his further satisfaction, looked over the packhorse, made more secure the fastenings of the load, and, taking the halter, mounted and rode stolidly away toward the north.

Rosa waited in her covert until they were far out of sight, then made her way hurriedly back to the house and climbed to a window where she could watch the trail for several miles. There, with a field glass, she kept watch until the procession had filed across the plains, down into a valley, up over a hill, and dropped to a farther valley out of sight. She looked at the sun and drew a breath of satisfaction. She had done it at last! She had got Margaret away before Forsythe came! There was no likelihood that the fraud would be discovered until her rival was far enough away to be safe. A kind of reaction came upon Rosa's overwrought nerves. She laughed out harshly, and her voice had a cruel ring to it. Then she threw herself upon the bed and burst into a passionate fit of weeping, and so, by and by, fell asleep. She dreamed that Margaret had returned like a shining, fiery angel, a two-edged sword in her hand and all the Wallis camp at her heels, with vengeance in their wake. That hateful little boy, Bud Tanner, danced around and made faces at her, while Forsythe had forgotten her to gaze at Margaret's face.

Chapter 29

To Margaret the day was very fair, and the omens all auspicious. She carried with her close to her heart two precious letters received that morning and scarcely glanced at as yet, one from Gardley and one from her mother. She had had only time to open them and be sure that all was well with her dear ones, and had left the rest to read on the way.

She was dressed in the khaki riding habit she always wore when she went on horseback, and in the bag strapped on behind she carried a couple of fresh white blouses, a thin, white dress, a little soft dark silk gown that folded away almost into a cobweb, and a few other necessities. She had also slipped in a new book her mother had sent her, into which she had as yet no time to look, and her chessmen and board, besides writing materials. She prided herself on having gotten so many necessaries into so small a compass. She would need the extra clothing if she stayed at Ganado with the missionaries for a week on her return from the trip, and the book and chessmen would amuse them all by the way. She had heard Brownleigh say he loved to play chess.

Margaret rode on the familiar trail, and for the first hour just let herself be glad that school was over and she could rest and have no responsibility. The sun shimmered down brilliantly on the white, hot sand and gray-green of the greasewood and sagebrush. Tall spikes of cactus like lonely spires shot up now and again to vary the scene. It was all familiar ground to Margaret around here, for she had taken many rides with Gardley and Bud, and for the first part of the way every turn and bit of view was fraught with pleasant memories that brought a smile to her eyes as she recalled some quotation of Gardley's or some prank of Bud's. Here was where they first sighted the little cottontail the day she took her initial ride on her own pony. Off there was the mountain where they saw the sun drawing silver water

221

above a frowning storm. Yonder was the group of cedars where they had stopped to eat their lunch once, and this water hole they were approaching was the one where Gardley had given her a drink from his hat.

She was almost glad that Bud was not along, for she was too tired to talk and liked to be alone with her thoughts for these few minutes. Poor Bud! He would be disappointed when he got back to find her gone, but then he had expected she was going in a few days, anyway, and she had promised to take long rides with him when she returned. She had left a little note for him, asking him to read a certain book in her bookcase while she was gone, and be ready to discuss it with her when she got back, and Bud would be fascinated with it, she knew. Bud had been dear and faithful, and she would miss him, but just for this little while she was glad to have the great out-of-doors to herself.

She was practically alone. The two sphinxlike figures riding ahead of her made no sign, but stolidly rode on hour after hour, nor turned their heads even to see if she were coming. She knew that Indians were this way; still, as the time went by she began to feel an uneasy sense of being alone in the universe with a couple of bronze statues. Even the papoose had erased itself in sleep, and when it awoke partook so fully of its racial peculiarities as to hold its little peace and make no fuss. Margaret began to feel the baby was hardly human, more like a little brown doll set up in a missionary meeting to teach white children what a papoose was like.

By and by she got out her letters and read them over carefully, dreaming and smiling over them, and getting precious bits by heart. Gardley hinted that he might be able very soon to visit her parents, as it looked as though he might have to make a trip on business in their direction before he could go further with what he was doing in his old home. He gave no hint of soon returning to the West. He said he was awaiting the return of one man who might soon be coming from abroad. Margaret sighed and wondered how many weary months it would be before she would see him. Perhaps, after all, she ought to have gone home and stayed them out with her mother and father. If the school board could be made to see that it would be better to have no summer session, perhaps she would even yet go when she returned from the Brownleighs'. She would see. She would decide nothing until she was rested.

Suddenly she felt herself overwhelmingly weary, and wished that the Indians would stop and rest for a while, but when she stirred up her sleepy pony and spurred ahead to broach the matter to her guide he shook his solemn head and pointed to the sun:

"No get Keams good time. No meet Aneshodi."

"Aneshodi," she knew, was the Indians' name for the missionary, and she smiled her acquiescence. Of course they must meet the Brownleighs and not detain them. What was it Hazel had said about having to hurry? She searched her pocket for the letter, and then remembered she had left it with Mrs. Tanner. What a pity she had not brought it! Perhaps there was some caution or advice in it that she had not taken note of. But then the Indian likely knew all about it, and she could trust to him. She glanced at his stolid face and wished she could make him smile. She cast a sunny smile at him and said something pleasant about the beautiful day, but he only looked her through as if she were not there, and after one or two more attempts she fell back and tried to talk to his wife; but she only looked stolid, too, and shook her head. She did not seem friendly. Margaret drew back into her old position and feasted her eyes upon the distant hills.

The road was growing unfamiliar now. They were crossing rough ridges with cliffs of red sandstone, and every step of the way was interesting. Yet Margaret felt more and more how much she wanted to lie down and sleep, and when at last in the dusk the Indians halted not far from a little pool of rainwater and indicated that here they would camp for the night, Margaret was too weary to question the decision. It had not occurred to her that she would be on the way overnight before she met her friends. Her knowledge of the way, and of distances, was but vague. It is doubtful if she would have ventured had she known that she must pass the night thus in the company of two strange creatures. Yet, now that she was here and it was inevitable, she would not shrink, but make the best of it. She tried to be friendly once more, and offered to look out for the baby while his mother gathered wood and made a fire. The Indian was off looking after the horses, evidently expecting his wife to do all the work.

Margaret watched a few minutes, while pretending to play with the baby, who was both sleepy and hungry, yet held his emotions as stolidly as if he were a grown person. Then she decided to take a hand in the supper. She was hungry and could not bear that those dusky, dirty hands should set forth her food, so she went to work cheerfully, giving directions as if the Indian woman understood her, though she very soon discovered that all her talk was as mere babbling to the other, and she might as well hold her peace. The woman set a kettle of water over the fire, and Margaret forestalled her next movement by cutting some pork and putting it to cook in a little skillet she found among the provisions. The woman watched her solemnly, not seeming to care, and so, silently, each went about her own preparations.

The supper was a silent affair, and when it was over the woman handed Margaret a blanket. Suddenly she understood that this, and this alone, was to be her bed for the night. The earth was there for a mattress, and the sagebrush lent a partial shelter, the canopy of stars was overhead.

A kind of panic took possession of her. She stared at the Indians and found herself longing to cry out for help. It seemed as if she could not bear this awful silence of the mortals who were her only company. Yet her common sense came to her aid, and she realized that there was nothing for it but to make the best of things. So she took the blanket and, spreading it out, sat down upon it and wrapped it about her shoulders and feet. She would not lie down until she saw what the rest did. Somehow she shrank from asking the bronze man how to fold a blanket for a bed on the ground. She tried to remember what Gardley had told her about folding the blanket bed so as best to keep out snakes and ants. She shuddered at the thought of snakes. Would she dare call for help from those stolid companions of hers if a snake should attempt to molest her in the night? And would she ever dare to go to sleep?

She remembered her first night in Arizona out among the stars, alone on the water tank, and her first frenzy of loneliness. Was this as bad? No, for these Indians were trustworthy and well known by her dear friends. It might be unpleasant, but this, too, would pass and the morrow would soon be here.

The dusk dropped down and the stars loomed out. All the world grew wonderful, like a blue jeweled dome of a palace with the lights turned low. The fire burned brightly as the man threw sticks upon it, and the two Indians moved stealthily about in the darkness, passing silhouetted before the fire this way and that, and then at last lying down wrapped in their blankets to sleep.

It was very quiet about her. The air was so still she could hear the hobbled horses munching away in the distance, and moving now and then with the halting gait a hobble gives a horse. Off in the farther distance the blood-curdling howl of the coyotes rose, but Margaret was used to them, and knew they would not come near a fire.

She was growing very weary, and at last wrapped her blanket closer and lay down, her head pillowed on one corner of it. Committing herself to her heavenly Father, and breathing a prayer for Father, Mother, and lover, she fell asleep.

It was still almost dark when she awoke. For a moment she thought it was still night and the sunset was not gone yet, the clouds were so rosy tinted.

She perceived, as she rubbed her eyes and tried to summon back her senses, that she was expected to get up and eat breakfast. There was a smell of pork and coffee in the air, and there was scorched corn bread beside the fire on a pan.

Margaret got up quickly and ran down to the water hole to get some water, dashing it in her face and over her arms and hands, the woman meanwhile standing at a little distance, watching her curiously, as if she thought this some kind of an oblation paid to the white woman's god before she ate. Margaret pulled the hairpins out of her hair, letting it down and combing it with one of her side combs, twisted it up again in its soft, fluffy waves; straightened her collar, set on her hat, and was ready for the day.

Margaret made a hurried meal and was scarcely done before she found her guides were waiting like two pillars of the desert, but watching keenly, impatiently, her every mouthful, and anxious to be off.

The sky was still pink-tinted with the semblance of a sunset, and Margaret felt, as she mounted her pony and followed her companions, as if the day was all turned upside down. She almost wondered whether she hadn't slept through a whole twenty-four hours, and if it were not, after all, evening again, till by and by the sun rose clear and the wonder of the cloud-tinting melted into day.

The road lay through sagebrush and old barren cedar trees, with rabbits darting now and then between the rocks. Suddenly from the top of a little hill they came out to a spot where they could see far over the desert. Forty miles away three square, flat hills, or mesas, looked like a gigantic train of cars, and the clear air gave everything a strange vastness. Farther on beyond the mesas dimly dawned the Black Mountains. One could even see the shadowed head of "Round Rock," almost a hundred miles away. Before them and around was a great plain of sagebrush, and here and there was a small bush that the Indians call "the weed that was not scared." Margaret had learned all these things during her winter in Arizona, and keenly enjoyed the vast, splendid view spread before her.

They passed several little mud-plastered hogans that Margaret knew for Indian dwellings. A fine band of ponies off in the distance made an interesting spot on the landscape, and twice they passed bands of sheep. She had a feeling of great isolation from everything she had ever known, and seemed going farther and farther from life and all she loved. Once she ventured to ask the Indian what time he expected to meet her friends, the missionaries, but he only shook his head and murmured something unintelligible about "Keams" and pointed to the sun. She dropped behind again, vaguely uneasy, she could not tell why. There seemed something so altogether sly and wary and unfriendly in the faces of the two that she almost wished she had not come. Yet the way was beautiful enough and nothing very unpleasant was happening to her. Once she dropped the envelope of her mother's letter and was about to dismount and recover it. Then some strange impulse made her leave it on the sand of the desert. What if they should be lost and that paper should guide them back? The notion stayed by her, and once in a while she dropped other bits of paper by the way.

About noon the trail dropped off into a canyon with high, yellow rock walls on either side, and stifling heat, so that she felt as if she could scarcely stand it. She was glad when they emerged once more and climbed to higher ground. The noon camp was a hasty affair, for the Indian seemed in a hurry. He scanned the horizon far and wide and seemed searching keenly for someone or something. Once they met a lonely Indian, and he held a muttered conversation with him, pointing off ahead and gesticulating angrily. But the words were unintelligible to Margaret. Her feeling of uneasiness was growing, and yet she could not for the life of her tell why, and laid it down to her tired nerves. She was beginning to think she had been very foolish to start on such a long trip before she had had a chance to get rested from her last days of school. She longed to lie down under a tree and sleep for days.

Toward night they sighted a great blue mesa about fifty miles south, and at sunset they could just see the San Francisco peaks more than a hundred and twenty-five miles away. Margaret, as she stopped her horse and gazed, felt a choking in her heart and throat and a great desire to cry. The glory and awe of the mountains, mingled with her own weariness and nervous fear, were almost too much for her. She was glad to get down and eat a little supper and go to sleep again. As she fell asleep she comforted herself with repeating over a few precious words from her Bible:

"The angel of the Lord encampeth round about them that fear Him and delivereth them. Thou wilt keep him in perfect peace whose mind is stayed on Thee because he trusteth in Thee. I will both lay me down in peace and sleep, for Thou Lord only makest me to dwell in safety. . . ."

The voice of the coyotes, now far, now near, boomed out on the night; great stars shot darting pathways across the heavens; the fire snapped and crackled, died down and flickered feebly, but Margaret slept, tired out, and dreamed the angels kept close vigil around her lowly couch.

She did not know what time the stars disappeared and the rain began to fall. She was too tired to notice the drops that fell upon her face. Too tired to hear the coyotes coming nearer, nearer, yet in the morning there lay one dead, stretched not thirty feet from where she lay. The Indian had shot him through the heart.

Somehow things looked very dismal that morning, in spite of the brightness of the sun after the rain. She was stiff and sore with lying in the dampness. Her hair was wet, her blanket was wet, and she woke without feeling rested. Almost the trip seemed more than she could bear. If she could have wished herself back that morning and have stayed at Tanners' all summer she certainly would have done it rather than to be where and how she was.

The Indians seemed excited—the man grim and forbidding, the woman appealing, frightened, anxious. They were near to Keams Canyon. "Aneshodi" would be somewhere about. The Indian hoped to be rid of his burden then and travel on his interrupted journey. He was growing impatient. He felt he had earned his money.

But when they tried to go down Keams Canyon they found the road all washed away by flood, and must needs go a long way around. This made the Indian surly. His countenance was more forbidding than ever. Margaret, as she watched him with sinking heart, altered her ideas of the Indian as a whole to suit the situation. She had always felt pity for the poor Indian, whose land had been seized and whose kindred had been slaughtered. But this Indian was not an object of pity. He was the most disagreeable, cruel-looking Indian Margaret had ever laid eyes on. She had felt it innately the first time she saw him, but now, as the situation began to bring him out, she knew that she was dreadfully afraid of him. She had a feeling that he might scalp her if he got tired of her. She began to alter her opinion of Hazel Brownleigh's judgment as regarded Indians. She did not feel that she would ever send this Indian to anyone for a guide and say he was perfectly trustworthy. He hadn't done anything very dreadful yet, but she felt he was going to.

He had a number of angry confabs with his wife that morning. At least, he did the confabbing and his wife protested. Margaret gathered after a while that it was something about herself. The furtive, frightened glances that the woman cast in her direction sometimes, when the man was not looking, made her think so. She tried to say it was all imagination, and that her nerves were getting the upper hand of her, but in spite of her she shuddered sometimes, just as she had done when Rosa looked at her. She decided that she must be going to have a fit of sickness, and that just as soon as she got in the neighborhood of Mrs. Tanner's again she would pack her trunk and go home to her mother. If she was going to be sick she wanted her mother.

About noon things came to a climax. They halted on the top of the mesa, and the Indians had another altercation, which ended in the man descending the trail a fearfully steep way, down four hundred feet to the trading post in the canyon. Margaret looked down and gasped and thanked a kind Providence that had not made it necessary for her to make that descent, but the mother stood at the top with her baby and looked down in silent sorrow—agony perhaps would be a better name. Her face was terrible to look upon.

Margaret could not understand it, and she went to the woman and put her hand out sympathetically, asking, gently: "What is the matter, you poor little thing? Oh, what is it?"

Perhaps the woman understood the tenderness in the tone, for she suddenly turned and rested her forehead against Margaret's shoulder, giving one great, gasping sob, then lifted her dry, miserable eyes to the girl's face as if to thank her for her kindness.

Margaret's heart was touched. She threw her arms around the poor woman and drew her, papoose and all, comfortingly toward her, patting her shoulder and saying gentle, soothing words as she would to a little child. And by and by the woman lifted her head again, the tears coursing down her face, and tried to explain, muttering her queer gutturals and making eloquent gestures until Margaret felt she understood. She gathered that the man had gone down to the trading post to find the "Aneshodi," and the woman feared that he would somehow procure firewater either from the trader or from some Indian he might meet, and would come back angrier than he had gone, and without his money.

If Margaret also suspected that the Indian had desired to get rid of her by leaving her at that desolate little trading station down in the canyon until such time as her friends should call for her, she resolutely put the thought out of her mind and set herself to cheer the poor Indian woman.

She took a bright, soft, rosy silk tie from her own neck and knotted it about the astonished woman's dusky throat, and then she put a silver dollar in her hand, and was thrilled with wonder to see what a change came over the poor, dark face. It reminded her of Mom Wallis when she got on her new bonnet, and once again she felt the thrill of knowing the whole world kin.

The Indian cheered up after a little, got sticks and made a fire, and together they had quite a pleasant meal. Margaret exerted herself to make the poor woman laugh, and finally succeeded by dangling a bright red knight from her chessmen in front of the delighted baby's eyes till he gurgled out a real baby crow of joy.

It was the middle of the afternoon before the man returned, sitting crazily his struggling beast as he climbed the trail once more. Margaret, watching, caught her breath and prayed. Was this the trustworthy man, this drunken, reeling creature, clubbing his horse and pouring forth a torrent of indistinguishable gutturals? It was evident that his wife's worst fears were verified. He had found the firewater.

The frightened wife set to work putting things together as fast as she could. She well knew what to expect, and when the man reached the top of the mesa he found his party packed and mounted, waiting fearsomely to take the trail.

Silently, timorously, they rode behind him, west across the great wide plain.

In the distance gradually there appeared dim mesas like great fingers stretching out against the sky; miles away they seemed, and nothing intervening but a stretch of varying color where sagebrush melted into sand, and sagebrush and greasewood grew again, with tall cactus startling here and there like bayonets at rest but bristling with menace.

The Indian had grown silent and sullen. His eyes were like deep fires of burning volcanoes. One shrank from looking at them. His massive, cruel profile stood out like bronze against the evening sky. It was growing night again, and still they had not come to anywhere or anything, and still her friends seemed just as far away.

Since they had left the top of Keams Canyon Margaret had been sure all was not right. Aside from the fact that the guide was drunk at present, she was convinced that there had been something wrong with him all along. He did not act like the Indians around Ashland. He did not act like a trusted guide that her friends would send for her. She wished once more that she had kept Hazel Brownleigh's letter. She wondered how her friends would find her if they came after her. It was then she began in earnest to systematically plan to leave a trail behind her all the rest of the way. If she had only done it thoroughly when she first began to be uneasy. But now she was so far away, so many miles from anywhere! Oh, if she had not come at all!

And first she dropped her handkerchief, because she happened to have it in her hand—a dainty thing with lace on the edge and her name written in tiny script by her mother's careful hand on the narrow hem. And then after a little, as soon as she could scrawl it without being noticed, she wrote a note which she twisted around the neck of a red chessman, and left behind her. After that scraps of paper, as she could reach them out of the bag tied on behind her saddle; then a stocking, a bedroom slipper, more chessmen, and so, when they halted at dusk and prepared to strike camp, she had quite a good little trail blazed behind her over that wide, empty plain. She shuddered as she looked into the gathering darkness ahead, where those long, dark lines of mesas looked like barriers in the way. Then, suddenly, the Indian pointed ahead to the first mesa and uttered one word—"Walpi!" So that was the Indian village to which she was bound? What was before her on the morrow? After eating a pretense of supper she lay down. The Indian had more firewater with him. He drank, he uttered cruel gutturals at his wife, and even kicked the feet of the sleeping papoose as he passed by till it awoke and cried sharply.

It seemed hours before all was quiet. Margaret's nerves were strained to such a pitch she scarcely dared to breathe, but at last, when the fire had almost died down, the man lay quiet, and she could relax and close her eyes.

Not to sleep. She must not go to sleep. The fire was almost gone and the coyotes would be around. She must wake and watch!

That was the last thought she remembered—that and a prayer that the angels would keep watch once again.

When she awoke it was broad daylight and far into the morning, for the sun was high overhead and the mesas in the distance were clear and distinct against the sky.

She sat up and looked about her, bewildered, not knowing at first where she was. It was so still and wide and lonely.

She turned to find the Indians, but there was no trace of them anywhere. The fire lay smoldering in its place, a thin trickle of smoke curling away from a dying stick, but that was all. A tin cup half full of coffee was beside the stick, and a piece of blackened corn bread. She turned frightened eyes to east, to west, to north, to south, but there was no one in sight, and out over the distant mesa there poised a great eagle alone in the vast sky keeping watch over the brilliant, silent waste.

Chapter 30

When Margaret was a very little girl her father and mother had left her alone for an hour with a stranger while they went out to make a call in a strange city through which they were passing on a summer trip. The stranger was kind, and gave to the child a large green box of bits of old black lace and purple ribbons to play with, but she turned sorrowfully from the somber array of finery, which was the only thing in the way of a plaything the woman had at hand, and stood looking drearily out of the window on the strange, new town, a feeling of utter loneliness upon her. Her little heart was almost choked with the awfulness of the thought that she was a human atom drifted apart from every other atom she had ever known, that she had a personality and a responsibility of her own, and that she must face this thought of herself and her aloneness for evermore. It was the child's first realization that she was a separate being apart from her father and mother, and she was almost consumed with the terror of it.

As she rose now from her bed on the ground and looked out across that vast waste, in which the only other living creature was that sinister, watching eagle, the same feeling returned to her and made her tremble like the little child who had turned from her box of ancient finery to realize her own little self and its terrible aloneness.

For an instant even her realization of God, which had from early childhood been present with her, seemed to have departed. She could not grasp anything save the vast empty silence that loomed about her so awfully. She was alone, and about as far from anywhere or anything as she could possibly be in the state of Arizona. Would she ever get back to human habitations? Would her friends ever be able to find her?

Then her heart flew back to its habitual refuge, and she spoke aloud and said, "God is here!" and the thought seemed to comfort her. She looked about once more on the bright waste, and now it did not seem so dreary.

"God is here!" she repeated, and tried to realize that this was a part of His habitation. She could not be lost where God was. He knew the way out. She had only to trust. So she dropped upon her knees in the sand and prayed for trust and courage.

When she rose again she walked steadily to a height a little above the camp fire, and, shading her eyes, looked carefully in every direction. No, there was not a sign of her recent companions. They must have stolen away in the night quite soon after she fell asleep, and have gone fast and far, so that they were now beyond the reach of her eyes, and not anywhere was there sign of living thing, save that eagle still sweeping in great curves and poising again above the distant mesa.

Where was her horse? Had the Indians taken that, too? She searched the valley, but saw no horse at first. With sinking heart she went back to where her things were and sat down by the dying fire to think, putting a few loose twigs and sticks together to keep the embers bright while she could. She reflected that she had no matches, and this was probably the last fire she would have until somebody came to her rescue or she got somewhere by herself. What was she to do? Stay right where she was or start out on foot? And should she go backward or forward? Surely, surely the Brownleighs would miss her pretty soon and send out a search party for her. How could it be that they trusted an Indian who had done such a cruel thing as to leave a woman unprotected in the desert? And yet, perhaps, they did not know his temptation to drink. Perhaps they had thought he could not get any firewater. Perhaps he would return when he came to himself and realized what he had done.

And now she noticed what she had not seen at first—a small bottle of water on a stone beside the blackened bread. Realizing that she was very hungry and that this was the only food at hand, she sat down beside the fire to eat the dry bread and drink the miserable coffee. She must have strength to do whatever was before her. She tried not to think how her mother would feel if she never came back, how anxious they would be as they waited day by day for her letters that did not come. She reflected with a sinking heart that she had, just before leaving, written a hasty note to her mother telling her not to expect anything for several days, perhaps even as much as two weeks, as she was going out of civilization for a little while. How had she unwittingly sealed her fate by that! For now not even by way of her alarmed home could help come to her.

She put the last bit of hard corn bread in her pocket for a further time of need, and began to look about her again. Then she spied with delight a moving object far below her in the valley, and decided it was a horse, perhaps her own. He was a mile away, at least, but he was there, and she cried out with sudden joy and relief.

She went over to her blanket and bags, which had been beside her during the night, and stood a moment trying to think what to do. Should she carry the things to the horse or risk leaving them here while she went after the horse and brought him to the things? No, that would not be safe. Someone might come along and take them, or she might not be able to find her way back again in this strange, wild waste. Besides, she might not get the horse, after all, and would lose everything. She must carry her things to the horse. She stooped to gather them up, and something bright beside her bag attracted her. It was the sun shining on the silver dollar she had given to the Indian woman. A sudden rush of tears came to her eyes. The poor creature had tried to make all the reparation she could for thus hastily leaving the white woman in the desert. She had given back the money—all she had that was valuable! Beside the dollar rippled a little chain of beads curiously wrought, an inanimate appeal for forgiveness and a grateful return for the kindness shown her. Margaret smiled as she stooped again to pick up her things. There had been a heart, after all, behind that stolid countenance, and some sense of righteousness and justice. Margaret decided that Indians were not all treacherous. Poor woman! What a life was hers—to follow her grim lord whither he would lead, even as her white sister must sometimes, sorrowing, rebelling, crying out, but following! She wondered if into the heart of this dark sister there ever crept any of the rebellion which led some of her white sisters to cry aloud for "rights" and "emancipation."

But it was all a passing thought to be remembered and turned over at a more propitious time. Margaret's whole thoughts now were bent on her present predicament.

The packing was short work. She stuffed everything into the two bags that were usually hung across the horse, and settled them carefully across her shoulders. Then she rolled the blanket, took it in her arms, and started. It was a heavy burden to carry, but she could not make up her mind to part with any of her things until she had at least made an effort to save them. If she should be left alone in the desert for the night the blanket was indispensable, and her clothes would at least do to drop as a trail by which her friends might find her. She must carry them as far as possible. So she started.

It was already high day, and the sun was intolerably hot. Her heavy burden was not only cumbersome, but very warm, and she felt her strength going from her as she went, but her nerve was up and her courage was strong. Moreover, she prayed as she walked, and she felt now the presence of her Guide and was not afraid. As she walked she faced a number of possibilities in the immediate future which were startling, and to say the least, undesirable. There were wild animals in this land, not so much in the daylight, but what of the night? She had heard that a woman was always safe in that wild western land, but what of the prowling Indians? What of a possible exception to the western rule of chivalry toward a decent woman? One small piece of corn bread and less than a pint of water were small provision on which to withstand a siege. How far was it to anywhere?

It was then she remembered for the first time that one word— "Walpi!" uttered by the Indian as he came to a halt the night before and pointed far to the mesa—"Walpi." She lifted her eyes now and scanned the dark mesa. It loomed like a great battlement of rock against the sky. Could it be possible there were people dwelling there? She had heard, of course, about the curious Hopi villages, each village a gigantic house of many rooms, called pueblos, built upon the lofty crags, sometimes five or six hundred feet above the desert.

Could it be that that great castle-looking outline against the sky before her, standing out on the end of the mesa like a promontory above the sea, was Walpi? And if it was, how was she to get up there?

The rock rose sheer and steep from the desert floor. The narrow neck of land behind it looked like a slender thread. Her heart sank at thought of trying to storm and enter, single-handed, such an impregnable fortress. And yet, if her friends were there, perhaps they would see her when she drew near and come to show her the way. Strange that they should have gone on and left her with those treacherous Indians! Strange that they should have trusted them so, in the first place! Her own instincts had been against trusting the man from the beginning. It must be confessed that during her reflections at this point her opinion of the wisdom and judgment of the Brownleighs was lowered several notches. Then she began to berate herself for having so easily been satisfied about her escort. She should have read the letter more carefully. She should have asked the Indians more questions. She should, perhaps, have asked Jasper Kemp's advice, or got him to talk to the Indian. She wished with all her heart for Bud, now. If Bud were along he would be saying some comical boy-thing, and be finding a way out of the difficulty. Dear, faithful Bud!

The sun rose higher and the morning grew hotter. As she descended to the valley her burdens grew intolerable, and several times she almost cast them aside. Once she lost sight of her pony among the sagebrush, and it was two hours before she came to him and was able to capture him and strap on her burdens. She was almost too exhausted to climb into the saddle when all was ready, but she managed to mount at last and started out toward the rugged crag ahead of her.

The pony had a long, hot climb out of the valley to a hill where she could see very far again, but still that vast emptiness reigned. Even the eagle had disappeared, and she fancied he must be resting like a great emblem of freedom on one of the points of the castlelike battlement against the sky. It seemed as if the end of the world had come, and she was the only one left in the universe, forgotten, riding on her weary horse across an endless desert in search of a home she would never see again.

Below the hill there stretched a wide, white strip of sand, perhaps two miles in extent, but shimmering in the sun and seeming to recede ahead of her as she advanced. Beyond was soft greenness—something growing—not near enough to be discerned as corn fields. The girl drooped her tired head upon her horse's mane and wept, her courage going from her with her tears. In all that wide universe there seemed no way to go, and she was so very tired, hungry, hot, and discouraged! There was always that bit of bread in her pocket and that muddy-looking, warm water for a last resort, but she must save them as long as possible, for there was no telling how long it would be before she had more.

There was no trail now to follow. She had started from the spot where she had found the horse, and her inexperienced eyes could not have searched out a trail if she had tried. She was going toward that distant castle on the crag as to a goal, but when she reached it, if she ever did, would she find anything there but crags and lonesomeness and the eagle?

Drying her tears at last, she started the horse on down the hill, and perhaps her tears blinded her, or because she was dizzy with hunger and the long stretch of anxiety and fatigue she was not looking closely. There was a steep place, a sharp falling away of the ground unexpectedly as they emerged from a thicket of sagebrush, and the horse plunged several feet down, striking sharply on some loose rocks, and slipping to his knees, snorting, scrambling, making brave effort, but slipping, half rolling, at last he was brought down with his frightened rider, and lay upon his side with her foot under him and a sensation like a red-hot knife running through her ankle.

Margaret caught her breath in quick gasps as they fell, lifting a prayer in her heart for help. Then came the crash and the sharp pain, and with a quick conviction that all was over she dropped back unconscious on the sand, a blessed oblivion of darkness rushing over her.

When she came to herself once more the hot sun was pouring down upon her unprotected face, and she was conscious of intense pain and suffering in every part of her body. She opened her eyes wildly and looked around. There was sagebrush up above, waving over the crag down which they had fallen, its gray-greenness shimmering hotly in the sun; the sky was mercilessly blue without a cloud. The great beast, heavy and quivering, lay solidly against her, half pinning her to earth, and the helplessness of her position was like an awful nightmare from which she felt she might waken if she could only cry out. But when at last she raised her voice its empty echo frightened her, and there, above her, with widespread wings, circling for an instant, then poised in motionless survey of her, with cruel eyes upon her, loomed that eagle—so large, so fearful, so suggestive in its curious stare, the monarch of the desert come to see who had invaded his precincts and fallen into one of his snares.

With sudden frenzy burning in her veins Margaret struggled and tried to get free, but she could only move the slightest bit each time, and every motion was an agony to the hurt ankle.

It seemed hours before she writhed herself free from that great, motionless horse, whose labored breath only showed that he was still alive. Something terrible must have happened to the horse or he would have tried to rise, for she had coaxed, patted, cajoled, tried in every way to rouse him. When at last she crawled free from the hot, horrible body and crept with pained progress around in front of him, she saw that both his forelegs lay limp and helpless. He must have broken them in falling. Poor fellow! He, too, was suffering and she had nothing to give him! There was nothing she could do for him!

Then she thought of the bottle of water, but, searching for it, found that her good intention of dividing it with him was useless, for the bottle was broken and the water already soaked into the sand. Only a damp spot on the saddlebag showed where it had departed.

Then indeed did Margaret sink down in the sand in despair and begin to pray as she had never prayed before.

Chapter 31

The morning after Margaret's departure Rosa awoke with no feelings of self-reproach, but rather a great exultation at the way in which she had been able to get rid of her rival.

She lay for a few minutes thinking of Forsythe, and trying to decide what she would wear when she went forth to meet him, for she wanted to charm him as she had never charmed anyone before.

She spent some time arraying herself in different costumes, but at last decided on her commencement gown of fine white organdie, hand-embroidered and frilled with filmy lace, the product of a famous house of gowns in the eastern city where she had attended school for a while and acquired expensive tastes.

Daintily slippered, beribboned with coral silk girdle, and with a rose from the vine over her window in her hair, she sallied forth at last to the trysting place.

Forsythe was a whole hour late, as became a languid gentleman who had traveled the day before and idled at his sister's house over a late breakfast until nearly noon. Already his fluttering fancy was apathetic about Rosa, and he wondered, as he rode along, what had become of the interesting young teacher who had charmed him for more than a passing moment. Would he dare to call upon her, now that Gardley was out of the way? Was she still in Ashland or had she gone home for vacation? He must ask Rosa about her.

Then he came in sight of Rosa sitting picturesquely in the shade of an old cedar, reading poetry, a little lady in the wilderness, and he forgot everything else in his delight over the change in her. For Rosa had changed. There was no mistake about it. She had bloomed out into maturity in those few short months of his absence. Her soft figure had rounded and developed, her bewitching curls were put up on her head, with only a stray tendril here and there to emphasize a dainty ear or call attention to a smooth, round neck, and when she raised her lovely head and lifted limpid eyes to his there was about her a demureness, a coolness and charm that he had fancied only ladies of the city could attain. Oh, Rosa knew her charms, and had practiced many a day before her mirror till she had appraised the value of every curving eyelash, every hidden dimple, every cupid's curve of lip. Rosa had watched well and learned from all with whom she had come in contact. No woman's guile was left untried by her.

And Rosa was very sweet and charming. She knew just when to lift up innocent eyes of wonder, when to not understand suggestions, when to exclaim softly with delight or shrink with shyness that nevertheless did not repulse.

Forsythe studied her with wonder and delight. No maiden of the city had ever charmed him more, and withal she seemed so innocent and young, so altogether pliable in his hands. His pulses beat high, his heart was inflamed, and passion came and sat within his handsome eyes.

It was easy to persuade her, after her first seemingly shy reserve was overcome, and before an hour was passed she had promised to go away with him. He had very little money, but what of that? When he spoke of that feature Rosa declared she could easily get some. Her father gave her free access to his safe, and kept her plentifully supplied for the household use. It was nothing to her—a passing incident. What should it matter whose money took them on their way?

When she went demurely back to the ranch a little before sunset she thought she was very happy, poor little silly sinner! She met her father with her most alluring but most furtive smile. She was charming at supper, and blushed as her mother used to do when he praised her new gown and told her how well she looked in it. But she professed to be weary yet from the last days of school—to have a headache—and so she went early to her room and asked that the servants keep the house quiet in the morning, that she might sleep late and get really rested. Her father kissed her tenderly and thought what a dear child she was and what a comfort to his ripening years, and the house settled down into quiet.

Rosa packed a bag with some of her most elaborate garments, arrayed herself in a charming little outfit of silk for the journey, dropped her baggage out of the window, and when the moon rose and the household was quietly sleeping she paid a visit to her father's safe, and then stole forth, taking her shadowy way to the trail by a winding route known well to herself and secure from the watch of vigilant servants who were ever on the lookout for cattle thieves.

Thus she left her father's house and went forth to put her trust in a man whose promises were as ropes of sand and whose fancy was like a wave of the sea, tossed to and fro by every breath that blew. Long ere the sun rose the next morning the guarded, beloved child was as far from her safe home and her father's sheltering love as if alone she had started for the mouth of the bottomless pit. Two days later, while Margaret lay unconscious beneath the sagebrush, with a hovering eagle for watch, Rosa in the streets of a great city suddenly realized that she was more alone in the universe than ever she could have been in a wide desert, and her plight was far worse than the girl's with whose fate she had so lightly played.

Quite early on the morning after Rosa left, while the household was still keeping quiet for the supposed sleeper, Gardley rode into the inclosure about the house and asked for Rogers.

Gardley had been traveling night and day to get back. Matters had suddenly arranged themselves so that he could finish up his business at his old home and go on to see Margaret's father and mother, and he had made his visit there and hurried back to Arizona, hoping to reach Ashland in time for commencement. A delay on account of a washout on the road had brought him back two days late for commencement. He had ridden to camp from a junction forty miles away to get there the sooner, and this morning had ridden straight to the Tanners' to surprise Margaret. It was, therefore, a deep disappointment to find her gone and only Mrs. Tanner's voluble explanations for comfort. Mrs. Tanner exhausted her vocabulary in trying to describe the "Injuns," her own feeling of protest against them, and Mrs. Brownleigh's foolishness in making so much of them, and then she bustled in to the old pine desk in the dining room and produced the letter that had started Margaret off as soon as commencement was over.

Gardley took the letter eagerly, as though it were something to connect him with Margaret, and read it through carefully to make sure just how matters stood. He had looked troubled when Mrs. Tanner told how tired Margaret was, and how worried she seemed about her school and glad to get away from it all, and he agreed that the trip was probably a good thing.

"I wish Bud could have gone along, though," he said, thoughtfully, as he turned away from the door. "I don't like her to go with just Indians, though I suppose it is all right. You say he had his wife and child along? Of course Mrs. Brownleigh wouldn't send anybody that wasn't perfectly all right. Well, I suppose the trip will be a rest for her. I'm sorry I didn't get home a few days sooner. I might have looked out for her myself."

He rode away from the Tanners', promising to return later with a gift he had brought for Bud that he wanted to present himself, and Mrs. Tanner bustled back to her work again.

"Well, I'm glad he's got home, anyway," she remarked, aloud, to herself as she hung her dishcloth tidily over the upturned dishpan and took up her broom. "I 'ain't felt noways easy 'bout her sence she left, though I do suppose there ain't any sense to it. But I'm *glad he's back!*"

Meantime Gardley was riding toward Rogers's ranch, meditating whether he should venture to follow the expedition and enjoy at least the return trip with Margaret, or whether he ought to remain patiently until she came back and go to work at once. There was nothing really important demanding his attention immediately, for Rogers had arranged to keep the present overseer of affairs until he was ready to undertake the work. He was on his way now to report on a small business matter which he had been attending to in New York for Rogers. When that was over he would be free to do as he pleased for a few days more if he liked, and the temptation was great to go at once to Margaret.

As he stood waiting beside his horse in front of the house while the servant went to call Rogers, he looked about with delight on the beauty of the day. How glad he was to be back in Arizona again! Was it the charm of the place or because Margaret was here, he wondered, that he felt so happy? By all means he must follow her. Why should he not?

He looked at the clambering rose vine that covered one end of the house, and noticed how it crept close to the window casement and caressed the white curtain as it blew. Margaret must have such a vine at her window in the house he would build for her. It might be but a modest house that he could give her now, but it should have a rose vine just like that, and he would train it round her window where she could smell the fragrance from it every morning when she awoke, and where it would breathe upon her as she slept.

Margaret! How impatient he was to see her again! To look upon her dear face and know that she was his! That her father and mother had been satisfied about him and sent their blessing, and he might tell her so. It was wonderful! His heart thrilled with the thought of it. Of course he would go to her at once. He would start as soon as Rogers was through with him. He would go to Ganado. No, Keams. Which was it? He drew the letter out of his pocket and read it again, then replaced it.

The fluttering curtain up at the window blew out and in, and when it blew out again it brought with it a flurry of papers like white leaves. The curtain had knocked over a paperweight or vase or something that held them and set the papers free. The breeze caught them and flung them about erratically, tossing one almost at his feet. He stooped to pick it up, thinking it might be of value to someone, and caught the name "Margaret" and "Dear Margaret" written several times on the sheet, with "Walpi, Walpi, Walpi," filling the lower half of the page, as if someone had been practicing it.

And because these two words were just now keenly in his mind he reached for the second paper just a foot or two away and found more sentences and words. A third paper contained an exact reproduction of the letter which Mrs. Tanner had given him purporting to come from Mrs. Brownleigh to Margaret. What could it possibly mean?

In great astonishment he pulled out the other letter and compared them. They were almost identical save for a word here and there crossed out and rewritten. He stood looking mutely at the papers and then up at the window, as though an explanation might somehow be wafted down to him, not knowing what to think, his mind filled with vague alarm.

Just at that moment the servant appeared.

"Mr. Rogers says would you mind coming down to the corral. Miss Rosa has a headache, and we're keeping the house still for her to sleep. That's her window up there—" And he indicated the rose-bowered window with the fluttering curtain.

Dazed and half suspicious of something, Gardley folded the two letters together and crushed them into his pocket, wondering what he ought to do about it. The thought of it troubled him so that he only half gave attention to the business in hand, but he gave his report and handed over certain documents. He was thinking that perhaps he ought to see Miss Rosa and find out what she knew of Margaret's going and ask how she came in possession of this other letter.

"Now," said Rogers, as the matter was concluded, "I owe you some money. If you'll just step up to the house with me I'll give it to you. I'd like to settle matters up at once."

"Oh, let it go till I come again," said Gardley, impatient to be off. He wanted to get by himself and think out a solution of the two letters. He was more than uneasy about Margaret without being able to give any suitable explanation of why he should be. His main desire now was to ride to Ganado and find out if the missionaries had left home, which way they had gone, and whether they had met Margaret as planned.

"No, step right up to the house with me," insisted Rogers. "It won't take long, and I have the money in my safe."

Gardley saw that the quickest way was to please Rogers, and he did not wish to arouse any questions, because he supposed, of course, his alarm was mere foolishness. So they went together into Rogers's private office, where his desk and safe were the principal furniture, and where no servants ventured to come without orders.

Rogers shoved a chair for Gardley and went over to his safe, turning the little nickel knob this way and that with the skill of one long accustomed, and in a moment the thick door swung open and Rogers drew out a japanned cashbox and unlocked it. But when he threw the cover back he uttered an exclamation of angry surprise. The box was empty!

Chapter 32

Mr. Rogers strode to the door, forgetful of his sleeping daughter overhead, and thundered out his call for James. The servant appeared at once, but he knew nothing about the safe, and had not been in the office that morning. Other servants were summoned and put through a rigid examination. Then Rogers turned to the woman who had answered the door for Gardley and sent her up to call Rosa.

But the woman returned presently with word that Miss Rosa was not in her room, and there was no sign that her bed had been slept in during the night. The woman's face was sullen. She did not like Rosa, but was afraid of her. This to her was only another of Miss Rosa's pranks, and very likely her doting father would manage to blame the servants with the affair.

Mr. Rogers's face grew stern. His eyes flashed angrily as he turned and strode up the stairs to his daughter's room, but when he came down again he was holding a note in his trembling hand and his face was ashen white.

"Read that, Gardley," he said, thrusting the note into Gardley's hands and motioning at the same time for the servants to go away.

Gardley took the note, yet even as he read he noticed that the paper was the same as those he carried in his pocket. There was a peculiar watermark that made it noticeable.

The note was a flippant little affair from Rosa, telling her father she had gone away to be married and that she would let him know where she was as soon as they were located. She added that he had forced her to this step by being so severe with her and not allowing her lover to come to see her. If he had been reasonable she would have stayed at home and let him give her a grand wedding, but as it was she had only this way of seeking her happiness. She added that she knew he would forgive her, and she hoped he would come to see that her way had been best, and Forsythe was all that he could desire as a son-in-law.

Gardley uttered an exclamation of dismay as he read, and, looking up, found the miserable eyes of the stricken father upon him. For the moment his own alarm concerning Margaret and his perplexity about the letters were forgotten in the grief of the man who had been his friend.

"When did she go?" asked Gardley, quickly looking up.

"She took supper with me and then went to her room, complaining of a headache," said the father, his voice showing his utter hopelessness. "She may have gone early in the evening, perhaps, for we all turned in about nine o'clock to keep the house quiet on her account."

"Have you any idea which way they went, east or west?" Gardley was the keen adviser in a crisis now, his every sense on the alert.

The old man shook his head. "It is too late now," he said, still in that colorless voice. "They will have reached the railroad somewhere. They will have been married by this time. See, it is after ten o'clock!"

"Yes, if he marries her," said Gardley, fiercely. He had no faith in Forsythe.

"You think—you don't think he would *dare!*" The old man straightened up and fairly blazed in his righteous wrath.

"I think he would dare anything if he thought he would not be caught. He is a coward, of course."

"What can we do?"

"Telegraph to detectives at all points where they would be likely to arrive and have them shadowed. Come, we will ride to the station at once, but, first, could I go up to her room and look around? There might be some clue."

"Certainly," said Rogers, pointing hopelessly up the stairs; "the first door to the left. But you'll find nothing. I looked everywhere. She wouldn't have left a clue. While you're up there I'll interview the servants. Then we'll go."

As he went upstairs Gardley was wondering whether he ought to tell Rogers of the circumstance of the two letters. What possible connection could there be between Margaret Earle's trip to Walpi with the Brownleighs and Rosa Rogers's elopement? When you come to think of it, what possible explanation was there for a copy of Mrs.

Brownleigh's letter to blow out of Rosa Rogers's bedroom window? How could it have gotten there?

Rosa's room was in beautiful order, the roses nodding in at the window, the curtain blowing back and forth in the breeze and rippling open the leaves of a tiny Testament lying on her desk, as if it had been recently read. There was nothing to show that the owner of the room had taken a hasty flight. On the desk lay several sheets of notepaper with the peculiar watermark. These caught his attention, and he took up and compared them with the papers in his pocket. It was a strange thing that that letter which had sent Margaret off into the wilderness with an unknown Indian should be written on the same kind of paper as this, and yet, perhaps, it was not so strange, after all. It probably was the only notepaper to be had in that region, and must all have been purchased at the same place.

The rippling leaves of the Testament fluttered open at the flyleaf and revealed Rosa's name and a date with Mrs. Brownleigh's name written below, and Gardley took it up, startled again to find Hazel Brownleigh mixed up with the Rogers. He had not known that they had anything to do with each other. And yet, of course, they would, being the missionaries of the region.

The almost empty wastebasket next caught his eye, and here again were several sheets of paper written over with words and phrases, words which at once he recognized as part of the letter Mrs. Tanner had given him. He emptied the wastebasket out on the desk, thinking perhaps there might be something there that would give a clue to where the elopers had gone, but there was not much else in it except a little yellowed note with the signature "Hazel Brownleigh" at the bottom. He glanced through the brief note, gathered its purport, and then spread it out deliberately on the desk and compared the writing with the others, a wild fear clutching at his heart. Yet he could not in any way explain why he was so uneasy. What possible reason could Rosa Rogers have for forging a letter to Margaret from Hazel Brownleigh?

Suddenly Rogers stood behind him looking over his shoulder. "What is it, Gardley? What have you found? Any clue?"

"No clue," said Gardley, uneasily, "but something strange I cannot understand. I don't suppose it can possibly have anything to do with your daughter, and yet it seems almost uncanny. This morning I stopped at the Tanners' to let Miss Earle know I had returned, and was told she had gone yesterday with a couple of Indians as guide to meet the Brownleighs at Keams or somewhere near there, and take a trip with them to Walpi to see the Hopi Indians. Mrs. Tanner gave me this letter from Mrs. Brownleigh, which Miss Earle had left behind. But when I reached here and was waiting for you some papers blew out of your daughter's window. When I picked them up I was startled to find that one of them was an exact copy of the letter I had in my pocket. See! Here they are! I don't suppose there is anything to it, but in spite of me I am a trifle uneasy about Miss Earle. I just can't understand how that copy of the letter came to be here."

Rogers was leaning over, looking at the papers. "What's this?" he asked, picking up the note that came with the Testament. He read each paper carefully, took in the little Testament with its fluttering flyleaf and inscription, studied the pages of words and alphabet, then suddenly turned away and groaned, hiding his face in his hands.

"What is it?" asked Gardley, awed with the awful sorrow in the strong man's attitude.

"My poor baby!" groaned the father. "My poor little baby girl! I've always been afraid of that fatal gift of hers. Gardley, she could copy any handwriting in the world perfectly. She could write my name so it could not be told from my own signature. She's evidently written that letter. Why, I don't know, unless she wanted to get Miss Earle out of the way so it would be easier for her to carry out her plans."

"It can't be!" said Gardley, shaking his head. "I can't see what her object would be. Besides, where would she find the Indians? Mrs. Tanner saw the Indians. They came to the school after her with the letter, and waited for her. Mrs. Tanner saw them ride off together."

"There were a couple of strange Indians here yesterday, begging something to eat," said Rogers, settling down on a chair and resting his head against the desk as if he had suddenly lost the strength to stand.

"This won't do!" said Gardley. "We've got to get down to the telegraph office, you and I. Now try to brace up. Are the horses ready? Then we'll go right away."

"You better question the servants about those Indians first," said Rogers, and Gardley, as he hurried down the stairs, heard groan after groan from Rosa's room where her father lingered in agony.

Gardley got all the information he could about the Indians, and then the two men started away on a gallop to the station. As they passed the Tanner house Gardley drew rein to call to Bud, who hurried out joyfully to greet his friend, his face lighting with pleasure.

"Bill, get on your horse in double-quick time and beat it out to camp for me, will you?" said Gardley, as he reached down and gripped Bud's rough young paw. "Tell Jasper Kemp to come back with you and meet me at the station as quick as he can. Tell him to have the men where he can signal them. We may have to hustle out on a long hunt, and, Bill, keep your head steady and get back yourself right away. Perhaps I'll want you to help me. I'm a little anxious about Miss Earle, but you needn't tell anybody that but old Jasper. Tell him to hurry for all he's worth."

Bud, with his eyes large with loyalty and trouble, nodded understandingly, returned the grip of the young man's hand with a clumsy squeeze, and sprang away to get his horse and do Gardley's bidding. Gardley knew he would ride as for his life, now that he knew Margaret's safety was at stake.

Then Gardley rode on to the station and was indefatigable for two hours hunting out addresses, writing telegrams, and calling up long-distance telephones.

When all had been done that was possible Rogers turned a haggard face to the young man. "I've been thinking, Gardley, that rash little girl of mine may have got Miss Earle into some kind of a dangerous position. You ought to look after her. What can we do?"

"I'm going to, sir," said Gardley, "just as soon as I've done everything I can for you. I've already sent for Jasper Kemp, and we'll make a plan between us and find out if Miss Earle is all right. Can you spare Jasper or will you need him?"

"By all means! Take all the men you need. I shan't rest easy till I know Miss Earle is safe."

He sank down on a truck that stood on the station platform, his shoulders slumping, his whole attitude as of one who was fatally stricken. It came over Gardley how suddenly old he looked, and haggard and gray! What a thing for the selfish child to have done to her father! Poor, silly child, whose fate with Forsythe would in all probability be anything but enviable!

But there was no time for sorrowful reflections. Jasper Kemp, stern, alert, anxious, came riding furiously down the street, Bud keeping even pace with him.

Chapter 33

While Gardley briefly told his tale to Jasper Kemp, and the Scotchman was hastily scanning the papers with his keen, bright eyes, Bud stood frowning and listening intently.

"Gee!" he burst forth. "That girl's a mess! 'Course she did it! You oughta seen what all she didn't do the last six weeks of school. Miss Mar'get got so she shivered every time that girl came near her or looked at her. She sure had her goat! Some nights after school, when she thought she's all alone, she just cried, she did. Why, Rosa had every one of those guys in the backseat acting like the devil, and nobody knew what was the matter. She wrote things on the blackboard right in the questions, so's it looked like Miss Mar'get's writing; fierce things, sometimes, and Miss Mar'get didn't know who did it. And she was as jealous as a cat of Miss Mar'get. You all know what a case she had on that guy from over by the fort, and she didn't like to have him even look at Miss Mar'get. Well, she didn't forget how he went away that night of the play. I caught her looking at her like she would like to murder her. *Good night!* Some look! The guy had a case on Miss Mar'get, all right, too, only she was onto him and wouldn't look at him nor let him spoon nor nothing. But Rosa saw it all, and she just hated Miss Mar'get. Then once Miss Mar'get stopped her from going out to meet that guy, too. Oh, she hated her, all right! And you can bet she wrote the letter! Sure she did! She wanted to get her away when that guy came back. He was back yesterday. I saw him over by the run on that trail that crosses the trail to the old cabin. He didn't see me. I got my eye on him first, and I chucked behind some sagebrush, but he was here, all right, and he didn't mean any good. I follahed him awhile till he stopped and fixed up a place to camp. I guess he must 'a' stayed out last night—"

A heavy hand was suddenly laid from behind on Bud's shoulder, and Rogers stood over him, his dark eyes on fire, his lips trembling.

"Boy, can you show me where that was?" he asked, and there was an intensity in his voice that showed Bud that something serious was the matter. Boylike he dropped his eyes indifferently before this great emotion.

"Sure!"

"Best take Long Bill with you, Mr. Rogers," advised Jasper Kemp, keenly alive to the whole situation. "I reckon we'll all have to work together. My men ain't far off," and he lifted his whistle to his lips and blew the signal blasts. "The kid here'll want to ride to Keams to see if the lady is all safe and has met her friends. I reckon mebbe I better go straight to Ganado and find out if them mission folks really got started, and put 'em wise to what's been going on. They'll mebbe know who them Injuns was. I have my suspicions they weren't any friendlies. I didn't like that Injun the minute I set eyes on him hanging round the schoolhouse, but I wouldn't have stirred a step toward camp if I'd 'a' suspected he was come fur the lady. 'Spose you take Bud and Long Bill and go find that camping place and see if you find any trail showing which way they took. If you do, you fire three shots, and the men'll be with you. If you want the kid, fire four shots. He can't be so fur away by that time that he can't hear. He's got to get provisioned 'fore he starts. Lead him out, Bud. We 'ain't got no time to lose."

Bud gave one despairing look at Gardley and turned to obey.

"That's all right, Bud," said Gardley, with an understanding glance. "You tell Mr. Rogers all you know and show him the place, and then when Long Bill comes you can take the crosscut to the Long Trail and go with me. I'll just stop at the house as I go by and tell your mother I need you."

Bud gave one radiant, grateful look and sprang upon his horse, and Rogers had hard work to keep up with him at first, till Bud got interested in giving him a detailed account of Fosythe's looks and acts.

In less than an hour the relief expedition had started. Before night had fallen Jasper Kemp, riding hard, arrived at the mission, told his story, procured a fresh horse, and after a couple of hours' rest started with Brownleigh and his wife for Keams Canyon.

Gardley and Bud, riding for all they were worth, said little by the way. Now and then the boy stole glances at the man's face, and the dead weight of sorrow settled like lead, the heavier, upon his heart. Too well he knew the dangers of the desert. He could almost read Gardley's fears in the white, drawn look about his lips, the ashen circles under his eyes, the tense, strained pose of his whole figure. Gardley's mind was urging ahead of his steed, and his body could not relax. He was anxious to go a little faster, yet his judgment knew it would not do, for his horse would play out before he could get another. They ate their corn bread in the saddle, and only turned aside from the trail once to drink at a water hole and fill their cans. They rode late into the night, with only the stars and their wits to guide them. When they stopped to rest they did not wait to make a fire, but hobbled the horses where they might feed, and, rolling quickly in their blankets, lay down upon the ground.

Bud, with the fatigue of healthy youth, would have slept till morning in spite of his fears, but Gardley woke him in a couple of hours, made him drink some water and eat a bite of food, and they went on their way again. When morning broke they were almost to the entrance of Keams Canyon and both looked haggard and worn. Bud seemed to have aged in the night, and Gardley looked at him almost tenderly.

"Are you all in, kid?" he asked.

"Naw!" answered Bud, promptly, with an assumed cheerfulness. "Feeling like a four-year-old. Get on to that sky? Guess we're going to have some day! Pretty as a red wagon!"

Gardley smiled sadly. What would that day bring forth for the two who went in search of her they loved? His great anxiety was to get to Keams Canyon and inquire. They would surely know at the trading post whether the missionary and his party had gone that way.

The road was still almost impassable from the flood; the two dauntless riders picked their way slowly down the trail to the post.

But the trader could tell them nothing comforting. The missionary had not been that way in two months, and there had been no party and no lady there that week. A single strange Indian had come down the trail above the day before, stayed awhile, picked a quarrel with some men who were there, and then ridden back up the steep trail again. He might have had a party with him up on the mesa, waiting. He had said something about his squaw. The trader admitted that he might have been drunk, but he frowned as he spoke of him. He called him a "bad Indian." Something unpleasant had evidently happened.

The trader gave them a good, hot dinner, of which they stood sorely in need, and because they realized that they must keep up their strength they took the time to eat it. Then, procuring fresh horses, they climbed the steep trail in the direction the trader said the Indian had taken. It was a slender clue, but it was all they had, and they must follow it. And now the travelers were very silent, as if they felt they were drawing near to some knowledge that would settle the question for them one way or the other. As they reached the top at last, where they could see out across the plain, each drew a long breath like a gasp and looked about, half fearing what he might see.

Yes, there was the sign of a recent camp fire, and a few tin cans and bits of refuse, nothing more. Gardley got down and searched carefully. Bud even crept about upon his hands and knees, but a single tiny blue bead like a grain of sand was all that rewarded his efforts. Some Indian had doubtless camped here. That was all the evidence. Standing thus in hopeless uncertainty what to do next, they suddenly heard voices. Something familiar once or twice made Gardley lift his whistle and blow a blast. Instantly a silvery answer came ringing from the mesa a mile or so away and woke the echoes in the canyon. Jasper Kemp and his party had taken the longer way around instead of going down the canyon, and were just arriving at the spot where Margaret and the Indian had waited two days before for their drunken guide. But Jasper Kemp's whistle rang out again, and he shot three times into the air, their signal to wait for some important news.

Breathlessly and in silence the two waited till the coming of the rest of the party, and cast themselves down on the ground, feeling the sudden need of support. Now that there was a possibility of some news, they felt hardly able to bear it, and the waiting for it was intolerable, to such a point of anxious tension were they strained.

But when the party from Ganado came in sight their faces wore no brightness of good news. Their greetings were quiet, sad, anxious, and Jasper Kemp held out to Gardley an envelope. It was the one from Margaret's mother's letter that she had dropped upon the trail.

"We found it on the way from Ganado, just as we entered Steamboat Canyon," explained Jasper.

"And didn't you search for a trail off in any other direction?" asked Gardley, almost sharply. "They have not been here. At least only one Indian has been down to the trader's."

"There was no other trail. We looked," said Jasper, sadly. "There was a camp fire twice, and signs of a camp. We felt sure they had come this way."

Gardley shook his head and a look of abject despair came over his face. "There is no sign here," he said. "They must have gone some other way. Perhaps the Indian has carried her off. Are the other men following?"

"No, Rogers sent them in the other direction after his girl. They found the camp all right. Bud tell you? We made sure we had found our trail and would not need them."

Gardley dropped his head and almost groaned.

Meanwhile the missionary had been riding around in radiating circles from the dead camp fire, searching every step of the way, and Bud, taking his cue from him, looked off toward the mesa a minute, then struck out in a straight line for it and rode off like mad. Suddenly there was heard a shout loud and long, and Bud came riding back, waving something small and white above his head.

They gathered in a little knot, waiting for the boy, not speaking, and when he halted in their midst he fluttered down the handkerchief to Gardley.

"It's hers, all right. Gotter name all written out on the edge!" he declared, radiantly.

The sky grew brighter to them all now. Eagerly Gardley sprang into his saddle, no longer weary, but alert and eager for the trail.

"You folks better go down to the trader's and get some dinner. You'll need it! Bud and I'll go on. Mrs. Brownleigh looks all in."

"No," declared Hazel, decidedly. "We'll just snatch a bite here and follow you at once. I couldn't enjoy a dinner till I know she is safe." And so, though both Jasper Kemp and her husband urged her otherwise, she would take a hasty meal by the way and hurry on.

But Bud and Gardley waited not for others. They plunged wildly ahead.

It seemed a long way to the eager hunters, from the place where Bud had found the handkerchief to the little note twisted around the red chessman. It was perhaps nearly a mile, and both the riders had searched in all directions for some time before Gardley spied it. Eagerly he seized upon the note, recognizing the little red manikin with which he had whiled away an hour with Margaret during one of her visits at the camp.

The note was written large and clear upon a sheet of writing-paper:

"I am Margaret Earle, schoolteacher at Ashland. I am supposed to be traveling to Walpi, by way of Keams, to meet Mr. and Mrs. Brownleigh of Ganado. I am with an Indian, his wife and child. The Indian said he was sent to guide me, but he is drunk now and I am frightened. He has acted strangely all the way. I do not know where I am. Please come and help me."

Bud, sitting anxious like a statue upon his horse, read Gardley's face as Gardley read the note. Then Gardley read it aloud to Bud, and before the last word was fairly out of his mouth both man and boy started as if they had heard Margaret's beloved voice calling them. It was not long before Bud found another scrap of paper a half mile farther on, and then another and another, scattered at great distances along the way. The only way they had of being sure she had dropped them was that they seemed to be the same kind of paper as that upon which the note was written.

How that note with its brave, frightened appeal wrung the heart of Gardley as he thought of Margaret, unprotected, in terror and perhaps in peril, riding on she knew not where. What trials and fears had she not already passed through! What might she not be experiencing even now while he searched for her?

It was perhaps two hours before he found the little white stocking dropped where the trail divided, showing which way she had taken.

Gardley folded it reverently and put it in his pocket. An hour later Bud pounced upon the bedroom slipper and carried it gleefully to Gardley, and so by slow degrees, finding here and there a chessman or more paper, they came at last to the camp where the Indians had abandoned their trust and fled, leaving Margaret alone in the wilderness.

It was then that Gardley searched in vain for any further clue, and, riding wide in every direction, stopped and called her name again and again, while the sun grew lower and lower and shadows crept in lurking places waiting for the swift-coming night. It was then that Bud, flying frantically from one spot to another, got down upon his knees behind some sagebrush when Gardley was not looking and mumbled a rough, hasty prayer for help. He felt like the old woman who, on being told that nothing but God could save the ship, exclaimed, "And has it come to that?" Bud had felt all his life that there was a remote time in every life when one might need to believe in prayer. The time had come for Bud.

Margaret, on her knees in the sand of the desert praying for help, remembered the promise, "Before they call I will answer, and while they are yet speaking I will hear," and knew not that her deliverers were on the way.

The sun had been hot as it beat down upon the whiteness of the sand, and the girl had crept under the sagebrush for shelter from it. The pain in her ankle was sickening. She had removed her shoe and bound the ankle about with a handkerchief soaked with half of her bottle of witch hazel, and so, lying quiet, had fallen asleep, too exhausted with pain and anxiety to stay awake any longer.

When she awoke again the softness of evening was hovering over everything, and she started up and listened. Surely, surely, she had heard a voice calling her! She sat up sharply and listened. Ah! There it was again, a faint echo in the distance. Was it a voice, or was it only her dreams mingling with her fancies?

Travelers in deserts, she had read, took all sorts of fancies, saw mirages, heard sounds that were not. But she had not been out long enough to have caught such a desert fever. Perhaps she was going to be sick. Still that faint echo made her heart beat wildly. She dragged herself to her knees, then to her feet, standing painfully with the weight on her well foot.

The suffering horse turned his anguished eyes and whinnied. Her heart ached for him, yet there was no way she could assuage his pain or put him out of his misery. But she must make sure if she had heard a voice. Could she possibly scale that rock down which she and her horse had fallen? For then she might look out farther and see if there were anyone in sight.

Painfully she crawled and crept, up and up, inch by inch, until at last she gained the little height and could look afar.

There was no living thing in sight. The air was very clear. The eagle had found his evening rest somewhere in a quiet crag. The long corn waved on the distant plain, and all was deathly still once more. There was a hint of coming sunset in the sky. Her heart sank, and she was about to give up hope entirely, when, rich and clear, there it came again! A voice in the wilderness calling her name: "Margaret! Margaret!"

The tears rushed to her eyes and crowded in her throat. She could not answer, she was so overwhelmed, and though she tried twice to call out, she could make no sound. But the call kept coming again and again: "Margaret! Margaret!" and it was Gardley's voice. Impossible! For Gardley was far away and could not know her need. Yet it was his voice. Had she died, or was she in delirium that she seemed to hear him calling her name?

But the call came clearer now: "Margaret! Margaret! I am coming!" and like a flash her mind went back to the first night in Arizona when she heard him singing, "From the Desert I Come to Thee!"

Now she struggled to her feet again and shouted, inarticulately and gladly through her tears. She could see him. It was Gardley. He was riding fast toward her, and he shot three shots into the air above him as he rode, and three shrill blasts of his whistle rang out on the still evening air.

She tore the scarf from her neck that she had tied about it to keep the sun from blistering her, and waved it wildly in the air now, shouting in happy, choking sobs.

And so he came to her across the desert!

He sprang down before the horse had fairly reached her side, and, rushing to her, took her in his arms.

"Margaret! My darling! I have found you at last!"

She swayed and would have fallen but for his arms, and then he saw her white face and knew she must be suffering.

"You are hurt!" he cried. "Oh, what have they done to you?" And he laid her gently down upon the sand and dropped on his knees beside her.

"Oh, no," she gasped, joyously, with white lips. "I'm all right now. Only my ankle hurts a little. We had a fall, the horse and I. Oh, go to him at once and put him out of his pain. I'm sure his legs are broken."

For answer Gardley put the whistle to his lips and blew a blast. He would not leave her for an instant. He was not sure yet that she was not more hurt than she had said. He set about discovering at once, for he had brought with him supplies for all emergencies.

It was Bud who came riding madly across the mesa in answer to the call, reaching Gardley before anyone else. Bud with his eyes shining, his cheeks blazing with excitement, his hair wildly flying in the breeze, his young, boyish face suddenly grown old with lines of anxiety. But you wouldn't have known from his greeting that it was anything more than a pleasure excursion he had been on the past two days.

"Good work, kid! Whatcha want me t'do?"

It was Bud who arranged the camp and went back to tell the other detachments that Margaret was found; Bud who led the packhorse up, unpacked the provisions, and gathered wood to start a fire. Bud was everywhere, with a smudged face, a weary, gray look around his eyes, and his hair sticking "seven ways for Sunday." Yet once, when his labors led him near to where Margaret lay weak and happy on a couch of blankets, he gave her an unwonted pat on her shoulder and said in a low tone: "Hello, Gang! See you kept your nerve with you!" and then he gave her a grin all across his dirty, tired face, and moved away as if he were half ashamed of his emotion. But it was Bud again who came and talked with her to divert her so that she wouldn't notice when they shot her horse. He talked loudly about a coyote they shot the night before, and a cottontail they saw at Keams, and when he saw that she understood what the shot meant, and there were tears in her eyes, he gave her hand a rough, bear squeeze and said, gruffly: "You shouldn't worry! He's better off now!" And when Gardley came back he took himself thoughtfully to a distance and busied himself opening tins of meat and soup.

In another hour the Brownleighs arrived, having heard the signals, and they had a supper around the camp fire, everybody so rejoiced that there were still quivers in their voices, and when anyone laughed it sounded like the echo of a sob, so great had been the strain of their anxiety.

Gardley, sitting beside Margaret in the starlight afterward, her hand in his, listened to the story of her journey, the strong, tender pressure of his fingers telling her how deeply it affected him to know the peril through which she had passed. Later, when the others were telling gay stories about the fire, and Bud lying full length in their midst had fallen fast asleep, these two, a little apart from the rest, were murmuring their innermost thoughts in low tones to each other, and rejoicing that they were together once more.

Chapter 34

They talked it over the next morning at breakfast as they sat around the fire. Jasper Kemp thought he ought to get right back to attend to things. Mr. Rogers was all broken up, and might even need him to search for Rosa if they had not found out her whereabouts yet. He and Fiddling Boss, who had come along, would start back at once. They had had a good night's rest and had found their dear lady. What more did they need? Besides, there were not provisions for an indefinite stay for such a large party, and there were none too many sources of supply in this region.

The missionary thought that, now he was here, he ought to go on to Walpi. It was not more than two hours' ride there, and Hazel could stay with the camp while Margaret's ankle had a chance to rest and let the swelling subside under treatment.

Margaret, however, rebelled. She did not wish to be an invalid, and was very sure she could ride without injury to her ankle. She wanted to see Walpi and the Hopi Indians, now she was so near. So a compromise was agreed upon. They would all wait in camp a couple of days, and then if Margaret felt well enough they would go on, visit the Hopis, and so go home together.

Bud pleaded to be allowed to stay with them, and Jasper Kemp promised to make it all right with his parents.

So for two whole, long, lovely days the little party of five camped on the mesa and enjoyed sweet converse. It is safe to say that never in all Bud's life will he forget or get away from the influences of that day in such company.

Gardley and the missionary proved to be the best of physicians, and Margaret's ankle improved hourly under their united treatment of compresses, lotions, and rest. About noon on Saturday they broke camp, mounted their horses, and rode away across the stretch of white sand, through tall cornfields growing right up out of the sand, closer and closer to the great mesa with the castlelike pueblos five hundred feet above them on the top. It seemed to Margaret like suddenly being dropped into Egypt or the Holy Land, or some of the Babylonian excavations, so curious and primitive and altogether different from anything else she had ever seen did it all appear. She listened, fascinated, while Brownleigh told about this strange Hopi land, the strangest spot in America. Spanish explorers found them away back years before the Pilgrims landed, and called the country Tuscayan. They built their homes up high for protection from their enemies. They lived on the corn, pumpkins, peaches, and melons which they raised in the valley, planting the seeds with their hands. It is supposed they got their seeds first from the Spaniards years ago. They make pottery, cloth, and baskets, and are a busy people.

There are seven villages built on three mesas in the northern desert. One of the largest, Orabi, has a thousand inhabitants. Walpi numbers about two hundred and thirty people, all living in this one great building of many rooms. They are divided into brotherhoods, or phratries, and each brotherhood has several large families. They are ruled by a speaker chief and a war chief elected by a council of clan elders.

Margaret learned with wonder that all the water these people used had to be carried by the women in jars on their backs five hundred feet up the steep trail.

Presently, as they drew nearer, a curious man with his hair "banged" like a child's, and garments much like those usually worn by scarecrows—a shapeless kind of shirt and trousers—appeared along the steep and showed them the way up. Margaret and the missionary's wife exclaimed in horror over the little children playing along the very edge of the cliffs above as carelessly as birds in trees.

High up on the mesa at last, how strange and weird it seemed! Far below the yellow sand of the valley; fifteen miles away a second mesa stretching dark; to the southwest, a hundred miles distant, the dim outlines of the San Francisco peaks. Some little children on burros crossing the sand below looked as if they were part of a curious moving picture, not as if they were little living beings taking life as seriously as other children do. The great, wide desert stretching far!

The bare, solid rocks beneath their feet! The curious houses behind them! It all seemed unreal to Margaret, like a great picture book spread out for her to see. She turned from gazing and found Gardley's eyes upon her adoringly, a tender understanding of her mood in his glance. She thrilled with pleasure to be here with him, a soft flush spread over her cheeks and a light came into her eyes.

They found the Indians preparing for one of their most famous ceremonies, the snake dance, which was to take place in a few days. For almost a week the snake priests had been busy hunting rattlesnakes, building altars, drawing figures in the sand, and singing weird songs. On the ninth day the snakes are washed in a pool and driven near a pile of sand. The priests, arrayed in paint, feathers, and charms, come out in line and, taking the live snakes in their mouths, parade up and down the rocks, while the people crowd the roofs and terraces of the pueblos to watch. There are helpers to whip the snakes and keep them from biting, and catchers to see that none get away. In a little while the priests take the snakes down on the desert and set them free, sending them north, south, east, and west, where it is supposed they will take the people's prayers for rain to the water serpent in the underworld, who is in some way connected with the god of the rain clouds.

It was a strange experience, that night in Walpi: the primitive accommodations, the picturesque, uncivilized people, the shy glances from dark, eager eyes. To watch two girls grinding corn between two stones, and a little farther off their mother rolling out her dough with an ear of corn, and cooking over an open fire, her pot slung from a crude crane over the blaze—it was all too unreal to be true.

But the most interesting thing about it was to watch the "Aneshodi" going about among them, his face alight with warm, human love, his hearty laugh ringing out in a joke that the Hopis seemed to understand, making himself one with them. It came to Margaret suddenly to remember the pompous little figure of the Reverend Frederick West, and to fancy him going about among these people and trying to do them good. Before she knew what she was doing she laughed aloud at the thought. Then, of course, she had to explain to Bud and Gardley, who looked at her inquiringly.

"Aw! Gee! *Him? He* wasn't a minister! He was a *mistake!* Fergit him, the poor simp!" growled Bud, sympathetically. Then his eyes softened as he watched Brownleigh playing with three little Indian maids, having a fine romp. "Gee! He certainly is a peach, isn't he?" he murmured, his whole face kindling appreciatively. "Gee! I bet that kid never forgets that!"

The Sunday was a wonderful day, when the missionary gathered the people together and spoke to them in simple words of God— their god who made the sky, the stars, the mountains, and the sun, whom they call by different names, but whom He called God. He spoke of the Book of Heaven that told about God and His great love for men, so great that He sent His son to save them from their sin. It was not a long sermon, but a very beautiful one; and, listening to the simple, wonderful words of life that fell from the missionary's earnest lips and were translated by his faithful Indian interpreter, who always went with him on his expeditions, watching the faces of the dark, strange people as they took in the marvelous meaning, the little company of visitors was strangely moved. Even Bud, awed beyond his wont, said, shyly, to Margaret:

"Gee! It's something fierce not to be born a Christian and know all that, ain't it?"

Margaret and Gardley walked a little way down the narrow path that led out over the neck of rock less than a rod wide that connects the great promontory with the mesa. The sun was setting in majesty over the desert, and the scene was one of breathless beauty. One might fancy it might look so to stand on the hills of God and look out over creation when all things have been made new.

They stood for a while in silence. Then Margaret looked down at the narrow path worn more than a foot deep in the solid rock by the ten generations of feet that had been passing over it.

"Just think," she said, "of all the feet, little and big, that have walked here in all the years, and of all the souls that have stood and looked out over this wonderful sight! It must be that somehow in spite of their darkness they have reached out to the God who made this, and have found a way to His heart. They couldn't look at this and not feel Him, could they? It seems to me that perhaps some of those poor creatures who have stood here and reached up blindly after the Creator of their souls have, perhaps, been as pleasing to Him as those who have known about Him from childhood."

Gardley was used to her talking this way. He had not been in her Sunday meetings for nothing. He understood and sympathized, and now his hand reached softly for hers and held it tenderly. After a moment of silence he said:

"I surely think if God could reach and find me in the desert of my life, He must have found them. I sometimes think I was a greater heathen than all these, because I knew and would not see."

Margaret nestled her hand in his and looked up joyfully into his face. "I'm so glad you know Him now!" she murmured, happily.

They stood for some time looking out over the changing scene, till the crimson faded into rose, the silver into gray, till the stars bloomed out one by one, and down in the valley across the desert a light twinkled faintly here and there from the camps of the Hopi shepherds.

They started home at daybreak the next morning, the whole company of Indians standing on the rocks to send them royally on their way, pressing simple, homely gifts upon them and begging them to return soon again and tell the blessed story.

A wonderful ride they had back to Ganado, where Gardley left Margaret for a short visit, promising to return for her in a few days when she was rested, and hastened back to Ashland to his work, for his soul was happy now and at ease, and he felt he must get to work at once. Rogers would need him. Poor Rogers! Had he found his daughter yet? Poor, silly child-prodigal!

But when Gardley reached Ashland he found among his mail awaiting him a telegram. His uncle was dead, and the fortune which he had been brought up to believe was his, and which he had idly tossed away in a moment of recklessness, had been restored to him by the uncle's last will, made since Gardley's recent visit home. The fortune was his again!

Gardley sat in his office on the Rogers's ranch and stared hard at the adobe wall opposite his desk. That fortune would be great! He could do such wonderful things for Margaret now. They could work out their dreams together for the people they loved. He could see the shadows of those dreams—a beautiful home for Margaret out on the trail she loved, where wildness and beauty and the mountain she called hers were not far away; horses in plenty and a luxurious car when they wanted to take a trip; journeys East as often as they wished; some of the ideal appliances for the school that Margaret loved; a church for the missionary and convenient halls where he could speak at his outlying districts; a trip to the city for Mom Wallis, where she might see a real picture gallery, her one expressed desire this side of heaven, now that she had taken to reading Browning and had some of it explained to her. Oh, and a lot of wonderful things! These all hung in the dream picture before Gardley's eyes as he sat at his desk with that bit of yellow paper in his hand.

He thought of what that money had represented to him in the past. Reckless days and nights of folly as a boy and young man at college; ruthless waste of time, money, youth; shriveling of soul, till Margaret came and found and rescued him! How wonderful that he had been rescued! That he had come to his senses at last, and was here in a man's position, doing a man's work in the world! Now, with all that money, there was no need for him to work and earn more. He could live idly all his days and just have a good time—make others happy, too. But still he would not have this exhilarating feeling that he was supplying his own and Margaret's necessities by the labor of hand and brain. The little telegram in his hand seemed somehow to be trying to snatch from him all this material prosperity that was the symbol of that spiritual regeneration which had become so dear to him.

He put his head down on his clasped hands upon the desk then and prayed. Perhaps it was the first great prayer of his life.

"O God, let me be strong enough to stand this that has come upon me. Help me to be a man in spite of money! Don't let me lose my manhood and my right to work. Help me to use the money in the right way and not to dwarf myself, nor spoil our lives with it." It was a great prayer for a man such as Gardley had been, and the answer came swiftly in his conviction.

He lifted up his head with purpose in his expression, and, folding the telegram, put it safely back into his pocket. He would not tell Margaret of it—not just yet. He would think it out—just the right way—and he did not believe he meant to give up his position with Rogers. He had accepted it for a year in good faith, and it was his business to fulfill the contract. Meantime, this money would perhaps make possible his marriage with Margaret sooner than he had hoped.

Five minutes later Rogers telephoned to the office.

"I've decided to take that shipment of cattle and try that new stock, provided you will go out and look at them and see that everything is all okay. I couldn't go myself now. Don't feel like going anywhere, you know. You wouldn't need to go for a couple of weeks. I've just had a letter from the man, and he says he won't be ready sooner. Say, why don't you and Miss Earle get married and make this a wedding trip? She could go to the Pacific coast with you. It would be a nice trip. Then I could spare you for a month or six weeks when you got back if you wanted to take her East for a little visit."

Why not? Gardley stumbled out his thanks and hung up the receiver, his face full of the light of a great joy. How were the blessings pouring down upon his head these days? Was it a sign that God was pleased with his action in making good what he could where he had failed? And Rogers! How kind he was! Poor Rogers, with his broken heart and his stricken home! For Rosa had come home again a sadder, wiser child, and her father seemed crushed with the disgrace of it all.

Gardley went to Margaret that very afternoon. He told her only that he had had some money left him by his uncle, which would make it possible for him to marry at once and keep her comfortably now. He was to be sent to California on a business trip. Would she be married and go with him?

Margaret studied the telegram in wonder. She had never asked Gardley much about his circumstances. The telegram merely stated that his uncle's estate was left to him. To her simple mind an estate might be a few hundred dollars, enough to furnish a plain little home, and her face lighted with joy over it. She asked no questions, and Gardley said no more about the money. He had forgotten that question, comparatively, in the greater possibility of joy.

Would she be married in ten days and go with him?

Her eyes met his with an answering joy, and yet he could see that there was a trouble hiding somewhere. He presently saw what it was without needing to be told. Her father and mother! Of course, they would be disappointed. They would want her to be married at home!

"But Rogers said we could go and visit them for several weeks on our return," he said, and Margaret's face lighted up.

"Oh, that would be beautiful," she said, wistfully, "and perhaps they won't mind so much—though I always expected Father would marry me if I was ever married; still, if we can go home so soon and for so long—and Mr. Brownleigh would be next best, of course."

"But, of course, your father must marry you," said Gardley, determinedly. "Perhaps we could persuade him to come, and your mother, too."

"Oh no, they couldn't possibly," said Margaret, quickly, a shade of sadness in her eyes. "You know it costs a lot to come out here, and ministers are never rich."

It was then that Gardley's eyes lighted with joy. His money could take this bugbear away, at least. However, he said nothing about the money.

"Suppose we write to your father and mother and put the matter before them. See what they say. We'll send the letters tonight. You write your mother and I'll write your father."

Margaret agreed and sat down at once to write her letter, while Gardley, on the other side of the room, wrote his, scratching away contentedly with his fountain pen, and looking furtively now and then toward the bowed head over at the desk.

Gardley did not read his letter to Margaret. She wondered a little at this, but did not ask, and the letters were mailed, with special-delivery stamps on them. Gardley awaited their replies with great impatience.

He filled in the days of waiting with business. There were letters to write connected with his fortune, and there were arrangements to be made for his trip. But the thing that occupied the most of his time and thought was the purchase and refitting of a roomy old ranch house in a charming location, not more than three miles from Ashland, on the road to the camp.

It had been vacant for a couple of years past, the owner having gone abroad permanently and the place having been offered for sale. Margaret had often admired it in her trips to and from the camp, and Gardley thought of it at once when it became possible for him to think of purchasing a home in the West.

There was a great stone fireplace, and the beams of the ceilings and pillars of the porch and wide, hospitable rooms were of tree trunks with the bark on them. With a little work it could be made roughly but artistically habitable. Gardley had it cleaned up, not disturbing the tangle of vines and shrubbery that had had their way since the last owner had left them and which had made a perfect screen from the road for the house.

Behind this screen the men worked—most of them the men from the bunkhouse, whom Gardley took into his confidence.

The floors were carefully scrubbed under the direction of Mom Wallis, and the windows made shining. Then the men spent a day bringing great loads of tree boughs and filling the place with green fragrance, until the big living room looked like a woodland bower. Gardley made a raid upon some Indian friends of his and came back with several fine Navajo rugs and blankets, which he spread about the room luxuriously on the floor and over the rude benches which the men had constructed. They piled the fireplace with big logs, and Gardley took over some of his own personal possessions that he had brought back from the East with him to give the place a livable look. Then he stood back satisfied. The place was fit to bring his bride and her friends to. Not that it was as it should be. That would be for Margaret to do, but it would serve as a temporary stopping place if there came need. If no need came, why, the place was there, anyway, hers and his. A tender light grew in his eyes as he looked it over in the dying light of the afternoon. Then he went out and rode swiftly to the telegraph office and found these two telegrams, according to the request in his own letter to Mr. Earle.

Gardley's telegram read:

Congratulations. Will come as you desire. We await your advice. Have written.—FATHER.

He saddled his horse and hurried to Margaret with hers, and together they read:

> Dear child! So glad for you. Of course you will go. I am sending you some things. Don't take a thought for us. We shall look forward to your visit. Our love to you both.—MOTHER.

Margaret, folded in her lover's arms, cried out her sorrow and her joy, and lifted up her face with happiness. Then Gardley, with great joy, thought of the surprise he had in store for her and laid his face against hers to hide the telltale smile in his eyes.

For Gardley, in his letter to his future father-in-law, had written of his newly inherited fortune, and had not only enclosed a check for a good sum to cover all extra expense of the journey, but had said that a private car would be at their disposal, not only for themselves, but for any of Margaret's friends and relatives whom they might choose to invite. As he had written this letter he was filled with deep thanksgiving that it was in his power to do this thing for his dear girl-bride.

The morning after the telegrams arrived Gardley spent several hours writing telegrams and receiving them from a big department store in the nearest great city, and before noon a big shipment of goods was on its way to Ashland. Beds, bureaus, washstands, chairs, tables, dishes, kitchen utensils, and all kinds of bedding, even to sheets and pillowcases, he ordered with lavish hand. After all, he must furnish the house himself, and let Margaret weed it out or give it away afterward, if she did not like it. He was going to have a house party and he must be ready. When all was done and he was just about to mount his horse again he turned back and sent another message, ordering a piano.

"Why, it's *great!*" he said to himself, as he rode back to his office. "It's simply great to be able to do things just when I need them! I never knew what fun money was before. But then I never had Margaret to spend it for, and she's worth the whole of it at once!"

The next thing he ordered was a great easy carriage with plenty of room to convey Mother Earle and her friends from the train to the house.

The days went by rapidly enough, and Margaret was so busy that she had little time to wonder and worry why her mother did not write her the long, loving, motherly good-bye letter to her little girlhood that she had expected to get. Not until three days before the wedding did it come over her that she had had but three brief, scrappy letters from her mother, and they not a whole page apiece. What could be the matter with Mother? She was almost on the point of panic when Gardley came and bundled her onto her horse for a ride.

Strangely enough, he directed their way through Ashland and down to the station, and it was just about the time of the arrival of the evening train.

Gardley excused himself for a moment, saying something about an errand, and went into the station. Margaret sat on her horse, watching the oncoming train, the great connecting link between East and West, and wondered if it would bring a letter from Mother.

The train rushed to a halt, and behold some passengers were getting off from a private car! Margaret watched them idly, thinking more about an expected letter than about the people. Then suddenly she awoke to the fact that Gardley was greeting them. Who could they be?

There were five of them, and one of them looked like Jane! Dear Jane! She had forgotten to write her about this hurried wedding. How different it all was going to be from what she and Jane had planned for each other in their dear old school day dreams! And that young man that Gardley was shaking hands with now looked like Cousin Dick! She hadn't seen him for three years, but he must look like that now, and the younger girl beside him might be Cousin Emily! But, oh, who were the others? *Father!* And MOTHER!

Margaret sprang from her horse with a bound and rushed into her mother's arms. The interested passengers craned their necks and looked their fill with smiles of appreciation as the train took up its way again, having dropped the private car on the side track.

Dick and Emily rode the ponies to the house while Margaret nestled in the backseat of the carriage between her father and mother, and Jane got acquainted with Gardley in the front seat of the carriage. Margaret never even noticed where they were going until the carriage turned in and stopped before the door of the new house, and

Mrs. Tanner, furtively casting behind her the checked apron she had worn, came out to shake hands with the company and tell them supper was all ready, before she went back to her deserted boarding-house. Even Bud was going to stay at the new house that night, in some cooked-up capacity or other, and all the men from the bunk-house were hiding out among the trees to see Margaret's father and mother and shake hands if the opportunity offered.

The wonder and delight of Margaret when she saw the house inside and knew that it was hers, the tears she shed and smiles that grew almost into hysterics when she saw some of the incongruous furnishings, are all past describing. Margaret was too happy to think. She rushed from one room to another. She hugged her mother and linked her arm in her father's for a walk across the long piazza; she talked to Emily and Dick and Jane, and then rushed out to find Gardley and thank him again. And all this time she could not understand how Gardley had done it, for she had not yet comprehended his fortune.

Gardley had asked his sisters to come to the wedding, not much expecting they would accept, but they had telegraphed at the last minute they would be there. They arrived an hour or so before the ceremony; gushed over Margaret; told Gardley she was a "sweet thing"; said the house was "dandy for a house party if one had plenty of servants, but they should think it would be dull in winter"; gave Margaret a diamond sunburst pin, a string of pearls, and an emerald bracelet set in diamond chips; and departed immediately after the ceremony. They had thought they were the chief guests, but the relief that overspread the faces of those guests who were best beloved by both bride and groom was at once visible on their departure. Jasper Kemp drew a long breath and declared to Long Bill that he was glad the air was growing pure again. Then all those old friends from the bunkhouse filed in to the great tables heavily loaded with good things, the abundant gift of the neighborhood, and sat down to the wedding supper, heartily glad that the "city lady and her gals"—as Mom Wallis called them in a suppressed whisper—had chosen not to stay over a train.

The wedding had been in the schoolhouse, embowered in foliage and all the flowers the land afforded, decorated by the loving hands of Margaret's pupils, old and young. She was attended by the entire school marching double file before her, strewing flowers in her way. The missionary's wife played the wedding march, and the missionary assisted the bride's father with the ceremony. Margaret's dress was a simple white muslin, with a little real lace and embroidery handed down from former generations, the whole called into being by Margaret's mother. Even Gardley's sisters had said it was "perfectly dear." The whole neighborhood was at the wedding.

And when the bountiful wedding supper was eaten the entire company of favored guests stood about the new piano and sang "Blest Be the Tie That Binds"—with Margaret playing for them.

Then there was a little hurry at the last, Margaret getting into the pretty traveling dress and hat her mother had brought, and kissing her mother good-bye—though happily not for long this time.

Mother and Father and the rest of the home party were to wait until morning, and the missionary and his wife were to stay with them that night and see them to their car the next day.

So, waving and throwing kisses back to the others, they rode away to the station, Bud pridefully driving the team from the front seat.

Gardley had arranged for a private apartment on the train, and nothing could have been more luxurious in traveling than the place where he led his bride. Bud, scuttling behind with a suitcase, looked around him with all his eyes before he said a hurried good-bye, and murmured under his breath: "Gee! Wisht I was goin' all the way!"

Bud hustled off as the train got under way, and Margaret and Gardley went out to the observation platform to wave a last farewell.

The few little blurring lights of Ashland died soon in the distance, and the desert took on its vast wideness beneath a starry dome, but off in the east a purple shadow loomed, mighty and majestic, and rising slowly over its crest a great silver disk appeared, brightening as it came and pouring a silver mist over the purple peak.

"My mountain!" said Margaret, softly.

And Gardley, drawing her close to him, stooped to lay his lips upon hers.

"My darling!" he answered.